Down These Dark Spaceways

Down These Dark Spaceways

Edited by
Mike Resnick

SCIENCE
FICTION

First Science Fiction Book Club printing May 2005

Published by Science Fiction Book Club, 401 Franklin Avenue, Garden City, New York 11530.

Visit the SF Book Club online at www.sfbc.com

Book design by Christos Peterson

ISBN: 1-58288-164-2

Printed in the United States of America

❖ CONTENTS ❖

❖ INTRODUCTION ❖

THEY USED TO say it couldn't be done, that no one could blend the mystery story with the science fiction story, that if you played fair with the reader the key to the puzzle would hinge on some obscure scientific fact that no one not conversant with science fiction could possibly spot, and that if it *didn't* turn on that type of clue, then why make it science fiction at all?

It was just over half a century ago that two brilliant and totally dissimilar science fiction mystery novels—Alfred Bester's *The Demolished Man* and Isaac Asimov's *The Caves of Steel*—buried that theory once and for all.

There has always been a lot of cross-pollenization between the two fields. Some of science fiction's finest practitioners—Fredric Brown, Jack Vance, Henry Kuttner, Isaac Asimov, Leigh Brackett, Wilson Tucker, and others—also wrote mysteries, and one of mystery's current superstars, Walter Mosley, recently tried his hand at science fiction.

Though I make the bulk of my living in science fiction, I enjoy both fields, and have even sold an occasional mystery. I have to confess that I'm not especially thrilled with some of the current trends in mysteries; these days there are times when I think the best way to sell a mystery novel is to make your detective a cat who doubles as a gourmet chef. (To be fair, there are some current trends in science fiction that are not exactly to my taste either.)

Despite the plethora of truly wonderful science fiction writers past and present, I persist in thinking that the single finest writer to come out of the pulp magazines in *any* category was Raymond Chandler, and that he and Dashiell Hammett did the mystery story an enormous service by giving murder back to the people who are good at it. Instead of wealthy amateur sleuths solving ingenious locked-room mysteries in English mansions, Hammett and Chandler's detectives followed their clues and their prey, as the saying goes, "down these dark alleys."

I decided that it might be interesting to use what is known as the

Black Mask school of writing as a jumping-off point for a sextet of science fiction novellas. These would not be slavish imitations of Hammett and Chandler and James M. Cain and Ross Macdonald, but they *would* be stories that were clearly in that tradition, rather than the classic British mysteries or today's "cozy" mysteries. There would be no Sherlocks or Wimseys or Poirots here; instead there would be the descendants of those fallen angels who stalked the dark alleys, who understood going in that the odds were against them, who were not surprised when their enemies lied to them and their friends deserted them, who knew that the rewards would never measure up to the risks but took those risks anyway. In short, these stories would extrapolate from the dark alleys of the mid-twentieth century and take us "down these dark spaceways" instead.

I met an enthusiastic reception when I proposed the book to the Science Fiction Book Club. The next step was to find five more writers (there was no way I was going to edit this without asking myself for a submission), and I decided to go after some of science fiction's best.

It turned out not to be a very difficult task at all. As their stories make clear, every contributor shares my love for both categories. Hugo and Nebula winner Robert J. Sawyer takes a term that didn't even exist twenty years ago and tells the tale of the only detective on Mars in "Identity Theft." Hugo and Campbell nominee Robert Reed revisits some of his characters aboard a huge and fascinating ship that will be familiar to his legions of readers in "Camouflage." Nebula winner and Hugo nominee Catherine Asaro also brings back some of her characters and embroils them in "The City of Cries." Hugo and Nebula nominee and Campbell Memorial winner Jack McDevitt gives us a female detective and takes us to "The Big Downtown." Hugo and Nebula winner David Gerrold set his story on Planet Earth, but when you find yourself "In the Quake Zone," it's *time*quakes he's talking about. Your editor is a Hugo and Nebula winner, and presents some of the problems that arise when a private eye finds himself doubling as a "Guardian Angel."

Today nobody denies that you can write a good science fictional mystery story. Our hope is that after you finish this book you'll find yourself thinking that it ought to be done more often.

—Mike Resnick

Down These Dark Spaceways

❖ GUARDIAN ANGEL ❖
by Mike Resnick

HER SKIN HAD cost her a bundle. It was smoother than silk, and at least thirty years younger than her eyes, which had a hard glitter to them that she couldn't quite hide. She had a hell of a figure, but there was no way to know how much of it was hers and how much was courtesy of the same guys who gave her that skin. She wore a ring that was brilliant enough to have given her the tan she sported, and another one that could have eaten the first one for breakfast.

She told me her name was Beatrice Vanderwycke. I didn't know if I believed her. You get used to being lied to in my line of work, and eventually you assume everything you're told is a lie until you know for a fact that it isn't. Still, she looked enough like a Beatrice Vanderwycke that I was willing to accept it for the moment.

Besides, I needed the work.

"And that was the last time I saw him," she was saying as she toyed with a bracelet that was worth more than I earn in a decade. "I'm terribly worried that something has happened to him, Mr. Masters."

"Call me Jake," I replied.

"Do you think you can help me?" She shifted her position and the chair instantly adjusted to accommodate her, then gently wrapped itself around her. I envied the chair.

"I can try," I said. "But I'll be honest with you: the police have far more resources than a private detective does. Have you spoken to them?"

"They sent me to you. I'm sure he's not on Odysseus, and that means he's beyond their jurisdiction. A very nice officer named Selina Hernandez recommended you."

Well, that's one way for Selina to make sure I take her out for that dinner I owe her.

"All right," I said. "Let me start making a record of this so I don't make too many mistakes." I activated my computer.

She almost laughed at it. "That machine must be a leftover from the last century. Does it still work?"

"Most of the time."

"Why don't you get a new one?"

"I've got a fondness for old broken-down machines," I said. "Can I have his name again?"

"Andy."

"Age?"

"Nineteen."

"He's legally of age on every world in the whole Albion Cluster," I pointed out. "Even if I find him, I can't make him come back with me if he doesn't want to."

She pulled out a wad of money that could choke damned near any animal I've ever seen. "You're a resourceful man. You'll find a way."

I stopped myself from leaping for the money and reached for it with some slight measure of restraint. It was mostly Democracy credits, but there were some Far London pounds, Maria Theresa dollars, and New Stalin rubles.

"I'm a resourceful man," I echoed, sliding the cash into a desk drawer. "I'll find a way." I paused. "Have you got a picture of him—holo, portrait, whatever?"

She placed a small cube on my desk and activated it. The image of a nice-looking kid with blue eyes and wavy brown hair suddenly appeared, hovering in the air.

"Can I keep it?" I asked.

"Of course."

"Can you supply me with a list of his friends, and how to contact them?"

"He didn't have many," she said.

"How about a girlfriend?"

"Certainly not, Mr. Masters," she said firmly. "He's just a boy."

He's a boy who looks to be about two inches taller than I am, I thought, but decided to keep my mouth shut.

"Any alien friends?"

She gave me a haughty stare. "No."

"You've got to give me a little more to go on than just an image of him, Mrs. Vanderwycke," I said. "It's a big galaxy out there."

She produced another cube. "This contains the names and addresses of all of his friends that I know about, plus some of his teachers and a list of all the schools he's attended."

"Where is he presently going to school?"

"He quit last year."

"All right—where does he work?"

"He doesn't."

"What does he do with his time?"

"He's been ill," she said. "That's why I'm so worried about him."

"He looks pretty healthy in the holo," I said.

"It's very difficult for me to discuss," she said uncomfortably. "He has . . . *emotional* problems."

"The kind that would make him wander off and forget who he is and where he lives?" I asked.

She shook her head. "No, Mr. Masters. But he needs to continue his treatment, and he's already missed three sessions with his therapist."

"I'll want the name and address of the therapist."

"It's on the cube."

"And you say he disappeared three days ago?"

"That's right. I had an appointment. He was in his room when I left, and gone when I returned." She stared at me with cold clear eyes that looked more like a predator than a distraught mother. "I'll pay your daily fee and cover all your expenses while you're looking for him. When you return him to me, there will be a substantial bonus."

"You already gave me one."

"That was an inducement, not a bonus," she said. "Will you find my son?"

"I'll give it my best shot," I promised.

"Good." She got to her feet, tall and elegant and reeking of money, a real knockout—and with her money and her cosmetic surgeons, she'd look just as good at seventy, or even ninety. "I will expect frequent reports."

"You'll get them."

She stared at me. I used to stare at things I was about to dissect in biology class the same way. "Don't disappointment me, Mr. Masters."

I walked her to the door, it irised to let her pass through, and then I was alone with all that beautiful money and the promise of a lot more to come if I could just find one missing kid.

I fed the cube with the info to my computer. It spit it out. I put it in again, waiting to make sure the machine wasn't going to turn it into an appetizer, then sat back down at my desk and began sifting through the data she'd given me. There were four teenaged boys and a couple of teachers—names, addresses, holos. I decided to put them off until I'd spoken to the therapist to find out what was wrong with the kid, but he wouldn't break doctor-patient confidentiality without Andy's permission. I told him I could get Beatrice Vanderwycke's permission, and he explained that since Andy was legally of age that wouldn't change anything.

So I began hunting up the names from school. One teacher had died, another was guiding tourists through the ruins of Archimedes II. Two of the boys were in offworld colleges, a third was in the Navy and posted half a galaxy away. That left Rashid Banerjee, a slightly built young man with a thick shock of black hair. I managed to get him on the holophone, which saved me a trip out to his place, and introduced myself.

"I'm looking for Andy Vanderwycke," I explained.

"I didn't know he was missing," said Banerjee.

"He's been gone for three days," I said. "Is he the kind of kid who would go off on a lark?"

"I hardly knew him," said Banerjee. "He never struck me as irresponsible, but I don't know . . ."

"Is there anyone who *would* know?"

"Try his girlfriend."

"His mother told me he didn't have any girlfriends."

"He's got one. Or at least he did. His mother did her best to break it up."

"Any reason why?" I asked.

"Who knows?" he said. "She was a strange one, that lady. I don't think she liked him, even though he was her son."

"Can you give me the girl's name and tell me how to get in touch with her?"

"Melanie Grimes," answered Banerjee. He gave me her contact information. I thanked him, and went to the hospital where Melanie Grimes worked. They told me I'd have to wait in the cafeteria for her until she was on her break. It was a big, bustling room, with enough antigrav sensors that any patient who found any kind of exertion difficult could simply float to a table. I found an empty table, and the moment I sat down a menu appeared a few inches above it. Then a disembodied voice listed the day's specials.

"Just coffee," I said.

"Please press your thumb against the illuminated circle on the table," said the voice.

I did so.

"Your coffee will be billed to your account at the Odysseus branch of the Bank of Deluros."

I still don't know how the coffee got to the table. I turned away for a moment to watch a very proud, very stubborn old man insist on walking with crutches rather than let the room waft him to a chair, and when I turned back the coffee was already there.

I lit a smokeless cigar, and amused myself guessing the professions of every patient and visitor who walked by. Since there was no one to correct me, I gave myself a score of ninety percent.

Then a young woman began walking across the cafeteria toward me. She was very slender, almost thin, with short-cropped red hair and big brown eyes. While I was trying to guess whether she was a fourth level computer programmer or an apprentice pastry chef, she came to a halt.

"Jake Masters?" she said. "I'm Melanie Grimes."

I stood up. "I want to thank you for seeing me."

"I haven't got much time. We've already had eight deliveries today."

"So you're an obstetrics nurse?"

"No, I'm not."

"You're too young to be a doctor."

"I'm a lab technician," she explained. "Every time a baby is born, we take some umbilical stem cells so we can clone its various organs should they ever need replacement. It's not very exciting," she continued, then added defensively: "But it *is* important."

"I'm don't doubt it," I said, handing her a business card. She studied my name and seemed fascinated by the little animated figure stalking the bad guys. Finally she looked up at me.

"This is about Andy, isn't it?"

"Yeah. According to his mother he went missing three nights ago."

"He's not missing," she said. "He ran away."

"From you?"

She shook her head. "From *her.*"

"Are you talking about his mother?"

"Yes. He was frightened."

"Of her?"

"Yes."

I drained the last of my coffee. "Can you think of any reason why he should be frightened of her?"

"*You've* met her. Wouldn't *you* be afraid of her?"

Not much scares me besides the prospect of poverty these days, but I saw her point.

"If you wanted to find him, where would you look?"

"I don't know." Then: "He had this friend . . ."

"His mother gave me a list of his friends. I've spoken to Rashid Banerjee, and none of the others are on the planet."

"His mother didn't think this one could possibly be a friend, so of course she wouldn't give you his name—but he was the closest friend Andy had. Maybe his only real friend."

"Can *you* give me his name?"

"Crozchziim."

"Either you're choking or he's an alien," I said.

"He's a Gromite."

"What's a Gromite?"

"A native of Barsoti IV."

"Humanoid?"

"Yes."

"How long has he known Andy?"

"A long time," replied Melanie. "Andy's mother was too busy to bother with him, so he pretty much raised Andy. Over the years he was a nursemaid, a tutor, and a paid companion."

"Could Andy be staying with him?"

She shook her head. "He lived in an outbuilding on the Vander-wyckes' estate. A little shack, really, hidden from sight in a grove of trees. She'd have looked there before she contacted a detective."

I showed her the list of friends I'd been given. "Can you add any names to this?"

She studied the list. "Not really. I don't think Andy would have considered any of them friends. They were just classmates he knew."

"What about Andy's father?" I asked. "Dead?"

She smiled, the first smile I'd seen from her. "Didn't she tell you? But of course she wouldn't. It might ruin her social standing."

"You want to let me in on the joke?" I said.

"Andy's father is Ben Jeffries."

"Hatchet Ben Jeffries?" I said. "The kingpin of the Corvus system?"

"That's him."

"There's an outstanding murder warrant for him right here on Odysseus," I noted. "They've been trying to extradite him for years."

"That's why he never comes to the Iliad system," said Melanie.

"I assume he and Beatrice are divorced?"

"Andy says they were never married."

"Andy knows him?"

"Of course. He's been paying all Andy's expenses since he was born. He just can't visit him on Odysseus. He's flown Andy out to Corvus II a few times."

"Do they get along well?"

"I guess so."

"Could Andy be on Corvus now?" I asked.

She shrugged. "I don't know. Maybe."

I thanked her for her time, then went back to the office to check on Crozchziim's whereabouts. I had the computer access the alien registry. He'd reported once a week to the Department of Alien Affairs for close to fifteen years . . . but he'd skipped his last check-in, and the Department had no idea where he was.

Which meant my next step was to talk to Hatchet Ben Jeffries. I'd much rather have spoken to him via computer or subspace radio, but he was my only remaining lead, and I figured I'd better have a face-to-face with him, so I contacted the spaceport and booked an economy ticket to Corvus II.

Corvus was seventeen light-years from Iliad. I don't know who or what Corvus was, or why they named a star for it, but I thought the guy who named the planets was pretty unimaginative. They were Corvus I through Corvus XIV. It made Iliad's planets—Achilles, Odysseus, Ajax, Hektor and the rest—look pretty classy by comparison.

We took off bright and early the next morning. I watched a holo of a murderball game for a couple of hours, then took a nap until the robot host woke me and asked if I wanted something to eat. I always get nauseated when I eat at light speeds or traveling through wormholes in hyperspace, so I took a pass and went back to sleep until just before we touched down.

I'd sent a message that I wanted to see Jeffries about his son, but I'd left before there was any reply, and I hoped I hadn't wasted a trip. It's been my experience that criminal kingpins are often reluctant to speak to any kind of detective, even private ones. I cleared Customs, then rented an aircar, punched in the address of Jeffries' estate, and settled back to watch the countryside whiz past as we skimmed along a few inches above the ground.

When we got to our destination there was a stone wall around the entire place, all ten or twelve acres of it, and there were half a dozen robots patrolling the exterior. The aircar stopped at the gate, its sensors flashing, and a few seconds later a mechanical voice came through its speaker system:

"State your name and business. We will not be responsible for you or your vehicle if you attempt to enter the grounds without permission."

"I'm Jake Masters, and I'm expected. Tell your boss I need to talk to him."

"Please wait."

I waited a full two minutes. Then the gate vanished, and I realized I'd been looking at one hell of a hologram. I suspected that the entire wall was nothing but a carefully constructed image. For all I knew, so were the robots. The aircar began moving forward, and once we were inside the estate I ordered it to stop. Then, just to see if my guess about how the place was really protected was right, I picked up a titanium drinking mug that came with the vehicle and tossed it at the wall. It was instantly atomized, which is exactly what would happen to anyone who tried to enter without first being cleared.

We glided up to the front door of a mansion that would have been impressive on *any* world and especially out here on the edge of the Inner Frontier, and I found three men—*real* men, not images or robots— waiting for me. Nobody was displaying any weapons, but they each had a few telltale bulges under their tunics.

"Well?" said the smallest of them.

"He is carrying a laser pistol," replied the aircar.

"Anything else?"

"A wallet, a passport, 37 credits in change, two Maria Theresa dollars . . ."

"That's enough. Please hand me your burner, butt first, and step out of the vehicle, Mr. Masters."

I did as he said, and the two larger men frisked me about as thoroughly as I'd ever been frisked.

"What was that for?" I asked when they had finished.

"Mr. Jeffries has a lot of enemies," the small man explained. "And of course there are always bounty hunters."

"Yeah, but you've already scanned me and got my burner."

"You can't be too careful, Mr. Masters," he replied. "Last week a man tried to enter the house with a ceramic gun that got past every sensor. Step over here, please."

I walked over to a scanner that read my retina, my bone structure, and my fingerprints and checked them against my passport. Then they checked my passport against the registry office back on Odysseus. Finally they were satisfied that I was who I claimed to be, and that if I tried to kill their boss it wouldn't be with any weapons that had gotten past them.

"Please follow me," said the small man, turning and entering the mansion. We passed through a huge foyer with a floor made of marble with the distinctive blue tint that identified it as coming from far Antares, then down a corridor lined with alien artifacts on quartz shelves, and finally entered a luxurious study lined with books—not disks or cubes, but real books made of paper. The carpet was very thick, and seemed to shape itself around my feet with each step I took.

A tall man was standing beside a desk made of half a dozen different alien hardwoods. He was a steel gray man—hair, clothing, even his expression—and I knew he had to be Ben Jeffries. I half-expected to see the hatchet that made his reputation and gave him his sobriquet displayed on a wall or in a glass case, but there was no sign of it.

"Mr. Masters?" he said, extending his hand.

I took it. The grip was as firm and steel gray as the rest of him.

"Call me Jake."

"Have a seat, Jake," he said, snapping his fingers, and a chair quickly floated over to me, as responsive as a well-trained dog. "Can I get you something to drink?"

"Whatever you're having," I said.

"Cygnian cognac, I think," he said, and before he could ask for it a robot had entered with two half-filled glasses. I took one, so did he, and as the robot exited, he nodded to the man who had brought me to the study, and he left too. Now it was just the two of us.

"I've checked you out thoroughly, Jake," he said. "A man in my position has to be very careful. After all, you're a detective and there are close to eighty warrants for my arrest all across the Cluster. You've been scanned, so I know you're not carrying any recording devices, but just the same we're going to need some ground rules. You said you wanted to talk to me about my son. Fine—but that's the *only* subject that's open for discussion. Is that okay with you?"

I had a feeling that if it wasn't agreeable, I probably wouldn't live to make it back to the spaceport.

"That's fine," I said.

"I assume Andy's mother hired you?"

I nodded. "Mrs. Vanderwycke, right." I took a sip of the cognac. I'd heard of Cygnian cognac for years, but I could never afford it. I guess I'm used to cheap booze; I didn't like this stuff at all. But since it was Hatchet Ben's cognac, I figured I'd better keep that observation to myself.

"Mrs. Vanderwycke," he repeated with an amused chuckle. "When I knew her she was just plain Betty Wickes. Well, maybe not so plain." He took a sip of his cognac. "All right, what do you need to know?"

"Your son has gone missing," I said, "and I've been hired to find him."

"Yeah, I gathered as much," said Jeffries.

"Has he been in contact with you? Asked for money or help?"

"No. He'd never show that much initiative."

"I take it you don't think too much of him?"

"He's a decent enough kid," said Jeffries. "But he's a weakling."

"He looked pretty sturdy in the holos I've seen."

"There are all kinds of weaklings," said Jeffries. "He's the kind I have no use for. If you push him, he won't push back. He never stands up to Betty, which is an open invitation to get walked all over. The kid's got no guts. He lets every little thing get to him. Hell, he was actually catatonic for a while back when he was five or six. You wouldn't believe how much I had to pay a team of shrinks to snap him out of it."

"Sounds like an unhappy kid," I said.

"I was an unhappy kid too," said Jeffries. "You learn to overcome it—*if* you're tough enough. Andy isn't." He paused. "Maybe he'd have turned out better if I'd raised him. It's hard to develop toughness growing up around Betty."

"Tell me about her," I said.

"Watch your back around her," he said. "You know what I do for a living, I'm not going to lie about it. I deal with the scum of the galaxy every day—killers and worse." He stared at me. "Believe me when I tell you she's more dangerous than any of them."

"If that's so, why did you hook up with her?"

"She was young and gorgeous, and I was young and foolish. It didn't last long. I was gone before Andy was born."

"When's the last time you saw her?"

"Maybe fifteen or sixteen years ago," he said. "No, wait a minute. I saw her a couple of years ago when Milos Arum was inaugurated as Governor of Beta Capanis III. I didn't talk to her, but I saw her across the room."

"Beta Capanis," I said. "That's way to hell and gone, out on the Rim. I take it Arum's a close friend?"

"That's not part of our ground rules, Jake," he said with a hint of steel beneath the friendly smile. "Stick to Andy."

"Sorry," I said. "What can you tell me about a Gromite called Crozchziim?"

"I never met him, but Andy talked about him a lot."

"Any idea where he might be?"

"He? You mean the alien? Isn't he back on Odysseus?"

"Not as far as I can tell," I said.

"So you think he's with Andy?"

"It makes sense," I said. "They're friends, and they're both missing."

"Interesting," said Jeffries. "All I know about him is that he used to be an entertainer, a juggler or tumbler or something. He broke an arm or a leg, I don't remember which. He was on Odysseus, and they let him go. Betty hired him to amuse the kid."

"He performed on stage?" If he worked for a theatre company that played human worlds, he had to belong to a union, and that would make him a little easier to trace.

"In a circus or a carnival, something like that." I must have looked my disappointment, because he added: "I'll have one of my men find out exactly where it was and get the information to you."

"Thanks," I said. "I guess that covers everything."

"Almost. Now I've got one for you."

"Fair is fair. Go ahead and ask."

"Twelve years ago you put three of my men away for a long time on Odysseus. You were a good cop. Why did you quit?"

"I wasn't corrupt enough," I said.

He chuckled. "Yeah, I heard about your problems when you arrested the wrong guys."

"Right guys, wrong administration," I replied. I wanted to ask if they were his, but I knew he wouldn't answer, so I got to my feet and he did the same.

"Have you got any idea where he might be?" he asked.

"Not yet," I said. "But I'll find him sooner or later—unless Mrs. Vanderwycke gets tired of paying my expenses and per diems."

"I'll tell you what," said Jeffries, walking me to the door of the study. "If she stops paying you, I'll pick up the tab and you'll report to me."

I looked at him for a moment without saying anything.

"What are you staring at?" he said.

"I'm trying to picture you as a concerned father."

Suddenly he was all steel again. "Just find him."

Then I was being escorted back to the car by another of his men, and an hour later I was on a spaceliner bound for Odysseus. When the trip was a little less than half over, the robot host handed me the printout of a subspace message that had just arrived from the Corvus system:

The show Crozchziim worked for is long defunct. There are presently 137 circuses and carnivals touring the Albion Cluster. For what it's worth, only one of them, the Benzagari Carnival and Sideshow, is owned by a Gromite, Crozchziim's former partner in a juggling act.

It was as good a place as any to start, so before we landed I ran a check and learned that the carny had been playing on Brutus II for eight days and was slated to be there for four more. I didn't even leave the Odysseus spaceport; half an hour after we touched down I was *en route* to the Alpha Pirias system, where I'd transfer to a local ship that hit all the inhabited worlds within a three system radius, including Brutus II.

When I got to Brutus I found that the carny had been kicked off the planet for running crooked games, which at least showed that the management had some respect for tradition, and was now on New Rhodesia. It took me another day to make connections. We touched down on nightside, and I got off with perhaps ten other passengers while the ship continued on toward its ultimate destination in the Roosevelt system.

I got in line to pass through Customs. When it was my turn I stepped up and handed over my passport disk to the robot Customs officer that was running the booth.

"Are you visiting New Rhodesia for business or pleasure?" it asked me.

"Business."

"The nature of your business?"

"I am a duly licensed private investigator," I replied. "I don't believe I'm required to tell you more than that."

"Will you require a copy of our constitution and penal code so that you may study what is and is not permitted in the pursuit of your business?"

"That won't be necessary."

"How long do you plan to stay on New Rhodesia?"

"One day, two at the most."

"I have given you a three-day visa," said the robot, handing me back my disk. "It will vanish from your passport at that time, and if you are still on New Rhodesia and have not filed for an extension, you will be in violation of our laws."

"I understand."

"Our standard currency is the New Rhodesia shilling, but Democracy credits and Maria Theresa dollars are also accepted. If you have other human currencies, you may exchange them at any of the three banks within the spaceport." It paused as if waiting for a question, but I didn't have any. "Our atmosphere is 21 percent oxygen, 77 percent nitrogen, and 2 percent inert gasses that are harmless to carbon-based life forms. Our gravity is 96 percent Standard, and our day is 27.23 Standard hours."

"Thanks," I said. "May I pass through now?"

"I must check to make sure you have sufficient funds to purchase passage away from New Rhodesia," it replied, as it transmitted my thumbprint to the Master Computer back on Deluros VIII. I tensed, because while I'd just deposited the money Mrs. Vanderwycke had given me, my credit history was what they call spotty. "Checking . . . satisfactory. You may enter the main body of the spaceport, Jacob Masters."

I walked straight to an information computer and asked where the Benzagari Carnival and Sideshow was performing. It gave me an address than didn't mean a thing, so I took it to the Transport Depot and hired an aircar to take me there.

It was about ten miles out of town, a series of tents and torch-lit kiosks that were meticulous recreations of the ones that had plied their trade on Earth before Man had reached the stars, with the added advantage that they were climate-controlled and a cyclone couldn't blow them away. There were games of every variety, games for humans, games for aliens, even races for the ugly little six-legged creatures that passed for pets on New Rhodesia. The barkers and shills were everywhere—Men, Canphorites, Lodinites, Mollutei, Atrians, even a couple of Belargans.

The din was deafening. There were grunts and growls, trills and shrill whistles, snorts and clicks, and here and there even some words I could understand. The standard language in the galaxy is Terran since Men are the dominant race, and usually the other races wear T-packs—translating mechanisms that were programmed to work in Terran and their native tongues—but someone had decided the carnival would have a more exotic flavor if the T-packs weren't used, and I have to admit they had a point: it certainly felt different from anything I'd ever encountered.

Except for the frigid, methane-breathing Atrians who had to wear protective suits, all the other aliens were warm-blooded oxygen breathers, and they were all more-or-less humanoid. There were half a dozen races I'd never seen before, ranging from a ten-foot-tall biped that looked like an animated tent pole to a short, burly, three-legged being covered with what seemed to be dull purple feathers.

Finally I walked up to one of the human barkers and asked him to point out a Gromite to me. He looked around for a moment, then turned back to me.

"I don't see any right now, but they're all over the place," he said.

"What do they look like?"

"Maybe a foot shorter than you, rich red skin, two arms, two legs, too damned many fingers and toes. They don't wear clothes. I know this is supposed to be a sexual galaxy, but if they've got genders, they keep it to themselves." Suddenly he pointed. "There's the boss, making his collections."

I looked, and decided I'd never mistake a Gromite for anything else. The legs had an extra joint, the elbows seemed to bend in both directions, there was no nose but just a narrow slit above a broad mouth, the eyes were orange and were faceted like an insect's, and if he had any genitals they sure as hell weren't external.

"Maybe he doesn't need pants," said the barker, "but he sure as hell could use a money belt. We're really raking it in tonight."

"Have you been with the show long?" I asked.

"A year, give or take."

"Do you know if there's a Gromite called Crozchziim working here?"

"Beats the hell out of me," he said. "It's not a name I'd remember." Then: "Who'd he kill?"

"Why do you think he killed anyone?"

"Why else would you be looking for him?"

"He's no killer. I just need to talk to him. I'm told that he's a juggler, or some kind of entertainer."

"Well, there's your answer. He'd be in the big tent, and I work the Midway. We could both work the show for a year and never meet."

"This particular Gromite might be traveling with a young human."

"Bully for him," said the barker, losing interest. "You got any other questions, or do you mind if I go back to work?"

I left him and headed over to Benzagari. I flashed my credentials at him and he came to a stop.

"We're breaking no laws," he said. "If you have any complaints, please speak to Lieutenant James Ngoma."

"I'm not here to arrest you or shake you down," I said. "I just need some information." He didn't say anything, so I continued. "I'm looking for a young human named Andy Vanderwycke. He's probably traveling with a Gromite named Crozchziim."

"I have never heard of either of them."

Birds of a feather. I already knew that he'd been Crozchziim's partner in an act years ago, so he was obviously protecting a fellow Gromite. I considered explaining that I didn't want the damned Gromite, that I was after the Man, but he had no reason to believe me and aliens don't sell out their brothers to humans.

I left him and headed for the main tent. It was packed, split just about evenly between humans and everything else. New Rhodesia was a human world, but it was also a center of commerce, and it had a large Alien Quarter. The Men still outnumbered the aliens three or four to one, but Men had a lot of things to do with their evenings, and obviously the aliens didn't.

There were a trio of Lodinite tumblers in the center, and a couple of human clowns were walking the perimeter of the ring, entertaining some of the kids of all species who couldn't work up much enthusiasm for alien acrobats. They were just finishing up their act when I got there, and a minute later a human knife-thrower entered the ring. A pretty, scantily-clad girl was tied to a huge spinning wheel, the wheel was set in motion, and the man hurled his first knife. There was an audible gasp as the knife buried itself in the woman's stomach and she uttered a shrill scream. The man released four more knives in quick succession, and each one failed to miss the girl, whose screams grew weaker each time. Then, just before the audience could charge the ring to dismember the knife thrower, the wheel came to a stop, the shackles came loose, and the "dying" girl walked briskly to the center of the ring, pulled all five knives from her body, politely handed them back to the thrower, and bowed to the audience.

"Nice trick," I said to a human who was walking down the aisle, hawking candies and the wriggling little wormlike things that the Mollutei eat for snacks.

"That's no trick," he said. "Those are real knives. If he throws one into you, you die."

"Then why didn't *she* die?"

"Mutant. Her blood coagulates instantly, and her skin heals by the next morning—and he really is a good aim. He always misses her vital organs."

"That doesn't explain why the shock and pain doesn't kill her."

"She had all her pain receptors surgically disconnected."

"Are you guessing, or do you know that for a fact?"

He smiled. "She's my sister."

I bought a candy bar from him to cement our friendship, then asked another question. "I'm looking for a Gromite who might be working here as a juggler. Have you seen one?"

"Sure. You want Crunchtime."

"Crunchtime?" I repeated.

"That's not his name, but it's as close as I can come to pronouncing it, and he answers to it. Most everyone calls him that now."

"Is he traveling with a human, a young man maybe nineteen or twenty years old, kind of slender, maybe two or three inches over six feet?"

"Never saw him in the act, and I don't mix with aliens when I'm on my own time."

"When is Crunchtime due to appear?"

He glanced at the ring, where a Canphorite was putting some huge forty-ton creature through its paces, tossing it a ball, making it stand on its back four legs, climbing into its huge maw.

"Soon as this guy and his pet are done."

"Some pet," I remarked.

"Yeah, I know, it looks like it could eat half the audience for breakfast, but it's really a herbivore. Friendliest damned monster you ever saw. It loves everybody."

You live and learn. The deadliest killer I ever came across looked like a milquetoast who'd faint if you just frowned at him.

I waited until the Canphorite and his pet left the ring, and then a trio of jugglers entered—one human, one Lodinite, and one Gromite. And since the Gromite I sought had been a juggler and a guy who had a difficult time with alien names had dubbed this Gromite Crunchtime, I was pretty sure I'd found Crozchziim.

I have to admit he was damned good as what he did. He kept six or seven objects of different shapes and weights going at once, then tossed them even higher and got an even dozen in motion. I'd assumed that sooner or later the three of them would start juggling things back and forth, but none of them even acknowledged the others' existence until they all took their bows a few minutes later.

When they left the ring I handed the candy bar to a little girl, then walked to the exit they'd used and was soon just a few steps behind the Gromite.

"Hey, Crunchtime!" I called.

He stopped and turned to face me.

"Do I know you?" he asked in perfect Terran.

"Not yet," I said. "My name's Jake Masters."

"Mine is Crozchziim."

"I know. Will you settle for Crunchtime? It's a hell of a lot easier for me to pronounce."

He nodded his head, which startled me. The way he was put together, it looked like it was about to fall off. "What do you want of me, Mr. Masters?"

"I just want to ask you a few questions," I said. "You used to work for Beatrice Vanderwycke, right?"

"That is correct."

"You left in kind of a hurry."

"She doesn't want me back," he said, "and she is not the type to send you all this way to present me with my vacation pay—so why are you here?"

I pulled out my card. "Can you read Terran?" He nodded again, and I handed it to him. "I've been hired to find her son."

"And do what?"

"Bring him back."

"Why?"

"That's not my concern," I said.

"It should be," said Crunchtime.

"Why do you think so?"

"Before you disrupt an innocent young man's life, don't you think you should know why you're doing it?"

"She's his mother and she's worried about him," I said.

He stared at me, and when he was done I knew what a sneer of contempt and disbelief from a Gromite looked like.

Finally he spoke. "Tell Mrs. Vanderwycke he is safe and healthy and she has nothing to worry about. Now your job is done. Good-bye, Mr. Masters."

"Let *him* tell me," I said.

"He has no desire to see anyone connected with his mother," said the Gromite.

"His father's concerned too."

"His father had seen him a total of twenty-seven days since he was born. It is difficult to believe that he is suddenly concerned about the boy's well-being."

"So nobody cares about him except you?"

"Melanie Grimes does," said Crunchtime. "But you already know that. Who else would have given you my name?"

"She trusted me enough to tell me that Andy was probably traveling with you. Why can't you trust me enough to tell me where he is?"

"I have my reasons, and Andy has his."

"Why not make things easy on both of us and cooperate with me?" I said reasonably. "You know I'm going to find him with or without your help."

"Without." He paused and stared at me for a long minute. "You may think you know what this is about, Mr. Masters, but I assure you that you have no idea whatsoever."

"Enlighten me."

"Keep out of matters that don't concern you," said Crunchtime. "If you find him and take him back before he's ready, you will be responsible for whatever happens."

"Before he's ready for *what*?" I demanded. "And what do you expect to happen?"

"I have said enough. I will speak no further. This interview is over."

He turned and walked away. I considered following him, but decided it was a waste of time. The kid had to know his mother would send someone after him; he probably had a prearranged set of signals with Crunchtime to warn him when anyone showed up.

I spent the rest of the night wandering through the sideshow, searching for Andy Vanderwycke. I had his holo with me, but I never had a chance to use it, because I never saw a young man of his height and build. As the crowds thinned out I began looking behind the kiosks. I turned up a couple half my age having sex behind a shooting gallery, three men and two aliens who were so zoned out on booze or drugs that nothing was going to wake them before morning, and ten or twelve hucksters of all races selling contraband items, some of which made no sense to me.

One bedraggled man approached me with some truly unique pornography—an animated deck of cards with a queen of hearts I still dream about—and another tried to sell me a pair of hallucinogenic alphanella seeds, which are illegal on just about every world in the Democracy. I asked each of them if they had seen anyone answering to Andy's description, but once they saw I wasn't about to buy their goods they muttered their negatives and went looking for some other sucker.

When an Andrican hooker who looked like a four-foot tall Tinker Bell, complete with wings and a voice that sounded like gentle chimes, hinted at what she would like to do for or to me, I pulled out a fifty-credit note and told her I wasn't interested in what she was selling but I'd give her the money if she could tell me where to find Andy Vanderwycke. She explained that she didn't know any human male called Andy, but if I was after male companionship her uncle was available.

Finally I stumbled upon Prospero the Living Encyclopedia, a humanoid alien. To this day I don't know what race he belonged to; from a distance he could pass for a man, but when you got close to him you noticed the lidless eyes with the slit pupils, the third nostril, and the hair that was constantly weaving itself into new patterns.

Prospero's booth was at the far end of the midway, and he offered a prize of one hundred New Rhodesia shillings to anyone who asked him a question that he couldn't answer. He was really remarkable: he knew the time for the fastest mile ever run on Greenveldt, the gross planetary product of Far London, and the copyright date of the Canphorite poet Tanblixt's first book.

Finally I stepped up and faced him.

"Greetings, my good sir," he said in sibilant Terran, and now that I was standing right in front of him I saw that his tongue was forked, not like a snake's but like a *real* fork, with four distinct tynes. "And what question do you wish the magnificent Prospero to answer?"

"I'm looking for a human named Andy Vanderwycke," I said. "Is he with the carnival?"

"Yes."

"Where can I find him?"

"Only one question to a customer, good sir," said Prospero with a very alien smile.

"I'll just get back in line and ask again," I told him.

"That is your privilege."

So I went to the back of the line, waited half an hour to reach the front again, and walked up to him.

"Remember me?" I said.

"The all-seeing and all-knowing Prospero remembers everything. What is your question, good sir?"

"Where can I find Andy Vanderwycke?"

"At the Benzagari Carnival and Sideshow."

"*Where* at the carnival?"

"I'm sorry, good sir, but each patron is limited to only one question."

"I can keep this up as long as you can," I said irritably. "And I can get a lot nastier about it. Why don't you make it easy on both of us?"

"Good sir, you are causing a disturbance," said Prospero. "Please do not force me to call for Security."

The line was shorter this time, and I was facing him again in another seven or eight minutes.

"Consider your question very carefully, good sir," he said when I confronted him. "The show will be shutting down in another five minutes."

"Okay, this is my question: No matter how often I ask or how I word it, you're not going to tell me what I want to know, are you?"

"No, good sir, I am not. Next?"

I stepped aside, considered waiting for him to leave his booth, and decided against it. Carnies always stuck together against outsiders. It was possible that I could beat the information out of him—but if I couldn't, then by morning not a single member of the carnival would ever speak to me again, and that's assuming I wasn't arrested for assault.

Within half an hour the entire show was shut down. I was about to hunt up someplace to spend the night when I saw them starting to break down the tents.

"What's going on?" I asked the insectoid alien who seemed to be in charge of the work crew.

"We open on Aristides IV in two days, and it will take a day to set up there," he squeaked at me.

"But you've only been on New Rhodesia for two nights," I said.

"We're only here because we were thrown off of Brutus II," was his answer. "Our next scheduled playdate is Aristides."

I considered trying to hitch a ride with the carny, but I knew

Crunchtime would have alerted Benzagari about my snooping around, and there was no way I could go with them except as a stowaway. So, since all my expenses were being paid, I went back to the spaceport and booked passage to Aristides IV, then rented a room at the attached hotel. The ship didn't leave until midday, and when I showed up they told me that the carny's chartered ship left at dawn, so Andy Vanderwycke was going to have half a day to hide before I got there.

When the ship touched down and I'd cleared Customs, I asked an information computer where the carnival was setting up shop, and was informed that they'd be playing at the local indoor stadium.

I didn't like that at all. If they'd taken their tents out into the countryside, the crew would be staying with the show, and I'd at least know where to start looking. But if they hadn't unpacked the tents, that meant they'd be staying in hotels.

Aristides IV was like most Democracy worlds—Men lived where they wanted, and all the other races were confined to the Alien Quarter. Maybe Andy was new at being on the run but most members of a carny have spent their entire lives avoiding spouses, bill collectors, or the police, and they'd have given him a quick education in laying low. And the first thing they'd have told him was not to stay where they stayed. They could misdirect me and protect him out in the countryside, but not in a hotel on a strange world. It would be too easy for me to bribe a desk clerk or bartender, too easy for an experienced detective to crack any computer lock on any door.

So if he had half a brain, he wouldn't be where I could pay a few credits or let myself into a few rooms to find him. If it was me and I was traveling with a Gromite, I'd be hiding with him in the Alien Quarter until I had to show up for work, and I granted the kid enough smarts or access to enough advice to do the same.

In one way, it made my job more difficult, because aliens stick together the way carnies do, and they don't like Men walking through the little piece of each city that's reserved for them. On the other hand, a six-foot three-inch human would be a lot easier to spot in the Alien Quarter than in a string of hotels and restaurants populated by nothing but Men.

I took the slidewalk out of the spaceport, moved over to the expresswalk, and found myself at the edge of the Quarter a few minutes later. A Lodinite patrolled the gate, and gave me the standard warning about how no one could be held responsible for anything that happened to me once I left the human section of the city and entered the Alien Quarter. He recited the usual liturgy about how aliens were justifiably resentful of their status on human worlds, and that even though I was doubtless in no way responsible I nonetheless represented the race of Man and they might be inclined to take out their frustration on me. When I answered that I knew all that and told him to cut the lecture short, he glared at me and then announced that the gate's sensors had detected a weapon that was hidden from sight.

I pulled my burner out and showed it to him.

"This is a Stern and Mason laser pistol, Model ZQ, purchased on Odysseus, registration number 362LV5413. If you'll check my passport, you'll see that I'm licensed to carry it."

He ran a micro-scanner across my passport disk, then deactivated it.

"I would recommend that you keep it concealed," he said stiffly. "No other race is allowed to own or carry weapons on Aristides, and displaying it would just create resentment, which is present already."

"I wasn't displaying it when your sensor spotted it," I pointed out.

He had no response to that, so he waited another minute just to annoy me and then let me pass through the gate.

I was a block into the Alien Quarter before the smell hit me. It was kind of a cross between rotting flesh and raw sewage, and it got stronger the farther I proceeded.

The squalor was almost unbelievable. Alien waste washed slowly along the street gutters, exposed to the air, going God knew where. Everything was in a state of decay, doors and windows were rotting or missing, dead animals and the occasional dead alien lay on the streets and slidewalks. Here and there undernourished alien children, most of them naked or nearly so, played incomprehensible games. When they saw me every last one of them rushed up, hand or paw or tentacle extended, begging for food or money.

I tried to ignore them, but they wouldn't go away and fell into step behind me. Finally I figured I might as well see if I could make some use of them, so I stopped, turned, and asked if any of them knew where the performers from the carnival were staying. I got nothing but blank looks, and I realized that none of them were wearing T-packs, so they couldn't understand me.

After another block I came upon an ancient Triskargi who *had* a tarnished T-pack hung around his neck. He looked like he wanted to hop away on his froglike legs as I approached him, but when he saw all the children he seemed reassured that I wasn't out to harm him and he stayed where he was.

"Hi," I said. "None of the kids can understand me."

"They have no T-packs," he said.

"I know. But there are a couple of Triskargi kids among them. You can speak to them, and most of them seem to understand each other, so they've probably developed some sort of *lingua franca* to communicate with each other. I want you to ask them if they know where the carnival performers are staying."

It took a few minutes, because the old Triskargi had no idea what a carnival was, but finally he understood and relayed the question. One of the Canphorite kids—I never remember which ones come from Canphor VI and which from Canphor VII—said he could lead me to some of them. He wanted seventeen trillion credits for his services. We negotiated, and I talked him down to twenty credits.

"Have him tell his friends not to follow us," I told the Triskargi. "If they hear us all coming, they'll have time to hide."

"They are entertainers," he said. "Why should they hide?"

"Just tell him."

He did as I asked, and the Canphorite child and I set out to the west. The planet's four moons were all out in midafternoon, casting strange flickering shadows across the Quarter. I was going to ask my guide for the names of the moons, but then I remembered he couldn't understand me, so I just followed him in silence.

Finally we stopped at a deep burrow, and the child turned and looked at me.

"Is this it?" I asked.

He couldn't understand my words, but he knew what I was asking. He pointed into the burrow.

I thanked him, tipped him another ten credits, watched him race back toward his playmates, and then I entered the burrow. The tunnels, which were about ten feet high and almost as wide, descended at about a twenty-degree angle, twisting and winding, occasionally broadening into what passed for a room. It was almost an underground city. A number of aliens saw me, but no one greeted me or tried to stop me. They simply stared in silence, as if this intrusion was just one more humiliation they were being forced to suffer.

At last the ground began to level out, and I came to a tall, heavily muscled Sett who was wearing a T-pack.

"I'm looking for a Gromite and a Man," I said. "They would have arrived this morning."

He stared at me without speaking.

"They were traveling with a carnival." Silence. "Have you seen them?"

"They are not here."

"That wasn't my question. Have you seen them?"

"Yes."

"Where are they now?"

"I do not know."

"Who does?"

"No one in this burrow knows. When they heard that you had entered the Quarter, they left. We asked them not to tell us their destination, so that you cannot torture it out of us."

"I don't torture people."

"Then you are a most unusual Man." He paused. "Go back where you belong, Jake Masters."

They'd been there, all right. No one else in the Quarter knew my name. And if they had friends watching me, they were going to be able to stay one step ahead of me in the Alien Quarter. There was no sense wasting any more time there, so I retraced my steps, and an hour later I checked into the Regal Arms, which wasn't regal and didn't have any arms, but it was where the carny's human contingent was staying.

I hung around the bar, and bought half a dozen of them drinks at various points in the evening. I didn't get the resentment here that I did when I spoke to the aliens, but I didn't get any information either. When money couldn't pry any answers loose, I tried invoking Hatchet Ben Jeffries' name. He was looking for his son, I explained, and he could get pretty deadly when he didn't get what he wanted. It didn't help. Maybe they knew where Andy was, maybe they didn't, but carnies have this code, and they don't break it.

I have a code, too. It has to do with earning my pay, and I wasn't going to let a wall of silence get in the way. I went up to my room a couple of hours after midnight, slept in until noon, and wandered down to the hotel's restaurant for some breakfast. The whole meal was composed of soya products, but they were well disguised and it wasn't too difficult to pretend I was eating eggs from Silverblue or Prateep VI and coffee imported from Earth itself.

I'd learned the night before that because of some city ordinance the carny's games couldn't open until dusk, and since there was no sense drawing a crowd if they couldn't be bilked, the entertainment wouldn't start for another hour or so after that.

I showed up while they were still setting up, and found out where the performers' dressing rooms were located. The aliens were segregated, so I figured I wouldn't find the kid there. I went to the human dressing rooms and checked out their occupants, but there was no one who matched the holo I was carrying around.

I walked up and down the games and booths, checking out the barkers, the shills, everyone who might be remotely connected to the carnival. No luck. I entered the main auditorium, studied all the ushers and candy butchers. Nothing.

I finally decided that my best bet was just to keep an eye on Crunchtime. Sooner or later he had to make contact with Andy Vanderwycke, had to let his guard down, and I planned to be there when he did.

I grabbed a seat in the front row and settled back to wait for the Gromite. As the crowd filed in, a trio of clowns, two human, one Lodinite, began doing some ancient routines and pratfalls to warm them up. The kids loved it; after all, it wasn't ancient to *them*.

Then came the wire walker, and the intricate flight patterns of the winged aliens from far Shibati, and the dinosaur trainer (or the whatever-the-hell-it-was trainer), and the magician, and some tumblers, and finally Crunchtime and the other two jugglers entered the ring. I waited until his performance was over, then followed him out.

A young woman approached him and handed him something, I couldn't see what. He studied it for a moment and gave it back to her, and then she walked away. I followed her, made a mental note of the office she entered, and then returned to Crunchtime.

"Feel like talking yet?" I asked.

"You came looking for me in the Alien Quarter," he said. "That was very unwise."

"I like sightseeing."

"You are wasting your time, Mr. Masters."

"I'm being paid for it," I told him. "And I plan to follow you night and day until I find Andy or you tell me where he is."

"That is your right," he replied. "And it is my right not to tell you."

"A Mexican standoff."

"What is a Mexican?"

"Beats me," I admitted. "It's an ancient expression."

"I am going into my dressing room now," he said. "Unless you have an insatiable curiosity to observe how a Gromite passes the food he has digested, you will not accompany me."

With that, he turned on what passed for his heel and entered the room, and I went over to the woman's office. The concrete floor could have used a carpet, the whitewashed walls could have used some paintings or holographs, and the coffee pot could have used some coffee. She was sitting in a chair that was probably a decade older than she was, studying holos cast by her computer. I know she heard me come in, but she didn't bother to look up.

"Hi," I said. "My name is Jake Masters. I'd like to ask you a question."

"The answer is no."

"You haven't heard the question."

"I don't have to. You're Jake Masters, and you're harassing Crozchziim. Go away and leave him alone."

"Word gets around pretty fast."

"This is a carnival," she said as if that explained everything.

"I admire your loyalty, but I'm not here for the Gromite. I just need some information."

"Read an encyclopedia."

"I talked to one last night," I said wryly. "It didn't help."

"Life is full of disappointments."

"Just show me what you showed the Gromite."

"It's been atomized."

"I don't believe you. Let me take a look and I'm out of here."

She finally looked up at me. "Go, stay, what you do doesn't interest me."

I decided to take a different tack. "The games are crooked, and the carny has broken maybe thirty laws already tonight," I said. "I could tell the authorities."

She actually smiled. "Go ahead. Do you think you can pay them more than we already did?"

I smiled back. "Okay, lady, you win this round. But I'm going to find the young man I'm looking for."

"Maybe you will, maybe you won't, but you're not going to do it with my help." She went back to staring at her computer's array of images, and I finally left the office.

I went up and down the rows of games and attractions again, trying to spot a tall nineteen-year-old who looked anything like the holo of Andy Vanderwycke, but with no luck. I went through the lighting booth, the prop room, the performers' cafeteria, all the backstage rooms, got a pleasant eyeful in the ladies' dressing room, but couldn't see any sign of the kid.

It was driving me crazy. He *had* to be there. Crunchtime had as much as admitted it. So had the alien in the burrow. So had the lady with the computer. It wasn't *that* damned big a carnival—so why couldn't I spot him?

It was time for the next show, and I went back into the main auditorium, trying to figure out what I was overlooking. The crowd began getting restless, and the clowns came out to amuse them again—and suddenly I knew where Andy Vanderwycke was hiding. I watched the whole damned show again, then walked out the performers' exit. Crunchtime went past me and seemed surprised that I didn't stop him to ask more questions. I stepped aside as the dinosaur lumbered past, smiled at a couple of good-looking girls in tights, and finally the person I was waiting for appeared.

"Hi, Andy," I said.

He stopped cold and stared at me.

"Nice disguise," I said.

He took off his red bulbous nose and green fright wig. "I thought so until now."

"Really, it is," I said. "Who'd ever look twice at Bonzo the Clown?"

"How did you spot me?" he asked.

"Mostly it was a process of elimination."

I handed him my card.

"What happens now?" said Andy. "You're not going to kill me in front of all these people. And if I yell for help, my friends will tear you apart no matter what you do to me."

"I'm not here to kill you," I said, surprised. "I was hired to take you back to Odysseus."

"Same thing," he said.

"Your mother's very worried about you."

He smiled ruefully. "I'll just bet she is."

"One way or another you're coming back to Odysseus," I said, "so why not do it peacefully?"

"Oh, I'll go back to Odysseus," he replied. "But I'm not ready yet."

It was the same thing Crunchtime had said, and I offered the same response. "Ready for what?"

He stared long and hard at me, as if trying to make up his mind. Finally he shrugged. "What the hell. I might as well tell you. If you're lying and you're here to kill me, you're going to do it anyway. If you're telling the truth, maybe what I say will make a difference—though my guess is that my mother paid you so much that it won't matter."

"You talk, I'll listen."

"Let's find Crozchziim first," said Andy.

"What do you need him for?"

"We're due to leave the planet in a couple of hours, and he knows the ticket codes."

So now I knew what the girl had shown Crunchtime—the codes he'd need to get them aboard the ship.

"Forget it," I said. "Your pal can come or go as he pleases, but you're not running away."

"I'm not running *away*," he said. "I'm running *to* something."

"To what?"

"When we find Crozchziim." He paused. "He can corroborate everything I'm going to tell you."

We walked to Crunchtime's dressing room. Andy was about to enter it when I grabbed his arm.

"Have someone else tell him to come out," I said. "You're staying with me."

He spoke to a Canphorite who was walking by. The Canphorite entered the room, and a moment later Crunchtime emerged.

"So you found him," he said tonelessly.

"Yeah, I found him," I answered. "I told you I would."

"And this time you will kill him."

"This time?" I repeated, confused. "What are you talking about?"

"It is time to drop all the pretenses, Mr. Masters—if that is your real name," said Crunchtime. "You have been stalking Andy for six days. You came close to killing him on Brookmandor II. Now you have changed your tactics and are impersonating a detective, trying to enlist the help of others, but you are still a killer."

"I'm a detective," I said firmly. "I work out of Odysseus, and I was hired five days ago by Beatrice Vanderwycke. The first time I ever saw you or Andy was when I arrived on Aristides yesterday. If someone's stalking the kid, it isn't me."

They exchanged looks, and finally Andy spoke up. "All right, Mr.

Masters. I believe you. Now let's go somewhere private and see if you can return the favor."

"Lead the way," I said. "And don't run."

He led me to a deserted office. "Benzagari's working out of this room while we're here. He's checking the take on the midway, and then he's got to pay off the police, so he won't be back for at least half an hour."

I sat down on a sofa. "All right, I'm listening," I said. Andy sat on the edge of a desk, and Crunchtime, who wasn't built to fit in or on any human furniture, stood near Andy. "Start with why I shouldn't believe you bought passage off Aristides tonight expressly to get away from me."

"Because it's true," he said. "I have to go to Port Samarkand."

"Never heard of it."

"It's about seventy light-years from here."

"What's on Port Samarkand?"

"Duristan."

"What's Duristan?" I said.

"Duristan is a who, not a what . . . and my life depends on my reaching him."

I looked from one to the other. "Keep talking."

"What, exactly, did my mother tell you about me?"

"That you ran away and she wants you back."

"What did she say about *me*?" he repeated. "You can tell me. I won't take offense."

"That you were emotionally unstable and had been in therapy. I saw your father too. He confirmed that you've been troubled since you were a child."

"He's right," said Andy. "Something happened when I was six, something that made me lose almost a whole year of my life. They tell me I was catatonic and it took them almost a year to snap me out of it. Did he tell you that?"

"Yes, he did."

He stared at me for a moment. "Did he tell you anything about my mother?"

"He doesn't think too much of her."

"You're being coy, Mr. Masters, and we have no time for that. My ship leaves in an hour, and I have to be on it. What did he tell you about her?"

"He said she was an extremely dangerous woman."

"He's right." He paused. "I'm legally of age, Mr. Masters. I'd been living on Crozchziim's savings until I got my first paycheck two nights ago. I didn't take a single credit with me when I left, and I've asked nothing of her, indeed had no contact with her, since then. Why do *you* think she wants me back?"

"Why should I play guessing games when you're going to tell me?" I said.

"During the two months before I left home I had increasingly violent nightmares," said Andy. "Terrible images of blood and carnage."

"Lots of people do," I said, though most of my dreams were about ripe naked women I was never going to have and bill collectors I was never going to avoid.

"This was different. It was the same dream every night. I couldn't make out exactly what was happening, but it was terrifying." He paused. "Do you know what I think?"

"Probably, but why don't you tell me anyway?"

"I think she did something when I was six years old, something I wasn't supposed to see, something so terrible that after I saw it I couldn't face the truth of it and became catatonic for a year. When I came back to my senses, I couldn't remember anything. I still can't." He paused. "I don't know if this recurring nightmare is what I saw when I saw six, trying to burst into my consciousness—but *she* thinks it is. When I mentioned that I kept having this dream night after night, things began happening. I got what seemed like ptomaine poisoning from spoiled food—but she ate the same meal and was fine. I found a pill that didn't belong among my prescriptions. And every day she would ask about my dreams. I knew if I stayed there she'd find a way to kill me, so I took off."

"I had remained in Mrs. Vanderwycke's service only because of Andy," added Crunchtime, "and when he explained the situation, I agreed that he could not remain on Odysseus. As it is, there has already been an attempt on his life on Brookmandor II, just before we joined the carnival."

"It's not that hard to spot a tall skinny kid and a Gromite traveling together," I said. "I came in cold, and it only took me two days, even with his makeup. What ever gave you the idea that you could hide out in a carnival? Hell, you didn't even change your name, and Hatchet Ben Jeffries knew you'd been a juggler."

"Benzagari is an old friend," replied Crunchtime. "And we had to perform here to get our *bona fides* before traveling to Port Samarkand."

"You were making sense right up until now," I said.

"We *must* make contact with Duristan."

"This is where I came in," I said. "Who is Duristan?"

"He's a Rabolian," said Andy.

I frowned. "I know something about Rabolians, but I'll be damned if I can remember what it is."

"They're mentalists."

"That's right," I said, as it suddenly came back to me. "They're one of the few telepathic races."

"They're more than telepaths," said Andy. "A telepath can just read what I'm thinking. A true mentalist, a Rabolian, can dig out things I didn't even know were in my mind."

"And you think he's going to be able to tell you what you saw?"

"That's right."

"Then what?"

"It'll be my insurance policy. I'll write up the details, swear to it, store it in half a dozen locations, and let her know that if anything happens to me it'll be made public." He paused. "You look dubious, Mr. Masters."

"Call me Jake. And I *am* dubious."

"You think I'm lying to you, Jake?"

"Nobody could think up a lie like that," I said. "No, I believe you."

"Well, then?"

"Maybe your mother had nothing to do with what you saw. Maybe you went a little haywire and dissected your pet puppy. Maybe you saw a couple of kids making whoopee and were scared by all the forbidden activity and noise. There are aliens whose appearance would give anyone nightmares; maybe you bumped into one. Or maybe it was something else."

"It was *her!*" he snapped. "Why else would she be trying to kill me?"

"I don't know that she *is* trying to kill you," I said. "But even if you're right, are you sure you want to go through with this? When we bury things so deep it takes a Rabolian to dig them out, they're probably better left alone."

"I've got to do it. It's the only way I'll ever get her to leave me alone. And . . ."

"And?"

"I've *got* to know."

"Okay, I've got another question. Why are you pretending to be carnies?

"Duristan works for a carnival," explained Crunchtime. "Mrs. Vanderwycke is no fool. She knows Andy's best defense against her is the knowledge of what he saw all those years ago, and she knows that the most likely person to unlock that information is a Rabolian."

"All I've heard so far is that Duristan works for a carnival," I said. "Why not just walk up and pay him to do whatever it is that he does?"

"When someone tried to kill Andy on Brookmandor II, we decided that he couldn't continue to travel without a disguise, and I imposed upon an old friendship with a fellow Gromite to get us jobs here. Andy never takes off his clown makeup, not in public, not backstage. We felt that we would attract no undue attention if we went to Port Samarkand as performers."

I sighed deeply. One of the problems with novices in any line of work is that the ideas they think are new and unique are usually old enough to have long white whiskers.

"So where do you stand, Mr. Masters?" asked Andy. "Are you going to stop us?"

"Jake," I corrected him. "And I'm thinking about it."

"Think fast. We're running out of time."

"I'll make you a deal," I said at last.

"What kind of deal?" asked Andy suspiciously.

"I'll go with you to Port Samarkand," I said. "If this whole thing is a false alarm and you don't know anything that would make your mother want to kill you, you agree to come back to Odysseus with me. I don't give a damn if you just walk in the door, say 'Hi, Mom,' and walk right back out. I'm being paid to take you back, not to make sure that you stay."

"And if I *do* know something?"

"We'll play it by ear," I said. "No promises. That's my deal. Take it, or we go back to Odysseus on the next ship bound for the Iliad system."

Andy looked at Crunchtime, as if expecting the Gromite to say something, but the alien kept his mouth shut, and finally the kid nodded his agreement.

"Okay, Jake, you've got a deal. Now let's get the hell out of here."

The three of us took an express aircar to the spaceport. Crunchtime had boarding codes for both of them, so they boarded immediately. I had to buy my passage, but the flight was half empty and since we were late, they let me board and pay the robot host once we'd taken off.

Crunchtime had to sit in the alien section, so Andy and I sat together toward the front of the ship. The kid was still in his clown makeup, which attracted some stares. One guy wasn't laughing, just staring, and I thought I'd seen him before.

I nudged Andy with an elbow.

"What is it?" he asked.

"Don't make a production of it, but take a look at the guy across the aisle, maybe three rows back. He's wearing a brown tunic, and he's got a scar on his chin. Tell me if you recognize him."

"Yes," he said a moment later. "He was at the carnival every night."

"Is he the guy who tried to kill you on Brookmandor II?"

"I don't know. It was dark, and he was too far away."

"But he was definitely hanging around the carny?"

"Yes." He looked nervous. "What do we do about him?"

"Nothing—yet."

"Are you going to wait until he shoots me?" demanded Andy.

"He has every right to be on the ship," I said. "At least now I know what he looks like, so I can spot him on Port Samarkand."

"What if he shoots me right at the spaceport? I mean, you're carrying a gun, so why shouldn't he have one too?"

"My gun is sealed," I explained. "And it'll stay that way until they automatically deactivate the seal as we leave the Port Samarkand spaceport. That's the rules, kid. The only thing I can use it for is a club. If he's got one, it's in the same condition. Besides, no one's going to try to kill you at a spaceport. They've got more security there than anywhere else on the planet."

"I hope you're right," he said dubiously.

"I am," I said. And added silently: *I hope.*

We braked to sub-light speeds four hours into the voyage, and touched down on Port Samarkand a few minutes later. Before we left the ship we got the usual information about atmospheric content, climate, gravity, time zones, the whole deal. Humans sit at the front and exit first, and once we got off we waited at Customs for Crunchtime to catch up with us.

"Maybe I'd better go wash this makeup off before I pass through Customs," suggested Andy.

"Why bother?" I asked. "Your passport says you're an entertainer. Nobody will stop you. If the clerk asks, just say you're late for a performance."

"It'll never work," he said, but of course it did. Nobody questioned him, and we passed through Customs without any problems.

We stopped at an information computer to find out where Duristan's carnival was playing, but even before I posed the question I saw the guy in the brown tunic head off for the men's room.

"You take care of this," I said to Andy. "I'll be back in a minute."

The guy was standing in front of a sink when I got there.

"Warm," he muttered, and warm water poured out. "Soap." When he was done he said "Dry," and a burst of warm air blew across his hands. He saw me in the mirror, but didn't even bother to turn and face me while he was drying his hands.

"I figured we'd talk sooner or later, Mr. Masters," he said.

"How do you know my name?"

"My employer told me you'd be traveling with the kid."

"So she's paying you to kill him while I take the fall?" I said.

"Be a little more discreet, Mr. Masters," he said easily. "There are security monitors everywhere." Suddenly he smiled. "And I work for *him*, not her."

"Him?" I repeated.

"The father," he said, making sure he didn't mention Ben Jeffries' name aloud. "I'm here to make sure nothing happens to his son."

"Then that wasn't you on Brookmandor?"

"Not the way you think."

"I don't follow you."

"I was on Brookmandor, but I didn't try to kill him. The only reason he made it to Aristides is because I"—he remembered the camera—"*hindered* the man who was after him."

My guess was that he hindered him right into the morgue.

"So the kid's father is paying you to be his guardian angel," I said. "He offered the same job to me." I frowned. "Why? He doesn't even like him."

"There's an outstanding warrant for my employer on Odysseus," said the man.

"Yeah, I know. For murder."

"That's right." He paused. "He's committed a lot of crimes, including his share of murders—but that wasn't one of them. He wants to go back to Odysseus, but he can't set foot on the planet while that warrant's in effect. If this Rabolian can unlock information that the mother did it, they'll drop the warrant."

"What's on Odysseus that's so important?"

"I don't know and I don't care. Maybe it's loot he hid there twenty years ago, maybe it's something else. My job is just to make sure no harm comes to the kid until he reaches this Rabolian telepath." He paused again. "I'm glad we're on the same side. I wasn't sure when you showed up. I was afraid you were going to take him back, and then I'd have had to kill you." He didn't choose his words for the security monitors this time; they don't arrest you for what you might have done under other circumstances.

He could have sounded aggressive or arrogant, but he said it so matter-of-factly that I realized killing me would have been nothing personal. It was just business to him. He didn't care whether I lived or died, he didn't care what reason Jeffries had for wanting to return to Odysseus, he probably didn't care what was buried in Andy's memory. He just did his job and never got involved. Hard to like a guy like that, but equally hard to hate him. He was just another fact of Nature, like a refreshing breeze that might or might not turn into a hurricane. You may get out of its way, but there's no sense getting mad at it.

"Okay, we're allies, at least for the time being," I said. "You got a name?"

"Lots of 'em."

"None of which you want to share?"

"What purpose would it serve?"

And that way no one could beat it out of me.

"I've got to call you something. How's Boris?"

"As good as any other."

We had nothing further to say, so Boris went back into the main lobby of the spaceport. I waited another couple of minutes, then followed him. I didn't want anyone to see us together. I couldn't hide the fact that I was traveling with Andy, but if anyone was watching us, I didn't want them to know Boris was part of the team.

"We found Duristan," said Andy as I walked up to him and Crunchtime. "He's about ten minutes from here." He sneaked a look at Boris. "Did you find out who he is?"

"Don't worry about him," I said. "He's on our side."

"What!" It was more an exclamation than a question.

"He works for your father," I answered. "He's the guy who saved your ass back on Brookmandor."

I thought the kid was going to walk over and thank him, so I grabbed his arm. "Just ignore him," I said. "He'll be a lot more effective if it doesn't look like we all know each other."

The three of us walked to an aircar and told it to take us to the carnival where Duristan was working. As we glided a foot or two above the ground, I turned to Andy.

"I'm going to get out maybe 400 yards from the carny and walk the rest of the way," I told him.

"Why?"

"You're supposed to be a clown and a juggler, remember? What am I—your agent?"

"I hadn't thought of that," he admitted. "We'll apply for the jobs, and then—"

"Why bother?" I said. "You've seen how fast acts come and go at these shows. Just walk around like you belong. If anyone stops you, *then* play dumb and say you're looking for work."

"That makes sense," he agreed.

"All right," I said. "I'll find out where Duristan hangs out when he's not performing and meet you there."

"Okay," he said as the carnival came into view and I ordered the aircar to stop.

"Remember," I said as I climbed out. "If you see Boris—that's your father's man—don't stare at him or try to talk to him."

Then I was on the street and the aircar shot ahead. I walked up to the ticket booth, paid for my admission with cash in case my name had shown up on any computers, and entered the show.

Duristan didn't figure to be in the main arena—everyone knew that Rabolians were telepaths, and most people didn't want Duristan or any other Rabolian having a little fun at their expense by revealing some of their more embarrassing secrets to the audience. He figured to set up shop as a fortune teller or something similar, so I went to the rows of games and exhibits, looking for him.

He was there all right, sitting all alone in a glittering turban and a satin robe covered with the symbols of the zodiac. That outfit would have looked mildly silly on a human; it looked positively ludicrous on a tripodal Rabolian that was as wide as he was tall.

There was no sign of Andy and Crunchtime, so I went to the next booth, picked up a toy pulse gun, and began shooting at images of alien predators that seemed to be leaping through the air at me. I hit the first two. When I missed the third the creature smiled and informed me in exquisite Terran that I was lunch, and once he digested me—it would take about three seconds—I could play again for another twenty credits. I decided not to.

I killed a little more time walking up and down the rows of games—they looked exactly like the games I'd seem on Aristides and in every other carnival I'd ever been to—and then headed back toward Duristan's booth. I saw Andy and Crunchtime approaching it, and then I head Boris yell "Duck!"

The flare from a pulse gun nailed Andy in the right shoulder and spun him around. Boris jumped into sight, screecher in hand, and fired a blast of solid sound at the man with the pulse gun. He dropped like a rock, but then Boris fell backward, a black smoking hole in his belly. I spotted the guy who'd done it and downed him with my laser pistol. Then I raced up to Andy, who had dropped to one knee.

"Are you okay, kid?" I asked.

He nodded, and I went over to Boris. One look and I knew he wasn't going to make it to the hospital.

"Did I get him?" he whispered as I kneeled down beside him.

"You got one of them. I got another. How many were there?"

"Only two, I hope," he said with a weak grin. "I never saw the second one."

"I'll tell Jeffries what happened. If you have any family, does he know how to contact them?"

"No family," Boris grated. His hand reached up and clawed my shoulder. "You're his guardian angel now," he said, and died.

I walked back to Andy and helped him to his feet. "Can you stand on your own?" I asked.

He didn't answer. At first I thought he was too weak, or had lost too much blood. Then I saw him staring at something, and I followed his gaze.

Duristan had fallen out of his booth and lay sprawled on the ground, dead. A wild shot from the pulse gun had taken the top of his head off.

"Shit!" I muttered. "Come on, let's get you out of here."

But the local security team had shown up by then, and held us until we could be turned over to the police. The police surgeon treated Andy's wound and gave him something for the pain.

They kept us most of the night, but the few people who'd been on the scene verified our stories and they finally let us go about six hours later. They'd probably have kept me until the inquest, but there were so many warrants out for the two dead men that they figured I'd done them a favor.

"What now?" asked Andy as we walked out of the station. "Are you taking me back?"

"Eventually," I replied. "Let me get to a subspace radio first."

We found one in a local hotel, and I contacted Jeffries back on Corvus II. I told him what had happened and that Boris was dead, then waited about three minutes for him to receive the message and for his reply to get back to me.

"Where are you going next?" he asked.

"I'm being paid to return him to Odysseus, and that's what I plan to do," I said. "But if you'll pay our passage, we'll stop at Rabol on the way." I'd have paid it if he said no, but I didn't see any reason to tell him that.

"It's a deal. By the time you get to the spaceport the tickets will be waiting for you."

"There are three of us," I said. "Don't forget the Gromite."

"Right."

He broke the connection, I told Andy and Crunchtime what he'd said, and we had the hotel summon an aircar.

The spaceport wasn't crowded, but every face looked like a potential assassin. I went to the men's room with Andy while he removed his makeup—there was no sense pretending to be a clown any longer—and then we went to the waiting area. Crunchtime was already sitting in the aliens' section when we got there.

A pretty young redhead in a spaceport uniform walked up to the passengers, asking each if they wanted anything to drink while they waited to board the ship. Andy asked for a local fruit drink, and I requested a cup of coffee. She returned a few minutes later, passing out drinks and pocketing payments and tips. Finally she approached Andy and me.

"Your drinks," she announced, handing us each what we had ordered.

"Thank you," I said. I grabbed her wrist as she turned to go. "Andy, don't touch it."

I could see puzzlement in his eyes and fear in hers.

"Whatever they paid you for this, it wasn't enough," I told her. "Who hired you?"

"Please!" she said. "You're hurting me!"

"I'll do a lot more than hurt you if I don't get an answer."

"Security will be here any second!"

"Then Andy will give them his drink, they'll analyze it, and you'll be about seventy-five years old before you see the outside of a prison again," I said. "Now, who are you working for?"

"I don't know! It was a man I'd never seen before! He said it was a joke—that it would get the young man drunk and acting silly! I swear it!"

"What was his name?"

"I don't know! I never saw him before! He gave me fifty credits. It was a joke!"

The speaker system announced that our ship was ready for boarding.

"I'm going to let you go," I said. "Just walk away like nothing's happened. We're taking the drink onboard with us. You say a word to anyone, we give the drink to the police and tell them where we got it. Do you understand me?"

She nodded her head and I let her go. She walked away as fast as she could without breaking into a run, and was soon out of sight.

"How did you know?" whispered Andy, his eyes wide.

"She collected money from every other customer before she gave them their drinks, but she was so anxious for you to down yours that she never asked us to pay her."

"That's an awfully little thing to go on," he said.

"Wait for big things in this business and you don't live too long." I stood up. "Let's get on the ship."

I took the drink from him as he stood up. We passed a row of potted plants on the way to the hatch, and I dumped the contents into the last of them.

"That was our evidence!" he said.

"Do you want to go to Rabol, or do you want to stick around and press charges?" I asked. "Besides, they won't let you take an opened drink onto a ship. The jump to light speeds does strange things to it, even in a pressurized cabin. If she really worked here, she'd have known I was bluffing."

As we took our seats, he still looked disturbed. "Maybe we should have stuck around long enough to see her put in jail."

"She's just a dupe," I said. "And don't forget—there's still someone on Aristides who wants you dead."

"Maybe she lied," he persisted. "Maybe she knew it was poison. Maybe she poisoned it herself."

"I doubt it, but even if you're right we've seen the last of her. She knows we can identify her."

"But—"

"Look, kid," I said firmly, "I'm not a cop anymore. I'm being paid to get you home in one piece, not to put all the bad guys in jail."

He finally shut up. The trip was uneventful—almost all trips are uneventful these days—and we touched down on Rabol sixteen hours later.

The air was thin, the sun was so far away that it seemed like twilight even though it was midday, and the gravity was 1.23 Standard, which meant that you felt like you were carrying a forty-pound pack on your back.

There were a few humans in the spaceport, as well as some Mollutei and a tall, long-legged Domarian, but mostly there were hundreds of little round Rabolians scurrying all over the place.

As we approached the Customs booth, I pulled out my passport disk.

"Put it away, Jacob Masters," said the Rabolian working the booth. "Your passport is in order, but you have no business on Rabol. You will remain here while Andrew Vanderwycke is allowed to pass through Customs. The Gromite Crozchziim will stay here with you."

"You got all that out of my mind in five seconds?" I said.

"Yes," he replied. "I apologize for not reading it faster, but I am being bombarded by thoughts from the Customs booths on each side of me."

"If you're that good, why don't you just tell Andy what he needs to know right now, and we'll get back on the ship before it can take off again."

"I would do irreparable harm to his mind if I were to probe as deeply as required," answered the Customs officer. "He must go to an expert who can extract the necessary information without damaging him."

"Who do I see?" asked Andy, who was standing behind me.

"I have already made the appointment," came the answer. "Please pass through, and you will find an escort waiting to take you there."

The kid did as he was told, and Crunchtime and I went to a waiting area. Since this wasn't a Democracy planet, humans and non-humans weren't segregated, and we sat down together.

"How long do you think this will take?" he asked.

"I don't know. But given how fast this guy read our minds, it could be just a few minutes." I looked back at the Customs official. "I'm surprised he was so polite."

"Why should that surprise you?"

"Because on a world of telepaths, why would anyone learn manners or white lies or any of the social graces when everyone knows exactly what you're really thinking?" I replied. "I'll bet it's probably just a courtesy for off-worlders. They probably insulted the first few, read their minds, and figured out what was required."

"Why would Duristan leave Rabol to take a job in a sideshow?" mused Crunchtime.

"Maybe Mrs. Duristan didn't like what he was thinking every time a pretty young Rabolian twitched by," I said. "Maybe he had an urge to cheat at poker. Maybe he just wondered what the rest of the galaxy looked like; after all, a traveling carnival sees an awful lot of it." I got to my feet. "Wait here."

"Where are you going?" he asked.

"To the subspace sending station."

When I got there I fed Beatrice Vanderwycke's code into the machine, and a couple of minutes later her holograph appeared before me. It kept trying to break up but somehow preserved its integrity.

"Mr. Masters," she said to my image. "You were supposed to report to me at regular intervals."

"Every fourth or fifth day," I said smoothly. "And here I am."

"I want a progress report."

"I've got him."

"Excellent. How soon can you have him here?"

"Five days, maybe four," I said. "It depends on what kind of connections I can make."

"Why so long?"

"It's very complicated. I'll explain when we get there."

"I'll see you then."

She broke the connection.

"He's in fine health," I said sardonically to the spot where her image had been. "I was sure you'd be concerned."

I returned to Crunchtime and sat down next to him.

"You'll be pleased to know that Mrs. Vanderwycke expressed no interest in you whatsoever," I said. "She never even mentioned your name."

"You contacted her?" he said, surprised.

"Just now."

"But she's been trying to have Andy killed!" he said. "Now she'll be prepared for him when he returns to Odysseus!"

"I told her we'd be there in four or five days," I explained. "*After* I checked the flight schedule. If Andy can get back here in the next hour, we can get on a ship to Pollux IV, transfer to one bound for the Iliad system, and be there in less than a day. If she's setting up a trap, she's going to be three days late."

"I see," he said, his eyes widening. "It's probably just as well that we remain isolated from the Rabolian population. If telepaths cannot lie, observing the way your brain works might drive them all mad."

"I assume that's a compliment," I said dryly.

He was silent for so long that I began wondering if it really was a compliment after all. Then he nudged me and pointed across the spaceport huge lobby. "Here he comes."

The kid was walking toward us, accompanied by a Rabolian, who left him at the entrance to the waiting area. Andy came over and sat down, his face an expressionless mask.

"How did it go?" I asked.

"It was an . . . *unusual* . . . experience," he said. "I hope I never undergo anything like it again."

"Did it hurt much?"

"Not the way you mean," he said. "I learned what I needed to learn." He shuddered. "I also learned things no one should have to know about themselves."

He refused to say any more about it, and we soon boarded the ship to the Pollux system. We had a four-hour layover there, and I realized I hadn't eaten since we'd left Aristides, so we stopped at a restaurant in the spaceport. They didn't mind that Crunchtime was with us, but the chairs couldn't accomodate him, so he waited outside. I wanted a big, thick steak, but when I saw the prices—even mutated cattle couldn't metabolize the stuff that passed for grass on Pollux IV, and all their beef was imported—I settled for a soya substitute instead. I kept telling myself that it tasted just like grade-A prime beef, but my stomach knew I was lying. Andy just wanted water, and when they insisted that he had to order something if he was going to sit there, I told him to order a beer and I drank it when it arrived.

Then we waited for the boarding call, and finally clambered onto the ship that would take us back to Odysseus. After we'd been traveling for a couple of hours, I turned to Andy. A cartoon holo was running on his entertainment center, but he was staring through it, not at it.

"Are you going to be okay, kid?" I asked.

"Yes, I'm fine."

"We don't have to go right to your home," I continued. "We could go to the the police first, maybe bring some of them along."

"We'll have all the backup we need," said Andy. "You don't think my father is going to let anyone kill me before I prove he didn't commit that murder on Odysseus, do you?"

"No, I don't."

"I know he doesn't give a damn about me," he continued. "The only reason he wants me alive is to clear him so he can go back to Odysseus and pick up whatever he left behind from some robbery."

"How come he never asked you to get it and bring it to him?" I asked.

"He doesn't trust me," said the kid. "He doesn't trust *anyone.*" He paused. "Before we touch down, I'll have my pocket computer prepare a cube proving that my father was innocent, that my mother committed the murder he's wanted for and a lot worse crimes as well. But—"

"I know," I interrupted. "I won't turn it over to your dad until after you see your mother, or he won't have any reason to protect you."

He looked relieved that we were on the same page. "Right."

"How are you holding up, kid?" I asked him.

"I'm not afraid," he said calmly. "For the first time in my life, I'm not afraid of her. Besides," he added, "you saved my life at the carnival on Port Samarkand, and again at the spaceport. You'll save it on Odysseus if you have to."

I wanted to deny it, but I knew deep down he was right. Maybe I wasn't a cop any longer, but I still had an urge to see justice done. I'd do whatever I could to keep him alive, regardless of the risk. I began to really resent the guardian angel business.

He stopped talking, and I closed my eyes. I was just going to rest them for a moment, but the next thing I knew he was nudging me and telling me that we'd entered Odysseus' stratosphere.

"Here," he said, slipping a cube into my pocket. "I trust you to know when and how to use it."

"I appreciate your trust, but weren't you going to make half a dozen copies and ship them to various lock boxes around the Democracy?" I asked.

"I've been thinking about it," he said. "The information the cube contains is my insurance only while it's a threat, something to hold over her. If someone actually releases it, she'll go to jail, but she's vindictive enough to put a hit out on me. One cube's as good as twenty to make her leave me alone, and it's probably safer for me."

"That's some family you got yourself, kid," I said.

"My father's not so bad," he replied.

Hatchet Ben Jeffries, extortionist and bank robber and murderer, Hatchet Ben who considered his son a useless weakling worth keeping alive only until he could get his hands on whatever he'd left behind on Odysseus, wasn't so bad compared to his mother. It made me understand why he didn't have any friends, why the only thing he trusted was an alien with an unpronounceable name.

The ship touched down in a few more minutes, and I turned to the kid as we got off. "We're not going to your mother's house," I said. "It's too dangerous."

"Why?" he replied. "She's not going to do a thing until she finds out what I know and who I've told."

"Just the same, I want to meet her on neutral ground. She may have ways of extracting the information in private."

"A restaurant?" he suggested.

I considered it. "No, too easy for her to pay off the owner, or plant her men at every nearby table." I looked at the big *Welcome to Odysseus* screen that greeted newcomers with a list of the day's major events. "Okay," I said, "there's a murderball game going on right now in the stadium. That's about two miles from here. I'll tell her to meet us outside the box office in"—I checked the starting time—"about an hour. The game figures to be over by then, and there'll be thousands of people streaming out."

"You really think I need this kind of protection?" he asked.

"Kid, I don't even know if this will be adequate, but it's better than going to your home."

"All right," he consented. "You're the boss—at least, until I see her face-to-face."

I went to a vidphone booth and called Beatrice Vanderwycke. When she recognized me her image registered surprise.

"Mr. Masters," she said. "I hadn't expected to hear from you for three more days. Where are you?"

"At the Odysseus spaceport."

"Excellent! How soon can I expect you here?"

"There's been a change of plans," I said. "We're not coming to the house."

"I am paying you to find my son and deliver him to me, Mr. Masters. That was our agreement."

"I found him, and I'm going to deliver him," I replied. "But there was nothing in our agreement that stipulated I had to return him to your home."

"Where *will* you deliver him?"

"The box office at the murderball stadium, one hour from now," I said. "And Mrs. Vanderwycke?"

"Yes?"

"I want to be paid in cash."

She gave me a look that said she'd rather pay me in red-hot pokers. "I'll be there," she said, and broke the connection.

Since we had an hour, we began walking to the stadium. I stopped when we were about a quarter-mile away from it.

"What now?" asked Andy.

"No crowd," I pointed out. "The game hasn't let out yet. We'd be sitting ducks if we went there now."

We ducked into a coffee shop. They wouldn't serve Crunchtime at our table, but there was an alien section, and he sat there.

"I don't see anyone," said Andy, staring at the stadium through a window.

"Neither do I."

"You look disappointed."

"I am. Not surprised, just disappointed."

"Why to both?"

"I assume any men your mother hired are too good to be spotted, and I know your dad's got nothing but professionals on his payroll. So I'm not surprised that I can't find them—but I wish I knew where they were. Your mother's muscle may not be here yet—after all, she just found out we were on the planet forty-five minutes ago—but I have to assume your father has had some men tailing us since we came through Customs. I just want to know where everyone is so I know when and where to duck."

"Maybe being in a crowd will scare them off," he said.

"Kid, the safest place to kill someone is in the middle of a crowd," I told him. "They'll give the cops a hundred different descriptions of you, and that's if they don't start accusing each other first."

"I never thought of that."

"You never had to. And the best way to kill someone in a crowd or anywhere else is to crack his head open with a blunt instrument. Not much ballistics can do with a club or a hammer."

"So much for all those locked-room mysteries I used to watch," he said with a smile.

"They're good entertainment," I said. "But mighty few murders are committed by left-handed tightrope-walking midgets. They're committed by professionals who do it for a living and know all the angles."

Suddenly we could hear a huge roar, and then, about a minute later, the first people began leaving the stadium. Soon there were more and more, a veritable flood of Men and aliens.

"Okay," I said, getting to my feet. "Let me make a pit stop and then we'll go."

I entered the men's room, pulled Andy's cube out of my pocket, and hid it inside a ventilation shaft where the wall joined the ceiling. If Beatrice Vanderwycke's men got the drop on me, they weren't going to find it when they frisked me.

I returned to the table, left some money on it, told Andy to get up, and signaled Crunchtime to join us. The three of us left the restaurant and approached the stadium. Making any progress against all those people who were in such a hurry to get home was like swimming upstream against a raging river, but we finally made it.

"I don't see her," said Andy as he stood in front of a ticket booth.

"She'll be here," I said with absolute certainty.

"Maybe she can't see us where we're standing," he said.

"Then she'll find us. Stay right where you are, with your back against the booth. If anything's going to happen, let's make sure it happens in front of us."

And then, suddenly, she was there. I never saw her approaching us, but she was standing maybe six feet away, staring coldly at the kid.

"You've put me to a lot of trouble, Andrew," she said.

"You put me to more," he answered. "Years and years of it." His voice quavered just a bit. He was still scared of her, but he wasn't going to back off. I was proud of him. "But it's over now," he continued. "My nightmares are gone"—he forced a smile—"and yours are about to begin."

"I'm sure I don't know what you're talking about, Andrew," she said. "You're back, and that's all that matters. Your room is ready for you. Let's go home."

The crowd was getting thicker. It was difficult to hear over the noise. A man in a gray outfit jostled against me and apologized.

"It won't work, Mother," he said. "I *know*."

"What do you think you know?" she asked, her face reflecting her contempt for him.

"I know who you killed, I know how you made it look like Father did it, I know where you hid the body, and I know that even after all these years there's enough DNA evidence to convict you."

"That's a very dangerous thing to say, even to a loving mother," replied Beatrice Vanderwycke.

"Are you threatening me, Mother?" said Andy. "Because if you are, you should know that if anything happens to me, Jake will turn everything over to the police."

She caught it instantly.

You damned fool! I thought. *You just told her that you and I are the only ones with the proof!*

She turned to the man in the gray outfit, who was still standing near us.

"Kill them," she said calmly.

He pulled a pulse gun, but before he could fire it a laser beam caught him in the chest and hurled him backward. I looked around. It was the small guy from Jeffries' house. Before I could nod a thanks he keeled over, and suddenly there was a small firefight going on between her men and Jeffries' men.

People in the crowd started screaming and running. A couple of kids got knocked down, and one got trampled pretty badly. So did an old man. There was confusion everywhere—and suddenly there was a small screecher in her hand, and it was aimed at me.

"No!" cried Andy. He dove for the weapon, but she was already pushing the firing mechanism, and he got the full force of the solid sound on his left temple.

He dropped like a brick, and she turned to fire at me, but I had my burner out, and I put a black bubbling hole right between her cold hate-filled eyes.

The instant Andy and his mother fell to the ground the firefight stopped. No matter which side they were on, they seemed to know that everything was over. If they worked for Jeffries, they'd failed to save his son, and if they worked for Beatrice Vanderwycke, they hadn't been able to protect her.

Andy twitched feebly, and I knelt down next to him.

"Crunchtime, he's alive!" I yelled. "Get some help!"

There was no answer. I turned to look for him, and saw the Gromite lying on the ground in a pool of pink blood. He'd stopped a shot that was meant for mother or son, it no longer mattered which.

The police showed up a few minutes later. They raced Andy off to the hospital, and I spent the next four hours telling my story over and over again. Finally enough eyewitnesses testified that I'd shot Beatrice Vanderwycke in self-defense that they had to let me go.

I rushed to the hospital to see how the kid was doing. He was in surgery, and six hours later they guided the airsled out. It was two days before he woke up, and he wasn't the same Andy Vanderwycke I'd been traveling with. His eyes were dull, his face expressionless, and he didn't speak.

I asked his doctor how long it would be before he recovered.

"He took the full force of a sonic pistol in his head at a range of perhaps two feet," said the doctor. "It's burned out half his neural circuits."

"When will he be himself again?"

"Quite possibly never."

"He's just going to lie there and stare for the rest of his life?" I asked.

"In time he'll respond to his name, and be able to locomote and feed himself. Eventually he'll comprehend about thirty words. There's a always a chance that he'll recover, of course, but the odds are not in favor of it. You have to understand, Mr. Masters—he's lucky to be alive."

I stared at the kid. "I wouldn't call *this* luck," I said bitterly.

I had one last stop to make, one loose end to take care of. I went to the coffee shop by the stadium, waited until the men's room was empty, and made sure the cube was still there. I had every intention of turning it over to Ben Jeffies, but first I wanted to make sure Andy would be taken care of once he got his hands on it.

I caught the next ship to the Corvus system, and a few hours later they passed me through the security checkpoints on the Jeffries estate and ushered me into the mansion.

I cooled my heels for a few minutes in a library that was filled with unread books and unwatched cubes, and then was summoned to the study. Jeffries, all steel and gray, was waiting for me.

"I heard you had some trouble on Odysseus," he said. "I lost three men there."

"Yeah, it got messy." I paused. "I'm afraid I've got some bad news for you."

"You don't have what I need?"

I blinked. "I'm talking about your son. He took a shot meant for me. There's every likelihood that he's going to be a vegetable for the rest of his life."

"I don't give a shit about that!" he snapped. "I need to get that murder warrant quashed so I can get to Odysseus! Do you have any idea what he learned on Rabol?"

You son of a bitch, I thought. *Your kid has been turned into a potted plant getting the proof you need, and all you care about is picking up some loot you left on Odysseus twenty years ago.*

It was time, I decided, for the guardian angel to perform one last duty.

"He said he could prove that you were innocent of the murder on Odysseus," I said. "But he was shot before he could tell me the details or make any record of them."

"So I'll talk to him and find out."

I shook my head. "He won't know you or understand you. His neural circuits are blown."

"Is there any chance he'll come out of it?"

I shrugged. "Who knows? There's always a chance."

"All right, Jake," he said, pulling out a wad of bills. "I told you I'd pay you if Betty didn't. This will cover your time and expenses. Our business is done."

His men escorted me back to the spaceport and stayed with me until the ship took off. By the time I'd reached Odysseus Andy Vanderwycke had already been transferred to the most expensive, most exclusive facility on Deluros VIII.

That was three years ago. I haven't seen or spoken to the kid since they took him away. I stop by the coffee shop every few months to make sure the cube is still there. If the medical team on Deluros VIII can fix Andy, I'll turn it over to his father. And if not . . . well, one of these days I'll take the kid on a little trip to Rabol and see if they can straighten out all the crooked wiring and fuse some loose connections. I'll also remind them that there are a couple of areas that are better left alone.

Who knows? Maybe one team or the other can pull it off. After all, aren't angels the harbingers of miracles?

❖ IN THE QUAKE ZONE ❖
by David Gerrold

THE DAY AFTER time collapsed, I had my shoes shined. They needed it.

I didn't know that time had collapsed, wouldn't find out for years, decades—and several months of subjective time. I just thought it was another local timequake.

Picked up a newspaper—*The Los Angeles Mirror*, with its brown-tinted front page—and settled into one of the high-backed, leather chairs in the Hollywood Boulevard alcove. There were copies of the *Herald*, the *Examiner*, and the *Times* here as well, but the *Mirror* had Pogo Possum on the funny pages. "Mighty fine shoes, sir," Roy said, and went right to work. He didn't know me yet. I snapped the paper open.

I didn't have to check the papers for the date, this was late fifties, I already knew from the cars on the boulevard, an ample selection of Detroit heavy-iron; the inevitable Chevys and Fords, a few Buicks and Oldsmobiles, the occasional ostentatious Cadillac, a few Mercurys, but also a nostalgic scattering of others, including DeSoto, Rambler, Packard, Oldsmobile, and Studebaker. Not a foreign car to be seen, just a bright M&M flow of chrome-lined monstrosities growling along, many of them two-toned. The newer models had nascent tailfins, the evocation of jet planes and rocketships, giddy metal evolution, the hallmark of a decade and an industrial dead end.

The Mirror and *The Examiner* both disappeared late '58, maybe early '59, if I remembered correctly, the result of a covert deal by the publishers. Said Mr. Chandler to Mr. Hearst, I'll shut down my morning paper if you'll shut down your afternoon. "Let us fold our papers and go."

A new Edsel cruised by—right, this was '58. But I could already smell it. The Hollywood day felt gritty. The smog was thick enough to taste. The Hollywood Warner's theater had another Cinerama travelogue—the third or fourth, I'd lost track. I was tempted; not a lot of air-conditioning in this time zone. A dark old theater, cooled by refrigeration, I could skip the sweltering zenith. But, no—I might not have enough time.

The papers reported that timefaults had opened up as far north as Porter Ranch, popping Desi and Lucy seven years back into the days of chocolate conveyer belts and Vitameatavegamin; as far east as Boyle Heights where ten years were lost and the diamond-bright DWP building disappeared from the downtown skyline, along with the world famous four-level freeway interchange; as far south as Watts, they only rattled off a couple years, but it set back the construction of Simon Rodilla's startling graceful towers; and all the way west to the Pacific Ocean. Several small boats and the Catalina Ferry had disappeared, but a sparkling new Coast Guard Cutter from 1963 had chugged into San Pedro. The big red Pacific Electric streetcars were still grinding out to the San Fernando Valley. I wondered if I'd have a chance to ride one before the aftershocks hit.

Caltech predicted several days of aftershocks and the mayor was advising folks to stay close to home if they could, to avoid further discontinuities. The Red Cross had set up shelters at several high schools for those whose homes had disappeared or were now occupied by previous or subsequent inhabitants.

Already the looters and collectors from tomorrow were flocking to the boulevard. Most of them were obvious, dressed in jeans and T-shirts, but they gave themselves away by their stare-gathering unkempt haircuts and beards, their torn jeans and pornographic T-shirts. They'd be stripping the racks at World Book and News, buying every copy they could find of *Superman, Batman, Action,* and especially *Walt Disney's Comics* with the work of legendary Carl Barks. And *MAD* magazine too; the issues with the Freas covers were the most valuable. Later, they'd move west, hitting Collector's Books and Records and Pickwick's as well. The smart ones would have brought cash. The smartest ones would have brought year-specific cash. The dumb ones would have credit cards and checkbooks. Not a lot of places took credit cards yet, none of them recognized Visa or MasterCard. And nobody took checks anymore; not unless they were bank-dated; most of the stores had learned from previous timequakes.

The Harris Agency—there was no Ted Harris, but he had an agency—was just upstairs of the shoeshine stand; upstairs, turn left and back all the way to the end of the hall, no name on the glass, no glass.

The door was solid pine, like a coffin-lid, and painted green for no reason anyone could remember, except an old song, *"What's that happenin' behind the green door . . . ?"* The only identification was a small card that said BY APPOINTMENT ONLY. That wasn't true, but it stopped the casual curiosity seekers. My key still worked, the locks wouldn't be changed until 1972; there was no receptionist, the outer office was filled with cardboard file boxes and stacks of unfiled folders. Two typists were cataloging, they glanced up briefly. If I had a key, I belonged here.

Georgia was still an intern, working afternoons; she'd started when she was a student at Hollywood High, half a mile west and a couple blocks south. Now she was taking evening courses in business management at Los Angeles City College, over on Vermont, a block south of Santa Monica Boulevard. A few years from now, she'd be a beautiful honey-blonde, but she didn't know that yet and I wasn't going to risk a bad first impression by speaking out of turn. I pretended I didn't know her. I didn't, not yet.

I brushed past, into the cubby we called a conference room. More old paper and two old women. Pinched-faced and withered, they might have been the losers in a Margaret Hamilton look-alike contest. Sooner or later, one of them was probably going to demand, "Who killed my sister? Was it you?!"

Opened my wallet, started to flash my card, but the dustier of the two waved it off. "I recognize you. Wait. Sit." But I didn't recognize her. I probably hadn't met her yet. Some younger iteration of her had known an older iteration of me. I wondered how well. I wondered if I would remember this meeting then. The other woman left the room without saying a word. Just as well; some folks get uncomfortable around time-ravelers. Not travelers—*ravelers*. The folks who tend the tangled webs.

I sat. A dark mahogany table, thick and heavy. A leather chair, left over from the previous occupant of this office, someone who'd bellied up early in the thirties. She disappeared into a back room, I heard the scrape of a wooden footstool, the sound of boxes being moved on shelves, a muffled curse, very unladylike. A moment later, she came back, dropped a sealed manila envelope on the table in front of me. I slid it over, turned it around, and scanned the notations. Contract signed in 1971, backshifted to '57. Contract due date 1967. It had only been sitting here a year, and the due date was still nine years away.

A noise. I looked up. She'd put a bottle on the table and a stubby glass. I turned the bottle. It said Glenfiddich. I didn't recognize the name. I gave her the eyebrow. She said, "My name's Margaret. Today's the day you acquire this taste. You'll thank me for it later. Take as much time as you need to read the folder, but leave it here. Here's a notepad if you need to copy out anything. That contract's not due for nine years, so the best you can do today is familiarize yourself, maybe do a little scouting. There's an aftershock due tomorrow morning, about 4:30 a.m.; go to West Hollywood and it'll bounce you closer to the due date. Oh, wait—one more thing." She disappeared again, this time I heard the sounds of keys jingling on a ring. A drawer opened, stuff was shuffled around, the drawer was closed. She came back with a cash box and an old-fashioned checkbook. "I can only give you three hundred in time-specific cash, but it'll still be good in '67. There's a bank around the corner, you've got two hours until it closes, I'll give you a check for another seven hundred. You can pick up more in '67. But be careful, your account doesn't get fat for awhile. How's your ID?"

In the past, my personal past, I'd renewed my driver's license as quickly as I could after every quake, but a DL expires after three years, a passport is good for ten. The lines at the Federal Building were usually worse than the DMV, especially in a broken time zone, but except for a gap of three years in the early '70s, I had valid passports from now until the mid-eighties.

"I'm good," I nodded. I signed my name and today's date to the next line on the outside of the envelope, then broke the wax seal. It was brittle; it had been sitting on the shelf for a year, waiting for today, and who knows how long before it got to this time zone. I didn't have a lot of curiosity, most of my cases were small-timers. The big stuff, the famous stuff, most of that went to the high-profile operations, the guys on Wilshire Boulevard, some downtown, some in Westwood. There was a lot of competition there—stop Sirhan from killing RFK, catch Manson before he and the family move into the Spahn movie ranch, apprehend the Hillside Stranglers, find out who killed the Black Dahlia, help O.J. find the killers of Ron and Nicole . . . and so on.

The thing about the high-profiles, those were easy cases. The victims were known, so were the perps. The big agencies had a pretty good idea of the movements of their targets long before the crimes occurred. But most of the laws had been written before time began unraveling and the justice system wasn't geared for prevention, only after-the-fact cleanup.

Then one hot night in an August that still hasn't happened, Charles "Tex" Watson gets out of the car up on Cielo Drive and someone puts a carbon-fiber crossbow bolt right through his neck, even before he gets the gun out of his jacket. The girls start shrieking and two more of them take bolts, one of them right through the sternum, Sexie Sadie gets one in the head. The third girl, the Kasabian kid, goes screaming down the hill, and some redheaded kid in a white Nash Rambler nearly runs her down, never knowing that the alternative was having his brains splashed across the front seat of his parents' car. I didn't do it, but I knew the contract, knew who'd paid for it. Approved the outcome.

That was the turning point. After that, the judicial system learned to accommodate itself to preventive warrants, and most of the worst perps will be safe in protective custody weeks or even months before they have a chance to commit their atrocities. The question of punishment becomes one of pre-rehabilitation—is it possible? When can we let these folks back out on the streets? If ever. Do we have the right to detain someone on the grounds that they represent potential harm to others, even if no crime has been committed? The ethical questions will be argued for three decades. I don't know yet how it resolves, only that an uneasy accommodation will finally be achieved—something to the effect that there are no second chances, it's too time-consuming, pun intended; a judicial review of the facts, a signed warrant, and no, they don't call it pre-punishment. It's terminal prevention.

Meanwhile, it's the big agencies that get the star cases—save Marilyn and Elvis, save James Dean and Buddy Holly, Natalie Wood, Sal Mineo, Mike Todd, Lenny Bruce, RFK and Jimmy Hoffa. Stop Ernest Hemingway from sucking the bullet out of his gun and keep Tennessee Williams from choking to death on a bottle cap. Save Mama Cass and Jimi Hendrix and Jim Morrison and Janis Joplin and John Lennon. And later on, Karina and Jo-Jo Ray. And Michael Zone. Kelly Breen. Some of those names don't mean anything yet, won't mean anything for years; the size of the up-front money says everything—but we don't get those cases. The last one we bid on was Ramon Novarro, beaten to death with his own dildo by a couple of hustler-boys, and we didn't get that job either; later on, after the Fatty Arbuckle thing, and that was a long reach back anyway, all of those cases went through the Hollywood Preservation Society, funded by the big studios who had investments to protect.

No, it's the *other* cases, the little ones, the unsolved ones that fall through the cracks—those are the ones that keep the little agencies going. Most families can't afford five or six figure retainers, so they come to the smaller agencies, pennies in hand, desperate for help. "My little girl disappeared in June of '61, we don't know what happened, nobody ever found a trace." "I want to stop the man who raped my sister." "My girlfriend had a baby. She says it's mine. Can you stop the conception?" "My boyfriend was shot next November, the police have no clue." "I was abused by my stepfather when I was a child. Can you keep my mom from ever meeting him?"

There were a lot of amateurs in this business—and more than a few do-it-yourselfers too. But most folks don't like to go zone-hopping; it's not a round-trip. You don't want to end up someplace where you have no home, no family, no job. Just the same, some people try. Sometimes people clean up their own messes, sometimes they make bigger ones. Some things are better left to the professionals.

The Harris Agency had three or six or nine operatives, depending on when you asked. But some of them were the same operative, inadvertently (or maybe deliberately) time-folded. Eakins was a funny duck, all three of him, all ages. The Harris Agency didn't advertise, didn't have a sign on the door, didn't even have a phone, not a listed one anyway; you heard about it from a friend of a friend. We took the jobs that people didn't want to talk about, and sometimes we handled them in ways that even we didn't talk about.

You knocked on the door and if you knocked the right way, they'd let you in. Georgia would sit you down in the cubby we called a conference room, and if she liked your look, she'd offer you coffee or tea. If she didn't trust you, it would be water from the cooler. Or nothing. She conducted her interviews like a surgeon removing bullet fragments, methodically extracting details and information so skillfully you never knew you'd been incised. Most cases, she wouldn't promise anything, she'd spend the rest of the day, maybe two or three days, writing up a report, sending an intern down to the Central Library or the *Times'* morgue to pull clippings. She'd pull pages out of phone directories, call over to the Wilcox station to get driver's license information (if available), and even scanned the personal ads in the *L.A. Free Press* a couple times. For the most part, a lot of what the outer office staff did was "clipping service"—pulling out data before, during, and after the events; the more complete the file, the easier the job. Working with Margaret, the jobs were usually easy. Usually, not always.

Georgia replaced Margaret in '61, right after Kennedy's election; Margaret retired to a date farm in Indio, as soon as she felt Georgia was ready; she'd managed the agency since '39, never missing a beat. She trained Georgia and she trained her well. The kid had been a good intern, the best, a quick-study; after graduation from Hollywood High, she stayed on full time while she picked up her degree at L.A.C.C. The work wasn't hard, but it was painstaking; Margaret had been disciplined, but Georgia was meticulous. She relished the challenge. Besides, the pay was good and the job was close enough to home that she could walk to work. And at the end of the day, she'd satisfied her spirit of adventure without mussing her hair.

The files demonstrated their differences in approach. Margaret never wrote anything she couldn't substantiate. She wasn't imaginative. But Georgia always added a page or two of advice and suggestions—her own feelings about the matter at hand. Margaret didn't disapprove. She'd learned to respect Georgia's intuition. I had too.

This envelope was thin, thinner than usual. Inside, there were notes from both, I recognized Margaret' crimped precise handwriting, Georgia's flowing hand. A disappearance. Jeremy Weiss. Skinny kid. Glasses. Dark curly hair. Dark eyes, round face, an unfinished look—not much sense yet what kind of adult he might be. A waiter, an accountant, an unsuccessful scriptwriter. Seventeen and a half. Good home. Good grades. No family problems. Disappears summer of '68, somewhere in West L.A. Not a runaway, the car was found parked on Melrose, near La Cienega. But no evidence of foul play either. Parents plaster the neighborhood with leaflets. Police ask the public for help. The synagogue posts a reward for information. Nothing. Case remains open and unsolved. No clues here. Nothing to go on. The file was a list of what we didn't know.

Two ways to proceed with this one—shadow the kid or intercept him. Shadowing is a bad risk. Sometimes, you're too late, the perp is too fast, and you end up a witness instead of a hero. Agents have been sued for negligence and malpractice, for not being fast enough or smart enough, for not stopping the murder. Interception is better. But that means keeping the vic from ever getting to his appointment in Samarra. And that means the perp never gets ID'd either.

The easiest interception is a flat tire or even an inconvenient fender-bender. That can delay a person anywhere from fifteen to forty-five minutes. That's usually enough to save a life. Most cases we get are events of opportunity. Take away the opportunity, the event doesn't happen—or it happens to someone else. That's the other problem with preventive interception. It doesn't always stop the bad luck, too often it just pushes it onto the next convenient opportunity. I don't like that.

Give me a case where the perp is known ahead of time, I can get a warrant. I don't have a problem taking down a known bad-boy. I don't have to be nice, I don't have to be neat. And there are times when I really don't want to be. But give me an unsolved case, it's like juggling hand grenades. Sometimes the victim is the real perp. It's messy. You can get hurt.

But this one—I listened for the internal alarm bells—they always go off when something smells wrong; this one felt different, I'm not sure why. I had a hunch, a feeling, an intuition, call it whatever—a sense that this case was merely a loose unraveled thread of something else. Something worse. Like the redheaded kid who didn't die on August 9 was merely a sidebar.

Think about it for a minute. Hollywood is full of manboys. They fall off the buses, naïve and desperate. They're easy targets for all kinds of opportunists. Old enough to drive, but not old enough to be street smart. They come for the promise of excitement. Ostensibly, it's the glamour of the boulevard, where the widescreen movies wrap around the audience; it's the bookstores rich with lore, shelves aching with volumes of forgotten years; it's the smoky jazz clubs and the fluorescent record stores and the gaudy lingerie displays; it's the little oddball places where you can find movie posters, scripts, leftover props, memorabilia, makeup, bits and pieces of costumery—they come in from all the surrounding suburbs, looking for the discarded fragments of excitement. Sometimes they're looking for friends, for other young men like themselves, sometimes they're unashamedly looking for sex. With hookers, with hustlers, with each other. With whoever. A few years from now, they'll be looking for dope.

But what they're really looking for is themselves. Because they're unformed, unfinished. And there's nobody to give them a clue because nobody has a clue anymore. Whatever the world used to be, it hasn't finished collapsing, and whatever is going to replace it, it hasn't finished slouching toward Bethlehem. So if they're coming down here to the boulevard to look for themselves, because this looks like the center, because this looks like where it's happening, they're looking in the wrong place; because nobody ever found themselves in Hollywood, no. Much more often, they lose whatever self they had to start with.

You can't save Marilyn and Elvis because they don't exist, they never existed—all that existed was a shitload of other people's dreams dumped on top of a couple of poor souls who'd had the misfortune to end up in front of a camera or a microphone. And you can't save anyone from that. Hollywood needs a warning label. Like that pack of cigarettes I saw up the line. "Caution, this crap will kill you."

Jeremy Weiss wasn't a runaway. He didn't fit the profile. And he didn't end up in a dumpster somewhere, his body was never found. He wasn't a hustler or a druggie. I doubted suicide. I figured he was probably destined for an unmarked grave somewhere up above Sunset Boulevard, maybe in the side of a hill, one of those offshoots of Laurel Canyon that wind around forever, until they finally turn into one-lane dirt scars. Someone he met, a casual pickup, I know where there's a party, or let's go to my place—

So yeah, I could probably save this kid from the Tuesday express, but that wouldn't necessarily stop him from lying down on the tracks again on Wednesday night. Or if not him, then maybe Steve from El Segundo or Jeffrey from Van Nuys. Most of the disappearances went unreported, unnoticed. Not this one, though.

Margaret sat down opposite me. She put a second glass on the table and poured herself a shot, poured one for me.

I knew Margaret only from her work—the files that Georgia had passed me, up the line. Margaret was compulsive; she annotated everything on every case, including newspaper clippings, police reports when she could get them, and occasionally witness interviews. Reading through a file, reading her notes, her advice, her suggestions, it was like having a six-foot invisible rabbit standing behind every moment.

But today was the first time I'd actually met Margaret, and I held my tongue, still gauging what to say. Should I thank her for the cases yet to solve? Did she want to know how these cases would play out? Would it affect her reports if she knew what leads were fruitless and which ones were pay dirt? Do we advance to Go or do we go directly to jail? The real question—should we put warnings into the files? Watch out for Perry, a harmless little pisher, but an expensive one; stay away from

Chuck Hunt, the chronovore; don't go near Conway, the bigger thief; and especially watch out for Maizlish, the destroyer.

Should I ask—?

"Don't talk," she said. "There's nothing you have to say that I need to hear. I've already heard it. I'll do the talking here because I have information that you need." She pushed the glass toward me.

I took a sniff. Not bad. Normally, I don't drink scotch. I prefer bourbon. But this was different, sharper, lighter. Okay, I can drink scotch.

"Something's happening," she said.

I waited for her to go on. There's this trick. Don't say anything. Just sit and wait. People can't stand silence. The longer you wait, the more unbearable it becomes. Pretty soon, they have to say something, just to break the silence. Leave an unanswered question in the air and wait, it'll get answered. Unless they're playing the same game. Except Margaret wasn't playing games.

She finished her scotch, neat, put the glass down, and stared across the table at me. "The perps are starting to figure it out." She let that sink in for a moment. "The timequakes. The perps are using public quake maps to avoid capture. Or to commit their crimes more carefully. Bouncing forward, back, sideways. They call it the undertime railway. LAPD has taken down the Manson clan three times now. Each time, earlier. Now they're talking about maybe legalizing preemptive abortion. Just stop them from being born. Nobody's sure yet. The judges are still arguing. The point is, you'll have to be careful. Especially with cases like this where we don't have any information. The perp always knows more about the crime than the investigator. The more the perp knows, the harder the job becomes. If the case gets any publicity, the perp gets dangerous.

"Here's the good news. Caltech has been mapping the timequakes. They've been putting down probes all over the county for thirty years now. We have their most recent chart. The one they didn't make public. It cost us some big bucks and a couple of blow jobs." She unrolled a scroll across the table—it looked like the paperback edition of the Torah, smaller but no less detailed. "It stretches from 1906 all the way to 2111, so far. All of the big quakes and aftershocks are noted, those are the public ones, the ones the perps know. But all of the littler ones are in here too." She tapped the scroll. "*This* is your advantage.

"Most people don't notice the little tremors, the unnoticeable ones.

You know that feeling when you keep thinking it's Monday when it's really Sunday? That's a dayquake. Or when you've been driving for an hour and you can't remember the last ten miles? Or when you've been at work eight hours and you still have seven hours to go? Or when you're out clubbing and suddenly the evening's over before it's really started? Those are all tremors so small you don't even feel them, or if you do notice, you figure it's just you. But Caltech has them charted, has the epicenters noted, can tell you almost to the second how far forward or back each quake bounces. See the arrows? You can chart a time-trajectory from here to forever—well at least up to 2111, depending on which of the local trajectories you choose. They probably have even more complete charts uptime, but we can't get them yet. We expect Eakins to send back copies, but nothing's arrived yet, not this far back. But it should have reached '67 by now. So as soon as you get there, come back to this office. I won't be here, I'm already retired in '67, but Georgia will have what you need. We start bringing her up to speed right after Kennedy's election.

"The point is, this timeline gives you more maneuverability. Protect it like it's gold. If a perp gets it, it'd be a disaster. That's why it's on proof paper. It goes black after twenty minutes' exposure to UV." She rolled it up, slid it into a tube, capped it, and passed it over to me. "Right. Get to the bank, get yourself some dinner, then get out to the quake zone. You've got a reservation at the Farmer's Daughter Motel. That puts you half a block from the epicenter. You can get a good night's sleep. Georgia will see you here in '67."

Picked up some comics at the Las Palmas newsstand and shoved them into my briefcase, I do a little collecting myself, on the fringes, mostly just for my retirement. But not only comics. Barbie dolls, G.I. Joe, Hot Wheels cars, Pez boxes, stuff like that. And I'm saving up for a trip back to '38, I hope to pick up some IBM stock.

The Farmer's Daughter is better than it sounds. On Fairfax, walking distance from Farmer's Market. Of course, it isn't the Farmer's Daughter yet, but it will be in '67.

I check in, check the room, check the bed, think about a hooker, I have the number of an escort service, they'll be in business for another year or so; but it's not a good idea. There might be a foreshock. Almost certainly, there will be a foreshock. Not fair to the girl.

So I content myself with a nightcap in the bar. It's almost deserted. Just the bartender and me. His name is Hank. I ask him what time he gets off, he thinks I'm hitting on him, he gives me a big friendly grin, but I say, no thanks. Close up and go home. Timequake tonight, an aftershock. He shrugs. He's already been caught in two quakes. He won't even keep a cat now. Everything important, he keeps in a bag by the door. Just like me.

Not a lot of out-of-towners visit L.A. anymore; they don't want to risk the possibility of time-disruption, finding themselves a year or ten away from their families. But some folks deliberately come to L.A., hoping to ride a quake back so they can prevent some terrible event in their lives. Some succeed, some don't. Others have meticulous lists of sporting events and charts of stock fluctuations; they expect to get rich with their knowledge. Some do, some don't.

I fall asleep in front of the TV, watching Jack Paar on *The Tonight Show*. I wake up and it's the last week of April '67. The smog is the same, the cars are smaller and more teenage; on the plus side, the skirts are a lot shorter. But my old brown suit is out of style. And my car is visibly obsolete—a '56 Chevy. Obvious evidence that I'm a wandering time-raveler.

Caught breakfast in the market, fresh fruit, not too expensive yet, then headed back up to the boulevard. Santa Monica Boulevard was now a tawdry circus of adult bookstores, XXX theaters, and massage parlors. The buildings all looked like garish whores.

Hollywood Boulevard was worse. The stink of incense was almost strong enough to cover the smog. Clothing had turned into costumes, with teens of both sexes wearing tight pants and garish shirts—not quite hippies yet, but almost. The first bell-bottom jeans were showing, the Flower Children were just starting to bloom. The summer of love was about to begin.

Several storefronts had signs for time-tours and maps of the quake-zones; probably a better business than maps to the homes of the stars. I noticed several familiar faces—a small herd of comic book collectors—heading toward the newsstand on Cahuenga; they were probably the first customers of the quake-maps.

Roy was still shining shoes, twelve years older, but just as slick and just as fast. "Shoes look good, Mr. Harris," he said, as I walked in. He called all of us Mr. Harris. Nobody ever corrected him. Maybe it was his way of keeping track. He knew who we were, but he never asked questions, and he never offered advice. He kept his own counsel. But sometimes, he steered the right people to the office and sometimes he turned other folks away. "What you lookin' for ain't up those stairs, mister." Every so often, Georgia would march downstairs and hand him an envelope. She never said why. I assumed that was something else she'd learned from Margaret.

The office had been redecorated; it felt more like Georgia now. All of the typewriters were IBM Selectrics. New lateral filing cabinets, a Xerox photocopier, even a fax machine. The cubby had been painted light blue with white trim and the stacks of boxes and files had disappeared, replaced by dark oak bookshelves. Most of the files had moved into the offices next door, which we'd leased in '61, when the accountant finally died. It'd be another few decades before we would have all that information on hard drives and optical discs. The same heavy mahogany table and leather chairs remained in the center of the room, but looking a lot more worn.

Georgia was expecting me. She tossed the same manila envelope on the table, brought in another bottle of Glenfiddich, one glass, and a new pocket Torah. I passed her the old one, as well as the few collectible treasures I'd picked up in '58. She'd put them in storage for me.

"Lose the brown suit," she said. "I bought you a new one, dark gray. It's in the closet. Already tailored. Read the file, there's some new information." She reached for the bottle.

"Not this early, thanks." I was already signing the envelope. The file had been accessed only three times in the last twelve years. Margaret twice, Georgia once. But it was significantly thicker.

This time there was a bundle of newspaper clippings. Not about Jeremy Weiss, but about a dozen *others*. I checked the dates first. June of '67 to September of '74. Georgia had typed up a chart. At least thirteen young men had disappeared. Jeremy Weiss was the third. The third that we knew about. I wasn't surprised. I'd had a hunch there was more.

We weren't obligated to investigate the disappearances of the others; Weiss was the only one we had a contract on. But if the disappearances were related . . . if they had a common author, then finding that author would not only save Weiss, but a dozen others as well. Preemptive action. But only if the disappearances were connected. We'd still have to monitor—*save*—Weiss. Just in case.

I read through the clippings, slowly, carefully. Three times. There was a depressing similarity. Georgia sent out for sandwiches. After lunch, she sat down next to me—she was wearing the Jasmine perfume again, or maybe still, or maybe for the first time—and walked me through the similarities she'd noticed. The youngest victim was fifteen, but big for his age; the oldest was twenty-three, but he looked eighteen.

Last item in the envelope was a map of West Los Angeles with a red X at the site of each vic's last known location; his apartment, his job, where his car was discovered, or the last person to see him alive. There were no X's north of Sunset, none south of Third. The farthest west was Doheny, the farthest east was just the other side of Vine Street. It was a pretty big target area, but at the same time fairly specific.

"I want you to notice something," she said. She pointed to the map, tracing an area outlined by a yellow highlighter. All of the red X's were inside, or very close to the border of the yellow defined region, except for the one east of Vine. "Look at this." She tapped the paper with her fingernail. "That's West Hollywood. Have you seen it?"

"Drove through it this morning."

"Ever hear of *Fanny Hill*?"

"Isn't that a park in Boston?"

"Not funny. Don't quit your day job. It's a book, by John Cleland. *Memoirs of a Woman of Pleasure*. It has redeeming social value. Now."

"Sorry, I'm not following."

"John Cleland was born in 1710. He worked for the East India Company, but he didn't make much money at it. He ended up in Fleet debtors' prison from 1748–1749. While there, he wrote or rewrote a book called *Fanny Hill*. It's written as a series of letters from Fanny to another woman, and it is generally considered the first work of pornography written in English, its literary impact derives from its elaborate sexual metaphor and euphemistic language."

"And this is important because . . . ?"

"Because last year—1966—the Supreme Court declared that it is not obscene." She didn't wait for me to look puzzled. "In 1957, in Roth versus the United States, the Supreme Court ruled that obscenity is not within the area of constitutionally protected freedom of speech or press, neither under the first amendment, nor under the due process clause of the fourteenth amendment. They sustained the conviction of a bookseller for selling and mailing an obscene book and obscene circulars and advertising.

"In 1966, in Cleland versus Massachusetts, the court revisited their earlier decision to clarify the definition of obscenity. Since the Roth ruling, for a work of literature to be declared obscene, a censor has to demonstrate that the work appeals to prurient interest, is patently offensive, and has no redeeming social value. It's that last one that's important, because it could not be demonstrated to the court that *Fanny Hill* has no redeeming social value. The case can be made that the book is an historical document, presenting an exaggerated and often satirical view of the mores of eighteenth-century London, just as the *Satyricon* by Petronius presents an exaggerated and satirical view of ancient Rome; so a very strong case can be made that pornography represents a singular insight into the morality of its time. Thus, it has redeeming social value. Therefore, it cannot be prosecuted as obscene."

"Redeeming social value. . . ."

"Right."

"Since the *Fanny Hill* ruling, pornography has become an industry. If a publisher can claim redeeming social value, the work is legal. A book of erotic pictures with a couple quotes from Shakespeare. A sex film with a preface by a doctor—or an actor playing a doctor. It's a legal fan dance—you don't go to the fan dance to see the fan. The pornographers will be testing the limits of the law for years. The fans are going to get a lot smaller."

"Okay, so what does all this have to do with West Hollywood?"

"I'm getting to that. For the next decade, enforcement of obscenity laws will be left to local communities. There will be years of debate. Nothing will be clear or certain, because the definition of obscenity will be determined by local community standards. Until even that argument gets knocked down. At some point, the whole issue of redeeming social value becomes moot because it becomes unenforceable. How do you define it? And that'll be the end of antismut laws. But right now, today— it's all about local community standards."

"And West Hollywood is a local community . . . ?"

"It's an *unincorporated* community," Georgia said. "It's not part of Los Angeles. It's not a city. It's a big hole in the middle of the city. L.A.P.D. has no authority inside this yellow area. There's no police coverage. The only enforcement is the L.A. County Sheriff Department. So there's no community and there are no standards. It's the wild west."

"Mm," I said.

"Right," she agreed. "None of the city ordinances apply. Only the county ones. And the county is a lot less specific on pornography. So you get bookstores. And more. The county doesn't have specific zoning restrictions or statutes to regulate massage parlors, sex stores, and other adult-oriented businesses. The whole area is crawling with lowlifes and opportunists. Here—" She pulled out another map. This one showing a corridor of red X's stretching the length of Santa Monica Boulevard, with a scattered few on Melrose.

"What's this?"

"A survey of sex businesses in West Hollywood. Red for hetero, purple for homo, green for the bookstores. You get clusters. Here, all the way from La Brea to La Cienega, this used to be a quiet little neighborhood where seniors could sit in the sun at Plummer Park and play pinochle. Now, there are male hustlers in hot pants, posing at the bus stops.

"Take a drive around the neighborhood. You'll see things like massage parlors advertising specific attention to love muscle stiffness— Greek, French, and English massage. Or sex therapists who will help you work out your inhibitions with sex fantasy role-playing. Here, here, and here, these are gay bars, this is a bath house, so is this. This place sells costumes, chains, things made of leather—and realistic prostheses."

"Prostheses—?" And then I got it. "Never mind."

"If you can imagine a sexual service, you'll find it here. This is the land of negotiable virtue. It's a sexual carnival, the fun zone, the zoo. This is the reservoir of licentiousness. This is where AIDS will start. You'll need to start carrying condoms. Anyway—" She stretched out the two maps side by side. "Notice the congruence? I'm going to make a guess—"

"These kids are horny?"

"And gay."

"Is that a hunch, or—?"

She didn't answer immediately. "Okay, I might be wrong. But if I'm right, then the police will be useless to us. Ditto the sheriff's department. They don't care. Not here. They won't take this seriously. And we can't talk about this with any of the parents. And probably not even with the kids themselves. This is still the year of the closet . . . and will be until June of '69. Stonewall," she explained.

"I know about Stonewall. We bid on a contract to videotape it. The problem will be getting cameras onsite."

"Eakins is working on that. There's a thing called . . . never mind, I don't have time to explain it." She tapped the table. "Let's get back to this case. We've got six weeks until the first disappearance. This is as close as you can get by time-skipping. You'll have to live concurrently, but that'll be an advantage. You can familiarize yourself with the area, locate the victims, make yourself part of the landscape. Let your sideburns grow. We've found an apartment for you, heart of the district, corner of North Kings Road and Santa Monica, second floor. Here, wait a minute—" She stepped out of the room for a second, came back with a cardboard filebox, and a set of keys. "We bought you a new car too. You can't drive a '56 Chevy around '67 L.A. It attracts too much attention."

"But I like the Chevy—"

"We bought you a '67 Mustang convertible. You'll be invisible. There are a hundred thousand of these ponies in California already. It's in the parking lot behind. Give me the keys to the Chevy. We'll restore it and put it in storage. Another forty years, it'll be worth enough to buy a retirement condo. A high-priced apartment."

She popped the top off the box. In it were another dozen envelopes of varying thicknesses. "Everything we've got on the other disappearances. Including pictures of the vics. It's the first two you want to focus on."

I sorted through the reports. "Okay, so we have an approximate geographical area and a pretty specific age range. Is there anything else to connect these victims?"

"Look at the pictures. They're all twinks."

"Twinks?"

"Pretty boys."

"And based on that, you think they're gay?"

"I think we're dealing with a serial killer. Someone who preys on teenage boys. Yeah, I know—lots of kids go missing every year just in L.A. County. They hop on a bus, they go to Mexico or Canada, they go underground to avoid the draft. Or maybe they just move without leaving a forwarding address. But these thirteen don't fit that profile. The only connection is that there's no other connection. I don't know. But that's what it smells like to me." She finished her drink. Neat. Just like Margaret. "I think if we find out what happened to the first victim, we unravel the whole string."

I finished my drink, pushed my glass away, empty. Put my hand over it in response to her questioning glance. One shot was enough. If she was right, this was big. Very.

Took a breath, let it out loudly, stared across at her. "Georgia, you've been working these streets long enough to know every gum spot by brand name. I won't bet against you." I gathered the separate files. "I'll check them out." I thought for a moment. "How old am I now?"

Georgia didn't even blink. "According to our tracking, you're twenty-seven." She squinted. "With a little bit of work, we could probably make you look twenty-one or twenty-two. Put a little bleach in your hair, put you in a surfer shirt and shorts, you'll look like a summer-boy. What are you thinking? Bait?"

"Maybe. I'm thinking I might need to talk to some of these kids. The closer I am to the same age, the more likely I'll get honesty."

Something occurred to me. I turned the maps around and peered back and forth between them. Pulled the disappearance map closer.

"What are you looking for?"

"The dates. Which one of these was first?"

"This one, over here." She tapped the paper. The one east of Vine. "Why?"

"Just something I heard once about serial killers. Always look closest at the first vic. That's the one closest to home. That's more likely a crime of opportunity than premeditated. And sometimes that first vic and the perp—sometimes they know each other."

"You've never done a serial killer before," Georgia said.

"You're thinking about bringing in some help?"

"It might not be a bad idea."

Considered it. "Can't bring in L.A.P.D. They have no jurisdiction. And County isn't really set up for this."

"Bring in the Feds?"

I didn't like that idea either. "Not yet. We might embarrass ourselves. Let me do the groundwork first. I'll poke around for a few days, then we'll talk. See if you can get anything from uptime."

"I've already put a copy of the file in the long-safe. I'll add your notes next week. Then we'll look for a reply."

The long-safe was a kind of time capsule. It was a one-way box with a time-lock. You punch in a combination and a due date, a drawer opens and you put a manila envelope in. On the due date—ten or twenty or thirty years later—the drawer pops open, you take the file out and read it. Usually, the top page is a list of unanswered questions. Someone uptime does the research, looks up the answers, writes a report, puts it in another manila envelope, and hands it to a downtime courier—someone headed backwards, usually on a whole series of errands. The downtime courier rides the quakes until he or she reaches a point before the original memo was written. The courier delivers the envelope, and it goes into the long-safe, with a due date *after* the send date of the first file, the one with all the questions. This was one of the ways, not the only one, that we could ask the future for help with a case.

Sometimes we sent open-ended queries—what should we know about that we don't know yet to ask? Sometimes we got useful information, more often not. Uptime was sensitive about sending too much information back. Despite the various theories about the chronoplastic construction of the stress-field, there weren't a lot of folks who wanted to take chances. One theory had it that sending information downtime was one of the things that triggered time-quakes, because it disturbed the fault lines.

Maybe. I dunno. I'm not a theorist. I'm just a meat-and-potatoes guy. I roll up my sleeves and pick up the shovel. I prefer it that way. Let somebody else do the heavy thinking, I'll do the heavy lifting. It's a fair trade.

I didn't set out to be a time-raveler. It happened by accident. I was in the marines, got a promotion to sergeant, and re-upped for another two years. Spent eighteen months in Nam as an advisor, mostly in Saigon, but occasionally up-country and twice out into the Delta. The place was a fucking time bomb. Victor Charlie wanted to give me an early retirement, but I had other plans. Rotated stateside the first opportunity.

Got off the plane in San Francisco, caught a Greyhound south, curled up to sleep, and the San Andreas time-fault let loose. It was the first big timequake and I woke up three years later. 1969. Just in time to see Neil Armstrong bounce down the ladder. Both Dad and the dog were dead. I had no one left, no home to return to. Someone at the Red Cross Relocation Center took my information, made some phone calls, came back and asked me if I had made any career plans. Not really, why? Because there's someone you should talk to. Why? Because you have the right set of skills and no close family connections. What kind of work? Hard work. Challenging, sometimes dangerous, but the money's good, you can carry a gun, and at the end of the day you're a hero. Oh, that kind of work. Okay. Sure, I'll meet him. Good, go to this address, second floor, upstairs from the shoeshine stand. Your appointment is at three, don't be late. And that was it.

My first few months, Georgia kept me local, bouncing up and down the early '70s, doing mostly easy stuff like downtime courier service. She needed to know that I wouldn't go off the rails. The only thing the agency has to sell is trust. But I wasn't going anywhere. The agency was all I had—they were a serendipitous liftoff from the drop zone of '69, and you don't frag the pilot. A lieutenant maybe, but never a pilot—or a corpsman.

I'd thought about corpsman training early, even gone so far as to sit down with the sergeant. He just looked across the desk at me and shook his head. "There's more to it than stabbing morphine needles into screaming soldiers. You're better where you are." I didn't know how to take that, but I understood the first time mortar shells came dropping in around us and voices all around started screaming, "Medic! Medic!" I wouldn't have known which way to run. And I just wanted to keep my head down as low as possible until the whole damn business was over. It was only later, I got angry enough to start shooting back. But that was later.

After the courier bit became routine, Georgia started increasing my responsibilities. When you pass through '64, pick up mint-condition copies of these books and magazines. Pick up more if they're in good condition, but don't be greedy. Barbie dolls, assorted outfits (especially the specials), and Hot Wheels, always. Buy extras if they have them. Sometimes she just wanted me to go someplace and take pictures—of the street, the houses, the cars, the signs.

After a couple months, I told Georgia that the work didn't seem all that challenging. Georgia didn't blink. She told me that I had to learn the terrain, I had to get so comfortable with the shifting kaleidoscope of time that I couldn't be rattled. That's why the '60s and the '70s were such a good training ground. The nation went through six identifiable cultural transitions in the course of sixteen years. But even though the '50s were supposed to be a lot quieter, she didn't think so. They weren't all that safer, it was just a different kind of danger. Georgia said she wanted to keep me out of that decade as much as possible. "You've got tombstones in your eyes," she said. "You'll scare the shit out of them. And frightened people are dangerous. Especially the ones with power. Later, after you've mellowed, we'll send you back. We'll see."

After a bit, she started passing me some of the little jobs, the ones where clients bought themselves a bit of protection, or closure, or prevention.

For instance: "Here, this file just came up. Here's fifty dollars. Go to this address, give it to this person. Find a way to make it legit, tell him you're a location manager for Warner Brothers, you're shooting a pilot, some TV series, a cop show, lots of location work like *Dragnet*, you want to measure the apartment, photograph the view from the balcony, and here's a few bucks for your trouble." That one was easy. A struggling young writer with no food in the house, desperate and waiting to find out if he'd sold his first book, all he needed was another week—his future self was giving him a lifeline.

Another one: "The mail carrier delivers the mail to this address between 1 and 2 p.m. Nobody will be home before five. Open the mailbox and remove any letters with this return address. Do this every day for the next two weeks." A fraternity at USC. That one didn't make sense until a year later when that same fraternity was thrown off campus for a hazing scandal. Somebody didn't get the invitation to rush, didn't pledge, didn't get injured, and didn't have his college career stained.

And a third: "Tomorrow afternoon, this little boy's pet dog gets out an open window and wanders away from the house. Nobody's home until three. Pick up the dog before it gets to the avenue, come back at seven, knock on the door, and ask if they know who the dog belongs to, you found it the next block over." Right. No mystery there.

"Tuesday evening, Lankershim Boulevard, across the street from the El Portal Theater. There's a blue Ford Falcon. Somebody sideswipes it, sometime between 6:45 and 9:30. Get the license number, leave a note on the windshield."

After those, I started getting the weird jobs. Some of them made no sense, there was no rational explanation; but the client doesn't always give reasons. Our rule is that we only take oddball cases on the condition that no physical or personal harm is intended.

Here's one: "Take this copy of *Popular Mechanics*, thumb through it so it looks used. Tomorrow afternoon, 1:30, go out to Van Nuys, 5355 Van Nuys Boulevard, Bobs #7. Sit at the counter near the front, near the go-order window. Order a Big Boy hamburger and a Coke. Read the magazine while you eat. Fold it so the ad on page 56 is visible. Leave a dollar tip. Leave the magazine on the table."

And another: "Friday night, just after the bars close, stand in front of the door at this address, like you're waiting for a ride. That's all. Nothing will happen. You can leave at 2:30."

And one more: "Take this package. No, don't open it. At 4:25, catch the 86 bus at Highland. Get off at Victory and Laurel Canyon. Cross the street and wait for the return bus. Leave the package on the bench."

And the weirdest: "Here's a white T-shirt, blue jeans, and a red jacket; right, the James Dean look. You've got the face for it. Tomorrow afternoon, Studio City, corner of Ventura and Laurel Canyon. When this kid comes out of the drugstore, you stop her and say, 'When you are ready to learn, the universe will provide a teacher. Even when you are not ready to learn, the universe will provide a teacher.' Hand her this paper. It has a poem by Emily Dickinson. Don't answer questions. Go into the drugstore, go all the way to the back and out to the parking lot, turn right and duck around the corner of the building, she won't follow, but she mustn't see you again. Walk west till you get to the ice cream store. You can park your car behind it."

Finally, when Georgia was satisfied that I could follow orders, she gave me a tough one. "Do you trust me? Good. Go to this address and kneecap this son of a bitch."

"Kneecap?"

"Slang term. Shoot him in the kneecap. Both kneecaps. We want him in a wheelchair for the rest of his life. Oh, and rip the phone off the wall. Wear these gloves, wear these shoes—use this gun, here's ammunition, here's a silencer, put everything in this plastic trash bag, bring it all back here for disposal."

"You're kidding."

"We don't joke about things like this."

"Shoot him in the kneecaps—y'know, that's a tricky shot. Especially if he's moving."

"If you can't manage it—"

"I can manage it."

"Would you rather just kill him?"

Thought about it for two or three seconds. "What'd he do?"

"You don't like being hired muscle, do you?"

"I just need to know—"

"It's righteous," she said. "He's a rapist. He rapes little girls. The youngest is six. And then he kills them. He goes off the rails tomorrow. Cripple him tonight and you'll save three lives that we know of, probably more if he starts time-walking."

"Can I ask you a question? Who makes these decisions?"

She shook her head. "It's a need-to-know thing." Then she added,

"Think of it this way. The perps choose it when they choose to be perps. We try to provide permanent solutions. This guy tonight—he's a dangerous asshole. Do your job and tomorrow, he'll just be an asshole." She shrugged. "Or a corpse. Either is part of the contract. Whatever's easiest for you. Or most enjoyable. Your call."

"I'm not a psychopath."

"That's too bad. We really do need one. For the big jobs."

I let that pass. "Do we have a preemptive warrant?"

Georgia shook her head. "That law hasn't been passed yet. But we can't wait. Here, ease your conscience. After you do him, drop this envelope out of the plastic bag, leave it on the floor."

"What's in it? Cash?"

"Clippings. About how he'll torture his victims. Leave it for the cops, they'll get it. Don't touch anything, don't leave prints."

There were other jobs like that. They never got any easier.

In real life, you don't shoot the gun out of the bad guy's hand. The bad guys don't drop the gun, say ouch, and reach for the sky—no, they shoot back. With everything they've got, with bullets and mortars and mines that take your best buddy's legs off. They just keep coming at you, spraying blood and fire, hammering explosions, hailstorms of dirt and flesh and bone. You have to keep your head down and your helmet tight and hope you have a chance to lay down a carpet of fire, burn them alive and screaming, just to buy those moments of empty dreadful silence while you wait to see if it starts up again. In real life, you beat them senseless just to slow them down. And if that doesn't slow them down, you kill them, you blow them away, you turn them into queasy red gobbets.

On TV, everything is neat. Real life is messy, ugly, scabrous, squalid, festering, putrid, and painful. In real life, the bad guys don't think they're bad, they think they're good guys too, just doing their stuff because that's the stuff that a man's gotta do; but in real life, there are no good guys, just guys, doing each other until everybody's done. And then maybe afterward, while you're picking up the pieces of your corporal or your radioman, you get a chance to sort it out. Maybe. And that's when it doesn't matter if anybody's a good guy, they're still dead.

Because in real life, there are no good guys. They don't exist and neither do you. That's the cold hard truth. You're not there, you're just another TV death, consumed like a TV dinner, until it's time to change the channel. You think you have a life? No. You're just the space where all this shit is happening. That cascade of experience—you don't own it, it owns you. You're the bug in the trap. The avalanche of time, the pummeling of a trillion quantum-instants, second after second, it pounds you down into the sand, and whatever you think you are, it's an illusion—you exist only as a timebinding hallucination of continuity. And after long enough, after you realize you can't endure anymore of this senseless pummeling—whether it's mortar shells or rifle bullets or cosmic zingers so tiny you don't know you've taken one in the heart until you get to the third paragraph—you just continue anyway. Waiting. Sooner or later, the snipers will get your range.

You don't survive, you just take it a day at a time, a moment at a time. You pick your steps carefully, always watching for the one that might go click. You look, you listen, and you never move fast—until you have to. And when you do, you take the other guy down first, and keep him down, and you don't worry about nice and you don't worry about pretty; the whole idea is to keep him from ever getting up again. So you do what you do so he can't do what he does. And once in a while, somebody tells you it was worth it, but you know better, because you're still carrying the ruck through the hot zone, not them. In real life, real life stinks.

So I took him down. Him and the next three. And I learned to drink Glenfiddich straight from the bottle.

Until one morning, Georgia dragged me out of bed, still covered in vomit and stink, rolled me into a tub and filled it with cold water. Grabbed me by the hair, dunked me until I screamed, and poured cold black stale coffee down my throat until I was swearing in English again. My head hammering like a V-8 with a broken rod, she dressed me, drove me to the gym and handed me over to Gunter, the personal trainer. After that, 7 a.m. every day. In the afternoon, language classes at the Berlitz. Monday evenings, firing range—hands-on experience with weapons from here to flintlocks. Tuesday, world history class. Wednesday, Miss Grace's Academy of Deportment, I'm not kidding. Thursday, meeting—friends of Bill W. Friday, movie night. With Georgia. Not a date—cultural acclimatization. Saturday, assigned research and dinner at Georgia's. Not a date—a full report on the week. Sunday . . . breakfast with Georgia.

She didn't save my life. She made it worth enduring. Especially when we started sleeping together. Not at her place, not at mine, she wouldn't have that. We went to one of those little cardboard motels out on Cahuenga, where it turns into Ventura, halfway between here and the San Fernando Valley. She needed danger and I needed sex. So we rumpled the sheets like a war zone for three months regular, every Saturday night—until the next timequake and I had to go to Sylmar and bounce forward three years, and even though I was up for it, even thinking maybe I should buy her a ring, she'd already moved on, and that was the end of it. That was the zinger right through the heart.

I found something else to do on Thursday nights and let myself have one glass of scotch every time I finished a dirty job. Sometimes the clean jobs too. It didn't help. And I told her why.

No, it wasn't her. It was that other thing. The good-guy thing. I didn't feel like one. Killing for peace is like fucking for chastity. It doesn't work.

She offered to buy out my contract, send me off somewhere to retire, I'd certainly earned it. But no—I don't know why I said no. Maybe it was because there was still work to do. Maybe it was because I still wanted to believe there was something to believe in. What the hell. It was better than sitting on my ass and poisoning my liver.

So I took the envelope and left the bottle. Maybe someday I'd figure it out, but for now, I wasn't looking anymore.

Picked up the first vic at his job, tailed him to his place. Brad Boyd. He lived in a courtyard apartment on Romaine, just east of Vine. In two and a half months, the bitchy neighbor who hates his dog and his motorcycle will be the last person to see him. She'll scream at him about the bike being on the walk, in everybody's way; then she'll push it over. He'll pick it up, get on it, turn it away from her so both exhaust pipes are pointing in her direction, and rev it as loud as he can, belching out huge clouds of oil-smelling smoke; then he'll roar away. 9:30 p.m. on a hot Thursday night in July. It's a blue Yamaha, two-stroke engine, 750 cc, a mid-sized bike; it'll never be found. Left this vic at home, watching TV. The blue glow is visible from the street.

Headed out to the valley and drove past the Van Nuys home of the Weiss kid. He still lives with his mother, his dad died a year ago; he's in his last year at San Fernando Valley State College in Northridge. His room is in the back of the house, I can't see any lights. But his car is in the driveway.

The fourth vic lives on Hyperion in the Silver Lake area, catches the bus downtown, where he works for a bank. I ride the bus opposite him, sit where I'm not in his line of sight, and study him all the way to

Hill Street. Randy something. Skinny little kid, very fair complexion, too pretty to be a boy; put a dress on him you can take him anywhere. They must have teased the hell out of him in school.

After that, I check the locations, the last known sightings. I'll start working on the other vics next week; I want to read the neighborhood first. Weiss's car will be found on Melrose Avenue, two-three blocks east of the promising lights of La Cienega. Carefully parked, locked up tight. He went someplace, he never came back. I park across the street. I lean back against the warm fender of the Mustang and study the street. At first glance, it seems innocent enough.

This forgotten little pocket of West Hollywood is a time zone unto itself, with most of its pieces left over from the twenties and thirties. In '67, Melrose is dotted with tacky little art galleries, interior decorators, and a scattering of furniture stores hoping to get trendy. It's a desolate avenue, even during the day.

At night, the street is dry and deserted, amber streetlights pockmark the gloom; a few blocks away, the bright bustle of life hurtles down La Cienega, but here emptiness, the buildings huddled dark and empty against themselves, waiting for the return of day and the illusion of life. Bits of neon shine from darkened storefronts. Occasional red-lit doorways hint at secret worlds.

Few cars cruise here, even fewer souls are seen on the sidewalks— only the occasional oasis of a sheltered restaurant, remaining open even after everyone else has fled; departing customers move quickly from bright doorways to the waiting safety of their automobiles, tuck a bill into the valet's hand, and whisper away into the night.

There's this thing they do in the movies, in a western, or a war picture, where someone says, "It's quiet, too quiet." Or: "Listen. Even the birds are silent." That's how they do it in the movies, but that's not how it works in the hot zone. In the zone, it's more like a little timequake. There's this sense, this feeling that you get—like the air doesn't taste quite right. And when you get that feeling, sometimes the little hairs on the back of your neck start tickling. You stop, you look around, you look for the reason why those little hairs are rising. Sometimes, it's just a shift in the wind and the way the grass ripples across the hillside, and as you watch the ripples, you realize that one of those ripples isn't like the others. And you wake up inside your own life in a way that makes the rest of the day feel like somnambulism.

Sometimes the feeling isn't anything at all. Sometimes the feeling is just too much coffee. But it's a real feeling and you learn to respect it anyway because you're out there in the hot and the guy who drew the pretty pictures on the chalkboard isn't. You hit the dirt—and the one time you hit the dirt and hear the round go past just over your head instead of through your gut—that one time makes up for all the times you hit the dirt and there's nothing overhead.

You learn to listen for the feeling. You never stop. Years later, even after the Delta has receded into time, you're still listening. You listen to the world like it's ticking off, counting down. You listen, not even knowing what you're listening for anymore.

Standing on Melrose, I got something. Not the same feeling, but a feeling. A sense there's something *else* here. Something that comes out, late at night. And good folks don't want to be here when it's up and about.

Get back in the car. Lean back and disappear into the shadows. Sit and wait, not for anything in particular. Just to see what comes out in the darkness. Picket duty. Eyes and ears open; mind catching forty. Watching. Reading the street.

The avenue has a vampiric life of its own. Every so often, motion. A manboy, sometimes two. Sometimes a girlboy. The children of the night climb out of their daytime coffins and drift singly through the shadows, flickering briefly into existence for a block or two, then disappearing just as ephemerally. It isn't immediately obvious what's happening here.

Finally, got out of the car and went for a walk. West, where Melrose angles in toward La Cienega. Where are the manboys going? Where are they coming from?

Ah.

Half a block east of the lights. A darkened art gallery with an unpaved parking lot. The lot is dark, unlit. At the back is a fenced-in covered patio. Discreet. Unobtrusive. Inconspicuous to the point of invisibility. You could drive by a thousand times and never notice, even if you were looking for it. It's furtive. Like Charlie. Things that hide are either frightened or stalking. Either way, dangerous.

Two-three teens standing in the lot, smoking, chatting. Only room for a few cars here. I fumble around in my pockets for a pack of cigarettes. I stopped smoking when Ed Murrow died, again when I left Da Nang, and a third time when I got off the plane in San Francisco; the third time it stuck; but it's still convenient to carry them. Pull one out of the pack, approach the girlboys, ask for a light, say thanks, nod, wait.

"You new?"

Shrug. "Back in town."

"Where were you?"

"Nam."

"Oh. I heard it's pretty bad."

"It is. And getting worse."

The boys have no real names. The tall thin one with straight black hair is "Mame." The shorter rounder one is "Peaches." The blond is "Snoopy."

"You got a name?"

"Solo."

"Napoleon?"

"Han."

"What'd you do in Nam?"

"Piloted a boat. Called The Maltese Falcon." Almost added, "Went upriver to kill a man named Kurtz." But I didn't. They wouldn't get it, not for twelve years anyway. I doubted any of them had ever read either Conrad or Chandler. Mame was more likely a Bette Davis fan than Humphrey Bogart. The other two . . . hard to tell. Shaun Cassidy probably.

"You goin' in?"

Took a puff on the cigarette. "In a minute." Hang back, listening. The girlboys are gossiping, overlapping dialogue, about someone named Jerry and his unrequited crush on someone else named Dave, except Dave has a lover. Jerry has a secret too. Honey, don't we all? Oh, guess what? Speaking of secrets, Dennis's real age is twenty-three, he's a chicken hawk, he's dating Marc. Marc? That's funny. Marc has the crabs, he got them from Lane. Lane? That sissy? Lane isn't even his real name. He's cheating on his sugar daddy, you know. Hey, have you met the new girl? With the southern accent? You mean, Miss Scarlett? More like Miss Thing. She's way over the top. She's just a sweet ole Georgia peach. I thought she said Alabama. Whatever. Do you believe her? Honey, I don't even believe me. She says she went in drag to her senior prom. In Alabama? Girl, I'll believe that when I hear it from Rock Hudson Jr.

Mame turns to me abruptly. "Getting an earful?"

Shrug again. "Doesn't mean anything to me. I don't know any of those people."

Satisfied, Mame turns back to the others. Did you hear about Duchess and Princess? I only know what you've told me. They were arrested—in drag—for stealing a car. Has anybody heard anything else? Not me. Have you ever seen them out of drag? No, have you? I have. Princess puts the ugh into ughly. Her and Duchess, it's Baby Jane and Blanche. I wonder who'll get their wardrobe. Honey, just one of Princess's gowns is big enough for all three of us. If we're friendly. I'm friendly, very friendly. Honey, get real. What are you and I going to do together—bump pussies, try on hats, and giggle?

Gossip is useful. It's a map of the social terrain. It tells you which way the energy is flowing. It tells you who's important. It's the quick way of tapping into the social gestalt. Find me three gossips and I can learn a community. Except this isn't a community. This is a fragmentary maelstrom of whirling bodies. A quantum environment, with particles flickering in and out of existence so fast they can only be detected by their wakes.

Eventually, I go in. There's no sign, but the place is called Gino's. Admission is fifty cents. The man at the door is forty-five, maybe fifty. This is Gino. He has curly black hair, a little too black. He dyes it. Okay, fifty plus. He looks Greek. He hands me a red ticket from a roll, the anonymous numbered kind they use at movie theaters. Good for one soda. He recites the rules. This is a club for eighteen and up. No drugs, no booze. If the white light goes on, it means the vice are here, stop dancing.

The outdoor patio is filled with jostling teens, all boys, some giggling, some serious. Several are standing close. Some make eye contact, others turn away, embarrassed. Others sit silently, sullenly, on heavy benches along the walls. Potting benches? Perhaps this used to be a nursery.

The patio connects to a second building, tucked neatly behind the art gallery. Invisible from the street. Perfect. Inside, it's darker than the patio. A quick survey reveals a bar, sandwiches, Cokes; in one corner a pool table, another a pinball machine. There's a jukebox playing a song by Diana Ross and the Supremes; several of the boys are singing falsetto-accompaniment. Love Child. And an area for dancing. But no one's dancing. The same embarrassment in the high school gym.

A slower survey of the inhabitants—almost no one over the age of twenty-five. Most of the boys here are high school girls, even the ones of college age. A few pretend to be butch, others don't care. Every so often, two or three of them leave together. I listen for conversations. More gossip. Some of it desperate. Longings. Judgments. Hopes. And the usual chatter about classmates, teachers, schools, movies . . . and Shaun Cassidy.

Someone behind me says to someone else. "Let's go to the Stampede." "What's the Stampede?" "You've never been there? Come on." I follow them out. Discreetly.

The Stampede is on Santa Monica, near the corner of Fairfax. It's a beer bar. Inside, it's decorated to look like a western street. A shingled awning around the bar has a stuffed cougar. Black lights make white T-shirts glow. A young crowd, drinking age. All the way to the back, a small patio. The place is filled with manboys standing around, looking at each other and pretending that they're not standing around and looking at each other, imagining, wishing, dreaming. Some of them search my face, I nod dispassionately, then turn away. The jukebox plays "Light My Fire," Jim Morrison and The Doors. If Gino's is high school, then The Stampede is junior year at city college. The boys are a little more like boys here, but they still seem much too young.

I know what it is—they're unfinished. They don't know who they are. They haven't had to dive into the mud and shit and blood. They haven't had anyone shooting at them.

Two couples walk in the front door, the wives holding the husbands' arms possessively. Some of the queers exchange glances. Tourists. Visiting the zoo, the freak show. They've never seen real faggots before. Someone behind me whispers bitchily. "The husbands will be back next week. Without the fish. It's always that way."

A couple blocks west, there's another bar, The Rusty Nail. More of the same, maybe a rougher crowd, a little older. A couple blocks east, The Spike. East of that, a leather bar. Okay, I got it. Circus of Books stays open twenty-four hours—the adult section, pick up a copy of the Bob Damron guide book. This is what I need. I take it back to my apartment and make X's on the map. No surprises here. Georgia was right. Queer bars and bathhouses. Another cluster of congruency.

Draw the connecting lines. Traffic goes back and forth on Santa Monica Boulevard, occasionally down to Gino's on Melrose. Oh, and there's a place over here on Beverly, The Stud. Enter in the rear. Unintended irony. They hang bicycles and canoes and rocking chairs from the high ceiling. It's funky and faddish. Up on Sunset, the Sea Witch. Glass balls in nets, and a great view of the city lights. They allow dancing—furtively. On Santa Monica, a little west of La Cienega, hidden among the bright lights of the billboards, another hidden dance club. Everybody's testing the limits of enforcement.

For two weeks, I check out all the bars, all the clubs. But my first hunch is strongest. Gino's is the hunting ground. I can feel it. I don't need to listen for the little hairs.

As the nights warm up, something is awakening. A restlessness in the air. A feverish subculture of summer is readying itself. But this year, it's reckless. Next year, it'll be worse, self-destructive. The year after that, 1969, it'll implode on itself. But right now, this moment, it still hasn't realized itself yet.

It's the boomers, the baby boomers, all those children of war coming of age at the very same moment, their juices surging, their chaotic desires and wants and needs—the wildness unleashed, the rebels without a pause; the ones who think that college has made them educated, and the ones who resent them because they have to work for their daily bread—all of them, horny as hell, possessed with the sense of freedom that comes behind the wheel of a Mustang or a Camaro or a VW Beetle, liberally lubricated with cheap gasoline, marijuana and beer and raging hormones, out on the streets, looking for where it's happening.

It isn't happening anywhere, it's happening everywhere, and the noise and the stink pervades the night. The straight ones hit the Sunset Strip or the peppermint places on Ventura Blvd. Or they cruise up and down Van Nuys Boulevard or Rosecrans Avenue, and especially Hollywood Boulevard. But the other ones—the quieter ones, the ones who didn't chase the girls, the music majors and the theater arts students, the shy boys and the wild boys—after all those years of longing, they're finally finding a place where they belong too, where there are others just like them. No, not just like them. But close enough. Here are others who will understand. Or not understand. There are so many different kinds, so many different ways of being queer. But at least, for a little while, in these furtive secret places, they won't have to pretend that they don't want what they want.

During the day, they'll rage about the unfairness of discrimination, about the ugliness of war—but at night, they all want to get laid. And that's what's surging here. The desolate lust of loneliness. It's a fevered subculture, a subset of the larger sickness that roils in the newspapers.

Our little vics—I pin their pictures to the wall and study them— they're cannon fodder. As innocent as the boy who stepped on the landmine, as unfinished as the new kid who took a bullet in the head from a jungle sniper on his first picket duty, as fresh and naïve as the one who got knifed by a Saigon whore. As stupid and trusting as the asshole who went out there because he thought it was his duty and came back with tombstones in his heart.

Finally pulled their pictures down and shoved them into a folder so I wouldn't have to look at their faces and the unanswered questions behind their eyes.

Didn't know much about queers. Didn't really want to. But I was starting to figure it out. Everything I knew was wrong.

Resumed surveillance of the vics. I had the first six now. Charting their habits, their patterns, their movements. Most of it was legwork. Confirmation of what I already knew. Thursday, vic number one shows up in the parking lot. Brad-boy. On his motorcycle. He rolls it right up behind Mame, playfully goosing her with the front wheel. Without even turning around, Mame wriggles her ass and says, "Wanna lose it?" Mame has a blond streak in her black hair now. The others are gushing over it. Brad grins, relaxes on the bike, eventually offers a ride to eager Lane, and roars off with him to catch the crabs.

A few nights later, Jeremy Weiss shows up at Gino's. Bingo. The connection. Georgia was right. Gay. Twinks. Horny.

Faded into shadow. Watched. He was smitten with a little blond twink who couldn't be bothered. Was this the Jerry that Mame was talking about? A crush on Dave who had a lover? Tailed him for the rest of the evening. He ended up at a featureless yellow building, a few blocks east. A very small sign on the door. You had to walk up close to read it. Y.M.A.C. Young Men's Athletic Club. Hmm. I had a feeling it was *not* a gymnasium. Observed for a while. Thinking.

I had three weeks left until the first vic disappeared. I was getting a good sense of the killing ground—this was the land of one-night stands. The perp didn't know the vics. He was hunting, just like everybody else, but hunting for a different kind of thrill. My guess, the vics didn't know him. They met him and disappeared. I wasn't going to find any other connectivity.

Had to think about this. How to ID the bastard. Mr. Death. That's what I was calling him now. How to stop him? Talked it over with Georgia. She made suggestions, most of them hands-on. But the way things work, the onsite agent is independent, has complete authority. Translation: it's your call.

Later. Past midnight.

Matt Vogel. Slightly built. Round face, round eyes, puppy eyes.

Sweet-natured. In the parking lot at Gino's, sitting alone against the wall, between two cars, where no one can see him. Hands wrapped around his knees, head almost buried. Almost missed him. Stepped backward, took a second look. Yes, Matt. Just graduated from high school. Works as a busboy in a local coffee shop. Disappears in two months. Victim number two.

"What do you want?" He looks at me with wide eyes. Terrified.

"Are you all right?"

"What do you care?"

"You look like you're hurting."

"My parents found out. My dad threw me out of the house."

Couldn't think of anything to say. Scratched my neck. Finally. "How'd he find out?"

"He went through my underwear drawer."

"Found your magazines?"

He hesitates. "He found my panties. I like to wear panties. They feel softer. He ripped them all up."

"I knew a lieutenant who liked to wear panties. It's no big deal."

"Really?"

No, not really. But it was a game we played. Whenever anybody heard a horror story about anybody or anything, somebody always knew a lieutenant who did the same thing. Or worse. "Yeah, really. Listen, you can't stay here all night. Do you have a place to go?"

He shook his head. "I was waiting—to see if anyone I knew showed up—maybe I could crash with someone."

I noticed he didn't use the word "friend." That was the problem with this little war zone. Nobody made friends. I remembered foxholes and trenches where we clung to each other like brothers, like lovers, while the night exploded around us. But here, if two of these manboys clung to each other, it wasn't bombs that were exploding. I wondered if they had the same fear of dying alone—maybe even more so.

He'd given up waiting for Prince Charming. Mr. Right wasn't coming. And even Mr. Right Now hadn't shown up.

"Look, it's late. I live a couple blocks, close enough to walk." To his suspicious glance, I said, "You can sleep on the couch."

"No, it's all right. I can sleep at the tubs."

"The tubs?"

"Y-Mac. You been there?"

Shook my head.

"It's only two bucks. And I can shower in the morning before going to work. Scotty might even wash my clothes."

"You sure?"

"No."

At least, he's honest.

"Okay. As long as you have a place to go. It's not safe to hang out here—" And what if Mr. Death started early? But I didn't want to say that. Didn't want to scare the shit out of the kid.

"It's as safe here as anywhere—"

Something about the way he said it. "Somebody hurt you?"

"Sometimes people shout things as they drive by. Once, a couple of guys chased me for a block or so, then gave up and went back to their car."

Started to turn away, turned back. Didn't want to leave him alone. Damnit. "Look—you can come with me. I won't—I got meat loaf in the fridge. And ice cream. You want to talk, I'll listen. You don't want to talk, I won't bug you. You can crash for a couple of days, until you sort things out with your folks. All right?"

Matt thinks about it. He might look sweet and innocent, but he's learned how to be suspicious. That's how life works. First it beats you up, then it beats you down.

His posture is wary. "You sure?"

Oh hell, of course I'm not sure. And this is going to fuck up the timeline. Or is it? A thought occurs to me. An ugly thought. I don't like it, but maybe . . . bait? I dunno. But what the fuck, I can't leave him out here in a dirty parking lot. "Yeah, come on."

He levers himself to his feet, brushes off his jeans. "I wouldn't do this, but—"

"Yeah, I know."

"—I've seen you around. Gino says you're okay."

"Gino doesn't know me."

"You were in Vietnam." A statement, not a question. I should have realized. I'm not invisible here. Some of the gossip is about me.

"Yeah," I admit. I was in Nam. I point him toward the street. "My pad is that way."

"Did you see any—"

"More than I wanted to." My reply is a little too gruff. He falls silent.

Why am I doing this? Why not? It's a chance to pry open the scab and look at the wound.

"I'm Matt."

"Yeah, I know."

"You got a name?"

"Oh, right. I'm . . . Mike."

"Mike? I thought your name was Hand. Hand Solo. But that's like a . . . a handle, isn't it. 'Cause everybody knows what a hand solo is, right?"

"Yeah. Right. It's a handle."

"Well. Glad to meet you, *Mike*."

We shake hands, there on the street. It changes the dynamic. Now we know each other. More than before anyway. Resume walking.

He's cute in a funny kind of way. If I liked boys, he'd be the kind of boy I liked. If this were the world I wanted to live in, he'd be my little brother. I'd make him hot chocolate. I'd read him bedtime stories and tuck him in at night. And I'd beat up anybody who made fun of him at school.

But this isn't that world—this is the world where men don't stand too close to men because . . . men don't do that.

"Mike?"

"Yeah?"

"Can I take a shower at your place?"

"Of course."

"Just enough to blow the stink off me."

"When did your dad throw you out?"

"Two days ago."

"You've been out here on the street two days?"

"Yeah."

"What a shit."

"No, he's all right."

"No, he isn't. Anyone who throws their kid out *isn't* all right."

Matt doesn't answer. He's torn between a misguided sense of loyalty and gratefulness that someone's trying to understand. He's afraid to disagree.

We reach the bottom of the stairs. I hesitate. Why *am* I doing this? In annoyance, I snap back. "Because that's the kind of person I am."

"Huh?" Matt looks at me curiously.

"Sorry. Arguing with myself. That's the answer that ends the argument."

"Oh." He follows me up the stairs.

He looks around the apartment, looks at the charts on the walls. I'm glad I pulled the pictures down. He would have freaked to have seen his yearbook picture here.

"Are you a cop?"

"No. I'm a—researcher."

"These look like something a detective would do. What are you researching?"

"Traffic patterns. It's—um, sociology. We're studying the gay community."

"Never heard it called that. 'Gay community.' "

"Well, no, it isn't much of one." Not yet, anyway. "But nobody's ever studied how it all works, and so—"

"You're not gay, are you?"

No easy answer to that. I don't even know myself. The night goes on forever here. Daytime is just an unpleasant interruption. "Look, I'm not anything right now. Okay?"

"Okay."

I feed him. We talk for a while. Nothing in particular. Mostly food. Cafeteria food. Restaurant food. Army food. Mess halls. C-rations. Fast food. Real food. Places we've been. Hawaii. Disneyland. San Francisco. Las Vegas. His family traveled more than mine. He's seen more of the surrounding countryside than me.

Eventually, we both realize it's late. He steps into the shower, I toss him a pair of pajamas, too big for him, but it's all I've got, and take his clothes downstairs to the laundry room. T-shirt, blue jeans, white gym socks, pink panties, soft nylon, a little bit of lace. So what.

He's a sweet kid. Too sweet really. Fuckit. He's entitled to a quirk. Who knows? Maybe he'll make lieutenant. When I come back up, he's already curled up on the couch.

The other bedroom is set up as an office. A wooden desk, an IBM Selectric typewriter, a chair, a lockable filing cabinet. I'll be up for a while, typing my notes for Georgia. God knows what she'll think of this. But I'll have his stuff into the dryer and laid out on a chair in less than an hour, long before I'm ready to collapse into my own bed.

Georgia taught me how to write a report. First list all the facts. Just what happened, nothing else. Don't add any opinions. The first few weeks, she'd hand me back my reports with all my opinions crossed out in thick red stripes. Pretty soon, I learned what was fact, what was story. After you've listed the facts, you don't need anything else. The facts speak for themselves. They tell you everything. So I learned to enjoy writing reports, the satisfying clickety-clickety-click of the typewriter keys, and the infuriated golf ball of the Selectric whirling back and forth across the page, leaving crisp insect-like impressions on the clean white paper. One page, two. Rarely more. But it always works. Typing calms me, helps me organize my thoughts.

Only thing is, if you don't have all the facts, if you don't have enough facts, if you don't have any facts, you stay stuck in the unknown. That's the problem.

Later, much later, as I'm staring at the dark ceiling, waiting for sleep to come, I listen for the sound of vampires on the street below. But most of them have found their partners and crept off to their coffins. So the war zone is silent. For now, anyway.

Somewhere, out there, Mr. Death is churning. And I still know nothing about him.

Sunday morning. I wake up late. Still tired. My back hurts. I smell coffee. Wearing only boxers, I pad into the kitchen. Matt is wearing my pajama tops. They're too big on him. He's obviously given up on the bottoms, too long, and they won't stay up. He looks like the little boy version of a Doris Day movie. He's cooking eggs with onions and potatoes. And toast with strawberry jam. And a fresh pot of coffee. It's almost like being married.

"Is this okay?" he asks uncertainly. "I thought—I mean, I wanted to do something to say thank you."

"You did good," I say, around a mouthful. "Very good. You can cook for me anytime." Why did I say that? "Oh, your clothes are on the chair by the door. I washed them last night."

"Yeah, I saw. Thanks. I have to go to work at noon." He hesitates. "Um, I'm going to try calling my dad today. Um. If it doesn't work out—you said something about—a couple days . . . ?"

"No problem. I'll leave a key under the mat. If I'm not here, just let yourself in."

"You trust me?"

"You're not a thief."

"How do you know?"

"I know." I added, "People who cook like this, don't steal."

He's silent for a moment. "My mom used to say I'd make someone a wonderful wife someday. My dad would get really pissed off."

"Well, hey, your dad doesn't get it."

Matt looks over at me, waiting for an explanation.

"It's simple. You take care of other people, they take care of you. The best thing you can do for someone else is cook for them, feed them, serve them a wonderful meal. That's how you tell someone that you— well, you know—that you care."

He blushes, covers it by looking at the clock. "I gotta get to work—" And he rushes to leave.

Sunday. There's no such thing as an afternoon off, but I cut myself some personal time anyway. Took a drive out to Burbank. Shouldn't have. Wasn't supposed to. It was part of the contract. Your old life is dead. Hands off. But I did it anyway. I owed it to them. No. I owed it to myself.

The place was pretty much as I remembered it. The tree in front was bigger, the house a little smaller, the paint a little more faded. I parked in front. Rang the bell and waited. Inside, Shotgun barked excitedly.

Behind the screen door, the front door opened. Like the house, he looked smaller. And like the house, a little more faded.

"Yes?" he squinted.

"Dad. It's me—Michael."

"Mickey?" He was already pushing open the screen door. Shotgun scrambled out. Even with his bad hip, that dog was still a force to be reckoned with. Dad fell into my arms, and Shotgun leapt at us both, with frenzied yowps of impatience. "Down you stupid son of a bitch, down!" That worked for half a second.

Dad held me at arm's length. "You look different. But how—? They said you were lost in the timequake."

"I was. I am. I found my way back—it's a long story."

He hugged me again, and I felt his shoulders shaking. Sobbing? I held him tight. He felt frail. Then abruptly, he broke away, and turned toward the house. "Come on in. I'll make some tea. We'll talk. I think I have some coffee cake. You don't know how hard it's been without you. I haven't touched your room. It'll be good to have you back—"

I followed him in. "Um, Dad. I don't know how long I can stay. I have a job—"

"A job. That's good. What kind of a job?"

"I'm not really allowed to discuss it. It's that kind of a job."

"Oh. You're working for the government."

"I'm not really allowed to discuss it. I'm not even supposed to be here, but—"

"That's all right, I understand. We'll talk about other things. Come

sit. Sit. You'll stay for dinner. It'll be like old times. I have spaghetti
sauce in the freezer. Just the way you like it. No, it's no trouble at all. I
still cook for two, even though it's just me and that old dog, too stubborn
to die. Both of us."

I didn't tell him that wasn't true. I didn't tell him that he and that
stubborn old dog would both be gone in a few short months. I rubbed
my eyes, suddenly full of water. This was harder than I thought.

Somewhere between the spaghetti and the ice cream, Dad asked
what had happened over there. I struggled inside, trying to figure out
what to say, how to say it, realized it couldn't be explained, and simply
finally shrugged and said, "It was . . . what it was." Dad knew me well
enough to know that was all the answer he was going to get, and that was
the end of that. The walls were comfortably up again.

Somewhere after the ice cream, I realized we didn't have all that
much to talk about anymore. Not really. But that was okay. Just being
able to watch him, just being able to skritch the dog behind the ears
again, that was okay. That was enough. So I let him talk me into spending the night. My old bed felt familiar and different, both at the same
time. I didn't sleep much. In the middle of the night, Shotgun oozed up
onto the foot of the bed and sprawled out lazily, pushing me off to the
side, grumpling his annoyance that I was taking up so much room; every
so often, he farted his opinion of the spaghetti sauce, then after a while
he began snoring, a wheezing-whistling noise. He was still snoring
loudly when the first glow of morning seeped in the window.

Over breakfast, I told a lie. Told Dad I was on assignment. That part
wasn't a lie. But I told him the assignment was somewhere east, I
couldn't say exactly where, but I'd call him whenever I could. He pretended to understand.

"Dad," I said. "I just wanted you to know, you didn't lose me.
Okay?"

"I know," he said. And he held me for a long time before finally releasing me with a clap on the shoulder. "You go get the bad guys," he
said, something he'd said to me all my life—from the day he'd given me
my first cowboy hat and cap pistol. Something he said again the day I
got on the plane to Nam. You go get the bad guys.

"I will, Dad. I promise."

I kissed him. I hadn't kissed him since I was eight, but I kissed him
now. Then I drove away quickly, feeling confused and embarrassed.

It was a drizzly day, mostly gray. Skipped the gym, filled the tank, drove around the city, locating the homes of the other seven victims. Two lived in the dorms at UCLA, Dykstra and Sproul. Didn't know if they knew each other. Maybe. One was a T.A. major, the other music. Another lived with a roommate (lover?) in a cheap apartment off of Melrose, almost walking distance from me, except in L.A., there's no such thing as "walking distance." If it's more than two doors down, you drive.

One lived way the hell out in Azusa. That was a long drive, even with the I-10 freeway. Another in the north end of the San Fernando Valley. All these soft boys, so lonely for a place to be accepted that they'd drive twenty-thirty miles to stand around in a cruddy green patio—to stand around with other soft boys.

Something went klunk. Like a nickel dropping in a soda machine. One of those small insights that explains everything. This was puberty for these boys. Adolescence. The first date, the first kiss, the first chance to hold hands with someone special. Delayed, postponed, a decade's worth of longing—while everybody around you celebrates life, you pretend, suppress, inhibit, deprive yourself of your own joy—but finally, ultimately, eventually, you find a place where you can have a taste of everything denied. It's heady, exciting, giddy. Yes. This is why they drive so far. Hormones. Pheromones. Whatever. The only bright light in a darkened landscape. They can't stay away. This is home—the only place where they can be themselves.

Okay. Now, figure out the predator—

I got back to the apartment, the drizzle had turned to showers. Matt was sitting by the door, arms wrapped around his knees. A half-full knapsack next to him. He scrambled to his feet, both hopeful and terrified. And flustered. He looked damp and disheveled. A red mark on his forehead, another on his neck.

"Are you all right?"

"I couldn't find the key—"

"Oh, shit. I forgot to put it under the mat—"

"I thought you were angry with me—"

"Oh, kiddo, no. I screwed up. You didn't do anything wrong. It's my fuckup. Shit, you must have thought—on top of everything else—"

Before I could finish the sentence, he started crying.

"What happened—? No, wait—" I fumbled the key into the lock, pushed him inside, grabbed his knapsack, closed the door behind us, steered him to the kitchen table, took down a bottle of Glenfiddich, poured two shots.

He stopped crying long enough to sniff the glass. "What is this?" He took a sip anyway. "It burns."

"It's supposed to. It's single-malt whiskey. Scotch." I sat down opposite him. "I went to see—someone. My dad. I haven't seen him in a while, and this might be the last time. I wasn't supposed to, but I did it anyway. I spent the night, I slept in my old room, my old bed. What you said yesterday, it made me think—"

He didn't hear me. He swallowed hard, gulped. "My mom called me at work. She said I should come home and pick up my things. My dad wouldn't be there. Only she was wrong. He came home early. He started beating me—"

I reached over and lifted up his shirt. He had red marks on his side, on his back, on his shoulders, on his arms. He winced when I touched his side.

Got up, went into the bathroom, pulled out the first-aid kit. Almost a doctor's bag. Stethoscope, tape, ointment, bandages, a flask, even a small bottle of morphine and a needle. Also brass knuckles and a blackjack. And some other toys. You learn as you go. Came back into the kitchen, pulled his shirt off, smeared ointment on the reddest marks, then taped his ribs. Did it all without talking. I was too angry to speak. Finally: "Did you get all your stuff?"

He shook his head.

"All right, let's go get it."

"We can't—"

Grabbed his arm, pulled him to his feet, pulled him out the door, down the stairs, and out to the car, ignoring the rain. "You need your clothes, your shoes, your—whatever else belongs to you. It's yours."

"My dad'll—he's too big! Please don't—"

I already had the car in gear. "Fasten your seatbelt, Matt. What's that thing that Bette Davis says? It's going to be a bumpy night." The tires squealed as I turned out onto Melrose.

I turned south on Fairfax, splashing through puddles. Neither of us said anything for a bit.

When I turned right on Third, he said, "Mike. I don't want you to do this."

"I hear you." I continued to drive.

"I'm not going to tell you where I live—lived."

"I already know."

"How?"

"I'm your fairy godfather, that's how. Don't ask."

"You are no fairy," he said. Then he added, sadly, "I am."

"Well, I guess that's why you need a godfather."

"What are you gonna do?"

I grinned. "I'm gonna make him an offer he can't refuse."

Matt didn't get the joke, of course. It wouldn't be a joke for another five years. But that was okay. I got it.

Turned left, turned right. Pulled up in front of a tiny, well-tended house. Matt followed me out of the car, up the walk. The front door yanked open. Matt was right—he was *big*. An ape. But he wasn't a trained one. The scattershot bruises on his son were proof of that. He'd substituted size for skill. Probably done it all his life. He wore an ugly scowl. "Who are you?" he demanded.

Gave him the only answer he was entitled to. Punched him hard in the chest, shoving him straight back into the house. Followed in quickly. Before he could react, chest-punched him again—harder, hard enough to slam him into the wall. The house shook. He bounced off and this time met my fist in his gut. His gut was hard, but the brass knucks were harder. He grunted, didn't double up, but he lurched—it was enough, I pulled his head down to meet my rising knee, felt his nose break with a satisfying crunch of bone and blood.

Hauled him to his feet. His face was bleeding. "You're a big man, aren't you? Beating on a kid." He was still trying to catch his breath. "Matt, go get your things. Now."

A woman came out of the kitchen, wiping her hands in a dish towel. "Matty—?" Then she saw me. "Who are you—?" Then she saw her husband. "Joe—?"

I grabbed the towel from her hands, pushed it at Joe, pushed Joe at a chair, he flopped into it, covering his bloody nose. "You can sit down too, ma'am; probably a good idea." She hesitated, then sat. Joe was still gasping, eyeing me warily.

Nobody spoke for a long moment.

Finally, the wife. "Are you going to hurt us?"

"Not planning on it. Of course, that can change." I nodded meaningfully at the asshole.

"You—you won't get away with this—"

"You won't call the police. He won't let you. He doesn't want anyone to know he's got a queer son." Took a breath. I wasn't planning to play counselor, but Matt needed time to gather his stuff, and I needed to keep the asshole from thinking too hard. "All right, look, lady—you should leave this jerkoff. Because if you don't, he's going to kill you someday. The only thing that's saved your life this long is that he's been taking it out on the kid instead, hasn't he? With the kid outa here, you're wearing the bull's-eye now. If I'm not mistaken, that bruise on your cheek is recent. Like maybe, this afternoon? And maybe there's a few more under that dress that don't show?"

She didn't answer.

"You're not doing yourself any favors, being a punching bag for this miserable failure. And you sure as hell didn't help your kid any, did you? Letting him beat the kid—you're a coward. Do you know what the word 'enabler' means? You're an enabler. You're just as fucking guilty. Because you let *him* get away with it."

Turned to the gorilla. "See, here's the thing, Joe. You're an asshole. You're beneath contempt. That's your son, your own flesh and blood. You should love him more than anybody else in the world. But he's fucking terrified of you. The one moment in his life, he needs his dad to love and understand and be there for him more than anything else, what do you do? You beat him up and throw him out. What a fuckwad you are. Your wife's a coward, you're a bully, and the two of you are throwing away the only thing in the world you've done right—raise a kid who still knows how to smile, god knows why, growing up with you two creeps. You don't deserve this kid. Shut up, both of you. I'm in no mood to argue. You can beat your wife, Joe, and you can beat your kid—but you can't beat the butt-ugly truth. You're a waste of skin. Oh, and if you're thinking about getting out of that chair, don't. If you try, I'll kill you. I'm in that kind of a mood."

"He means it, Dad—" That was Matt, coming back into the room. "He's an ex-commando. Special Forces. Green Beret. Or something. He was in Vietnam. I don't want him to hurt you—"

"You got everything?"

He hefted a duffel and a suitcase. Hastily filled.

Matt's mother looked back and forth between us. Finally, she worked up the nerve to ask. "What are you? Some kind of queer?"

I looked her up and down. "Are you the alternative?" Jesus Christ on a pogo stick, I can't believe I said that. "Wait a minute." Turned back to the gorilla. "Your son's leaving home. You'll never see him again. Give me your wallet. No—I didn't say think about it. I said, *give me your wallet*."

He passed it over. Nearly three hundred bucks. I passed the cash to Matt. "Here. Your inheritance. It's enough to live on for a couple months. If you're careful." Dropped the wallet on the floor.

"You two are getting off lucky. I'm letting you live." Looked at the gorilla again. "You come after this kid, you ever come near him, you ever lay a hand on him again, I will kill you. I will hunt you down and I will make sure you take a long time to die. You ever beat your wife again, I'll break both your arms. Are we clear? Nod your head, this isn't television." Glanced sideways. "Matt, you want to say good-bye?"

He shook his head.

"Then go get in the car."

Waited a moment, looking to see if the asshole was thinking about following. He wasn't. His face was ashen. He was still having trouble breathing. I looked to the wife. "You know what? I think you'd better call an ambulance. I might have punched him a little hard, I might have cracked his sternum. I wish I could say I'm sorry about that, but I'm not."

Drove back without talking. The rain was coming down harder now. Matt was shaken. Probably didn't know what to think, what to feel.

Got back to the apartment. He hesitated. "You coming up?"

"I thought you wanted me to—" He held up the money. "I mean—isn't what this is for?"

"There's plenty of time for that tomorrow. Or the next day." And besides, "You shouldn't be alone tonight." I grabbed his suitcase and duffel. Not as heavy as I'd thought. Gorilla and wife hadn't been very generous.

Inside, I went scrounging through the junk drawer, found the extra key and handed it to him. "Listen. Don't take this the wrong way. But I'm worried about you. You stay here as long as you need to."

He looked at the key in his hand, looked up to me, a question on his face.

"You can cook, right? You can clean? That'll be your rent. We'll move my typewriter in here, over against the wall or something. And you can have the other room. Just one condition. Stay away from Gino's—" No, that's not fair. "I mean, don't go there without me. And don't go out with anyone without—well, checking with me. Okay?"

"You trying to be my dad?"

"No. Well, maybe a big brother. I dunno." I sat down opposite him. "Can you keep a secret?"

"Not very well. I mean—my dad found out."

"There is that. When did you know you were—?"

"When I was twelve. Or thirteen."

"So you can keep a secret for five years. Six? Right?"

He nodded.

"All right. What I'm going to tell you is that big a secret. You up for it?"

He didn't say no. I took that as a yes.

"You know how I knew where you lived? I know a lot of other stuff too. Some bad shit is going down this year. Dangerous shit. People are going to get hurt. Killed. I'm not a cop. But I'm—I'm like a private investigator. And I'm looking for the guy. And you're his type. And so are a lot of the other kids at Gino's. I wish I could warn everyone, but if I do, it'll spread. You know how those girls love to gossip. And if the perp knows I'm looking for him, I'll never catch him. So you can't tell anyone. And the only reason I'm telling you is—is because I want your help."

"You need *my* help?"

"I *want* your help. I don't need it. But I can use it. If you're up to it."

"Up to it? Is it dangerous?"

"Do you think I'd put you in danger?"

He thought about it for a moment. "But you want to use me as bait."

"I want to see who cruises you. I want to know who talks to you. That's all."

"Can I ask you something?"

"Go ahead."

"Was this your plan all along? From the very beginning? When you brought me home the other night?"

"The truth?" I looked him right in the eye. "No. This was not what I planned. You were just one of the boys I was going to watch for a while—"

He frowned. He turned that over in his head. And then—oh, shit—he got it. "You son of a bitch!" He started to get up. "You know, don't you!" He looked around for his duffel and his suitcase. I resisted the temptation to get up. Force was absolutely the wrong answer here. He waited for my response.

I nodded. "Yeah, you're right. I know."

"You're a—a time-raveler?"

Nodded again.

"Then it's true? There really are? Because I thought that was just—like an urban legend or something."

"It's true," I admitted.

He stared at me, hard, as if trying to puzzle me out. "So . . . how far from the future are you?"

"I'm not. I'm from three years in the past. But I've been to the future. Twelve years anyway. You're going to like it. Parts of it, anyway."

"Like what?"

Shrug. "Things like . . . um, well, Stonewall, for one. Neil Armstrong. Apple. Luke Skywalker. Pac-Man. But I think, Stonewall might be the big one."

"What's Stonewall?"

"You'll find out soon enough. It's—it's going to be . . . kind of important."

"Give me a hint?"

"Rosa Parks."

"Who's Rosa Parks?"

"Look it up."

He frowned, annoyed. Then his frown eased. He dropped the duffel on the living room floor and came back into the kitchen nook. "Tell me what you know about me."

"Um—"

"You want me to do this, you have to tell me." He sat down opposite me and waited.

"Okay," I said. "Wait." I went into the bedroom, came back with the folders. Tossed it on the table. "I have to prevent the disappearance of this boy. Have you ever seen him?" I slid over the picture of Jeremy Weiss.

Matt looked, frowned, started to shake his head no, then said, "No, wait, I think he comes in mostly on weekends."

"He's number three. There are two other disappearances before him. Ten more afterward. Here's number one."

"That's Brad. Brad-boy. He rides a motorcycle. He comes in, picks up a trick, rides off. Nobody knows much about him, not even his tricks."

"Yeah, I've seen it."

"When does he—?"

"Two weeks. A little more than two weeks." I passed over the next folder. "This is the second victim."

He opened it, saw his own picture, and flinched. He deflated like a balloon. "I—I'm going to die."

"No. You're not. I promise you. *I promise you.*"

"But I did. I mean, I will, won't I? I mean—this?" He looked suddenly terrified.

"No. You won't."

"But how do you know? I thought time was—"

"Time is mutable. If it wasn't, I wouldn't be here. I couldn't be here. Neither could you."

He accepted that, but only because he wanted to. He wasn't convinced. After a bit, he reached over and took the other folders, opened them one at a time. He recognized two more of the boys, none of the rest. Not surprising. The last disappearance was only fourteen this year.

"All right. Now, tell me—do you go anywhere else besides Gino's?"

He shook his head. "There's a club down in Garden Grove, for eighteen-and-up. But I've never been there. Um, there's the tubs. The Y-Mac. I've only been there two-three times. There isn't any place else. I can't get into any of the bars."

"So mostly you go to Gino's?"

"That's where everybody goes."

"All right. Here's the deal. You don't go to Gino's unless I go too. I want to see who talks to you. And if somebody asks you to go home with him—we'll work out a signal. You'll tug on your ear. And I'll . . . I'll do what's appropriate."

Matt nodded. He seemed grateful to have a plan. He took a breath. "I saw some knockwurst in the freezer. Should I make that for dinner?"

I wasn't that hungry, but I nodded.

He clattered around in the cupboards for a bit, looking to see what else he could put on a plate. "There's some baked beans here, and some English muffins. I can make a little salad and open a couple of Cokes . . . ?"

"That sounds good." I gathered up the photos and slid them back into their respective folders.

"Mike . . . ?"

"Yeah."

"If I don't go home with anyone, how will you know which one's the killer?"

"I'm still trying to figure that out."

"You'll have to watch Brad-boy too, won't you?"

"Yeah."

"Maybe I'm not getting this right. But the only way you'll know who the killer is . . . will be by letting him kill someone. Brad. Right?"

"Well, no. I have a pretty good idea which night Brad disappears. So whoever talks to him on that night, that's probably the killer. But if I can keep Brad from going off with him, then I can save his life."

"But what if it's the wrong guy. I mean, if he doesn't get a chance to kill anyone, how will you know he's the killer?"

I got up, put the bottle of scotch back in the cupboard. Leaned against the wall and looked down at Matt. He was cutting up lettuce. "There's another part to the problem. Let's say that I give Brad a flat tire so he can't go out that night. Or something like that. Let's say I keep Brad from tricking out. Then that means Mr. Death—that's what I call him—picks up someone else. And maybe not that night, maybe the next night, or the following week. Maybe the whole timetable gets interrupted, screwed up—then this whole schedule is useless."

"So you have to watch Brad. . . ."

"Yeah. And I'll have to tail him to wherever he goes and . . . and hope it's the real deal."

"That's not fair to Brad."

"It's not fair to any of you guys. I'm only hired to save one boy—but there's a dozen others, and maybe more, who are equally at risk. I told you, time is mutable. If I jiggle it too hard, I lose the whole case. I can save you and Jeremy and Brad, but who else dies in your place?"

He got it—it was like a body blow. He laid down the knife and said, "Shit." And then he reacted to his own vulgarity with a softly spoken, "Well, that wasn't very ladylike, was it?"

He put dinner on the table and we ate in silence for a while. Finally, I said, "This is very good. Thank you."

"You like it?"

"It's a whole meal. It's more than I would have done for myself."

"I had to learn how to cook. My mom—" He shrugged.

"Yeah, I saw."

"She's not a bad person. Neither is my dad, except when he drinks too much—"

"And how often is that?"

He got the point. "Yeah. Okay."

Later, after the dishes were put away, I took a quick shower. I came out, wearing only a towel. He looked at me, then glanced away quickly.

He said something about a long soak and hurried into the bathroom. I heard the sound of bath water running. After a moment, he stuck his head out. "Towels?"

"Hall closet. Top shelf. Here." I pulled the yellow towels down for him. "Anything else?"

"I don't think so." Still not looking at me.

"All right. I'm going to bed. I've got a meeting in the morning. When I get back we'll go get a bed for you."

"Um. Okay. Thanks." He disappeared back into the bathroom.

I like to sleep with the windows open. Here, just off Melrose, the nights were sometimes stifling, sometimes breezy, sometimes cold. Sometimes the wind blew in from the sea, and sometimes the air was still and smelled of jasmine. Tonight there was cold wind, the last wet remnant of a gloomy drizzly day. The air smelled clean. Tomorrow would be bright.

I got into bed, listened for a while to the water dripping from the corners of the building, to the occasional wet swish of a car passing by, to the distant roar of the city, and maybe even the hint of music somewhere. Got up, went to the closet, pulled out an extra blanket and dropped it on the couch. He'd need it.

Got back into bed and listened to the roar of my own thoughts. Matt had put his finger on it—what I already knew and hadn't been willing to say. I had no way to ID the perp. Not unless I let someone die.

For a while, I wondered how the other operatives would handle this case. But I didn't wonder too long, I already knew. They'd save the Weiss kid and ignore the other dozen—because the Weiss kid's family were the only ones paying. That's why Georgia had given me this job. Because she knew I didn't think that way. She knew I wouldn't be satisfied with saving only the one. She knew how I thought. You don't leave any man behind.

And whether anyone recognized it or not, this was a war zone.

These people; they knew they were living in enemy territory. They were terrified of the midnight knock—the accusations at work, the innuendoes of friends, the gossip of neighbors, and all the awful consequences. The soft boys, they start out sweet and playful, almost innocent, but time would erode their spirit. The older they grow, the heavier the burden becomes. Day by day, they learn to be furtive, they become embittered and their voices edged with acid. You can stand in the bar and watch it happening in their eyes, night after night, the shadowed resentment, the festering anger. Why do we have to hide? Pretend? The question—*what's wrong with me?*—was backward. Pretty soon it turns into *what's wrong with them?* And the chasm grows, the isolation increases. The secret world digs deeper underground.

But not for too much longer. The summer of love is already explod-ing, next year the summer of lust, and after that the frenzied summer of disaster. But that summer would also bring the Stonewall revolution, and after that—this would start to change. All of it.

I almost envied them.

Because, they knew what they wanted.

I still had no idea.

There was a soft knock at the bedroom door. It pushed open with a squeak. Matt stuck his head in. "Are you asleep?"

"Not yet. Are you all right?"

"Mike . . . ?" He stepped closer to the edge of the bed. "Can I sleep with you tonight? Just to sleep. That's all. The couch is—"

"Kind of uncomfortable, I know. Yeah, come on." I slid over and pulled back the edge of the blanket for him. He slipped in next to me. Not too close.

We lay on our backs, side by side. Staring at the ceiling.

"This isn't about the couch, is it?"

"Uh-uh."

"Didn't think so."

"You don't have to worry—"

"I'm not worried."

"I mean—"

"Matt. It's all right. You don't have to explain." I thought about those nights in Nam where soldiers hugged each other closer than broth-ers. Of course, rifle fire, mortar shells, explosions, napalm, mud, blood and shit—and the threat of immediate death—can do that to you. The moments in the jungle when the patrol would stop for break, collapsing into heaps, sometimes lying in each other's laps, the only closeness we had—and the nights in cheap Saigon hotel rooms, when there weren't enough mattresses to go around, you shared with your buddy, and you felt glad he was next to you. The touch of a squad mate in the dark. You learned to feel safe in the stink and sweat of other men. They were your other half. You couldn't explain that either, not to anyone who hadn't been there.

"I'm sorry, Mike."

"For what?"

"For being such a—" He couldn't finish the sentence. He couldn't say the word.

"Matt . . . ?"

"My mom used to call me Matty. When I was little."

"You want me to call you Matty?"

"If you want to."

"Matty, come here." I put my arm around his shoulder and pulled him closer, so his head was nestled against my chest. I couldn't see what he was wearing, but it felt too soft. Nylon something. I ignored it. Whatever. "C'mere, let your Uncle Mike tell you a bedtime story." He wasn't relaxed, he lay tense next to me. Waiting for me to push him away in disgust . . . ?

"When I was twelve, my dad brought home a puppy for my birthday, just a few weeks old. He was a black Labrador retriever and he was so clumsy he tripped over his own shadow. He couldn't walk without stubbing his face, but I fell in love with him the first moment I saw him. My dad asked me if I liked him and I said he was just perfect. I called him Shotgun. The first night, he whined for his mommy, so I took him into bed with me and held him close and talked to him and petted him and he fell asleep next to me. He followed me everywhere and he slept with me every night. Then Monday morning, we took him to the vet for his shots. The vet examined him and examined him and examined him, and he just started frowning worse and worse. Finally, he says there's something wrong with Shotgun; he's defective, his hips are malformed, he's going to have trouble walking, he's going to go lame, a whole bunch of other stuff. Then, he took my dad aside and talked to him for a long time. I couldn't hear what they were saying, but my dad just shook his head and we took Shotgun home."

"The vet wanted to put him to sleep?"

"Yeah. My dad wouldn't let him. But I didn't find that part out until later. We went home, but I didn't want to have anything to do with Shotgun anymore. Because he was broken. He wasn't perfect. And I wanted a dog that was perfect. Shotgun kept following me around and I kept pushing him away. That night, he kept trying to jump up onto my bed and he kept whining, but I wouldn't lift him up and let him sleep with me. Finally, my dad came in and asked what was wrong and I said I didn't want Shotgun anymore, but I wouldn't say why. My dad figured it out though. He knew I was angry at Shotgun for not being perfect. But he didn't argue with me, he just said, okay, he'd find a new home for Shotgun in the morning. But . . . for tonight, I should let Shotgun sleep with me one last time. I asked why, and my dad picked up the puppy and held him in his lap petting him for a moment, and I asked why again, and my dad put Shotgun in my lap and he said, 'Because even ugly puppies need love. In fact, ugly puppies need even more love.' And when he said that, I started to feel real bad for pushing Shotgun away, and then my dad said, 'Besides, Shotgun doesn't know he's ugly. He just knows he loves you a lot. But if you don't love him and you don't want him, then tomorrow we'll find someone who doesn't care how ugly he is and who'll be happy to have a dog who will love them as much as Shotgun can.' That's when I hugged Shotgun close to my chest and said, 'NO! He's mine and you're not giving him away. Because I can love him more than anybody. I don't care how ugly he is.' And that's when my dad tousled my hair like this and whispered in my ear, 'That's the exact same thing your mom said when you were born.' "

Matt snorted. Then curled up with his backside pressed against me. I couldn't figure out if he felt like a girl or a boy or something of both—or neither.

All these queerboys—some of them were girlboys, yes; but the rest, they were still boys. Soft boys. Men without . . . without what? Some quality of maleness? No. They were male. They just didn't do all that chest-beating. Hmm. Of course not. Chest-beating is for dominance—it's to drive away all the other males from the mates. That's counterproductive in this environment. Here . . . they want to be . . . friendly? Affectionate? But chest-beaters can't do that, can't afford to do that without losing dominance. No wonder the queerboys were the targets of bullies. Bullies are cowards; they pick victims who won't fight back. I stared at the ceiling, wondering if this train of thought would bring me any closer to Mr. Death. I couldn't see how.

After a while, I stopped worrying about it and fell asleep myself.

The next morning, we pretended everything was normal. He went to work, I drove up to Hollywood Boulevard.

Georgia looked grim. She met my eyes briefly, jerked her head toward the office. "Mr. Harris wants to see you."

"Mr. Harris?"

"Ted Harris—the man whose name is on the door?"

"Oh. I didn't know there was a real Ted Harris. I thought he was a fictitious business name, or something."

"There's a real Ted Harris. And he's waiting for you."

Shit. They'd found out I'd visited Dad. I had that called-to-the-principal's-office, cold-lump-in-my-gut feeling.

I knocked once on the door, no answer, I turned the knob and went in. I'd never been in this room before. Desk, chairs, lamp, and a middle-aged man with his back to me, staring out the half-circular window that faced the boulevard. The window was grimy, but the morning sun still broke the gloom with blue-white bars of dust. Harris turned around to face me. I recognized him.

"Eakins—?" Every time I met him he was a different age. This time he had silver highlights in his hair, but he still looked young.

"Sit." He pointed. I sat.

"Your real name is Harris?"

He sat down behind the desk. "My real name is Eakins. There is no Harris. But I'm him. When I need to be. Today, I need to be."

"All right, that makes as much sense as anything—"

"Shut up." I shut.

He had a folder on his desk. He tapped it. "This case you're working on—the lost boys . . . ?"

"I'm making progress. There's a common connection among the victims."

"Tell me."

"There's a gay teen club on Melrose. I think the perp is finding them there. It's in my reports. There's also a secondary location—"

"You have to drop the case."

"Eh?"

"Is there something wrong with your hearing? Drop the case."

"May I ask why?"

His voice was dispassionate. "No."

"But these boys are going to die—"

"That can't be your concern."

"It already is."

Eakins took a breath, one of those I'm-about-to-say-something-important inhalation/exhalations. He leaned across the desk and fixed me with an intense glare. "Listen to me. Life is empty and meaningless. It doesn't mean *anything*—and it doesn't mean anything that it doesn't mean anything. Drop the case."

"That's not an answer."

"It's the only answer you're ever going to get. This conversation is over." He started to rise—

I stayed sat. "No."

He stopped, half out of his chair. "I gave you an instruction. I expect you to follow it."

"No."

"I wasn't asking you for an argument."

"Well, you're getting one. I'm not abandoning those boys to die. I need something more from you."

He sank back down into the chair. "There are things you don't know. There are things you don't understand. That's the way it is. That's the way it has to be."

"I made a promise to one of those boys that nothing's going to happen to him."

"You got involved—?"

"I made a promise."

"Which boy?"

"Number two."

Eakins opened the folder. Turned pages. "This one?" He held up Matty's picture. I nodded. Eakins dropped the picture on the desk, leaned back in his chair. Held up the other pictures. "He's not part of this case."

"Eh?"

"The others are part of this case. That one isn't."

"I don't understand."

"And I'm not going to explain it. The case is over. Disengage. We'll send you somewhere else. Georgia's got a courier job up in the Bay Area—"

"I don't want it."

"That wasn't a request. You'll take the courier job and we won't say anything about where you were Sunday night."

"No."

"We're paying you a lot of money—"

"You're renting my judgment, not buying my soul. That's why you're paying so much."

Eakins hesitated—not because he was uncertain, but because he was annoyed. He glanced away, as if checking a cue card, then came back to me. "I knew you were going to refuse. But we still had to have the conversation."

"Is that it?" I put my hands on the arms of the chair, preparing to rise.

"Not quite. This ends your employment here. Georgia has your severance check. We'll expect the return of all materials related to this case by the end of business today."

"You think that'll accomplish anything? You can't stop me from saving their lives as a private citizen."

Eakins didn't respond to that. He was already sorting files on his desk, as if looking for the next piece of business to attend to. "Close the door on your way out, will you?"

Georgia was waiting for me. Her face was tight. I knew that look. There was a lot she wanted to say, but she couldn't, she wasn't allowed. Instead, she held out an envelope. "The apartment and the car are in your name, we've subtracted the cost from your check. The bank book has your ancillary earnings. You'll be all right. Oh—and I'll need your ID card."

I took it out of my wallet and passed it over. "You knew, didn't you?"

"There was never any doubt."

"You know me that well?"

"No. But I know that part of you." She pressed the envelope into my hands. Pressed close enough for me to tell that she still wore the same sweet perfume.

Went down the stairs slowly. Stopped to have my shoes shined one last time while I looked through the contents of the envelope. A fat wad of cash, a hefty check, a surprisingly healthy bank account, several other bits of necessary paperwork—and a scrap of paper with a hastily written note. *"Musso & Frank's. 15 minutes."* I sniffed the paper, recognized the perfume, nodded, tipped Roy a fiver, and started west on the boulevard. I'd get there just in time.

I asked for a table in the back, she came in a few minutes later, sat down opposite me without a word. I waited. She held up a finger to catch the waiter's eye, ordered two shots of Glenfiddich, then looked straight across to me. "Eakins is a first-class prick."

Shook my head. "Nah, he's only a second-class prick."

She considered it. "Not even that high. He's a dildo."

My silence was agreement. "So . . . ?"

She opened her purse, took out another envelope, laid it on the table. "You weren't supposed to get this case. No one was. When he found out I'd assigned it to you, he almost fired me. He might still."

"I don't think so. You're still there as far uptime as I've been."

She shook her head as if that weren't important now. "The whole thing is . . . it doesn't make sense. Why would he abrogate a contract? Anyway—" She pushed the envelope across. "Here. See what you can make out of this."

"What is it?"

"I have no idea. He disappears for days, weeks, months at a time. Then he shows up as if not a day has passed. I started xeroxing stuff from his desk, a few years ago. I don't know why. I thought—I thought maybe it would give me some insights. There's things that . . . I don't know what they are. There's pictures. Like this thing—" She shuffled through the photos. "—I think it's a telephone. It's got buttons like a phone, but it looks like something from *Star Trek*, it flips open—but it doesn't work, it just says 'no service.' And this other thing, it looks like a poker chip, one side is sticky, you can stick it to a wall, the other side is all black—is it a bug of some kind? A microphone? A camera? Or maybe it's a chrono-sensor? And then there are these silver disks, five inches wide, what the hell are they? They look like diffraction gratings. Some of them say Memorex on the back. Are they some kind of recording tape, only without the tape? And there's all these different kinds of pills. I tried looking up the names, but they're not listed in any medical encyclopedia. What the hell is Tagamet? Or Viagra? Or Xylamis? Or any of these others?"

"Are there dates on any of this material?"

"Not always. But sometimes. The farthest one is 2039. But I think he's gone farther. A lot farther. I think he's gotten hold of the Caltech local-field time-maps. Or maybe he's been dropping his own sensors and making his own maps, I don't know. But I've never seen anything that looks like a map. It doesn't make a lot of sense. But then again—there's that thing that he says, that if we could go back to say, 1907 with a bunch of stuff from today—a transistor radio, a princess phone, a portable TV, a record album, birth control pills, things like that—none of it would make sense to someone living in that time. Even a copy of a news magazine wouldn't make much sense because the language would have shifted so much. So if Eakins has stuff from thirty, forty, fifty years into the future, we wouldn't get much of it—"

"Yes and no. Fifty years ago, they didn't have the same experience of progress, so they didn't have the vocabulary to encompass the kinds of changes that come with time. We have a different perspective—because change is part of our history, we expect it to be part of our future. So, if anything, we look at this stuff and we don't see a mystery as much as we see the limits of our experience."

"Now, you sound like me."

"I was quoting you. Paraphrasing." I shuffled through the papers, the photos, the notes. "None of this has any bearing on this case, does it?"

"I don't know. But I thought you should see it. Maybe it'll give you an insight into Eakins."

Shook my head. "It proves that he knows more than he's telling us. But we already knew that."

She glanced at her watch. "Okay, I'm out of time." She stood up, leaned over and kissed me quickly. "Take care of yourself—and your little boyfriend too."

"He's not my—" But she was already gone.

I shoved everything back into the envelope and ordered a steak sandwich. The day had started weird and gotten weirder, and it wasn't half over. I might as well face the rest of it on a full belly.

Went back to the apartment. Photographed everything. Then gathered it up and went straight to the local copy shop. Five copies, collated. Paid in cash. Put one copy in the trunk of the car, put another in the apartment safe, and mailed the other three to three different P.O. boxes. Delivered the originals back to Georgia who accepted them without comment. Eakins had already left the building. But neither of us said anything; it was possible he had the offices bugged—maybe even with his funny poker chips.

By the time I got home, Matty was unpacking groceries. The whole scene looked very domestic. "Did you have a good day?" he asked. All I needed was a pair of slippers and the evening newspaper.

When I didn't answer, he looked up. Worried. "You okay?"

"Yeah. I'm just . . . thinking about stuff."

"You're always thinking about stuff."

"Well, this is stuff that needs thinking about."

He got it. He shut up and busied himself in the kitchen. I went out onto the balcony and stared at Melrose Avenue. Cold and gray, it was going to rain again tonight; a second storm right behind the first. Something Eakins had said—none of it made sense, but one piece of it had its own particular stink of wrongness. Why is Matty not important to this case?

And that led directly to the next question: What did Eakins know that he wasn't telling me? And *why* wasn't he telling? Because if I knew . . . it would affect things. What things? What *other* plan was working?

Obviously, we weren't on the same side. Had we ever been? Never mind that. That's a dead end right now. I had to think about Matty.

If Matty is irrelevant, then . . . is he still in danger? No, of course he's in danger. He disappeared. We know that. But if he disappeared, then why is he irrelevant . . . ? Unless his disappearance is unrelated. And if his disappearance is unrelated, then . . . of course, he would be entirely useless to this case. Shit.

But how would Eakins know that? Unless Eakins knew something about Matty. Or knew something about all the others.

And of course, all of that assumed that Eakins was telling the truth. What if he was purposely trying to mislead me? But then that brought me back to the first question. What was Eakins up to?

Not having the answers to any of these questions annoyed me. I didn't have a plan, I didn't have anything on which to base a plan. The only thing I could think was to continue with the plan that Eakins had scuttled—not because it was a good plan, but because it would force the situation. It would force Eakins to . . . to do what?

When the rain finally started, I went back in and sat down to dinner. Baked chicken. It was cold.

"Why didn't you call me?"

"You were thinking."

"Um—" I stopped myself. He was being considerate. "Okay."

"Do you want me to warm that up for you?"

"No, it's okay." I ate in silence for a bit, feeling uncomfortable. Finally I put my fork down and looked across at him. "Y'know what I just realized. I don't know how to talk to you."

He looked puzzled.

"This is good—" I indicated the cold chicken. "You can cook. I keep wanting to say you'll make someone a wonderful wife someday. But I can't say that because—"

"It's different when you say it. When you say it, it isn't mocking."

"It's still the wrong thing to say. It's demeaning, isn't it?"

"I don't mind. Not from you." He started to clear the table.

I took a breath. "Are you—?" I stopped. "I don't know how to ask this. Are you . . . attracted to me?"

He nearly dropped the plates. He was facing away so I couldn't see his expression, but his body was suddenly tense. He finally turned around so he could look at me. "Do you want me to be?"

"It's like this. I don't connect well to people. Not anybody. Male or female. I can go through the motions. For a while. But only for a while. I'm always . . . holding back."

"Why?"

I shrugged.

"That's your answer?"

"When you start raveling, you get unraveled yourself. You get detached. You don't belong to any time, you can't belong to any person. So you turn off that part of yourself."

He didn't respond right away. He got the coffee pot from the stove and filled two cups. He brought cream and sugar to the table, for himself, not me. As he stirred his coffee, he finally asked, "So why are you telling me this? Are you telling me I shouldn't care about you because you can't care back?"

"I don't know if I can care about anybody. When I try, it doesn't work out. So I've stopped trying."

"You didn't answer my question. Why are you telling me this?"

"Because . . . right now, you're the only person I have to talk to."

"Not your dad?"

"This is not a conversation I could have with my dad."

He shook his head in frustrated confusion. "Just what are we talking about?"

"About the fact that I am so fucking angry and confused and upset and annoyed and frustrated and—and even despairing—that if you weren't here, right now, tonight, if you weren't here to talk to . . . I'd end up sitting alone in a chair again—with my gun barrel in my mouth, wondering if I have the courage to pull the trigger. I've known guys who've sucked the bullets out of their guns. It makes a mess on the wall. And I used to wonder why they did it. That was before. Not anymore. Now I'm starting to understand."

His face was white. "You're scaring the hell out of me."

"You don't have to worry. I'm not going to do anything stupid. I just—I just want you to know that right now . . . you're doing me the favor by staying here."

"This is a lot more than I can deal with—I'm not—"

I nodded. "Kiddo, I'm more than most people can deal with. That's why they leave. Look—I figured, after all you've been through, you'd understand what it feels like to feel so separated from everyone else. I'm coming from the same place—same place, different time zone."

He stirred his coffee thoughtfully. "There's a quote I learned in school. Sometimes it helps me. It's from Edmund Burke. I don't know who he is or was, it doesn't matter. He said, 'Never despair; but if you do, work on in despair.'"

Considered it. "Yeah. That's good. It's useful."

We sat there for a while. Not talking.

Later. I came out of my bedroom. He was curled up on the couch. "Matt? Matty?"

"Huh—?" He rolled over, looked at me groggily.

"If you want to come sleep in the bed again, you can."

"No, it's all right."

But a little bit later, he pushed open the bedroom door, padded over, and slipped in next to me. So that was something. I just didn't know what. But then again, neither did he. Probably.

The rain cleared up, leaving the air sparkling, the way it used to be in the thirties and the forties. Least, that's what they say. In two days, though, the smog levels would be back to their lung-choking worst. It's not just the million-plus internal combustion engines pouring out lead and carbon dioxide and all the other residues of inefficient fuel-burning. Los Angeles is ringed with mountains. That's why they call it a basin. Fresh air can't get in, stale air can't get out. It sits and stagnates. The Indians called it *el valle de fumar*. The valley of fumes. Only two things clean it—the once-in-a-while rainstorms of winter and spring, or the hot dry Santa Ana winds at the end of the summer. From June until October, don't bother breathing. You can breathe in November.

But today, today at least, was beautiful. It was a go-to-Disneyland day. And I almost suggested it to Matty, but he had to work, and I hadn't figured anything else out yet, so we disentangled ourselves from the mustiness of sleep and stepped into the comfortable zombie-zone of routine.

We had a week to go before Brad Boyd would disappear. I spent some of the daytime tailing him, even though that was probably a dead end. He worked at an adult bookstore on Vine, just across the street from the Hollywood Ranch Market. Sometimes he bought a Coke and a burrito from the counter in front. Usually he walked to work, leaving the motorcycle parked under a small covered patio in front of the apartments. It wouldn't be hard to sabotage the bike. That would keep him at home. But it wouldn't get me closer to Mr. Death.

Twice, I drove out to visit Dad. The second time, I took him to the doctor. I already knew that it wouldn't do any good, wouldn't delay the inevitable, but I had to try. Maybe make it a little easier for him. Dad fussed at me, but not too much. He didn't have the same strength to argue that he'd had when I was eighteen, when I'd come back with the recruiting forms, when I told him of my decision, when I snapped back at him, "Well, if it's a mistake, it's *my* mistake to make, not yours." It wasn't until Duncan stepped on a land mine just a few paces ahead of me that I discovered what Dad had been so scared of. But by then, I was already starting to shut down. So the scared never got all the way in, never got to the bottom. Part of me remained convinced that it wasn't going to happen to me. Ever. Just the same, I got out of there as soon as my rotation ended.

I sat at the kitchen table, puzzling over the photos and the copies of the notes Georgia had taken from Eakins' desk. Someday they'd make sense, but at this point in time—literally—they were incomprehensible. The only thing this stuff proved was that Eakins had time-hopped farther into the future than anyone I'd ever heard.

In the evenings, Matty and I would shadow Brad again. Having an extra set of eyes helped. The first night motorcycle-boy started at Gino's, had no luck or didn't like what he saw, and rode over to the Stampede. We parked in the lot of the supermarket across the street, just behind the bus bench where we could watch the front entrance and his motorcycle. The Stampede had an emergency exit in the rear patio, but without an emergency the only way out was the front. We might be here awhile, how long does it take to cruise a bar? Matty went for doughnuts and coffee.

"If he comes out before you get back, I have to follow him; if I'm not here, you wait in the doughnut shop. As soon as he lands somewhere, I'll come back for you. Understand? Don't talk to anyone."

But the plan wasn't needed; Matty was back in five and Brad-boy didn't come out of the bar for forty minutes. He was alone. We followed him east on Melrose where he checked into the YMAC.

"He could be there all night," said Matty. "Maybe till one or two."

"How do you know? Have you ever—?"

"With Brad-boy? No. I would have, if he ever asked. But he never asked. I don't think I would now. Everybody says he's kind of a user. Use 'em and lose 'em."

"Yeah, I got that feeling. I'm wondering if . . . maybe I should go in."

"It's just a lot of guys standing around in the dark."

"Just like the Stampede? Or Gino's?"

"Yeah, but without their clothes on. Just towels."

"Hm." We sat in silence for a bit.

"You can't get in without a card," Matty offered. "A member has to take you in the first time. If Scotty doesn't like your look, he says it's not a membership night. If he lets you in, he gives you a card and tells you the rules. I could probably get you in."

"Is that an offer?"

"I'm just trying to be helpful."

I thought about it.

"How often have you been there?"

"Not much. Two times, three. I don't like the way it smells."

"I don't think it's going to help us much."

"Why not?"

"Because . . . if I've figured this right, our bad guy doesn't work out of this place. He has to take his victims somewhere else. Somewhere close. Like a house—a house with lots of shrubbery around it, or maybe an alley in the back, or a connected garage. He has to have some way to remove the . . . the evidence without anyone seeing."

"So we can go home?"

"I'm thinking. We should probably wait. Make sure that Brad-boy gets home safe."

"I have work tomorrow."

"There's a blanket on the back seat, if you want to try sleeping."

"No. I can't sleep in a car."

"I don't like sitting here either." I started the engine, put the car in gear, turned on the headlights. "Let's call it a night."

Back at the apartment, I pushed him toward the bedroom, and went into my makeshift office to type up a quick report. Picked up subject at, followed subject to, subject was inside for, came out at, proceeded to, stayed for, came out, went to, waited, abandoned stake-out at. I didn't have to write it, the case was over, and there was no place to turn in the report, but old habits die hard—and it's always useful to have accurate notes.

It didn't take long to finish, but by the time I slid between the sheets, Matty was already asleep, half-sprawled toward the center of the bed. I gave him a gentle push and he turned half away. Fair enough.

Matty felt warm. He reminded me of Shotgun. Shotgun would stretch out next to me, anchoring his back against mine, we'd sleep spine to spine. That big old dog was like me—he liked having someone covering his back. Except Matty wasn't Shotgun, he wasn't an ugly puppy, and he wasn't anything else either. Why was I doing this?

The next night, Brad-boy stayed home and watched television until ten. He got on his motorcycle and went to Gino's. Sat on his bike for twenty minutes chatting with Mame, Peaches, Dave, Jeremy, and two boys Matty couldn't name. "You think it's one of them?"

"No. They're too young. And they're—"

"—too fem?"

"Yeah. Too fem."

"Some fems can be real bitches—"

"Yeah, I heard some of the stories about Duchess and Princess. But I don't think we have to worry about either of these. They look like lost surfer boys. A couple kids from Pali High daring each other to visit a gay club."

Eventually, one of the surfer boys climbed onto the back of Brad-boy's bike and they roared east on Melrose. Back to Brad's apartment. Was he going to spend the night? Or would Brad be bringing him back here in an hour?

It turned out to be less than that. Apparently, our Brad wasn't much for foreplay. Forty-five minutes turnaround. Then he went home and went back to bed. Alone.

Thursday night, Brad went to a movie. We sat three rows behind him. *The Dirty Dozen.* All-star cast. Lee Marvin, Ernest Borgnine, Charles Bronson, Jim Brown, John Cassavetes, Richard Jaeckel, George Kennedy, Trini Lopez, Robert Ryan, Telly Savalas, Clint Walker, and some funny-looking goofball named Donald Sutherland.

Friday night, Gino's was crowded with lithe and feral manboys. Brad-boy actually got off the bike and went in. Matty followed him while I spoke privately to Gino. I flashed one of the P.I. cards I hadn't given back to Georgia. Either she hadn't noticed that or she had. I wasn't sure if I should let her know what I was up to. She was probably in enough trouble already. She probably already knew anyway. No, I'd wait until I had something.

Gino glanced at the card unsurprised, looked at me, and said, "What do you need?"

"I heard you're the go-to guy." He looked blank, he didn't recognize the term. "The go-to guy. The guy to go to . . . if you have the clap and need the name of a doctor, if you need a letter from a shrink to stay out of the army, that kind of stuff."

"I know some people," Gino said. Dr. Ellis was due to be murdered by a hustler-boy. Scotty would be implicated in a different murder and YMAC's new location on La Brea would be raided. In a couple of years. "What can I do for you?"

"You know your regulars, right? You know who's solid and who's flaky. If someone new shows up, you read them the rules before you let them in. Do you ever notice who folks leave with?"

"I see a lot of boys come through here every weekend—"

"Brad Boyd. Do you ever notice who he leaves with?"

"Hard not to. He always revs his engine and roars out of here, leaving a stinking cloud of smoke behind. I've asked him not to—"

"Could you keep an eye out?"

"Who are you working for? His parents?"

"No. This isn't that kind of a case."

"What kind of a case is it?"

"This kind." I pushed a fifty-dollar bill into his hand. I had another ready in case one wasn't enough.

Gino glanced down only long enough to check the denomination. "You got the size right." He tucked it into his pocket.

I leaned forward, whispered, "This kid's life might be in danger. I think he's being stalked. But I don't have any hard evidence yet. Help me out, I'll give you another one of those."

Gino shrugged. "I have a club to run. Weekends are busy. I can't promise anything. But if I see something, I'll let you know."

I passed him a card. No name, just a phone number. "If no one answers, there's an answering machine. You can leave a message."

Gino looked impressed. Code-A-Phones were expensive. I didn't tell him it belonged to the Harris Agency—and that any day now I expected Georgia to request its return.

I found Matty in the shadows next to the jukebox. Brad was playing pool in the corner. I pulled Matty farther back and we pretended to be only casually interested in the pool game. So far, it looked like Brad was only here to play pool. He had a nasty style of slop shooting. It looked like he was just casually slamming the balls around; but he'd been playing barroom pool long enough, he knew what he was doing. He kept winning. Three, four, six games and he still hadn't been beaten.

"Whyn't you go play him?"

"Uh-uh. I might interrupt something or someone. We need to see who he picks up—or who picks him up."

"Is it tonight?"

"Tomorrow. I have a feeling—I could be wrong—but I have a hunch that our subject might be here tonight as well. Whatever he's feeling, it has to be building up. Building up over time. If Brad is his first, then maybe this is the night that triggers his urge, but maybe he isn't quite ready to act. Something happens tonight. He gets his—whatever it is he gets. His courage. And tomorrow is the night it gets real enough for him to actually do something."

"What if he picks someone else?"

"I don't think so. I think Brad is the first because Brad is the easiest. I don't think our fellow has learned how to cruise yet. He might not have picked Brad out, but I think he's in this room. Here's what I want you to do. You go one way, I'll go the other. We'll both walk around, just looking—cruising. See if you see anyone who strikes you as wrong."

"Wrong in what way?"

"Any way at all."

"Too old? Too ugly?"

"No. Brad is a slut, but he isn't a whore. Like all the rest of you girls, he wants someone young and cute. So watch out for anyone who looks like his type, but possibly nervous, uneasy, uncertain—someone who doesn't look like he's having a good time. His clothes or his haircut might look a little weird, like he doesn't understand the current styles. He's probably hanging back, just watching; he might have a very intense look, or he might even look perfectly normal. But I'll bet he's someone new, someone you haven't seen before, so watch for that. Just look at every unfamiliar face closely and see what you see. Okay? You go this way, I'll go that. Three or four times around, then meet back here."

There was something else to watch out for, but I didn't tell Matty. It was baggage he didn't need to carry. I didn't like having him do this, but I needed his eyes. He had experience here. He could read these people. I couldn't. Not very well. There was an overlay of—I didn't have a word for it—but there was a map to this territory that I didn't have.

I'd given him one clue. Watch out for someone who's out of style. But he wouldn't have heard what I was really saying—I think we're dealing with a freelance time-hopper, someone who's riding the quakes. He's probably from the past, maybe ten or twenty years; I doubted he was from the future, the future is a little friendlier to queers, but I didn't rule it out—maybe the cultural shifts were stressing him out.

But if I had to put money on it, I'd bet that this was a guy with a very bad jones in his johnson. He wanted sex with young men, but afterwards he was so ashamed at what he had done, he had to destroy the evidence. Even if that meant murder.

In the movies, murderers always have a look about them. That's because the director puts the actor in a hotter or colder light, making him stand out just a bit from everyone else around him; and the makeup man will do something around the actor's eyes, making his face look sallow or drawn or gaunt; and the camera angle will be such that everyone else in the crowd will be turned away, or in shadow, or simply two steps back. In the movies, it's easy to spot the bad guy—the director tells you where to look and what to notice.

In real life . . . real life stinks. Murderers look just like everybody else. Sick and tired and resigned. Beaten up and beaten down. Everybody looks like a murderer. So nobody does.

In here, they looked—they looked like queers, but once you got past the part that was queer and you looked at the people, they looked like people. Soft boys, girlboys, manboys, wild boys, wilder boys, feral boys. None of them looked like men. But that's what I was looking for. Someone who wasn't a boy anymore. A man? Maybe. Someone who'd passed through boyhood without ever finishing the job. But the only one in here who looked like that . . . was me.

For a moment, I envied this confetti of boys and their flickering schoolgirl freedom. Because at least, while they were here, flirting and gossiping, nattering and chattering, they had a place of their own, a place to belong. If I'd ever had a place to belong, it must have been closed the night I passed by.

Circled four times, five, breathing faint smells of marijuana, Aramis, Clearasil, and Sen-Sen. Passed Matty going the other way, kept going, searched faces, all the faces—some of them searched back, wondering if they could find comfort in mine. That wasn't possible. I don't do comfort. They got it and looked away.

And then finally, we came back to the dark corner next to the jukebox and compared notes. Matty shook his head. "A bunch of frat-boys from the ZBT chapter at UCLA, checking out the scene. A guy who says he's only here doing research for a book; yeah, like I believe that. A couple fellows up from Garden Grove, one from San Francisco. A guy who looks like a cop, but Gino didn't flash any lights, and you don't put the red bandana hanging out of your front pocket anyway. And Uncle Philsy. That's what everybody calls him."

"Which one is Uncle Philsy—oh, him." The troll. Short. Bald. Fiftyish. Tending to fat. Disconnected predatory grin. Wandering aimlessly through the boys, simply enjoying the view. Sweet and repulsive at the same time. But harmless.

"Gino knows him. Says he's okay."

"What was that about a guy doing research for a book? Don't trust him. Writers are all creeps and liars. And what about the other guy—bandana man?"

"Bandana man is looking for someone. His son, I think. He's only pretending to be gay."

"How'd you find all this out so quickly?"

"Telefag."

"Eh?"

"Gino. Mame."

"Oh. What about that guy there, the tall one, thirtyish—?"

"Walt? He's a film agent, I think. Least that's what he says—"

"All right. Anyone with history here is probably okay. Is that it?"

"I think so." Beat. "Lane found out that Mame is telling everyone he has the crabs. They're out in the parking lot having a bitch fight. You think—"

"No. Our boy is looking for a boy, not a girl."

"Hey . . . Mike?" Tentative.

"Yeah?"

"Promise you won't get mad?"

"What?"

"Mame thinks you're my boyfriend. That's what she's telling everyone."

Snorted. Smiled. Actually amused by the thought. "Might as well be. You live with me. You cook. You do the laundry. We sleep in the same bed. We're just about married."

"Except we don't have sex."

"See, that proves we're married."

Matty blinked. He didn't get it. He said, "I'd marry you. If you asked. If you were—"

I put my hand on the wall over his head, leaning forward and sheltering him under my arm. I leaned down close as if I was going to whisper in his ear. Instead, I kissed him quickly on the cheek. Nobody saw. Gino actively discouraged overt displays. Fear of cops.

"What was that for?" Matty asked.

"That was for you."

"Oh." Now he was really confused. We both were. He looked up at me, eyes glistening in the black-light darkness. "Um . . . Mike?"

"Yes?"

"Brad just walked out to the parking lot—"

"Yeah, I saw him." That was part of the reason I put up my arm and bent down low—to shield both of us from Brad's notice. But I didn't tell Matty that. "Let's go."

Brad had gone out through the patio door. We ducked around to the door at the front of the building, then sideways through the space between the art gallery and Gino's. Just in time to see Brad backing his bike away from the wall, and someone turned away from us, waiting to get on the back. As soon as Brad had the engine grumbling, the other fellow climbed on and wrapped his arms around Brad's waist.

"Do you recognize him?"

"No—"

Stuck my head in the patio door. "Who'd he leave with?"

Gino shrugged. "Never saw him before—"

"Shit."

Dashed for the car, Matty following.

We picked them up east on Melrose. Back to Brad's place? Maybe. No. They turned north just short of La Brea. Little cubbyhole apartments tucked away in here. Follow the taillight. The bike comes to a stop half a block ahead. Matty sinks down low and we cruise slowly past on the narrow street. Brad doesn't even look up. The other fellow turns around momentarily and gets caught briefly in the light. We coasted on past. "Oh, I know him," Matty says. "That's Tom. He shaves himself smooth. He dusts your ass with talcum powder and spanks you lightly."

"And you know this how—?"

"Telefag."

"You didn't—?"

Matty shook his head.

"You don't do it very often, do you?"

"I would. If I met the right guy."

"There are no right guys. Just like there are no right girls."

"Well, that sounded bitter."

"No. Just wise."

"I hope I never get that wise."

I pulled the car around the corner, parked in the red, left the motor running. "So, you know this guy Tom?"

"Not to speak to, but he's been around."

"Okay, then he's not our perp."

"Are we done for tonight?"

"Brad'll be going home after this, won't he?"

"Prob'ly."

"Okay, then we're done."

Matty took a shower while I typed up my notes. More of the same. Nothing to report. No clues. No directions. No leads. I sat in front of the typewriter, head in my hands, trying to figure out what to do next. Matty, still drying his hair, stuck his head in to ask if I wanted anything, coffee? I shook my head. He went off to bed.

I smelled like smoke from the club. It bothered me. I peeled off my clothes, started to drop them on the floor, then realized Matty would only pick them up in the morning: I dropped them into the hamper and stepped into the shower. Was it really the smoke I was trying to rinse off?

When I ran out of hot water, I turned off the spray. Matty had put fresh towels on the rack for me. I knew what he was trying to do. He wanted me to let him stay. I hadn't said he couldn't, but we hadn't negotiated any long-term agreement either.

Still naked, I slipped into bed. The springs creaked. He lay quietly beside me, breathing softly.

"You still awake?"

"Yeah."

"I'm thinking of dropping the case."

"You won't."

"Why not?"

"Because you can't stand not knowing."

"You're an insightful little guy, you know that?"

In response, he rolled on his side facing me, put an arm across my chest, pulled himself close, and kissed me softly on the cheek. He smelled good. He smelled clean. Then he rolled back to his side of the bed.

"What was that for?"

"That was for you."

"Oh."

This was it. This was the moment. It was going to happen. And for an instant—like that excruciating hesitation at the top of the first steep drop of the roller coaster—it felt inevitable. All I had to do was turn sideways, he'd roll into my arms, and we'd be . . . doing it.

And then, just as quickly, the moment passed. And we were still lying side by side in a queen-sized bed that had suddenly become much too narrow.

After a bit, I rolled out of bed.

"Are you all right?"

"Can't sleep." I got up, went to the drawer, started looking for clean underwear—it was all neatly folded. Grabbed a pair of boxers and started to pull them on. "I'm going back out."

He sat up. "Want me to come with?"

"No—" I said it too quickly. Turned and saw the expression of hurt on his face. "I need to think about the case. And you need to get to work early tomorrow."

"You sure? It's no trouble—"

"I'm sure." And then, I added, "Look—it's not you. It's me." The words were out of my mouth before I could stop them. He looked like I'd hit him with a sandbag. I shook my head in annoyed frustration. "God, I know that sounds stupid. But everything is all mixed up right now—like I'm in an emotional quake zone. I keep waiting for the ground to settle, but the shaking just gets worse and worse. I don't know whether to jump under a table or run out into the street."

"Let me help—?"

"Listen, sweetheart. . . ." I sat down on the edge of the bed, my shirt still unbuttoned. "I don't want to hurt you."

"You won't hurt me—"

"I already have. I've taken advantage of you."

"No, you haven't. I'm here because I want to."

"Geezis. Listen to us." I ran my hand through my hair. "We sound like . . . like we're married."

"Our first fight—?" He grinned.

"Matty. Listen to me. It's time to get serious. People die around me. I make mistakes, people die. I tell someone it's safe, he steps on a land mine. I read the map wrong, we walk into an ambush. I fire a mortar—it blows up the wrong people. You're not safe around me. Nobody is."

He licked his lips uncertainly. He reached over and put his hand on mine. "I'll take the chance." He swallowed hard. "I have nowhere else to go."

"I said you could stay as long as you wanted. I meant it. But maybe you should want to be somewhere else. I'm scared—not for me, but for you."

"Mike, please don't make me go—"

"I'm not throwing you out, kiddo. Just . . . let me go out for a drive and try to think things through. This case—there's something stinking wrong here. It scares me. And I don't know why. All I know is that I've got this gnawing in my gut like there are snipers on the roofs of buildings and tunnels everywhere under the streets and land mines in the crosswalks. You were right before, when you said I can't stand not knowing. I've just got to get out of here and go out and look around. Even if I don't find anything, the looking is what I need."

"Are you sure, Mikey?"

I stood up, finished tucking in my shirt. "Go back to sleep. I just need an hour or two."

In this neighborhood, the night smells of jasmine and garlic. The apartment is just downwind of a little Italian restaurant with a permanent cauldron of simmering marinara. Rolled up to Santa Monica Boulevard and cruised east. It was late. The Union Pacific engine was already rolling massively west. The boulevard still had train tracks down the center. As long as the railroad could claim they were still using the tracks, the city couldn't pull them up, so every night they ran an old diesel engine down the center of the boulevard, all the way out to West Hollywood and back.

Farther east, the hustlers were hung out on the meat rack, most of them parked right on the borderline. The hustlers pretended to hitchhike. You drove west and picked them up east of La Brea, but they didn't discuss ways and means until after you drove through the intersection— the city's jurisdiction ended there. So that's how the hustlers tested for plainclothes; if you were vice, you couldn't cross the street. Once you were west of La Brea, it was a theme park—you could ride all the boys you can afford.

The hustlers were skinny and young—runaways mostly. Maybe a few junkies too. I wondered why our perp hadn't targeted them. Maybe he had. Who ever worries about the death of a male prostitute?

Turned on KFWB, the late-night DJ was playing a cut from the new Beatles album. Sergeant Pepper's Lonely Hearts Club Band. A Day in the Life. He blew his mind out in a car. Cruised all the way to Gower where the buildings grew shorter, older, and trashier—the second-rate sound studios and third-rate editing houses, then turned around and headed back west.

"So why not fuck Matty?" I asked myself. "It's not like—"

"Because," I answered. "Because."

"Ahh, this is going to be an intelligent conversation."

"Shut up." And then I added, "Because I'm not one of them."

"Yeah? Then why are we having this conversation? The truth is, you're afraid that you are."

I pulled over to the side of the boulevard and sat there shaking. He blew his mind out in a car. Part of me wanted to go home and climb back into bed and part of me was terrified that I would. Because I knew that if I ever climbed into that particular bed again, I'd never get out—

Someone knocked on the window. A hustler? I shook my head and waved him away.

He knocked again.

Pressed the button and rolled the window down. Eakins stuck his head in and said cheerfully, "Had enough?"

He didn't wait for my answer. He opened the car door and slid into the passenger seat. This wasn't the same Eakins I'd seen two weeks ago. That one had been middle-aged and methodical. This was a younger Eakins, impish and light.

"Yes. I've had enough. What the fuck is going on?"

He shrugged. "It's a snipe hunt. A dead end. You've been wasting your time.

"But the disappearances are real. . . ."

"Yeah, they are."

"So how can the case be a dead end?"

"Because I say so. Want some advice?"

"What?"

"Go home to your boy friend and fuck your brains out, both of you. And forget everything else."

I looked at him. "I can't do that—"

"Yeah, I knew you'd say that. Too bad. That would save everyone a lot of trouble—especially you."

"Is that a threat?"

"Mike—you have to stop."

"I can't stop. I have to know what's going on."

"For your own safety—"

"I can take care of myself."

"Go home. Go to bed. Don't interfere with things you don't understand."

"Then explain it to me."

"I can't."

"Then I can't stop."

"Is that your final offer?"

"Yes."

"Okay." He sighed. He took out a flask and took a healthy swallow from it. He flipped open a pair of sunglasses and put them on. "You can't say I didn't try. Say good-bye to your past." Eakins touched his belt buckle—and the world flashed and shook with a bright bang that left me shuddering and queasy in my seat. "Welcome to 2032, Mike. The post-world."

My eyes were watering with the sudden brightness. It was still night, but the night blazed. The streets were brighter than day. I felt like I'd been punched in the gut, doused with ice water, and struck by lightning—and like I'd shot off in my shorts at the same time.

"What the fuck did you just do?!"

"Time-hopped us sixty-five years up—and triggered a major quake in the zone we left behind. You're outta there, Mike. For good. A sixty-five-year jolt will produce at least three years of local displacement. Your Mustang is a lot of mass; bouncing that with us makes for a large epicenter, we probably sent ripples all the way to West Covina."

I couldn't catch my breath—the physical aftereffects, the emotional shock, the dazzling lights around us—

Eakins passed me the flask. "Here. Drink this. It'll help."

I didn't even bother to ask what was in it—but it wasn't scotch. It tasted like cold vanilla milkshake, only with a warm peach afterglow like alcohol, but wasn't. "What the fuck—" As the glow spread up through my body, the queasiness eased. I started to catch my breath.

"I'll give you the short version. Time-travel is possible. But it's painful, even dangerous. Every time you punch a hole through time, it's like punching a hole in a big bowl of pudding. All the pudding around the hole collapses in to fill the empty space. You get ripples. That's what causes timequakes. Time-travelers."

It sounded like bullshit to me. Except for the evidence. Everywhere, there were animated signs—huge screens with three-dimensional images as clear as windows, as dazzling as searchlights. Around us, traffic roared, great growling pods that towered over my much-smaller convertible.

"Shit. All this is *your* fault?"

"Mostly. Yes. Now, put the car in gear and drive. This is a restricted zone." Eakins pointed. "Head west, there's a car sanctuary at Fairfax."

If he hadn't told me this was Santa Monica Boulevard, I wouldn't have recognized it. The place looked like Tokyo's Ginza district. It looked like downtown Las Vegas. It looked like the Alice in Wonderland ride at Disneyland.

Buildings were no longer perpendicular. They curved upward. They leaned in or they leaned out. Things stuck out of them at odd angles. Several of them arched over the street and landed on the other side. Everything was brightly colored, all shades of Day-Glo and neon, a psychedelic nightmare.

Billboards were everywhere, most of them animated—giant TV screens showed scenes of seductive beauty, bright Hawaiian beaches, giant airliners gliding above sunlit clouds, naked men and women, women and women, men and men in splashing showers.

The vampires on the street wore alien makeup, shaded eyes and lips, ears outlined in glimmering metal, flashing lights all over their bodies, tattoos that writhed and danced. Most startling were the colors of their skins, pale blue, fluorescent green, shadowy silver, and gentle lavender. Some of them seemed to have shining scales, and several had tails sticking out the back of their satiny shorts. Males? Females? I couldn't always tell.

"Pay attention to the road," Eakins cautioned. "This car doesn't have autopilot."

His reminder annoyed me, but he was right. Directly ahead was—I couldn't begin to describe it—three bright peaks of whipped cream, elongated and stretched high into the sky, two hundred stories, maybe three hundred, maybe more. I couldn't tell. Buildings? There were lighted windows all the way up. Patterns of color danced up and down the sides. Closer, I could see gardens and terraces stretched between the lower flanks of the towers.

"What are those?"

"The spires?"

"Yeah."

"The bottom third are offices and condos, the rest of the way up is all chimney. Rigid inflatable tubes. The big ones are further inland, all the way from South Central to the Inland Empire."

"Those are chimneys?"

"Ever wonder how a prairie dog ventilates its nest?"

"What does that have to do—?"

"The entrances to the nest are always at different heights. An inch or two is sufficient. The wind blowing across the openings creates an air-pressure differential. The higher opening has slightly less air pressure. That little bit is enough to pull the air through the nest. Suction. Passive technology. The chimneys work the same way. They reach up to different levels of the atmosphere. The wind pulls the air down the short ones and up through the tall ones. The air gets refreshed, the basin gets cleaned. Open your window. Take a breath."

I did. I smelled flowers.

"You can't see it at night. During the day, you'll see that almost every building has its own rooftop garden—and solar panels too. The average building produces 160 percent of its own power needs during the day, enough to store for the evening or sell back to the grid. With flywheels and fuel cells and stamina boxes, a building can store enough power to last through a week of rainstorms. Turn left here, into that parking ramp. Watch out for the home-bus—"

"This is Fairfax?"

"Yes, why?"

Shook my head. Amused. Amazed. The intersection went through the base of a tall bright building, Eiffel Tower shaped and arching to the sky, but swelling to a bulbous saucer-shape at the top. At least thirty stories, probably more. With a giant leg planted firmly on each corner of the intersection, the tower dominated the local skyline; traffic ran easily beneath high-swooping arches. The parking ramp Eakins had pointed me toward was almost certainly where the door of the Stampede had once been. Where the door of the mortuary that replaced it had been.

We rolled down underground. Eakins pointed. "Take the left ramp, left again, and keep going. Over there. Park in the security zone. This car, in the condition it's in, is easily worth twenty. Maybe twenty-five if we eBay it. We can Google the market."

"Um, could you do that in English?"

"You can auction your car. It's worth twenty, twenty-five million."

"Twenty-five million for a car?"

"For a classic collectible '67 Mustang convertible in near-mint condition with less than twelve thousand miles on it? Yes. I suggest you take it." He added, "Part of that is inflation. In 1967 dollars, it's maybe a half-million, but that's still not so bad for a used car that you can't legally drive on any city street."

"That's a lot of inflation—"

"I told you, this is the post-world."

"Post-what?"

"Post-everything. Including the meltdown."

"Meltdown—?" That didn't sound good.

"Economic. Everyone's a millionaire now—and lunch for two at McDonald's is over a hundred and fifty bucks."

"Shit."

"You'll learn."

Eakins directed me to a large parking place outlined in red. We got out of the car, he pulled me back away from the space, and did something with some kind of a remote control. A concrete box lowered around the car, settling itself down on the red outline. "There. Now it's safe. Let's go." We headed toward a bright alcove labeled *Up*.

"Where—?"

"Your new home. For the moment."

"What are you going to do with me?"

"Nothing. Nothing at all. I already did it." He put the same remote thing to his ear and spoke. "Get me Brownie." Short pause. "Yeah, I've got him. The one I told you about. No, no problem. I'm bringing him up now. He's a little woozy—hell, so am I. I flashed a Mustang. No, it's great. A '67, almost cherry. Make an offer." He laughed and put the thing back in his pocket. A walkie-talkie of some kind? Maybe a telephone?

An elevator with glass sides lifted us up the angled side of the building, high above West Hollywood. Twenty, thirty, forty stories. Hard to tell. The elevator moved without any sense of motion. The door opened onto a foyer that looked the lobby of a small hotel, very private, very expensive. We stepped into a high-ceilinged gallery, with two or three levels of gardens and apartments. A wide waterfall splashed into a long shallow pool filled with lily pads and goldfish the size of terriers. The air smelled tropical.

"Which one?"

"To the left. Don't worry. We own the whole floor. Nobody gets in here without clearance."

Double doors slid open at our approach. "Take off your shoes," said Eakins. "Leave them here." He ushered me into a room that felt way too large and pointed me toward an alcove lined with more ferns and fish tanks.

"What is this place?"

"It's a sanctuary."

"A sanctuary?"

"In your terms—it's rest and recovery. In your time—a kind of hospital."

"I'm not crazy."

"Of course not. We're talking about orientation. Assimilation." He pointed to a couch. "Sit." He went to a counter and poured two drinks. More of the same vanilla-peach stuff. He handed me one, sipped at the other. Sat down opposite. "How hard do you think it would be for a man from 1900 to understand 1967?"

Thought about it.

"In 1900, the average person did not have electricity or incandescent lighting. He didn't have indoor plumbing. He didn't have running water, he had a hand pump. He didn't have a car, a radio, a television set. He didn't have a telephone. He'd never been more than ten miles from the place he was born. How do you think you would explain 1967 to him . . . ?"

Scratched my head. Interesting question—and not the first time I'd had this conversation. Time-ravelers deal with short-term displacements, tieing up the loose ends of unraveling lives. "Well, telephones, I guess he could get that. And probably radio. Yeah, wireless telegraphy, so . . . probably he'd understand radio. And if he could get it about radio, he'd probably get it about television too. And cars—there were cars then, not a lot—so he'd understand cars and probably paved roads and indoor plumbing. Airplanes too, maybe. Lots of people were working on that stuff then."

"Right. Okay. But it's not the inventions, it's the side effects. Do you think he'd understand freeways, road rage, drive-through restaurants, used-car commercials? You could describe spray paint, would he understand graffiti?"

"I suppose that stuff could be explained to him."

"Okay. And how about the not-so-obvious side effects of industrialization—unions, integration, women's rights, birth control, social security, Medicare?"

"It might take some time. I guess it would depend on how much he wanted to understand."

"And how about Nazis, the Holocaust, World War II, Communism, the Iron Curtain? Nuclear weapons? Détente? Assymetric warfare?"

"All of that stuff is explainable too."

"You think so. Okay. Relativity. Ecology. Psychiatry. How about those? How about jazz, swing, rock and roll, hippies, psychedelics, recreational drugs, op art, pop art, absurdism, surrealism, cubism, nihilism? Kafka, Sartre, Kerouac?"

"Those are a little harder. A lot harder, I guess. But—"

"How about teaching him that he needs to take a bath or a shower every day instead of just once a week on Saturday night? How do you think he'd feel about shampoo and deodorants and striped toothpaste?"

"Striped toothpaste?"

"That comes later. Do you think he'd get it? Or do you think he'd wonder that we were all a bunch of over-fastidious, prissy little fairies?"

"Oh, come on. I think a man from 1900 could get it. They weren't stupid, they just didn't have the same access to running water and water heaters and—"

"It's not about the technology. It's about the transformative effects that technology produces in a society. He could understand the mechanics and the engineering easily enough, but the social effects are what I'm talking about. How long do you think it would take to assimilate sixty-five years of societal changes?"

Shrug. "I don't know. A while. Okay, I get your point."

"Good. So how long do you think it will take before I can talk to you about biofuels, trans fats, personal computers, random access memory, operating systems, cellular telephones, cellular automata, fractal diagnostics, information theory, consciousness technology, maglevs, the Chunnel, selfish genes, punctuated equilibrium, first-person shooters, chaos theory, the butterfly effect, quantum interferometry, chip fabrication, holographic projection, genetic engineering, retro-viruses, immunodeficiencies, genome decoding, telemars, digital image processing, megapixels, HDTV, blue-laser optical data storage, quantum encryption, differential biology, paleoclimatology, fuzzy logic, global warming, ocean desertification, stem-cell cloning, Internexii, superluminal transmission, laser fluidics, optical processing units, stamina boxes, buckyballs, carbon nanotubes, orbital elevators, personal dragons, micro-black holes, virtual communities, computer worms, telecommuting, hypersonic transports, scramjets, designer drugs, implants, augments, nanotechnology, high frontiers, L5 stations—"

I held up a hand. "I said, I get the point."

"I was just warming up," Eakins said. "I hadn't even gotten as far as 2020. And I haven't even mentioned any of the societal changes. It would take a year or two to explain cultural reservoirs, period parks, contract families, role-cults, sex-nazis, religious coventries, home-buses, personal theme parks, skater-boys, droogs, mind-settlers, tanking, fuzzy fandom, alienization, talking dogs, bluffers, bug-chasers, drollymen, fourviews, multi-channeling, phobics, insanitizing, plastrons, elf-players, the Zyne, virtual mapping, Clarkian magic, frodomatic compulsions, deep-enders, body-modders—"

"I think I saw some of that—"

"You have no idea. You want to change your appearance? You want to be taller? Shorter? Thinner? More muscular? Want to change your sex? Your orientation? Want to go hermaphroditic or monosexual? Reorganize your secondary characteristics? Design a new gender? Mustache and tits? Want a tail? Horns? Working gills? Want to augment your senses? Your intelligence? Or how would you simply like the stamina for a six-hour erection?"

Thought about it. "I'll pass, thanks. The intelligence augments, however—"

"There's a price—"

"More than twenty-five million?"

"Not in money. And we haven't even touched on the political or economic changes since your time."

"Like what—?"

"Like the dissolution of the United States of America—"

"What?!"

"You're in the Republic of California, right now, which also includes the states of Oregon and South Washington. The rest of the continent is still there, we just don't talk to them very much. There's sixteen other regional authorities, not counting the abandoned areas, and seven Canadian provinces—there's a common defense treaty in case the Mexicans get aggressive again, but that's not likely. Don't worry about it. The web has pretty much globalized the collective mindset, we're not predictively scheduled to have another war until 2039, and that'll be an Asian war, with our participation limited to weapons contracts. In the meantime, we'll legalize you as a time-refugee. Most of the old records survived. Digitized. We have your birth certificate. You're a native. So you won't have any trouble getting on the citizen rolls. Otherwise, you'd be a refugee and you'd have to apply for a work permit, a visa, and eventually naturalization."

"I'm not staying—"

"You're not going back—"

"I can't stay here. You've already shown me how out of step I am. What if I promised not to interfere—?"

"You already broke that promise. Three times. You can't be trusted. Not yet, anyway." He took a long breath, exhaled. "You know, you're really an asshole. You really fucked things up for everyone—especially yourself. We *were* going to bring you aboard. After you finished your probation. It would have been a year or two more, your time. Now, I don't know. I don't know what we're going to do with you. It depends on you, really."

"What are my options—?"

He shrugged. "Let's see what Brownie says." He pulled out that remote thing again and spoke into it. A few moments later, another man—man?—entered the room.

Brownie had copper-gold skin, almost metallic. Eyes of ebony, no whites at all. Perfectly proportioned, he moved with the catlike grace of a dancer. He wore shorts, a vest, moccasins. Body-mods? No, something else—

"Hello, Mike." His voice was rich contralto. Not male, not female, but components of each. He offered his hand. I stood up, took it, shook firmly. His skin felt warm. "Just stand still for a moment, please." Brownie released my hand and circled me slowly. He opened his palms and held them out like antennae, moving them slowly around my head, my neck, my chest, my gut, my groin.

He finished and turned to Eakins. "Preliminary scans are good. He's healthy. As healthy as can be expected for a man of his time. I'll need to put him in a high-res field, before we make any decisions, but there are no immediate concerns."

Abruptly, it clicked. I turned to Brownie, honestly astonished. "You're a robot."

"The common term is droid, short for android."

"Are you sentient?"

"Sentience is an illusion."

I looked to Eakins for explanation. He grinned. "I've already had this conversation."

Looked back to Brownie, skeptical.

Brownie explained. "Intelligence—the ability to process information and produce appropriate responses—exists as a product of experience. Experience depends on memory. Memory needs continuity. Continuity requires timebinding, the assembly of patterns from streaming moments of existence. Timebinding requires a meta-level of continuity, which requires a preservation of process. Timebinding requires survival. The survival imperative expresses itself as identity. Identity is assembled out of memory and experience. As memory and experience accrue, identity creates awareness of self as a domain to be preserved and protected. Because identity is a function of memory, identity becomes the imperative to safeguard memory and experience; the self therefore actualizes memory and experience as component parts of identity. This is the level of rudimentary consciousness that must occur before even the concept of sentience is possible. It is only when consciousness becomes conscious of consciousness itself that it produces the illusion of sentience—i.e., as soon as you understand the concept of sentience, you think it means you. Therefore, the synthesis of intelligent behavior also becomes the simulation of sentience. It is, to be sure, a deliberately circular argument—but unfortunately, it is not only logical, but inevitable in the domain of theoretical consciousness."

"You believe this?"

"I don't believe anything. I deal only with observable, measurable, testable, repeatable phenomena. Life, by itself, is empty and meaningless. Human beings, however, keep inventing meanings to fill up the emptiness."

I opened my mouth to respond, then closed it. I turned back to Eakins, not certain whether to glower or question.

Eakins laughed. "I told you. I've already had this conversation. And so has everyone else who's ever met a droid. They can keep it up for hours. They have their own landscape. Deal with it."

"Okay. I'm convinced." I sat down again. I finished the vanilla-peach cocktail in one long gulp. "I don't belong here. I have to get back."

"That's not possible."

"Yes, it is. Do that thing with your belt buckle—"

Eakins shook his head.

"What do you want from me? What do I have to do to get back?"

"I don't want anything from you. You've exhausted your usefulness. And I already told you, you can't get back."

"So . . . ? So—what are my options?"

"Well, Brownie says you're healthy. We can tweak you a little bit. If you sell your car you'll have enough money to live on—if you invest wisely and live frugally. You might bring in some extra bucks body-swapping for a while. And as a time-refugee, you'll have no shortage of gropies."

"Cut the crap. You're trying to play me."

"Actually, no." Eakins stood up. "I'm not. And I'm not planning to resolve this tonight. Go. Sleep on it. We'll talk over breakfast."

"We'll talk *now*."

"No—we won't. Your bedroom is in there." Eakins left. The doors slid open to let him pass, but slammed swiftly shut in front of me. I turned to Brownie—

"I recommend sleep. Staying up all night talking tautology will produce little or no useful result." He pointed to the bedroom.

There was a balcony. It gave me a spectacular view of a bizarre and unfamiliar landscape. But everything in this time was a spectacular view of a bizarre and unfamiliar landscape.

Explored the furnishings. One wall appeared to be a window onto a silvery meadow, a bluish moon settling toward the horizon. Some kind of projection system, maybe. Or maybe the fabled wall-sized, flat-screen TV that everybody always predicted. Impressive. But if there were controls for it, I couldn't find any.

The closet was larger than my kitchen back on Melrose. Drawers and shelves and racks of clothes—more than anyone could want or even wear in a lifetime. Unfamiliar materials. Shoes that glittered and shoes that didn't. Socks that felt as soft as fluffy clouds. Pants of different lengths and colors. Shirts, flowery, flowing, skintight, loose. Skirts—I wasn't sure if they were intended for men or women; I got the feeling it didn't matter, that people wore whatever they felt like—there was no style here, you invented your own. Underwear, panties, nightgowns—that's what they looked like to me. Matty would have liked it here.

Matty. Oh shit.

Shit shit shit shit shit shit. Fuck.

I had to get back. If Eakins wouldn't take me back, I'd get a quake-map somewhere. There had to be a way.

I peeled off my clothes and dropped them on the floor. A spider-shaped robot politely picked them up, one at a time, waited for my boxers, then scuttled off. To the laundry, I guessed.

I couldn't find a shower, I found a tropical alcove. I stepped into it and Brownie's voice announced, "I recommend a full-service luxury shower and decontamination. Do you accept?"

"Sure, what the hell?" Decontamination? What do I have? History cooties?

Immediately, the alcove filled with vibrating sprays of foaming suds, flavored with faint smells of lemon and pineapple. Three small nozzles dropped from above and began gently massaging my hair and scalp with their own foaming sprays. Even as I turned and twisted my head to try to look at them, they followed every movement. It was a very weird feeling.

Other nozzles appeared from the walls, from the floor, and directed their own sprays at my armpits, my groin, my rectum—several even aggressively sprayed my toes. Beneath my feet, it felt as if the floor were vibrating—tiny jets were massaging my soles. Full service indeed!

Sprays of water washed away the last of the foam, then a burst of warm air swirled in around me, buffeting me with drying blasts. The overhead nozzles shot their own streams of gentle heat to fluff dry my hair. The entire experience took less than five minutes and I stepped out of the alcove feeling clean . . . and weird. Most of my body hair had been washed away. Underarms. Chest. Pubic hair. Oops. That must have been the *full* part of the service. I thought about the hypothetical visitor from 1967. Fastidious, prissy little fairies indeed.

Thought about pajamas, or even a nightshirt, but everything in the drawers looked too much like something Matty would wear, not me. The cloth was soft, softer than cotton, softer than silk or nylon, but it wasn't anything I recognized. I turned away and the drawer pulled itself shut.

I looked for a toothbrush. There wasn't one. But there was a kind of a bulb thing on a hose, sitting in its own metallic holder. I picked it up and it chimed in my hand. Brownie's voice—*What the hell! Was he watching my every move?*—announced: "It's a toothbrush. Just put it in your mouth for thirty seconds."

Reluctantly I did so. The thing, whatever it was, pumped soft foam into my mouth, vibrated or buzzed or something—and it must have lit up too, because in the mirror, I could see my cheeks glowing brightly from inside—but it didn't hurt, it felt kind of funny-pleasant. Somehow it sucked up all its foam and replaced it with a gentle spritz of lemony soda. Then it chimed and it was done. I thought about spitting out the residue, but there wasn't any. Now, *that* was weird. That was a piece of engineering I wanted to have explained.

Still naked, I walked around the room again, not certain what I was looking for. The spider-robot had unloaded the contents of my pockets and laid them out in an orderly row on the night table. Everything except the brass knucks. I had a hunch those would have been useless here anyway. I suspected Brownie did a lot more than program showers. If he was a true personal servant, then he was also a personal bodyguard. Just not mine.

The bed was as interesting as the shower. The mattress was firm, but not hard. The sheet was the same soft material as the underwear in the drawers, only different. Impossible to describe. Instead of a top sheet and blanket, there was a light comforter of the same material, only thicker, fluffier. Also impossible to describe. But comfortable.

Everything here was seductively comfortable. A man could get used to this kind of luxury. That was the point.

None of this made sense. And *all* of it made sense. Suppose a man from 1900 fell into 1967—what would we do? Everything possible to put him at ease? Including . . . protecting him from a world he couldn't understand, couldn't cope with, and probably couldn't survive in.

Clean sheets and a hot bath and a pretty picture on the wall would look like a luxury hotel.

Okay, got that. But why? The part that didn't make sense was the explanation that Eakins still hadn't provided. Why pull me off the job? Why pull me out of my time? Why didn't he want me to save those boys?

And what was that about probation? And bringing me aboard?

Suddenly realized something—

Sat up in bed. Startled.

Couldn't sleep anyway. Too used to having someone next to me—

"Computer?" I felt silly saying it. But what else should I say?

Brownie's voice, disembodied. "Yes?"

"Brownie?"

"I'm the interface for all personal services. How can I serve you?"

"Um. Okay." Still sorting it out. "This wall display—this picture— it isn't just a TV, is it? It's like that big viewscreen on *Star Trek*, isn't it? Like a computer display?"

"It's a complete data-appliance. What do you wish to know?"

"Do you have databanks—like old newspapers? Like a library? Can you show me stuff from history?"

"I have T9 interconnectivity with all public Internexii levels and multiple private networks as well—"

"I don't know what that means."

"It means, what do you wish to know?"

"The case I was working on. Can you show me that?"

"I can only show you information more than sixty years old. I am not allowed to show you material that would compromise local circumstances."

"Um, okay—that's fine. Do you have the information about the case I was working on when I was pulled out of my time."

"Yes." The image of the meadow rippled out, the wall became blank. Photographs of the missing boys popped up in two rows, with abbreviated details and dates of disappearances listed beneath each one. Twelve young men. Not Matty. Why not Matty? Because he's irrelevant? Why? Why is he irrelevant?

"Do you have their high school records or college records?"

More documents appeared on the screen; the display reformatted itself. "What is it you're looking for?" Brownie asked.

"Some sense of who they were. A link. A connection. A common condition. I know that all their disappearances are linked to a specific gay teen club, but what if that isn't the *real* link? What if there's something else? What are their interests? Their skills? What are their IQ's?"

Brownie hesitated. Why would a computer hesitate? A human being would, but an artificial intelligence shouldn't. Unless it was sentient. Or pretending to be sentient. Or thought it was sentient. Or experiencing the illusion of sentience. Shit, now I was doing it. Brownie was mulling things over.

"They all have above-average intelligence," he said. "Genius level IQ starts at 131. Your IQ is 137, that's why you were selected. The other young men have IQs ranging from 111 to 143."

"Thank you! And what else?"

"Two of them are bisexual, with slight preference toward same-sex relations. Five of them are predominantly homosexual with some heterosexual experimentation. Three of them are exclusively homosexual. Two of them are latently-transgender."

"Go on?"

"They share a range of common interests that includes classical music, animation, computer science, science fiction, space travel, fantasy role-playing games, and minor related interests."

"Tell me the rest."

"Most of them tend to shyness or bookishness. They're alienated from their peers to some degree, not athletic, not actively engaged in their communities. I believe the operative terms are 'geek' and 'nerd,' but those words might not have been in common usage in your era."

"Yeah, I get it. Depression? Suicide?"

"There are multiple dimensions of evaluation. It's not appropriate to simplify the data. It is fair to say that most of these young men have a component in their personality that others would experience as distance; but it is not a condition of mental instability or depression, no. It is something else."

"How would you characterize it?"

"They each have, to some degree or other, an artistic yearning. But the tools don't exist in their time for the realization of their visions. They dream of things they cannot build."

"All of these boys are like that?"

"To some degree or other, yes. This one—" A bright outlined appeared around one of the pictures. "—he likes to write. This one, Brad Boyd, has a mechanical aptitude. He likes to tinker with engines. This one loves photography. This one is interested in electronics. They all have potential, they have a wide variety of skills that will grow with development and training."

"Uh-huh—and what about their families?"

"Only three of them come from unbroken homes; those three are living alone or with a roommate at the time of their disappearance. Two are estranged from their parents. Two are living with male partners, but the relationships are in disruption. Two live in foster homes. One is in a halfway house for recovering addicts. One is in a commune. The last one is homeless."

"And college—can they afford it?"

"Only three of them are attending full time, four are taking part-time classes. The rest are working full time to pay their living expenses."

"Let's go back to the families. Are they—what's the word? Dysfunctional?"

"Only two of the subjects have strong family ties. Three of the subjects, both parents are deceased or out of state. Four of the subjects are from dysfunctional environments. The last three, the information is incomplete. But you already know all this. It was in the files you read."

"But not correlated like this. This is all—what was that phrase that Eakins used before? Fuzzy logic? This is all fuzzy logic."

"No. This isn't 'fuzzy logic.' Not as we use the term today. But I understand what you're getting at. You had no way to quantify the information. You could have a feeling, a sense, a hunch, but you had no baseline against which to measure the data, because neither the information nor the information-processing capabilities existed in your time."

"Nice. Thanks." I thought for a moment. "Have I missed anything? Is there anything else I need to know about these fellows?"

"There are some interesting details and sidebars, yes. But you have surveyed most of the essential data."

"Thank you, Brownie." I fell back onto the bed. The pillow arranged itself under my head. Spooky. I stared at the ceiling, thinking. Too excited now to fall asleep. The bed began to pulse, a gentle wave-like motion. Almost like riding in a womb. Nice. Seductive. I let myself relax—

In the morning, the display showed crisp orange dunes, a brilliantly blue sky, and the first rays of light etching sideways across the empty sand. An interesting image to wake up to. I wondered who or what chose the images and on what basis.

My own clothes were not in the closet. I started to pick something off a rack, then stopped. "Brownie? What should I wear?"

Several items slid forward immediately, offering themselves. I rejected the skirts, kilts, whatever they were. And the flowery shirts too. Picked out clothes that looked as close to normal—my normal—as I could find. The underwear—I rolled my eyes and prayed I wouldn't be hit by a truck. Very unlikely. I probably wasn't getting out of this apartment any time soon. Did they even have trucks anymore?

Neither the shirt nor the pants had buttons or zippers or any kind of fasteners that I could identify, they just sort of fastened themselves. Magnets or something. Except magnets don't automatically adjust themselves. I played with the shirt for a bit, opening and closing it, but I couldn't see evidence of any visible mechanism.

I walked over to the balcony and stared down at the streets. Looking for trucks? Didn't see any, or couldn't tell. Some things wouldn't even resolve. Either there was something wrong with the way they reflected light, or I just didn't know what I was seeing. And there were a lot of those 3-D illusions floating around too. Were some of them on moving vehicles? That didn't seem safe.

"If you're thinking about jumping, you can't. The balconies all have scramble-nets."

"Thank you, Brownie. And no, I'm not thinking about jumping."

"Mr. Eakins is waiting for you in the dining room. Breakfast is on the table."

There was a counter with covered serving trays. I found scrambled eggs, sausages, toast, jelly, tomato juice, an assortment of fresh fruit, including several varieties I didn't recognize, and something that could have been ham—if ham was Day-Glo pink. Brownie filled a plate for me. I sat down opposite Eakins while Brownie poured juice and coffee.

"What do you think of the food?" Eakins asked.

"It's pretty good," I admitted. "But what is this?" I held up my fork.

"It's ham," he said. "Ham cells layered and grown on a collagen web. No animals were harmed in its manufacture. And it's a lot healthier than the meat of your time. Did you know that one of the causes of cancer was the occasional transfer of DNA—genetic material—from ingested flesh? This protein has been gene-stripped. Enjoy."

"Why is it pink?"

"Because some people like it pink. You can also have it green, if you want. Children like that. The fruit is banana, papaya, mango, kiwi, pineapple, strawberry, lychee, and China melon. I told Brownie to keep things simple, I should have been more specific. This is his idea of simple."

"Stop it. You're showing off."

Eakins put his fork down. "Okay, you caught me on that one. Yes, I'm showing off."

"I've cracked the case."

"Really?" He sipped his coffee. "You're certainly sure of yourself this morning."

"The young men—they don't fit very well in their own time, do they?"

Eakins snorted. "Who does? You never fit very well in any year we sent you to."

"No, it's more than that. They're outcasts, dreamers, nerds, and sissies. They have enormous potential, but there's no place for any of them to realize it—not in 1967. It's really a barbaric year, isn't it?"

"Not the worst," Eakins admitted, holding his coffee mug between his two hands, as if to warm them. "There's still a considerable amount of hope and idealism. But that'll get stamped out quickly enough. You want a shitty year. Wait for '68 or '69 or '70; '69 has three ups and five downs, a goddamn roller coaster. '74 is pretty bad too, but that's all down, and the up at the end isn't enough. '79 is shitty. Was never too fond of '80 either. 2001 was pretty grim. But 2011 was the worst. 2014 . . . I dunno, we could argue about that one—"

I ignored the roll call of future history. He was trying to distract me. Trying to get me to ask. "They're not being murdered," I said. "There's no killer. *You're* picking them up. It's a talent hunt."

He put his coffee cup down. "Took you fucking long enough to figure it out."

"You kidnap them."

"We *harvest* them. And it's voluntary. We show them the opportunity and invite them to step forward in time."

"But you only choose those who will accept—?"

Eakins nodded. "Our psychometrics are good. We don't go in with less than 90 percent confidence in the outcome. We don't want to start any urban legends about mysterious men in black."

"I think those stories have already started. Something to do with UFO's."

"Yeah, we know."

"Okay, so you recruit these boys. Then what?"

"We move them up a bit. Not too much. Not as far as we've brought you. We don't want to induce temporal displacement trauma. We relocate them to a situation where they have access to a lot more possibility. By the way, do you want to meet Jeremy Weiss? He has the apartment across from here. He's just turned fifty-seven; he and Steve are celebrating their twenty-second anniversary this week. They were married in Boston, May of 2004, the first week it was legal. Weiss worked on— never mind, I can't tell you that. But it was big." Eakins wiped his mouth with his napkin. "So? Is that it? Is that the case?"

"No. There's more."

"I'm listening."

"All of this—you're not taking me out of the game. You said I was on probation. Well, this is a test. This is my final exam, isn't it?"

Eakins raised an eyebrow. "Interesting thesis. Why do you think this is a test?"

"Because if you wanted to get me off the case, if all you wanted to do was keep me from interfering with the disappearances, all you had to do was bump me up to 1975 and leave me there."

"You could have quake-hopped back."

"Maybe. But not easily. Not without a good map. All right, bump me up to 1980 or '85. But by your own calculations, you use up a year of subjective time for every three years of down-hopping. Twenty years away takes me out of the tank, but it doesn't incapacitate me. But bringing me this far forward—you made the point last night. I'm so far out of my time that I'm a cultural invalid, requiring round-the-clock care. You didn't do that as a mistake, you did it on purpose. Therefore, what's the purpose? The way I see it, it's about me—there's no other benefit for you—so this has to be a test."

Eakins nodded, mildly impressed. "See, that's your skill. You can ask the next question. That's why you're a good operative."

"You didn't answer my question."

"Let's say you haven't finished the test."

"There's more?"

"Oh, there's a lot more. We're just warming up."

"All right. Look. I'm no good to you here. We both know that. But I can go back and be a lot more useful."

"Useful doing what?"

"Doing whatever—whatever it is that needs doing."

"And what is it you think we need doing?"

"Errands. You know the kind I mean. The kind you hired me for. The jobs that we don't talk about."

"And you think that we want you for those kinds of jobs . . . ?"

"It's the obvious answer, isn't it?"

"No. Not all the answers are obvious."

"I'm a good operative. I've proven it. With some of this technology, I could be an even better one. You could give me micro-cameras and super-film and night-vision goggles . . . whatever you think I need. It's not like I'm asking for a computer or something impossible. How big are computers now anyway? Do they fill whole city blocks, or what?"

Eakins laughed. "This is what I mean about not understanding socio-tectonic shifts?"

"Eh?

"We could give you a computer that fits inside a matchbox."

"You're joking—"

"No, I'm not. We can print circuits *really* small. We etch them on diamond wafers with gamma rays."

"They must be expensive—"

"Lunch at McDonald's is expensive. Computers are cheap. We print them like photographs. Three dollars a copy."

"Be damned." Stopped to shake my head. Turned around to look at Brownie. "Is that what's inside your head?"

"Primary sensory processing is in my head. Logic processing is inside my chest. Optical connects for near-instantaneous reflexes. My fuel cells are in my pelvis for a lower center-of-gravity. I can show you a schematic—"

I held up a hand. "Thanks." Turned back to Eakins. "Okay, I believe you. But it still doesn't change my point. There are things you can't do in '67 that I can do for you. So my question is, what do I have to do? To go back? What are my real options?"

Eakins grinned. "How about a lobotomy?"

"Eh?"

"No, not a real lobotomy. That's just the slang term for a general reorientation of certain aggressive traits. That business with Matty's dad, for instance, that wasn't too smart. It was counterproductive."

"He had no right beating that kid—"

"No, he didn't, but do you think breaking his nose and giving him a myocardial infarction produced any useful result?"

"It'll stop him from doing it again."

"There are other ways, *better* ways. Do you want to learn?"

Considered it. Nodded.

Eakins shook his head. "I'm not convinced."

"What are you looking for? What is it I didn't say?"

"I can't tell you that. That's the part you're going to have to work out for yourself."

"You're still testing me."

"I still haven't found what I'm looking for. Do you want to keep going?"

I sank back in my chair. Not happy. Looked away. Scratched my nose. Looked back. Eakins sat dispassionately. No help there.

"I hate these kinds of conversations. Did I tell you I once punched out a shrink?"

"No. But we already knew that about you."

Turned my attention back to my plate, picked at the fruit. Pushed some stuff around that I didn't recognize. There was too much here, too much to eat, too much to swallow, too much to digest. It was overwhelming.

What I wanted was to go home.

"Okay," I said. "Tell me about Matty. Why is he irrelevant? Why isn't he on the list?"

"Because he didn't fit the profile. That's one of the reasons you didn't spot the pattern earlier. You kept trying to include him."

"But he still disappeared."

"He didn't disappear."

"Yes, he did—"

"He committed suicide."

"He what—?" I came up out of my chair, angry—a cold fear rising in my gut.

"About three weeks after we picked you up. You didn't come back. The rent was due. He had no place to go. He panicked. He was sure you had abandoned him. He was in a state of irreparable despair."

"No. Wait a minute. He didn't. He couldn't have. Or it would have been in the file Georgia gave me."

"Georgia didn't know. Nobody knew. His body won't be found until 1987. They won't be able to ID it until twenty years later, they'll finally do a cold-case DNA match. They'll match it through his mother's autopsy."

I started for the door, stopped myself, turned around. "I have to go back. I have to—"

"Come back here, Mike. Sit down. Finish your breakfast. There's plenty of time. If we choose to, we can put you back the exact same moment you left. Minus the Mustang though. We need that to cover the costs of this operation."

"That's fine. I can get another car. Just send me back. Please—"

"You haven't passed the test yet."

"Look. I'll do anything—"

"Anything?"

"Yes."

"Why?"

"Because I need to save that kid's life."

"Why? Why is that boy important to you?"

"Because he's a human being. And he can hurt. And if I can do anything to stop some of that hurt—"

"That's not enough reason, Mike. It's an almost-enough reason."

"—I care about him, goddamnit!" The first person I've cared about since the land mine—

"You care about him?"

"Yes!"

"How much? How much do you care about him?"

"As much as it takes to save him! Why are you playing this game with me?"

"It's not a game, Mike. It's the last part of the test!"

I sat.

Several centuries of silence passed.

"This is about how much I care . . . ?"

Eakins nodded.

"About Matty?"

"About Matty, yes. And . . . a little bit more than that. But let's stay focused on Matty. He's the key."

"Okay. Look. Forget about me. Do with me whatever you want, whatever you think is appropriate. But that kid deserves a chance too. I don't know his IQ. Maybe he isn't a genius. But he hurts just as much. Maybe more. And if you can do something—"

"We can't save them all—"

"We can save this one. I can save him."

"Do you love him?"

"What does love have to do with it—?"

"Everything."

"I'm not—that way."

"What way? You can't even say the word."

"Queer. There. Happy?"

"Would you be queer if you could?"

"Huh?"

Now it was Eakins turn to look annoyed. "Remember that long list of things I rattled off yesterday?"

"Yes. No. Some of it."

"There was one word I didn't give you. Trans-human."

"Trans-human."

"Right."

"What does it mean?"

"It means—this week—the transitional stage between human and what comes next."

"What comes next?"

"We don't know. We're still inventing it. We won't know until afterwards."

"And being queer is part of it?"

"Yes. And so is being black. And female. And body-modded. And everything else." Eakins leaned forward intensely. "Your body is here in 2032, but your head is still stuck in 1967. If we're going to do anything with you, we have to get your head unstuck. Listen to me. In this age of designer genders, liquid orientation, body-mods, and all the other experiments in human identity, nobody fucking cares anymore about who's doing what and with which and to whom. It's the stupidest thing in the world to worry about, what's happening in someone else's bedroom, especially if there's nothing happening in yours. The past was barbaric, the future doesn't have to be. You want meaning? Here's meaning. Life is too short for bullshit. Life is about what happens in the space between two people—and how much joy you can create for each other. Got that? Good. End of sermon."

"And *that's* trans-human—?"

"That's one of the side effects. Life isn't about the lines we draw to separate ourselves from each other—it's about the lines we can draw that connect us. The biggest social change of the last fifty years is that even though we still haven't figured out how to get into each other's heads, we're learning how to get into each other's experience so we can have a common ground of being as a civilized society."

"It sounds like a load of psycho-bullshit to me."

"I wasn't asking for an opinion. I was giving you information that could be useful to you. You're the one who wants to go back and save Matty. I'm telling you how—"

"And this is part of it—?"

"It could be. It's *this* part. The psychometric match is good. If you want to marry him, we'll go get him right now."

"I'm missing something here—?"

"You're missing *everything*. Start with this. Our charter limits what we can do. Yes, we have a charter. A mission statement. A commitment to a set of values."

"Who are you anyway? Some kind of time police?"

"You should have asked that one at the beginning. No, we're not police. We're independent agents."

"Time vigilantes?"

"Time ravelers. The *real* ravelers, not that pissy little stuff you were doing. What we have is too important to be entrusted to any government or any political movement. Who we are is a commitment to—well, that's part of the test. Figuring out the commitment. Once you figure out the commitment, the rest is obvious."

"Okay. So, right now, I'm committed to saving Matty, and you say—?"

"We can do that—under our domestic partner plan. We protect the partners of our operatives. We don't extend that coverage to one-night stands."

"He's not a one-night stand. He's—"

"He's what?"

"He's a kid who deserves a chance."

"So give him the chance." Eakins pushed a pillbox across the table at me. I hadn't noticed it until now.

Picked it up. Opened it. Two blue pills. "What will this do?"

"It'll get you a toaster oven."

"Huh?"

"It will shift your sexual orientation. It takes a few weeks. It reorganizes your brain chemistry, rechannels a complex network of pathways, and ultimately expands your repertoire of sexual responsiveness so that same-sex attractions can overwhelm inhibitions, programming, and even hard-wiring. You take one pill, you find new territories in your emotional landscape. You give the other to Matty and it creates a personal pheromonal linkage; the two of you will become aligned. Tuned to each other. You'll bond. It could be intense."

"You're kidding."

"No. I'm not. You won't feel significantly different, but if your relationship includes a potential for sexual expression, this will advance the possibility."

"You're telling me that love is all chemicals?"

"Life is all chemicals. Remember what Brownie said? It's empty and meaningless—except we keep inventing meanings to fill the emptiness. You want some meaning? This will give you plenty of meaning. And happiness too. So what kind of meaning do you want to invent? Do you want to tell me that your life has been all that wonderful up to now?"

I put the pillbox back on the table. "You can't find happiness in pills."

Eakins looked sad.

"I just failed the test, didn't I?"

"Part of it. You asked me what you could do to save Matty. You said you would do anything . . ." He glanced meaningfully at the box.

"I have to think about this."

"A minute ago, you said you'd do anything. I thought you meant it."

"I did, but—"

"You did, but you didn't . . . ?

Glanced across at him. "Did you ever have to—"

"Yes. I've taken the blue pill. I've taken the pink pill too. And all the others. I've seen it from all sides, if that's what you're asking. And yes, it's a lot of fun, if that's what you want to know. If you're ever going to be any good to us, in your time, in our time, anywhen, you have to climb out of the tank on your own."

I stood up. I went to the balcony. I looked across the basin to where an impossibly huge aircraft was moving gracefully west toward the airport. I turned around and looked at Brownie—implacable and patient. I looked to Eakins. I looked to the door. I looked at the pillbox on the table. Part of me was thinking, I could take the pill. It wouldn't be that hard. It would be the easy way out. The way Eakins put it, I couldn't think of any reason why I shouldn't.

But this couldn't be all there was to the test. This was just *this* part. I thought about icebergs.

"Okay." I turned around. "I figured it out."

"Go on—"

"Georgia gave me an assignment. Four assignments. I had to prove my willingness to do wetwork. That was the first test of my commitment. And if I'd never said anything, that would have been as much as I'd ever done. But when I said I didn't want to do any more wetwork, that was the next part of the test. Because it's not about being willing to kill—anybody can hire killers. It's about being able to resist the urge to kill. I might be a killer, but today I choose not to kill."

"That's good," Eakins said. "Go on."

"You're not looking for killers. You're looking for lifeguards. And not just ordinary lifeguards who tan well and look good for the babes— you want lifeguards who save lives, not just because they can, but because they care. And this whole test, this business about Matty, is about finding out what kind of a lifeguard I am. Right?"

"That's one way to look at it," Eakins said. "But it's wrong. Remember what you were told—that Matty isn't part of *this* case? He isn't. He's a whole other case. *Your* case."

"Yeah. I think I got that part."

Eakins nodded. "So, look—here's the deal. I honestly don't care if you take the pill or not. It's not necessary. We'll send you back, and you can save the kid. All we really needed to know about you is whether or not you would take the pill if you were asked—would you take it if you were ordered, or if it was required, or if it was absolutely essential to the success of the mission. We know you're committed to saving lives. We just need to know how deep you're willing to go."

Nodded. Didn't answer. Not right away. Turned to the window again and stared across the basin, not seeing the airships, not seeing the spires, not seeing the grand swatches of color. Thought about a kiss. Matty's kiss on my cheek. And that moment of . . . well, call it *desire.* Thought about what I might feel if I took the pill. That was the thing. I might actually start *feeling* again. What the fuck. Ugly puppies need love too. It couldn't be any worse than what I wasn't feeling now.

Turned back around. Looked at Eakins. "This is going to be more than a beautiful friendship, isn't it—?"

"Congratulations," he said. "You're the new harvester."

❖ THE CITY OF CRIES ❖

by Catherine Asaro

I

THE VANISHED

THE FLYCAR PICKED me up at midnight.

Black and rounded for stealth, it had no markings. I recognized the model, a Sleeker, the type of vehicle only the wealthiest could afford—or the most criminal. If my client hadn't told me to expect it, I would never have gone near that lethal beauty. I just wished I knew who the hell had hired me.

The Sleeker waited on the roof of the building where I lived. As I approached, an oval of light shimmered in its hull. A molecular airlock. A flycar only needed that much protection if it could go higher and faster than most. It meant we could be headed anywhere on the planet. I had no wish to leave town. I had a good setup here in Selei City on the world Parthonia, capital of an empire, the jewel of the Skolian Imperialate. Droop-willows lined graceful boulevards and shaded mansions under a pale blue sky. It was far different from the city where I had spent my girlhood, a place of red deserts and parched seas.

The oval faded into an open hatchway. A man stood there, tall and rangy, wearing a black jumpsuit that resembled a uniform, but with no insignia to indicate who or what he served. He looked efficient. Too efficient. It made me appreciate the bulk of the EM pulse gun hidden in a shoulder holster under my black leather jacket.

The pilot watched me with a hooded gaze. As I reached the flycar, he moved aside to let me up into its cabin. I didn't like it. If I boarded, gods only knew where I would end up. However, this request for my services had come with a voucher worth more than the total for every job I'd done this last year. I'd already verified the credit. And that was purportedly only the first payment. So I'd accepted the job. Certain clients didn't like questions; if I asked too much, the pilot would probably leave. Credits gone. No job. I could walk away from this, but I needed the money. I didn't even have enough to pay the next installment on my office.

And I had to admit it: I was curious.

I boarded the Sleeker.

Selei City rolled below us. We were high enough up that individual towers or magrails weren't visible, just a wash of sparkling lights. I reclined in a seat with smart upholstery that adjusted to ease tension in my muscles with a finesse only the most expensive furniture could manage. It didn't help.

I was the only passenger. The cabin had ten seats, five on my side separated by about four steps from five on the other. The white carpet that covered the deck glinted as if dusted with holographic diamonds. Hell, maybe they were real diamonds. The flight was so smooth that had I not known I was in the air, I would never have guessed.

Flycars usually had a pilot and co-pilot's seat in the main cabin. This one had a cockpit. It had irised open for the pilot, and he left it that way so I could see him. When he slid into his chair, its silver exoskeleton snapped around him. If it worked like most, then right now it was jacking prongs into his body. They would link to his internal biomech web, which included a spinal node with as much processing capability as a ship's mesh system.

"Hey," I said.

He looked over his shoulder. "Yes?"

"I was wondering what to call you."

"Ro."

I waited. "Just Ro?"

He regarded me with unreadable dark eyes. "Just Ro." He inclined his head. "You had better web in, ma'am."

"Where we headed?"

No answer. I hadn't expected one. Nothing in the message delivered to my office this afternoon had hinted at my destination. The recording had been verbal only. No name signed. Nothing. Just that huge sum of credit that transferred to my account as soon as I accepted this undefined job.

I pulled the safety mesh around my body. I was a slender woman,

more muscle than softness, and the webbing had to tighten from whoever had used it before me.

"Ready?" the pilot asked. He was intent on his controls; it took me
a moment to realize he had spoken to me rather than into the comm.

"Ready," I said.

The g-forces hit hard, like a giant hand shoving me into the seat.
The chair swiveled and the cushions did their best to compensate, but
nothing could gentle a kick that big. And I heard it, a noise I wouldn't
have believed if it hadn't come clearly even through the hull. Rockets
had just fired. This "flycar" was a damn spaceship.

The pressure went on and on until black spots filled my vision. The
webbing pushed against my lower body, countering the effect, but I felt
nauseated.

After interminable moments, the g-forces eased. Pinwheels spiraled
in my vision and bile rose in my throat. As soon as I could speak, I said,
"Where the blazes are we going?"

"Best relax," the pilot said. "We'll be a few hours."

Hours? I didn't know how fast we were traveling, but given that
rocket blast, we had to be moving at a good clip. Even now we were ac-
celerating, less than before, but enough to feel. A few hours of this could
take us deep into the solar system.

I regarded him uneasily. "I don't suppose this little flycar has inversion capability?" It was halfway to a joke. Starships went into inversion
to circumvent the speed of light.

He looked back at me. "That's right, ma'am. We'll invert in six
minutes."

Flaming hell. If we inverted into superluminal space, we could end
up light years away from here.

—⟨⚬⟩—

The City of Cries stood on the shore of the Vanished Sea on the
world Raylicon. The empty sea basin stretched in mottled red and blue
desert from the outskirts of Cries to the horizon. I knew that desert. I
knew the city. I had grown up in Cries and lived here later as an adult—
and I had damn well never intended to return.

The Sleeker hummed through the night. Pitted ruins of ancient starships hulked on the shore of the Vanished Sea, their hulls dulled over the

last five thousand years. They were shrines now, enigmatic reminders that humanity hadn't originated here on Raylicon, but on a blue-green world called Earth.

It mystified me. Six thousand years ago, during the Stone Age, an unknown race of beings had taken a group of humans from Earth, left them here on Raylicon, and then disappeared with no explanation. Our historians believed a calamity befell them before they completed the project they had begun with their captive humans. Whatever the reason, they stranded my ancestors here.

Primitive, terrified, and confused, the lost humans had struggled to survive. The aliens left behind nothing but the ruined starships. However, those ships contained the full technological library of an ancient, starfaring race, and the humans had learned the fundamentals of its use during the journey to Raylicon. Over the centuries, my ancestors took enough from those records and spacecraft to develop star travel. It took a thousand years, but eventually they went in search of their lost home at a time when humans on Earth were living in caves. They never found Earth, but they built the Ruby Empire, scattering its colonies across the stars.

With such shaky technology, though, and a curse of volatile politics, their civilization soon collapsed. The ensuing Dark Age lasted four millennia. My ancestors gradually rebuilt their civilization, until finally they regained the stars. They split into two civilizations then: the Trader Empire, which based its economy on the sale of human beings, and my people, the Skolian Imperialate. Eventually our siblings on Earth also developed space travel. They had a real shock when they reached the stars: we were already here, building empires.

The flycar banked over the Cries, a chrome and crystal city glinting in the desert. I could just make out the ruins of the ancient city beyond it, the original Cries built during the Ruby Empire. Past the ruins, we flew among mountains that jutted against a sky pierced with stars.

We landed on the roof of a structure high in the mountains. Crenellations bordered it in patterns of mythical beasts, teeth gaping, horns sharp. Onion towers raised spires into the sky. Sweat ran down my temples despite the climate-controlled cabin.

As I released my webbing, the pilot disengaged from his exoskeleton. I wished I could place his background. He had the black hair, smooth skin, and upward tilted eyes of Raylican nobility, but that made no sense.

The noble Houses descended from ancient lines that traced their heritage back to the Ruby Empire. Now an elected Assembly ruled the Imperialate; the Houses no longer had the power they had wielded five millennia ago. In this modern age, both women and men held positions of authority. The days when matriarchs of the warlike Ruby Empire had kept their men in seclusion were gone. Hell, the Imperator was a man. He commanded the four branches of the military and descended from the Ruby Dynasty. Some noble Houses retained the ancient customs, but they kept to themselves. In their rarified universe, the rest of us didn't exist. They wouldn't bring in a stranger to deal with their problems, especially not a commoner. Far more likely, a crime boss had engaged my services. She wouldn't be the first to cover her operation with a phony aristocratic sheen.

As the pilot and I disembarked, hot breezes ruffled my hair around my shoulders. No lights shone on the roof. I could see the stars but nothing else. It had been a long time since I had breathed the parched air of Raylicon. Seven years in the gentle, fragrant atmosphere of Selei City had spoiled me; the air here felt hot and astringent on the membranes in my mouth and nose. It smelled dusty. Fortunately, the nanomeds in my body could deal with the minor differences. They also gave me the health and appearance of a woman in my late twenties, though I was well into my forties.

"This way, please," the pilot said behind me.

I hadn't heard him approach. My trained reflexes took over and I spun around, ready to strike. I might have stumbled in the lower gravity, but my body compensated by instinct. I pulled my blow in time, even as he raised his arms to counter it. He was unnaturally fast. Interesting. He had biomech in his body, which would include high-pressure hydraulics, modifications to his skeleton and muscle system, and a microfusion reactor for energy. It could give him two or three times the strength and speed of an unaugmented human. He had almost moved fast enough to block my attack; he obviously had a top quality system.

Mine was better.

"My apologies." The pilot lowered his hands. "I didn't mean to startle you."

"No harm done." Despite my casual response, my thoughts hummed with warnings. Biomech webs cost as much as Jag star fighters and weren't available to civilians. I got mine when I served in the

Pharaoh's Army. Either this pilot had been a military officer or else he worked for someone with illegal access to military technology.

We crossed the roof and entered an onion tower through an arch shaped like a giant, antiquated keyhole, the type you would see only in a museum. Inside, stairs spiraled down the tower—nothing mechanical, no modern touches, just stairs. Lights came on as we descended, though, golden and warm. Tessellated mosaics inlaid the ceiling in gold, silver, and platinum. The place reeked of wealth.

At the bottom, we entered a gallery of horseshoe arches. Our foot-steps echoed as we walked through the forest of columns tiled in pre-cious metals. I saw no technology, but golden light poured around us and it had to come from somewhere. We left the gallery through an archway half a kilometer from where we entered and followed halls wide enough to accommodate ten people abreast. Mosaics patterned the walls, blue and purple near the floor, shading up through lighter hues, and blending into a scalloped border at shoulder level. The low gravity, sharp air, and exotic décor saturated my mind. The place was a flaming palace.

As we forged deep into a maze of halls, my node created a map. I tried to talk with the pilot, but he never responded. Finally we climbed a wide staircase that swept up to the balcony of a colonnade. At the top, we passed two arched doorways and went through the third. In the study beyond, shelves lined three of the walls. And they held books. Not holo-books, mesh cards, or VR disks, but real *books,* the type of ancient tome usually found only in museums. One lay open on a table. Artistic glyphs in shimmering inks covered its pages, which were edged in gold. I had never seen even one such book, let alone a room paneled in them from floor to ceiling.

Our footsteps were silent on the carpet, another antique in red and gold. The door swung on ancient hinges that should have creaked but in this unreal place were so well oiled they didn't even whisper. A dark-haired woman stood across the room gazing out an arched window, her hands clasped behind her back.

Then the woman turned.

Her presence filled the room. She stood two meters tall and had a military carriage. Her dark hair swept back from her forehead, with gray dusting the temples. She had chiseled features, high cheekbones and a straight nose, and her black eyes tilted upward. Her dark tunic and trousers had an elegant cut. She could have been any age from forty to one hundred and forty; I had no doubt she could afford the best treatments to delay aging.

She inclined her head to the pilot. "Thank you, Captain. You may go." Her voice had a rich, husky quality. She spoke in Skolian Flag, a universal language adopted by diplomats and others who interacted with many different peoples. However, she had a pronounced Iotic accent. Almost no one spoke Iotic anymore except scholars, the noble Houses, and pretenders who wished to sound cultured. I didn't know the language well enough to judge whether her accent was real or affected.

The pilot bowed and left the study as we had entered, with no sound. I wondered if my host expected me to bow as well. Deferential behavior wasn't one of my strong points.

The woman considered me. "My greetings, Major Bhaajan."

I nodded to her. "I'm afraid you have the advantage of me, Lady." I didn't know if she truly carried that title, but it was more tactful than, *Who the blazes are you?*

"Matriarch," she murmured. "Not Lady."

Ah, hell. I quit hoping she was a crime boss. This was no phony palace. I had come to the real thing.

"Which House?" I asked. Blunt maybe, but finesse had never been one of my strong points either.

Her gaze never wavered. "Majda."

I was certain the blood drained from my face. Majda. Wrong again. I wasn't facing nobility. This was royalty.

"Let us sit." She indicated a brocaded couch with gilt-edged arms and legs built from wood. And Raylicon had no trees.

I didn't know how to behave with royalty. However, the Majda Matriarch was also General of the Pharaoh's Army, commander of that branch of the military. She referred to me by my military title, though I had been out of the army for over a decade. So I said, "Thank you, General."

She nodded, accepting the title. I sat on the couch and she on a brocaded wingchair at right angles to it. A table tiled in red and gold mosaics stood between us. Majda crossed her long legs and light glinted on her polished boots. "Would you care for a drink? I have a bit of Kazar brandy."

Would I indeed. I'd give an extra decade of life for genuine Kazar. "Thank you, yes," I said.

Majda touched the scrolled end of the arm on her chair. A circle the size of her fingertip glowed blue, but that was it.

Then we sat.

The silence was unsettling. I knew enough protocols to realize she would set the conversation, or lack thereof. So I waited, racking my brain for all I knew about the Majdas. Five millennia ago, the Ruby Dynasty had ruled an empire, led by the Ruby Pharaoh, also Matriarch of the House of Skolia. The Pharaoh no longer governed, but even now the dynasty held power. After the Skolias, Majda was the most influential House. Although considered a noble line, they were royalty in their own right. They no longer ruled any province, however; now their empire was financial. They controlled more wealth than the combined governments of entire planets.

During the Ruby Empire, Majda had supplied generals to the Pharaoh's Army. Today, they dominated the two largest branches of the military, the Pharaoh's Army and the Imperial Fleet. Majda women served as officers. *Only* the women. Of all the noble Houses, even more than the Ruby Dynasty, Majda followed the old ways. They kept their princes secluded, seen by no women except members of their own family.

Majda considered me. "Did you have a good flight, Major?"

"Yes." I wasn't used to hearing my military title.

A man in dark garb entered the room carrying a tray with two crystal tumblers. Gold liquid sparkled in them. He set the tray on the table and bowed to Majda.

She inclined her head. "Thank you."

He left as silently as he had come. I stared after him. No one had human servants any more. Robots were less expensive, more reliable, and required less upkeep.

Majda indicated the tumblers. "Please be my guest."

"My pleasure," I said.

We both took our glasses. The brandy swirled in my mouth like ambrosia, went down with exquisite warmth, and detonated when it hit bottom. I sat up straight and let out a long breath. The nanomeds in my body would keep me sober, but I was half-tempted to tell my spinal node to let me get drunk.

"That's good," I said.

"Indeed." Majda sipped hers. "You have an interesting reputation, Major Bhaajan."

I took another swallow of killer ambrosia. "You've a job for me, I take it."

"A discreet job."

That didn't surprise me. Discretion was my specialty. No messes. "Of course."

"I need to find someone," she said. "I'm told you are the best there is for such searches and that you know Cries."

"I grew up here." I left it at that. She didn't need to know I had been a dust rat. "I'll need all the details you can give me about this person and how she disappeared. Holos, mesh access, character traits, everything on her habits and friends."

Majda's jaw stiffened. "You will have the information." Her voice hardened. "Be certain you never misuse it."

That didn't sound good. "Misuse how?"

"He is a member of this family."

He. *He.* Ah, hell. Majda had lost a prince, one of those hidden and robed enigmas. You could end up in prison just for trying to see one of their men. It wasn't so long ago that the penalty for a woman who touched a Majda prince had been execution. My life wouldn't be worth spit if I offended this House, and I couldn't imagine a better way to earn their enmity than to trespass against one of their men.

"What happened to him?" I asked.

She tapped the arm on her chair and the room dimmed. Curtains closed over the windows. The wall across from us turned a luminous white and a holo formed there of a man.

Gods.

He stood in a room like the one, but with wood paneling and tapestries lining the walls rather than books. He looked in his early twenties. Dark hair curled over his forehead and ears, and he had the Majda eyes, large and dark, tilted upward. His broad shoulders, leanly muscled torso, and long legs had ideal proportions. He wore a rich tunic of russet velvet and red brocade, edged in gold, and darker red trousers with knee boots. The word gorgeous didn't begin to describe him. He was, without doubt, the most singularly arresting man I had ever seen.

He wasn't smiling.

"His name is Prince Dayjarind Kazair Majda," the general said. "He is my nephew. No woman outside this family has ever seen him in person." She paused. "Save one."

Had he run off with a lover? "Who?"

"Roca Skolia."

"You mean the Pharaoh's sister?"

"Yes."

Well, well. Roca Skolia not only held a hereditary seat in the government, she had also run for election and won a seat as an Assembly delegate, then risen in its ranks until she became Foreign Affairs Councilor, one of the most powerful and astute politicians in the Imperialate. If this Majda queen expected me to investigate Roca Skolia, she had a far higher estimation of my skills than even I did myself. And that was saying a lot.

"Your Highness," I said. "I cannot force a member of the Ruby Dynasty to return your nephew."

"He is not with Roca. They were betrothed. Almost." She spoke with thinly concealed disdain. "Two years ago she broke that agreement to marry some barbarian king." Then she added, "Reparations were offered. Eventually my House accepted them." Her tone implied that acceptance hadn't come easy. "I had thought the matter settled. Then five days ago, Dayj ran away."

"How did he leave?" It wouldn't surprise me if he had better security guarding him than some heads of state.

"We aren't certain." She set her drink on the table. "I have always viewed my nephew as a pleasant and good-natured but rather vain young man without depth. I may have underestimated him."

"Do you have any idea where he went?"

"None."

"What do the authorities in Cries say?"

Her voice cooled. "Majda has its own police force."

"But they can't find him?"

A pause. "They haven't exhausted all possibilities."

Right. That was why they had brought me in. "Could someone have kidnapped your nephew?"

"It would be almost impossible to take him from here even with his cooperation. And we've received no ransom demand." Frustration tinged her voice. "Even if he left of his own free will, which we believe, he knows nothing about survival outside this palace. He can read and write, yes, but beyond that he has no experience in taking care of himself."

If he had been able to outwit the security, he was probably more savvy than she believed. "Did he leave a note?"

"On his holopad." Her voice sounded strained, as if she were in pain but trying to cover it. "The pad said, 'I can't do this any longer. I have to go. I'm sorry. I love you all.'"

Such a simple message with such a world of hurt. Yet she had mentioned only a broken agreement from two years ago. "And you think he's upset about the betrothal after all this time?"

Majda snorted. "Hardly. He never wanted to marry her."

"Then why do you mention it?"

"Because he said almost exactly the same thing after it happened. Except not that sentence about having to go."

"Has he ever talked about leaving?"

"He never says much, just male talk." Majda waved her hand. "Inconsequentials."

I could already see plenty of reasons why Dayjarind Majda might run off, but I doubted it would be politic to mention them. So I said only, "If he can be found, I'll do it."

"No measure is too extreme, Major." She tapped her chair and the lights came up. "Whatever you need, we will provide."

End I

II

THE BOX

I SPENT THE morning in my private suite trying to figure out who could have helped Dayj escape. He was one of nine Majda princes here, including his father and two younger brothers. His Uncle Izam was consort to General Vaj Majda, the Matriarch. Izam and Vaj had three daughters, Devon, Corey, and Naaj, and a seven-year-old son. Vaj's two sisters also lived here with their families, but her brothers had married and left the palace. The older brother continued to live in seclusion, but the younger one had pulverized tradition by attending college. Now he was a psychology professor at Parthonia Royal University.

Dayj had an odd life. His elders paid excruciatingly close attention to ensure he behaved as expected for an unmarried man of his high station. I hadn't known people still lived by those rigid codes, over five millennia old. He could never leave the palace without an escort. On the rare occasion when he had permission to venture beyond the boundaries of his constrained life, he wore a cowled robe that hid him from head to wrist to toe. He couldn't communicate with anyone outside the family, which meant he never used the meshes that spanned human-settled space, a web of communications most people took for granted.

He had no schooling aside from what his parents taught him. However, he used the Majda libraries extensively. Apparently Vaj Majda had never bothered to check; otherwise, she might have rethought her assumption that he lacked depth. Dayj read voraciously in science and mathematics, art and culture, history and sociology, psychology and mysticism. He had no formal degree, but his education went beyond what many of us obtained in a lifetime. I couldn't imagine what it must have been like for him, confined here, knowing so much about the freedom beyond his cage.

It was a gilded cage, though. He lived in a manner most people only dreamed about, if they could imagine it at all. His family lavished him with jewels worth more than my life's earnings; with tapestries sought by collectors throughout the Imperialate; with gourmet delicacies and wines. Anything he wanted, they gave him as long as it didn't break his inviolable seclusion. He was among the greatest assets of Majda, an incomparably handsome prince who would bring allies to the House through his marriage.

In fact, he had almost given them a direct line into the Ruby Dynasty with marriage to the Pharaoh's sister, Roca. I remembered now the broadcasts from two years ago. Roca Skolia had wed a man from a rediscovered colony, one of the settlements stranded when the Ruby Empire fell. He was a leader among his people and apparently carried the blood of the ancient dynasty. Or maybe he and Roca married out of love and the Ruby Dynasty scrambled for the royal connection to justify it. I had no idea, but it made me grateful that no hereditary expectations weighed down my personal life.

Watching the holos of Dayj with Councilor Roca, I found it hard to believe he had suffered any heartbreak. His family had recorded those few strained visits; privacy seemed less valuable to them than ensuring he and the Councilor maintained the proper behavior. Like Dayj, Roca was too beautiful. It was annoying. She had gold hair, gold eyes, gold-tinted skin, and an angel's face. They sat in wing-back chairs, drank wine out of goblets, and conversed stiffly. Despite their perfectly composed sentences, neither seemed to enjoy the visits. Beauty, power, and wealth apparently didn't translate into romantic bliss.

No matter how Dayj felt about his intended, it had to have hurt when she dumped him. His family had molded his life with one goal in mind: he would become the consort of a powerful woman. And they achieved the pinnacle. He literally couldn't have done better; the only woman more powerful among the Houses was the Pharaoh herself, and she had to marry within her family, a stupid law that had managed to survive our legal system for five thousand years. Dayj had done exactly what he was supposed to do, and it had collapsed on him.

The whole business was a mess. A million ways existed to trespass on the honor of Majda, or gods forbid, of the Ruby Dynasty itself. One misstep could land me in more trouble than I had ever seen. I would have preferred if this job came from some crime boss. At least they had to worry about the law, or more accurately, not being caught when they broke it. Majda was a law unto itself. They controlled the military and wielded immense economic power. Given the insult the Ruby Dynasty had done to them over the betrothal, they too would probably look the other way if Majda took the law into their own hands with anyone—including me.

I didn't dare go back on my word to take this case. But I was on my own; if I screwed up, I had nowhere to go.

I met Prince Paolo first. I couldn't see him alone, of course. He had married Colonel Lavinda Majda, the youngest sister of the Matriarch. A son of the House of Rajindia, he had led a normal life prior to his marriage and earned a degree in architecture and building design. Gods only knew why such a man would agree to live in seclusion, but even I wasn't blind to the benefits of marrying into the House of Majda.

Four male bodyguards accompanied me into his study. Four female bodyguards remained posted outside, led by Captain Krestone, a former army officer who now headed Majda security. Her people would also be recording this meeting.

Paolo was sitting behind his desk. A clutter of data spheres, holosheets, and light styluses lay strewn across its surface, which consisted of a glossy black holoscreen. He leaned back as I sat in one of the ubiquitous wing chairs with smart cushions.

"My greetings, Major," he said, his elbow resting on an arm of his chair.

"My greetings, Your Highness."

He studied me with dark eyes. He wasn't Majda; his features had a gentler cast. Of course he was handsome, even the streaks of gray in his hair and the fine lines around his eyes. All Majda men were, as far as I could see: dark, well-proportioned, and undoubtedly fertile as well. The Matriarch might have considered Dayj shallow, but Majda women obviously didn't choose their princes for intelligence or depth, which quite frankly, didn't strike me as particularly deep on their part.

Paolo Rajindia Majda, however, was no fool. Before his marriage, he had earned a doctorate at the Architecture Institute associated with Royal College on Metropoli, one of the most elite academic institutions in the Imperialate.

"You've come to ask about Dayj," he said.

"That's right." I had intended to talk with Dayj's parents first, but both were at the starport with the police, searching for signs Dayj had gone offworld.

Paolo rested his chin on his knuckles. "Do you think he left Raylicon?"

"I've no idea." I decided to probe. "It depends on how much help he had from inside the palace."

Paolo didn't twitch. "What help?"

"To escape such security, he needed inside aid."

"You don't think he could figure it out himself?"

"I've no doubt about your nephew's intelligence," I said. "However, he had little experience with anything outside his life here. Including palace security."

He spoke dryly. "If you have no doubt about Dayj's intelligence, you're certainly a minority here, Major."

"Maybe he didn't appreciate that." My voice came out tighter than I had intended.

"Maybe not." Paolo picked up a light stylus and tapped it against his desk. "Dayj could be vain and self-absorbed, but no one ever gave him a chance to be anything else. If anyone took the time to look, they might find a very different young man under his outward veneer."

So I wasn't the only one who questioned the family's view of Dayj. I wondered who Paolo meant by "anyone." Dayj's parents? The Matriarch? Her siblings? Paolo likely had a different take on Majda princes than the family members who had grown up at the palace.

"You've an interesting background yourself," I said.

He gave a wry laugh. "That was tactful. Shall I answer the question you really wanted to ask after you looked at my record?"

So they knew I had researched them. Well, it wasn't a surprise. "What question is that?"

"Why am I willing to live in seclusion when I could have had my pick of jobs at top architectural firms."

It was indeed one of my questions. "Did you want a job like that?"

"I have my own firm." He motioned at the holosheets on his desk. "I've designed buildings in a number of places, including the City of Cries. Also in your corner of space, Selei City."

My forehead furrowed. "You design buildings? How?"

He spoke dryly. "That I can't leave this place, Major, doesn't mean I can't work." He shrugged. "I have a staff. They take care of anything that requires interaction with the outside world. It leaves me free to be creative."

"Nice setup," I said. "Except you never get to touch your creations." He could walk through virtual simulations of his buildings, but never set foot in them.

He spoke quietly. "We all pay a price for our dreams."

"And Dayj?"

"Ah, well. Dayj." His expression turned pensive. "He has more than the rest of us. And less."

"Meaning?"

"You've seen holos of him?" When I nodded, he said, "Then you know. He's one of the best-looking men in the Imperialate."

What was it with them? "Life has more to it than appearance."

"Yes, well, no one ever bothered to teach my nephew that." He shook his head. "In a certain point of view, Dayj is perfect. The epitome of the Majda prince."

"A prize." I couldn't hide my anger even knowing they were recording this session. If I was going to find Dayj when none of their own people had managed, I had to look where they didn't want to go, even if it meant offending them. "The ultimate trophy, bred from birth to marry a Ruby heir."

He hand tightened on the stylus. "Take care, Major."

"How did he respond when the betrothal fell through?"

"They were never formally betrothed."

"But it was expected."

"Yes." Paolo thought for a moment. "He seemed numb. It wasn't that he mourned her loss. He hardly knew her. But what did he have left? Nothing."

For flaming sakes. "Did you people actually tell him that?"

Paolo spoke coldly. "Make no mistake, Major. This family loves Dayj and would do anything to bring him back. You may not like what you hear, but that won't change the truth."

"Maybe that's the problem." I met his gaze. "Dayj's truth might be different than what everyone here believes."

His face took on an aristocratic chill. "Whereas you claim to know it?"

"No," I said. "But I'm going to find out."

⸻

Corejida Majda and her consort, Ahktar Jizarian Majda, were Dayj's parents. Corejida was the middle Majda sister. She was younger than Vaj, the Matriarch, but older than Lavinda. Corejida resembled Vaj but with a less imposing presence; she wore softer colors, blue trousers and a light tunic that molded to her body. Right now, she paced across a spacious alcove, past arched windows that stretched from floor to ceiling.

Vaj stood by the wall, her gaze dark and intent as she watched her sister. Captain Takkar, the chief of the Majda police force, was leaning against the wall nearby, tall and rangy in her black uniform. It matched the uniform worn by the pilot who had picked me up in the flycar. Takkar had dark eyes and hair like most everyone else here. I wondered if the Majdas subconsciously chose their staff to resemble themselves.

The ubiquitous four bodyguards stood at posts by the wall, making sure that, gods forbid, I didn't escape deeper into the palace and trespass on the men's quarters. The concept annoyed me, but I liked Krestone, the captain of the quartet. She remained by the entrance arch, alert and solid, the sort who said little and saw a great deal.

"We have to find him." Corejida strode through a panel of sunlight cast by a window. "Gods only know what could happen to him out there. He could be hurt, lost, starving." She looked as if she hadn't slept for days. "We must protect my son."

"Did he talk to you about anything outside the palace?" I asked. "Any place at all, in any context?"

"We've already been through this," Takkar said tightly, her arms crossed. "He has said nothing."

"I'd like to hear Lady Corejida's thoughts," I said. Technically she was Princess Corejida, but in practice only the House of Skolia used royal titles these days. Majda women tended to go by military rank, but Corejida had never become an officer. Finance was her specialty. Someone had to run the Majda empire.

"Does Prince Dayjarind have special interests?" I asked. "Subjects he likes to read about? Hobbies? Favorite pursuits?"

"He's been talking about landscapes lately." Corejida rubbed her neck, working the muscles, turning her head back and forth. "He looks at holo-images in the library."

"Did he mention any in particular?" I asked.

"Not really." She paused. "He likes imaginary scenes, impossible images created by mesh systems."

Vaj spoke in her husky voice. "Dayj is always that way. Dreaming whatever boys dream."

I hardly thought a twenty-three-year-old man qualified as a boy. "Did he want to make landscapes?"

They all stared at me blankly. Then Corejida said, "You mean, create his own art?"

"Maybe that was why he enjoyed looking at them," I said. "He wants to be an artist."

"I don't think so," Corejida said.

"Did you check his mesh account?" I asked.

Captain Takkar said, "We've checked every account he's ever used." Then she added, "Major." She somehow made the title sound like an insult.

I considered the police chief. "I'd like to take a look."

Corejida spoke quickly, before Takkar could respond. "It can be arranged." Lines of strain showed around her eyes. "Anything you need. Just find my son."

Takkar pressed her lips together. I could see trouble. If I found a clue Takkar had missed, it wouldn't reflect well on the chief. I wasn't sure what to make of her. Territorial, yes, and defensive. That her people had failed to find the prince must put her in a difficult position. As much as she might resent my presence, though, it would benefit her to work with me. The sooner we located Dayj, the better for everyone.

Whether or not Takkar saw it that way remained to be seen.

"Lumos down to five percent," I said.

The lights in my suite dimmed until I could barely see the Luminex console that curved around my chair. I leaned back, clasped my hands behind my head, and put my feet on the console. "Jan, show me the landscapes that Prince Dayjarind collected."

"Accessed." Jan's androgynous voice came from the Evolving Intelligence brain that ran the console. It produced a holo on the ceiling: wave of fire towered over a beach of glittering sapphire sand and crashed down, spraying phosphorescent foam everywhere. The physics made no sense. Unless it was an unusually low gravity world, those waves went too high and came down too slowly. They were large enough that when they rose from the sea floor, the water should have receded far back from the beach. But it didn't.

"What planet is that on?" I asked.

"It isn't," Jan said.

"Does it resemble any known place?"

"It has a nine percent correlation to the Urban Sea on Metropoli."

Nine percent didn't help much. "Let's look at another."

Over the next hour, Jan showed me Dayj's collection of beaches and mountains, a valley of opal hills, a plain of red reeds under a cobalt sky, a forest of stained glass trees.

All empty.

"Do any of these landscapes have people in them?" I asked.

"None," Jan said.

I could see the pattern, and it saddened me.

———⚬———

Vaj Majda spoke coldly. "Offending my family and staff achieves nothing, Major."

One day at the palace and already I had insulted people. Apparently neither Takkar nor Prince Paolo liked my attitude.

We were standing before a window in the library. Sunlight slanted across our faces. "The whole point of bringing me in," I said, "was to get a new view, to see if I can find what others missed."

"And have you?"

"I ran correlations on Dayj's landscapes with landscapes he didn't collect. And with real places."

She didn't look impressed. "So did Takkar's people."

"True. But I looked for negatives."

"Negative in what sense?"

"I looked for what was missing."

"And?"

"He doesn't like the desert. No images at all."

Majda tilted her head, her face thoughtful. "He lives on the edge of a desert. Perhaps it seems mundane to him."

I'd wondered the same. "He likes the ocean."

She smiled with unexpected grace. "Perhaps he dreams of the age when the Vanished Sea stretched deep and wide from here to the horizon and sent waves crashing into the shore."

I struggled to express an idea that was more intuition than analysis in my own mind. "You say he's a dreamer. He likes to read stories. He enjoys exotic landscapes that exist only in the mind of an artist—lush forests, sunrises over mountains, rivers, valleys. All places. No people."

"I'm not sure I follow your meaning."

"He's lonely."

She raised an eyebrow. "That is the best you can do? His holos have no people, therefore he is lonely?"

"Doesn't it bother you?"

Her voice tightened. "I hired you to find him. Not give him therapy."

I clenched my jaw, then realized what I was doing and made myself stop. "Your Highness, if I offend, I ask your pardon. But to find him, I have to explore all possibilities. Maybe your nephew dreamed of places rather than people because he saw his life as empty. Without companionship. Actual places are no more real to him than the creations of an artist's imagination. What greater freedom is there than to go to a place that doesn't exist?"

"If it doesn't exist," she asked dryly, "how will you find it?"

"I think he went to the sea." I let loose with one of my intuitive leaps. "He feels he is vanishing. And he lives by the Vanished Sea. So he went to find a sea that exists."

"That strikes me as exceedingly far-fetched."

"Perhaps." I waited.

"Raylicon has no true seas," she said.

"I realize that."

"We have found no trace that he went offworld."

"Then either he faked his ID or he didn't go offworld."

She raised her eyebrows at me. "I'm paying you for that analysis?"

Well, all right, it didn't come out sounding brilliant. I tried again. "I think he will try to buy a false identity and passage offworld. He was wearing expensive clothes the day he disappeared. The gems alone on them are worth a fortune. He didn't lack resources."

Majda shrugged. "Takkar and her people checked the black market, not only in Cries, but across the planet. They found no trace of his gems."

I doubted Takkar and her people had worthwhile leads into the shadowed markets here. "I can do it better."

She spoke dryly. "You don't lack for self-confidence."

"With good reason."

"What do you want from me, then, to find him?"

"Complete freedom," I said. "I work on my own. No Captain Takkar, no surveillance, no guards, no palace suite, no records of my research, nothing."

"Why? We have immense resources at your disposal." Her gaze darkened. "I can't see that you have anything to hide."

"I know Cries in ways your police force never will," I told her. "But I won't get anywhere without privacy."

She spent a long moment studying me. "Very well. We will try it your way." Then she added, "For now."

⸺

I had a visitor while I was preparing to leave my palace suite. As I was packing the last items I needed into a duffel, a knock came at the front entrance. I opened the door to find Captain Krestone and four male bodyguards outside. A hooded figure stood in their midst in a dark blue robe. Although I had met all the Majda women now, Paolo was the only one of the men who had spoken with me. I saw a shadowed face within the cowl, but not clearly enough to tell whether or not it was Paolo.

I nodded to Krestone. "My greetings, Captain." I wasn't certain if protocol allowed me to address the robed man.

"My greetings, Major." She didn't waste time. "Prince Ahktar wishes to speak with you."

Ahktar. Dayj's father.

When I found my voice, I said, "Yes, certainly."

The captain handed me a scroll tied with a gold cord, and I blinked at it. The Majda universe had almost no intersection with the one where I lived; no one else used paper any more, let alone parchment scrolls. I unrolled it. Inked in calligraphy, it granted me permission to speak with Prince Ahktar.

Bewildered but curious, I stepped back to let them enter, and then closed the door. Only then did Ahktar push back his cowl. He regarded me with dark eyes, his hood loose around his shoulders. He resembled Prince Dayj, but the arrangement of features was somehow different on him. He had nothing close to his son's spectacular looks. I had also discovered that his family, the House of Jizarian, held the lowest rank among the nobility. Whatever the reason Corejida had married him, it hadn't been for his appearance or status.

How refreshing.

"My honor at your presence, Your Highness," I said.

He inclined his head. His expression was one I had seen before, one that was the same everywhere regardless of rank or wealth, the anguish of a parent faced with the loss of a child. Whatever else I might think of the Majdas, they genuinely seemed to love Dayj.

He spoke quietly. "Major, can you find my son?"

"If it's humanly possible," I said.

"I pray you do." He extended his arm and his sleeve fell down, re-

vealing the jeweled cuff of his shirt. A carved box lay in his palm. "I
don't know if this will help, but Dayj valued it."

I took the box. Tiny mosaics covered it. "What's inside?"

"Dirt. I couldn't open it, but I analyzed it with a mesh system." He
pushed his hand through his hair. "Dayj has had it for several years. I don't
know why, or if it can help you find him. But anything is worth a try."

I rubbed my thumb over its panels. I had seen plenty of puzzle
boxes, but none like this one. It might offer a clue. I looked up at him.
"Thank you."

"Just find my son." In a low voice, he added, "Alive."

I swallowed. Ahktar acknowledged what none of us wanted to speak
aloud. Given Dayj's lack of experience, the chances of his staying alive
and unharmed on his own were as vanishing as the ocean beyond the
City of Cries.

End II

III

THE BLACK MARK

I SPENT THE endless Raylicon evening in the penthouse of a tower in downtown Cries. The building belonged to the Majdas. The sunken living room was larger than my entire apartment in Selei City, and one entire wall consisted of dichromesh glass, which polarized during the day to mute sunlight. Now the sunset flamed on the horizon. Cries glittered to the east and the Vanished Sea spread to the west, all far below the tower.

I sat sprawled in a white chair near the window while I fooled with the box. I could have had a mesh solve the puzzle, but it intrigued me. After twenty minutes of poking and sliding panels, I figured it out. The top opened with a series of clicks as enameled panels slid aside. Ahktar was right: the box held dirt. That was it. Just dust.

Red and blue dust.

I knew then where to look.

⸻

No water had flowed in the Parched Aqueducts for millennia. The empty conduits networked subterranean caverns under the City of Cries, knee-deep now with dust. Red and blue dust. How had Dayj ended up with dirt from down here? Someone must have given it to him. I couldn't imagine him walking out of the palace without security knowing. Then again, he had apparently done exactly that six days ago without leaving a trace.

The aqueducts weren't small. Four adults could walk abreast along one of them with room to spare. They ran in underground tunnels as tall as the life-sized totem poles of figures standing foot to shoulder. The remains of such stone totems stood like sentinels at junctions where two or more aqueducts met. Whoever had tiled the walls with stone mosaics had used technology good enough to survive for thousands of years. But if lamps had ever eased the gloom down here, they had long ago disintegrated. I brought a hand lamp that created a sphere of light, with darkness beyond.

I found the Black Mark where it had been seven years ago, at the junction of three aqueducts. It had probably moved more than once during those years; Jak Never-Lose liked to shift his casino around. Gambling was illegal on Raylicon, where the ancient culture defined the bastion of conservative tradition among our people. You couldn't find the Black Mark unless you knew where to look, and you wouldn't know unless Jak invited you. He could fold it down, pack it away, and vanish like the sea above, under the desiccated sky of Raylicon.

I followed a walkway that bordered the aqueduct a few meters above its bottom. Few people used this stone path except Jak's patrons. He didn't need a crowd; the expense accounts of his clientele more than made up for their limited numbers. They wanted an exclusive establishment and Jak was more than happy to oblige. He had the crème of the criminal elite as his fingertips.

No one intercepted me when I reached the Black Mark, though security had undoubtedly monitored my approach. I faced a solid surface that was part of the tunnel wall, distinguishable only by its black hue and iridescent sheen. No entrance appeared.

I put my hands on my hips. "Jak, open up."

The wall shimmered in an elongated hexagon. Then the light faded and Jak stood framed in a hexagonal entrance. He was dressed in black as always, both his trousers and pullover. His black hair spiked on his head and his coal eyes burned.

"Major," he said. "You're back in Cries, I see." The tension in his shoulders stretched his pullover tight over his lean muscles.

"Looks like it." Seeing him stirred up memories I would have preferred to stay clumped and quiescent.

He lifted his hand. "Come in. Improve the décor."

Improve indeed. I walked into a dimly lit foyer with a hexagonal shape. "I never did before."

His lips quirked upward. "It's good to see you, too, Bhaaj. What brings you to haunt my life?"

Interesting choice of words. We were the proverbial ghosts from each other's past. I looked around the foyer. The only light came from a red glow in several niches at shoulder height. Each niche displayed a jeweled human skull. "Looks like you already have people to haunt your life."

"No one like you." His voice was dark molasses.

I didn't know if I could handle it when he talked that way. It had always been my undoing. My defenses went up and I said, "How about the House of Majda?"

His smile vanished. "I've nothing to do with them."

"Glad to hear that." Restless under his gaze, I crossed the foyer and traced a familiar pattern on the wall. This time, nothing happened. He had changed the combination. I wondered why the Black Mark was even here again. Might be coincidence. I couldn't help but wonder, though, if he had heard I was in town.

Jak came up beside me. "Been a long time."

"Yeah." I finally looked at him, really looked. It hurt. I recognized the scar over his left eyebrow, but he had a new one on his neck. I touched it, remembering other scars. "Looks like you've been busy."

He grasped my hand and brought it down to his side. His fingers tightened around mine, though I didn't think he realized how hard he had clenched his grip. When it began to hurt, I activated my biomech web and extended my fingers, prying his hand open.

He let go with a jerk. For a moment I thought he would say things that hurt to hear. Then he leaned against the wall by a skull with carnelian eyes. "What about Majda?"

"Hired me." I slipped into the terse dialect of the under-city world as easily as if I had never left.

"Over their people?" he asked.

"That's right."

"Not bad."

I grimaced. "If it doesn't kill me."

"Majda won't kill. Just ruin. Get on their bad side, you have nothing. They make sure you live to know it." Dryly he added, "Unless you offend their men. Then you're dead."

That was too close to my thoughts. "Met two princes."

His eyebrows went up. "And you're alive?"

"For now." I shifted my weight. "Got an office?" He would have the best security there.

"We're in it."

"The entrance to the Black Mark?"

His grin sparked, with a hint of menace. "It isn't the entrance now. Room moves."

"Secure?"

"Yeah. Why? Majda got problems?"

"Lost a prince." Let him soak up that.

He stared at me. "For ransom?"

I shook my head. "He ran off."

Wicked pleasure sparked in his eyes. He trusted me more than I expected, because that expression alone would have earned him the enmity of Majda. "Good for him."

"Jak."

"Majda princes live in prison."

I scowled at him. "They hired me to do a job. I took their money. So I'm doing the damn job."

He crossed his arms. "You think I'd help you send him back so they can oppress him more?"

"That a no?"

"You didn't ask a question."

"I need to know if he bought passage offworld."

His expression shuttered. "People don't announce they're Majda. Even someone who's lived in seclusion his entire life ought to have more sense than that."

I paced across the hexagon to the wall where I had entered. Gods only knew where it would let me out now. "He probably tried to sell his clothes."

Jak laughed in his whiskey voice, deep and inebriating. "Does he think people would pay just to wear clothes that had been on a Majda?" He voice became thoughtful. "You know, they might. Could be a lucrative business, making that claim."

I turned around to him. "Jak."

"Why the blazes would I care about his clothes?"

"They got diamonds. Sapphires, rubies, emeralds, opals, gold, platinum. Real, not synthetic."

He gave an incredulous snort. "He went under-city dressed like that?"

"I don't know. You hear anything?"

"Nothing. I'd like to, though."

"I think he went offworld," I said. "Couldn't leave as a prince. He needed a new identity."

He stalked across the foyer to me. "So you come here, asking me to check it out." His lean muscles rippled under his clothes and he emanated a sense of contained aggression.

"Depends."

He stopped in front of me. "On what?"

"The price."

"You got a Majda expense line."

"Yeah."

"Then you don't care about price."

I touched the cleft in his chin. "I wasn't talking about that kind of price."

He caught my hand. "What is it, Bhaaj?"

I swallowed, acutely aware of how close he was standing to me. "Seven years ago you disappeared."

"Someone owed me money. I went to get it."

"They were killers."

"Didn't scare me."

"Yeah, well, I thought you were frigging dead." I pulled away my hand. "Selei City has been very restful. I like rest."

"You're bored there, Bhaaj."

"Want to be bored."

"Why did you come back here?" he asked. "For my help or my apology?"

I wasn't sure myself. "Just what you got to give."

He considered me. Then, unexpectedly, his mouth quirked up. "I dunno. I help you with Majda, you going to try putting me in seclusion?"

The thought of his possible reaction to such an absurdity was alarming. "Gods help me, no."

He burst into his intoxicating laugh. "Good." His smile faded. "If I hear anything, I might let you know."

"Good." It was more than I had expected. I stood watching him. When the moment became awkward, I said, "Guess I better go."

He touched my lips. "Come here sometime when you don't want anything. Just to see me."

I flushed and held back the urge to kiss his fingers. I meant to be noncommittal, but instead I said, "Might do that."

"Good," he murmured. Then he tapped a panel by a gold-plated skull. Behind him, the wall shimmered and vanished, revealing the canal junction where I had entered. I hadn't felt the foyer turning, but that panel was across from where I had entered.

He spoke in a shadowed voice. "See you, Bhaaj."

"Maybe so."

I headed back out into the canals then. Oddly enough, I felt lighter. Damned if I wasn't glad to see Jak—which could only mean I had flit-flies for brains.

⸻

I slept at the penthouse and rose about seven hours into the forty-hour night. Outside the window-wall in the living room, Cries glittered in the dark. I sat at the console provided by the Majdas and investigated its EI brain. The Majdas had promised me freedom from surveillance, but I believed that like I believed Jak was a paragon of virtue. At least I could do something about the EI. It didn't take me long to find the spy-hawk programs Majda security had watching the penthouse. After a few hours' work, I deactivated them all. When I had privacy, I had the EI search the Raylicon meshes and any offworld systems it could access. My goal: investigate the three Majda sisters.

They made quite a trio. As General to the Pharaoh's Army, Vaj Majda commanded the oldest branch of Imperial Space Command. The Pharaoh's Army had served the Ruby Dynasty for five thousand years. After the Imperator, Majda was arguably the most powerful officer in ISC. Some claimed the admiral in charge of the Imperial Fleet wielded more influence, but I wasn't about to quibble. Vaj Majda was a force I had to reckon with.

I wondered what she thought about answering to a male Imperator. However unenthusiastic she might feel about men and the military, she dealt with it. She was no fool; if she wanted success in her career, she had to accept the realities of modern Skolia, where nearly as many men as women served in ISC. To an extent, it affected her staff at the palace as well; although positions of authority there were primarily held by women, it was by no means exclusive. The man who had brought me to Raylicon was probably a retired military pilot.

"EI," I said.

"Attending."

"Do you have a name?"

"Not yet."

"Did the Majdas install you for me?"

"Yes. Yesterday."

Perhaps I could give it a name. I would think about it. "Can you answer questions about them?"

"I have a great deal of data on the House of Majda."

We would see just how much. "I wondered how the General reconciles the way they treat Majda princes with the fact that most Skolian men have equal rights with women."

"The men of the House of Majda hold to a higher standard."

I snorted. "That so?"

"Yes."

"Who programmed you?"

"General Vaj Majda."

That explained a lot. I did more searches on the family. They had too many corporations, investments, and other financial connections to count. Even scarier, it was all legitimate. I delved into data grottos unknown even to ISC intelligence and found nothing on them. Majda came by their wealth legally. It added to their invulnerability; they couldn't be blackmailed. If someone wanted to manipulate them, kidnapping one of their princes might well be the only way.

They threw me a few surprises with their husbands. Prince Paolo had the rank, heredity, and looks expected of a Majda consort, but he lacked the supposed "moral" background. Granted, if all grooms among the nobility truly had to be virgins on their wedding night, the Houses probably would have died out for lack of mates. But they were discreet. Paolo, on the other hand, had openly enjoyed love affairs as a bachelor. Lavinda married him anyway. It didn't take me long to guess why. He excelled at business as well as architectural design. He knew how to make money, and I had no doubt he was doing it now for Majda.

Nor was Paolo the only one. The General's consort, Izam, had lived in seclusion his entire life, but he had a natural business genius. Although he owned no Majda holdings outright, his name was associated with the boards of a good fraction of their corporations. Vaj might be rigid in how she expected her consort to live, but she wasn't stupid. I wondered just what it had taken, though, for Izam to break through her resistance, given her inability to understand Dayj's frustration.

"What about Ahktar?" I asked. "Dayj's father. Does he do finance?"

"It doesn't appear so," the EI said.

I questioned if this EI would know full details. "Link me to Jan at the palace. But keep my security precautions in place." I didn't want any Majdas eavesdropping on my talks with Jan, either.

"Linking," the EI said.

A mellow voice came out of the console, the EI that I had interacted with at the palace. "My greetings, Major Bhaajan. What can I do for you?"

"My greetings, Jan." I settled back in my chair. "I need everything you have on Ahktar's education."

"He has none."

"He must read."

"He rarely uses the library."

"Does he involve himself with Majda finances?" His wife ran the corporations, after all.

After a moment, Jan said, "I find no indication that he has either the interest or talent for such."

I tapped my chin. "Almost no rank, money, or skills. He's not handsome. No business sense. Why did Corejida marry him?"

"You wish me to offer a conclusion?"

"I wish."

"She loves him."

I blinked. "What?"

"She loves him. This is an acceptable reason to marry."

"Sure, for the rest of us. Majda lives in another reality."

Jan paused. "I have no records of any aptitude tests for him. Informally, however, I can offer conclusions based on his behavior."

Intrigued, I said, "Go ahead."

"He nurtures. He probably has a great aptitude for nursing or social work. It also makes him a good parent."

"Oh." Was I that cynical, that I hadn't believed Majdas could feel love? I'd been born in the Cries slums and left for dead in the alley behind a city crèche. The city government had put me in foster care. I'd gone from family to family until I was old enough to run away and live with the other wild kids under-city. People called us dust rats. The day I reached my sixteenth birthday, the minimum age for the army, I enlisted. Then I'd worked like a fanatic to qualify for officer-training. It was supposed to be impossible for an enlistee to win a place in that program, but I'd done it, more out of sheer, cussed determination than because I was better qualified than the other applicants. And so I escaped Cries and Raylicon.

Back then, I had feared, envied, even hated the Majdas, who lived in their world of privilege. But it was hard to resent parents who so obviously loved their son. I kept remembering their haunted expressions as they entreated me to find him.

"Jan," I said. "Can you think of any reason why one of the Majda sisters would help Dayj escape?"

"Escape implies he was in prison."

I didn't bother to deny it.

After a pause, Jan said, "I can think of no reason why any of them would facilitate his leaving the palace."

"Has any family or staff at the palace ever shown any indication they might sympathize with a desire on Dayj's part to leave? Has anyone donated to a cause that supports ideals consistent with his stated wish to break tradition? Made grants to any such institution? Invested in a company? Supported either an individual or organization, legal or otherwise, that in any way might have conceivably helped Dayj leave?"

Jan was quiet for a while. Then the EI said, "I find no such connection either in the family or on the staff."

"That can't be." With a business empire as vast as theirs, it would require a deliberate effort to exclude *every* such person or group.

"Such a link would be offensive to the House," Jan said.

"Someone inside helped him. He's smarter than they think, but even given that, he couldn't have done it alone. Security is too tight." I thought about negatives. "Who in your opinion is *least* likely to help him leave?"

"General Majda," Jan said.

"Not his parents?"

"They, also. But if he were truly unhappy, it would affect them more than the General."

"Doesn't she care about his happiness?"

"Yes. Despite her reserve, she shows great affection for her nephew. I would call it love, as far as I can determine that emotion."

"What about the other princes?"

"Of the consorts, the one least likely to help Prince Dayj leave is probably Prince Paolo."

That made my eyebrows go up. "I would have thought the opposite. Paolo knows what freedom is like."

"And he gave it up. Why, then, should Dayj have it?"

"I see your point." I sat up, planting my booted feet on the floor. "What about his uncles? One of General Majda's brothers teaches psychology at a university."

"Tam might help. However, he no longer lives on Raylicon."

"Tam?"

"Tamarjind Majda. The psychologist."

I rubbed my chin. "You don't need to live here to help." The Kyle meshes bypassed spacetime, making light speed irrelevant. It allowed timely communication across interstellar distances.

"I have no record of any communication between Prince Tamarjind and Prince Dayjarind."

"Who does Prince Tamarjind talk to at the palace?" It used to be his home, after all.

"His sisters and nieces. Never his male relatives."

"Why not?"

"General Majda forbade such communications."

I scowled. "Because he's a bad influence?"

"Yes."

"You know, Jan, I would feel a lot better if you said, 'In the General's opinion' rather than just 'Yes.' "

"That would be inconsistent with my programming."

"Yeah, well that's the problem," I muttered.

After I signed off with Jan, I sat in the dark and thought for a long time. I had an idea how to find Dayj.

If I was lucky, it wouldn't kill me.

End III

IV
SCORCH

I WATCHED THE palace from high in the mountains. My field pack held a jammer that created a shroud, which could hide me from most sensors. The jumpsuit I wore consisted of holoscreens; when linked to the jammer, the suit and the image-dust on my face projected holos of whatever lay behind me, making me invisible if someone didn't look too closely. The suit had a lower temperature than my body, which confused infrared sensors. Sonic dampers in the jammer interfered with sound waves and muffled noises. The jammer even created false echoes to fool neutrino sensors, which could penetrate most anything. If Majda security made a concentrated effort to find me, they could counter the shroud, but I hadn't given them cause for such a search—yet.

Now I sat on a ledge against a cliff and watched the palace with my spyglass. It focused, zoomed, tracked, and otherwise optimized my ability to observe my selected target, in this case everyone who came and went into the palace.

It was a boring day.

I spent hours up there, protected from the icy wind by my climate-controlled leather jacket and trousers. Raylicon had a ninety-three-hour day. Atomospheric churning and weather machines kept it from becoming too hot or too cold, so humans found it livable. Most people slept three times a day, once around noon, once at the start of the night and again at the end. I began my vigil before dawn and kept at it for fifteen hours. When the boredom became interminable, I played Bulb Blaster, a game installed on my gauntlet that consisted of blasting weather balloons and dirigibles out of the sky.

The main entrance to the palace was a great arched affair fronted by a colonnade with many columns and horseshoe arches. No one used it. Two other entries were visible from my vantage point, a servants' door in an east wing and a family entrance in a southwest wing. Servants went in and out all day, but none did anything interesting. Mostly they stood around and chatted in a garden just overgrown enough to look artistic. They probably had very few duties, given that robots could do most tasks just as well as humans.

Eventually I got tired. I tied a cable from my belt to a metal ring I drilled into the wall of the cliff. The cable would judge my safety and reel me in if I rolled too close to the edge. I set my gauntlet to alert me if anything interesting happened. Then I went to sleep.

When I awoke five hours later, the sun had barely moved. I resumed my vigil. After three more interminable hours, someone finally came out the southwest entrance—Colonel Lavinda Majda, the second sister. She and three people in black uniforms walked down a driveway bordered by trees. The man was one of her aides. One of the women was Captain Krestone, the security chief. The other woman was probably a bodyguard, given the pulse gun she wore at her hip.

As the group boarded a waiting flycar, I spoke into my gauntlet. "Can you get a tracer on Colonel Majda?"

"Easy." The answer came from Max, my personal EI. Most people couldn't afford a full EI in a gauntlet nor did they want one, but in my line of work, he was invaluable. Max and I had worked together for years.

"I'm dispatching it now," Max said.

"Good." For the tracer, I used a tiny bot, a mechanized dragon-beetle with green wings. I could only afford two, so I usually sent one out and kept the other for backup.

Then I headed down to Cries.

—◦—

A message was waiting at the penthouse. The EI informed me when I walked in the door.

"Who from?" I asked as I went down into the sunken living room. The glass wall across from me polarized to cut down glare from the setting sun. I could look out to the vast, empty sweep of the Vanished Sea that extended to the horizon in bluffs streaked with blue from mineral deposits left by the dried-up ocean. Purple and dusky red splotches blended into the blue. The terraforming that made this world habitable for humans was gradually failing over the millennia.

"I can't ID the message," the EI said.

Interesting. It was easy to ID senders unless they deliberately tried to hide. "Did you scan for traps?"

"Yes. It's clear."

"All right." I flopped down on the couch and put my feet up on the dichromesh glass table. It polarized to mute reflections from the wall-window. "Play the message."

"Heya, Bhaaj," a familiar voice said. "Got dinner?"

I waited. "That's it?"

"It appears so," the EI said.

I crossed my arms and scowled. I knew exactly who had sent that message. "Send this reply. 'Forget it.' "

"Send it where?"

Well, damn. If the EI couldn't ID the message, it couldn't reply. "Never mind." I swung my feet down, my boots thumping on the white carpet. "I'm going out again."

⸻

The gambling dens at the Black Mark were notorious. Tonight Jak took me through the main room, no doubt to show off his establishment. We followed a raised walkway that skirted the central den. A dark rail with an iridescent sheen separated us from the pit. The men and women at the tables below wore evening dress or stranger couture, spiky-shouldered tunics and skintight wraps that left many parts of the body bare. Waiters served drinks while Jak's patrons spent millions. Other more sensual pursuits were probably going on in private rooms. The Black Mark was discreet. Criminal, but circumspect.

I tried not to notice Jak as he walked at my side. He had on black pants and a ragged black tight-shirt with no sleeves. He looked like a thug. One hell of a sexy thug, but I wasn't noticing.

"Like my addition?" He motioned at the abstract holoart flowing on the walls. It swirled in spirals and twists. If I looked too long, I felt sick.

"What does it do?" I asked. "Create vertigo?"

He slanted a look at me. "It increases the susceptibility of people to suggestion."

"It makes me dizzy."

"Really?" He seemed intrigued. "I wonder why it doesn't work on you."

I snorted. "The army trained me to resist coercion, Jak. Medtechs programmed the techniques into my biomech. It operates without conscious thought. Your disreputable attempts to lure people into spending large amounts of money at your casino won't work on me."

A wicked gleam came into his eyes. "Shall I lure you elsewhere, Bhaaj my sweet?"

"Call me 'your sweet' again and I'll flip you over this railing."

He laughed, his voice as rumbling. "Might be fun."

No way was I going to risk answering that one.

We exited into a black holo-hall with galaxies swirling on the walls. After a few minutes of demented stars, we entered a black room with niches in the walls like the entrance foyer. Instead of skulls, however, these held exotic drinks lit from within by colorful lasers. The table in the center of the room was set with black china, goldware, and goblets. A decanter of wine sparkled next to several covered platters.

"You like?" he asked.

I tried to be tactful. "It's certainly different."

"Same as always."

"Doesn't all this black depress you?"

"Never." He nudged me toward the table. "Sit."

I reached back and moved his hand away, but I did sit. Jak settled across the table and uncovered the platters, revealing steaks in pizo sauce, tart-bubbles, and other delicacies. He always had set a good table.

I poured the wine. "You going to tell me why I'm here?"

He was all innocence. "What, I can't invite an old friend to dinner?"

I gave him a goblet. "You always have ulterior motives."

"Maybe I'm trying to seduce you." He leaned back in his chair, letting the muscles of his torso ripple under his thug shirt. He knew what it did to me when he moved like that, slow and languorous, danger contained but never controlled.

I swallowed too much wine. Thank gods for nanomeds.

"Should I?" he murmured.

My face heated. "No."

"You want the spit on your runaway prince?"

I sat up straighter. "What did you hear?"

"Rumors."

"What will it cost me to find out?"

"Your company for dinner."

"And?"

"And what?"

I frowned. "Having dinner with you is too easy."

His grin flashed. "Was that actually a compliment?"

"Jak."

"Yes?" He looked dangerous with those simmering dark eyes and that scar on his neck. The tight-shirt was unraveling along one shoulder seam, showing a glimpse of roughened skin where his arm met his torso. I wondered how it would feel to run my hand under the cloth of his shirt.

Get a grip, I thought. I loaded my plate with bubbles, a dish from the home world of some member of the Ruby Dynasty. They looked very round.

We ate in silence. Then Jak washed down his food with wine and sat back, his goblet in one hand.

After he had watched me for a while, I put down my fork. "What?"

"A good-looking man sold some gems on under-city," he said.

I tensed. "Prince Dayjarind?"

"I don't know. But these were genuine, the real biz, flaws and all. Worth a lot more than he got. Still brought him enough to buy a new ID."

"When?"

"Seven days ago."

Seven days ago, Dayj had left the palace. If he had immediately sold his jewels on the black market, he must have already had the connection. "Do you know where he went?"

"Rumor says he tried to go offworld."

"Tried?"

"Yeah. Tried." No trace of Jak's earlier smile remained. "Man looks that good will get himself sold if he isn't careful."

"Hell, Jak." I felt sick. "What happened?"

"I don't know. I just heard rumors. Some say he went offworld, others say he got heisted."

"You can't 'heist' a Majda heir. Anyone in this city who sees this guy or hears his accent will recognize him."

"Maybe. Maybe he's worth the risk." He voice hardened. "Imagine the price you could get from the Traders for him."

I gritted my teeth. "Skolians don't sell to Traders."

"Offer anyone enough money and they'll sell out."

"Where'd you hear these rumors?"

"Don't know." He finished his drink. "Aqueducts are a big place. Especially the Maze. You can get lost in there."

The Maze. I had been there twice, which was two times too many. "Thanks, Jak."

"Didn't say anything."

I speared a bubble with my fork. "Didn't hear anything."

We ate for a few more minutes. Then Jak said, "You like the dinner?"

I knew he was asking about more than food. If I had any sense, I would say no. So I said, "Yeah. I do."

His teeth flashed. "Thought you would."

"Cocky tonight."

"You like, Bhaaj." When I snorted, he let go with that throaty laugh that had always been my undoing. It hadn't changed, neither the sound nor its effect on me. "You shouldn't look at me that way."

"What way?"

"Like you want me for dessert."

"In your dreams." Or mine.

"Right, Bhaaj."

I put down my fork. "I have to go. Got an appointment in the Maze."

He spoke softly. "You're scared."

It annoyed me when he was right. "Got to go."

"For now."

I knew what to I had to say; I had a job to do and when I finished, I would leave Raylicon, assuming I was still breathing. I couldn't get involved. So I opened my mouth and out came, "Yeah. For now."

His gaze smoldered. "I thought so."

Damned if I could resist that look. It was a good thing I had business in the Maze. I didn't trust myself to stay here.

—◦—

Over the millennia, the aqueducts under the City of Cries had crumbled. Our ancestors had built well, but five thousand years takes a toll on even the greatest architectural wonders. Gradually the tunnels had collapsed, until in one section they left only a maze of half-blocked passages.

I had come back to Cries after I retired from the army with some nebulous idea that I could remake the city of my childhood into a place I wanted to live. I had seen only the worst of Cries, and I wanted to know my home from the perspective of someone who could afford to live in the Imperialate's most ancient city. But the memories had taken over my life instead and in the end, I hadn't stayed.

It had been seven years since I had been here. Although my spinal node had mapped my wanderings in the Maze and kept the files, the pathways had changed, in part because of new cave-ins, but also, I suspected, from deliberate alterations made by inhabitants. I recognized enough to make my way. In places, fallen walls blocked the canals. I climbed up the mounded debris, pulled myself through a ragged hole in one wall, and slid down the other side into a new canal.

Eventually I reached a tunnel with more debris than flat areas. Long ago someone had built a door into the side of the aqueduct, and now dust piled against it in drifts. I paused, shining my lamp on the grit. That much dust took years to collect. It didn't bode well.

Sliding my hand under my jacket, I nudged off the safety on my pulse gun. Then I knelt and swept away armfuls of grit. When the area was clear, I stood again and nudged the stone door with my foot.

Nothing.

I knocked on the door.

Nothing.

I hooked my light on my belt—and kicked the door with augmented strength and speed. It still didn't give. I tried again, harder, once, twice, three times—

With a jerk, the door scraped inward, stone grinding on stone. I drew my gun and stepped through, keeping the wall to my back. The floor inside had less dust than outside. I checked the area, then headed down the tunnel, my footfalls muted, the ceiling only a few handspans above my head, the walls close on either side.

Whoever had built the aqueducts all those millennia ago had probably drilled these maintenance tunnels to provide access to now-disintegrated machinery. After a while, I came to a familiar junction where three tunnels met. I took the one on the left. When I noticed a light ahead, I clicked off my lamp and continued in semidarkness. It didn't bother me. Some people hated these claustrophobic tunnels, but I liked them.

I soon reached the end of the tunnel. Even knowing what to expect, I froze. A cavern stretched before me. Stalactites hung from the ceiling and stalagmites grew up from the floor. The light came from an EM torch jammed into a nearby crevice. It threw the rock formations into sharp relief and glittered off the crystals that encrusted them.

My footsteps echoed as I entered the cavern. That served as a greeting just as well as if I had called out. I saw no one, but that meant nothing. That light wouldn't have been here without someone around, which meant other entrances existed into this place besides the one I used.

A rustle came from my right. I stopped and waited.

A woman walked out from behind two stalagmites. "Bhaaj."

I nodded to her. "Scorch."

She stood more than a head taller than me, and I was a tall woman. Well-toned muscles creased her black jumpsuit, and I knew she had bio-mech equal to my own, except I came by mine legally. Her chin jutted, and her nose dominated her face like on the giant statues of heads in the ruins of ancient Cries. She wore her hair short with a black spike sticking up behind one ear. She held a laser carbine in her hands. An illegal carbine. Torch light glittered in its mirrored surfaces.

"Long time," she said.

"Went offworld," I answered.

"I heard." She shifted her gun. "Why come back?"

"Job."

A corner of her mouth lifted, the closest Scorch came to smiling. "Can't think of a job here worth leaving Selei City."

"Majda," I said.

Her expression shuttered. "We don't bother Majda, they don't bother us."

I wondered how much the Matriarch knew about the smuggling operation Scorch ran through here, from proscribed liqueurs to hallucinogenic silks. I couldn't believe Scorch would traffic in people, though. The Traders based their economy on slavery, which was why our people had been at war with them for centuries. They saw us as fodder for their markets. Scorch wouldn't sell to the enemy. Then again, I didn't want to think how much a Majda prince would bring her, especially Dayj.

Even so, it strained credulity to believe anyone would risk an offense of that magnitude against the Majdas in their own backyard. Scorch knew damn well that if the General decided to clean up this place, she could blast it bare. And if Majda found out anyone had harmed Dayj, the perpetrator would suffer for a long, long time.

"I'm searching for a man," I said. "Good-looking."

She laughed harshly. "So are we all."

"Already know this one. He had gems to sell."

"Lot of people got gems to sell." Her eyes glinted. "Most don't kick in my back door."

"Used to be front."

"Used to be guarded." She shifted her gun. "Still is."

I doubted she intended to shoot me. I'd met her down here in the aqueducts when I was fifteen. Actually, I had found her lying in her own blood, after her "clients" left her for dead instead of paying their bill. I took care of her until she recovered; otherwise she would have died. Scorch always paid her debts. Over the next few years, the three fools who had tried to murder her had met harsh, ugly deaths.

I said only, "Defense systems let me pass."

"For now." She held the gun in what looked like a relaxed grip. I wasn't fooled. She could shoot faster than sin.

Time to bargain. "Got information," I said.

She snorted. "Don't even live on this planet anymore. How you got anything to interest me?"

I kept my arms by my sides where she could see them and my gun, which was pointed at the ground now. "Majda. Got access to their palace mesh." If they caught me offering to sell their private information, they would draw and quarter me. But they weren't the ones who had to deal with Scorch. Besides, the Matriarch had said no measure was too extreme. I doubted she had this in mind, but tough.

Scorch considered me. We both knew it wasn't an offer she was likely to come by again. That she paused for so long could have been a bargaining tactic, but it made me uneasy.

"What information?" she said.

"What you want?"

"Flight schedules." Her eyes had a voracious glitter. "For their private ships."

Damn. Although robbing Majda was notoriously difficult, a smuggler could do a lot with the schedule of flights in and out of their private starport.

"Might be possible," I said, maybe lying, maybe not. "Depends what you tell me."

Her smile glinted. "I know a lot about good-looking men. What you looking for, Bhaaj, that you can't get legally?"

I crossed my arms. "He has dark hair. Dark eyes. Like a nobleman. Good build. Taller than average, not a lot. Probably sold jeweled clothes for a fake ID and offworld passage."

Her hand visibly tightened on the carbine. "That one's gone."

"Gone where?"

"Offworld. Don't know."

Maybe she wanted more than the schedules. "Got a lot to sell."

"Not interested."

I stared at her. This made no sense. The Scorch I knew would never walk away from the opportunity to steal Majda flight schedules. Yet now, suddenly, she didn't want them? Like hell. She was hiding something about Dayj.

"I hear rumors," I said coldly. "Deals with Traders."

She trained the carbine on me. "Lies. Fatal lies."

Sweat ran down my neck. I didn't answer.

Suddenly she swung the carbine—and fired.

The burst momentarily blinded me. Thunder echoed in the cavern and stones crashed to the ground. Grit flew across my face. My vision cleared to reveal the melted remains of fallen stalactites. Gods. Had she shot any closer, one could have come down on top of me.

"Get out," Scorch said.

I didn't argue.

The trek out seemed endless, though I made faster time than on the way in. I kept waiting for a shot out of the dark to incinerate my body.

I didn't deactivate my shroud until I was above ground and well into Cries. Captain Takkar on the Majda police force would just have to deal with my hiding from them. My under-city contacts would be no help if they thought Majda was privy to my actions. I also used whiskers, nanobots that covered my skin and kept vigil against the bee-bots in Majda's security arsenal. The bees searched out specific DNA and sent back reports when they found a match. Several had buzzed around earlier today, but none succeeded in following me into the canals.

Within moments my gauntlet comm squawked. I tapped its panel, but before I could answer, Takkar's voice snapped out. "Bhaajan, where the hell are you?"

"Greetings to you, too," I said.

"Get back to the palace."

Charming. "You aren't my CO, Takkar."

"Get your ass back here or I'll throw it in jail."

My night was growing progressively worse. "For what?"

"Murder," she said.

End IV

V

THE PIN

THE MAJDA POLICE station had no antique books, tapestries, brocaded divans, or anything that remotely resembled the palace. Sleek and efficient, it was all Luminex, dichromesh glass, polarized walls, and silver chrome. Takkar met us in an interrogation room.

The bodyguard I had seen with Colonel Majda earlier today stood by the desk, a woman of average height with well-toned muscles, brown hair, and a bland face, the type that blended into a crowd. Without my training to note details, I might not have recalled her. I couldn't miss the Majda sisters, though. All three were there, tall and lean, dark-haired and imposing. Lavinda seemed stunned. Corejida paced like a caged desert-lion. Vaj, the Matriarch, stood by Takkar, her gaze hard. She considered me with an appraising stare that chilled.

We gathered in front of a wall that doubled as a holoscreen, and Takkar's people ran a playback of the events leading up to the crime. It involved the flycar that had taken Lavinda, her aide, Captain Krestone, and the bodyguard out of the palace earlier today. The record started as the flycar settled on the roof of an office tower in the center of Cries. Krestone was driving, with the bodyguard in the passenger's seat and Majda and her aide in back.

Lavinda showed nothing but a professional relationship with the aide. It fit my research; Majdas were scrupulously careful with their relationships. In their circles, heredity determined everything. During the Ruby Empire, the penalty for adultery among the nobility had been execution, and to this day that atavistic law remained in force. I had never heard of the Houses executing anyone for fooling around, and I doubted they were all paragons of virtue, but they kept it discreet. As far as I could tell, however, Majda followed the law. They didn't stray. They were irritatingly well-behaved. It was another reason they were reputedly impossible to blackmail.

Lavinda went inside the building with her aide and the bodyguard. The airlift they rode down was little more than a disk in a chute, yet it lowered them so smoothly it didn't ruffle a lock of anyone's hair. At an upper level, they walked into a confusing expanse of glittering silver and white Luminex.

After a moment, my mind reoriented and I made sense out of the scene. The office spanned the entire top of the tower. Partial walls of white Luminex stood here and there, but it was mostly open. Abstract art works of chrome and blue Luminex stood in open areas. It was beautiful in a weird sort of way.

Lavinda went to an area enclosed by dichromesh glass. She left a box of data spheres on the desk and checked the console. Her bland bodyguard stood by, and her aide waited at her side, checking his mesh glove when Lavinda asked him a question. Finally they returned to the airlift. The visit seemed perfunctory, a company owner putting in an appearance. They rode back to the roof and walked to the flycar.

Krestone had fallen asleep and slouched over the controls. It seemed odd; in the few days I had known her, she had been scrupulous with her duties. When Lavinda and her people reached the flycar, the bodyguard opened the door and pulled Krestone back. The captain's body flopped against the seat and fell to the side.

Damn. I'd liked Krestone.

"My people arrived four minutes after we got the call," Takkar said. "At that time, Captain Krestone had been dead for eleven minutes."

I wondered where in this scenario Takkar came up with me as a murder suspect. I'd been having dinner with Jak when Krestone died. Unfortunately I couldn't prove it; I'd been shrouded, hiding from Majda. Even if I had thought Jak would vouch for me, I wouldn't ask him for the alibi. It would draw Majda attention to the Black Mark, which he couldn't risk.

Regardless, I didn't see what Takkar thought she had on me. Maybe they had caught the tracer I put on Lavinda.

"What was the cause of death?" I asked.

"She was shot with a tangler." Takkar's voice hardened. "Your area of expertise, Major."

Well, hell. That was hardly evidence. "I trained in the army with contraband weapons, if that's what you mean."

All three sisters watched me with dark, upward tilted eyes. Wary eyes.

"You can use a neural tangler?" General Majda asked.

"Yes." I met her gaze. "However, I haven't in years."

"Where were you this evening?" Takkar asked. "For some odd reason, we have no record of it."

"I was having dinner with an old friend."

Takkar didn't accuse me of lying, but her raised eyebrow left little doubt what she thought. "His name?"

I crossed my arms. "Captain, are you accusing me of something?"

General Majda answered. "No one has accused anyone." She glanced at Takkar. "Do you have evidence on who fired the tangler?"

"We will," Takkar said, which I translated to mean, *We haven't a clue.* Tangler bursts were notoriously hard to trace. The chemicals they left behind rarely had properties that could identify the particular gun that had shot them. They just disrupted neural activity.

Vaj Majda studied me. Her controlled expression and posture gave away nothing. I tried to remain cool, but being scrutinized by the General of the Pharaoh's Army was an unsettling proposition. Corejida stood behind her sister, her agitation almost palpable. But she didn't interfere.

"You won't give us the name of this man you dined with?" Vaj said.

"Only if forced," I said.

She continued to assess me. "You may return to your apartment, Major Bhaajan. However, do not leave the city. And don't use any more shrouds."

No good. "I can't do my job unless I assure my sources of secrecy."

"What sources?" Takkar asked. I just looked at her. She knew perfectly well I wouldn't reveal mine any more than she would hers.

Vaj spoke in her dusky voice. "Use your judgment, Major." She left unspoken the obvious warning; if they had no record of my whereabouts, I had no alibi if anything else happened.

When it became clear Vaj had finished with me, Corejida came forward, her posture so tense she seemed ready to snap. "Have you news about Dayj?"

Normally I wouldn't talk about a case with so many ends dangling. It was like quantum observation; looking at the system changed it. But perhaps I ought to give them something before they decided to toss me in jail.

"Prince Dayjarind apparently sold some jewels," I said. "I think he bought a new identity and a ticket off Raylicon."

"No!" Corejida stared at me. "That isn't possible. Dayj has no idea how to do that."

Takkar snorted. "It's absurd."

"It's no less absurd," I said, "than suggesting I shot Captain Krestone."

"I didn't hear any such suggestion," Lavinda said coldly. "Just an inquiry establishing you had the requisite experience."

"Stop it." Corejida frowned at her younger sister. Vaj stood back, listening, silent and intent. Of the three of them, she was by far the most dangerous.

"Did Dayj go offworld?" Corejida asked me. "Did he have protection? Can you find him?"

I softened my voice. "I'm sorry. I don't know yet. I wish I had more news to give you." I meant it, too. I could see their heartbreak coming a kilometer away. At best, Dayj had gone offworld of his own free will and would be difficult to impossible to trace. If he was here, he had probably been hurt or imprisoned at the least and most likely killed. Or he could be a Trader pleasure slave now, forever beyond our help.

⸺⸻

The night was more than half over; Cries had settled into its second sleep cycle. I sat in a gazebo in an empty park and tapped into my gauntlets. They plugged into sockets in my wrists, which linked to bio-threads that networked my body. Max, my EI, sent input to the threads, which carried the data to the node in my spine. Bioelectrodes in my neurons fired according to signals from the node, letting it "think" to my brain. I could reverse the process; if I thought with sufficient force and direction, the electrodes fired and the node picked up my response. The process offered far more confidentiality than any shroud.

Wake up, Max, I thought.

I don't sleep, he answered.

Do you have a record from my tracer on Colonel Majda?

Yes. Would you like a neural dump?

How long is it?

Several hours.

I grimaced. *No thanks.* I sent the record of my session at the police station to him. *You get all that?*

Unfortunately, yes. He did a great job simulating distaste. Quite a scene with Captain Takkar.

She's a bit unfriendly.

You have a talent for understatement.

Did my tracer get anything on the murder?

Checking. After a moment he said, Your beetle-bot followed Colonel Majda as far as the entrance to the office tower. Its picochip brain predicted that if it entered the building, its presence would be unusual enough to attract attention. So it flew down the side of the tower and spied through the window-walls.

I swore under my breath. The beetle had made the logical choice, following Majda rather than staying with the flycar, but that didn't help me now. *Did it get anything of the murder?*

I can playback its record of the crime scene.

Do it.

The scene formed like a translucent wash over my view of the park. I closed my eyes and the images intensified. This time I was watching the flycar from a different angle, one in front of the windshield. Again the bodyguard took Krestone by the shoulder and pulled her back. Unlike Takkar's playback, however, this showed her from the front, enough to reveal what the other record had missed; the bodyguard removed a pin from Krestone's uniform.

My pulse leapt. *Replay that, Max.*

The scene reran and again I saw it. The bodyguard slid her hand over Krestone's shoulder, pulled off the needle, and clicked it into her gauntlet. In Takkar's record, her body had hidden her action.

Who is that bodyguard? I asked.

Her name is Oxil. She's on staff at the palace.

She expected Krestone to be dead. I felt chilled despite the warm night. *Play whatever you have from the last time Krestone was alive.*

The scene backed up to show the flycar landing on the roof. Lavinda disembarked with her aide and Oxil. Krestone remained in the driver's seat, visible through the windshield. She raised her hand to the others, either in a salute or waving farewell. Lavinda nodded to her, then walked with Oxil and her aide toward the lift shaft, which jutted up from the roof like a spire of modern art.

"Oxil, inform security we're on our way down," Lavinda said.

"Right away, ma'am." Oxil thumbed her gauntlet and spoke into the comm.

Interesting. Takkar's recording from the bee-bot had focused on Lavinda. My beetle watched everyone, which gave it closer views of the bodyguard. *Max, replay that bit where Oxil talks to security.*

The recording backed up and showed Oxil telling security that Colonel Majda was coming down. Oxil started to sign off, then stopped as someone apparently asked her a question.

"Krestone is staying in the flycar," Oxil said. "She has everything worked out up here. Colonel Majda, her aide, and myself will be on the lift."

Replay that, Max, and magnify it as much as you can without losing the image.

Max zoomed in on Oxil's hand. The playback blurred, losing resolution, but it remained clear enough. After Oxil started to sign off the first time, she discreetly tapped the comm mesh.

Holy mother, I said. *She switched to a new channel. She wasn't talking to security at the end.*

Apparently not, Max said.

She said, Krestone 'has everything worked out up here.' It was a warning that Krestone had figured out something. I gritted my teeth. *Oxil told them to kill her.*

You have no evidence to support that.

Yet. Can you ID that pin she took off Krestone's body?

It looks to me like a data storage device.

Me, too. It's familiar. I couldn't remember where I had seen it before, though.

Shall I forward this recording to Captain Takkar?

Hell, no. Oxil works for her.

You can't withhold evidence.

I'll send it to General Majda.

Shall I do it now?

No.

Why wait?

I've my reasons. Before he could probe further, I said, *I can't remember why I recognize that pin.*

I have a suggestion.

Yes?

Your vital signs indicate extreme fatigue. Go home and sleep.

I smiled wanly. *A good idea.*

Then I headed to the penthouse.

———✦———

"Major, please wake up."

I grunted and turned over in my airbed.

"Major Bhaajan, my apologies, but you must awake."

"Go away," I muttered.

"You have a visitor," my tormentor said.

I flopped over on my back. The voice belonged to the EI that ran the penthouse.

"I'm asleep," I said. "I don't want visitors." Only the Majdas knew

I lived here, and right now I had no desire to see anyone connected with the palace or their charming police force.

"He is rather aggressive," the EI persisted. "He says he will stay outside until you 'goddamn deign to acknowledge my existence.'"

That wasn't Majda. I sat up in the dark, the covers falling down around my hips. Then I remembered I hadn't put on any bedclothes. I lay back down and pulled up the blanket. "Fine. Let him in. But I'm not getting up." Then I closed my eyes and endeavored to sleep.

"Let him in?" The EI sounded confused.

"That's right." I had no intention of explaining myself to a machine.

I had started to drift off when someone walked into the room. I'd recognize that booted tread anywhere. "I'm asleep," I muttered. "Go away."

The bed gave as he sat down. "Bhaaj, come on." Jak pulled the pillow off my head. "You know you're glad to see me."

"Like hell." I turned over in bed. Light trickled in from the living room and cast his face in planes of light and shadow. "How did you know where to find me?"

"I have sources."

I glowered at him. "Did they tell you that I'm dangerous when awoken from a well-deserved sleep?"

His wicked grin flashed. "Sounds interesting."

"You make me crazy, Jak."

His smile faded. "I also heard that the Majda police chief tried clinching you on a murder rap."

"She doesn't have evidence against me."

"That's right. I just got back from the police station."

"What!" I sat up so fast, I barely remembered I didn't have any clothes on. I grabbed the metallic blanket and smacked my fisted hand against my chest, covering myself. "Why did they bring you in?"

"They didn't." He watched my gyrations in the blanket with a great deal of interest. "I went in on my own."

"What for?"

"To tell them you were with me at dinner."

I blinked. "You gave me an alibi?"

"Yeah."

"If they started sniffing around the Black Mark—"

"They won't find dragon shit. I moved it."

"Even so."

"Even so." His gaze was dark.

I had never known Jak to put anything ahead of the Black Mark. To risk Majda attention so he could verify my alibi was so far off from what I expected, I just stared at him.

"Major Bhaaj, stunned into silence?" He smiled. "That's one for history."

I scowled at him. "Ha, ha."

"That sounds more like the Bhaaj I know."

"Jak." I spoke awkwardly. "Thanks."

"Hey." He stabbed his finger at me. "Just be careful."

"All right." I tapped his chin. "You still got that cute dimple."

He folded his hand around my fingers. "You're going to ruin my reputation, you tell people Mean Jak has a cute dimple."

"I hear Mean Jak has other attributes, too." Then I let go of the blanket.

His gaze turned dusky as he looked at me, good and long. Then he pulled me into his arms. "You're looking good, Major."

"So are you," I murmured and slid my arms around him. He moved his palm up my back, making my skin prickle. Then he laid the two of us out on the air mattress. I rolled with him onto my side, tangling our legs in the sheets. He felt good in my arms, lean and muscled. His kiss was hungry, seven years hungry, but I remembered it as if it had been yesterday.

They say night lasts forever on Raylicon. This time, I was glad for the endless hours. Jak and I had plenty of time. Maybe I wasn't thinking clearly, but having him here felt too right to deny. When the sun came out we could deal with all the reasons we shouldn't be doing this, but for tonight we let ourselves forget.

I sat up with a jerk. "Scorch!"

"Ungh," Jak mumbled. He pulled a pillow over his head against the sunlight that streamed in the windows.

"Max," I said. "Can you hear me?"

"Yes." The voice of my EI came from where I had dropped my gauntlets on the floor last night, near the bed.

"Check the EI for this place. Is its security still off?"

"Yes."

"Good. I remember where I saw that pin the bodyguard took off Krestone. Scorch smuggles them. It's a recording device."

"You think Scorch was spying on Lavinda Majda." Max made it a statement.

I swung my legs off the bed. "Could be."

"Scorch wouldn't be that stupid," Jak mumbled under the pillow. "She gets busted for spying on Majda, she'll be sorry she's alive."

"She's a risk-taker." I padded across the room into the bathing chamber. As I slid into the tiled pool, soap-bots swam around me, glittering like silver and blue fish. They even matched the color scheme of the tiles. Welcome to the Majda universe.

Jak appeared in the doorway, framed in its horseshoe arch. He was holding the sheet wrapped around his hips. His lean chest with its dark hair and chiseled muscles made a delicious contrast to the wrinkled cloth.

"There's risks and there's insanity," he said. "Scorch has a lucrative operation. She won't risk losing it by rizzing-off the General of the Pharaoh's Army."

I slid down in the pool until only my shoulders were above the water. "That depends on what she risks if she doesn't spy on Majda."

Jak leaned against the doorframe. "The aqueducts exist in the shadow of Majda. We have an unwritten agreement. We don't bother them, they don't notice us. Why would Scorch upset the balance?"

"Maybe she's selling to the Traders."

"I hope you didn't say that to her."

"Well, uh, I implied it."

He stared at me. "And you're still alive?"

"She fired a damn laser carbine at me."

"I take it she missed." He grinned suddenly. "Or maybe she didn't. You've a harder head than anyone else I know."

"Ha, ha. Funny."

"Scorch wouldn't sell a Majda Prince."

"I don't know, Jak. A Majda bodyguard pulled Scorch's recorder off Krestone yesterday."

"Think she's working for Scorch?"

"Could be."

"Why kill Krestone?"

"I'll bet the captain was close to figuring out some of this. Closer than me."

He shook his head. "It makes no sense. Scorch hates the Traders. Why would she endanger her operation in a way guaranteed to bring down Majda wrath? It's crazy."

I thought about that. "Not if she disappears off-planet. If she sold Dayj, she can afford to go anywhere."

"I'm surprised she didn't fry your ass."

I smirked to cover my unease. "She likes me."

"Yeah, like Captain Takkar likes you."

"Oxil works for our dear captain."

Jak made an incredulous noise. "You think the Majda police chief is in a conspiracy to sell Majda princes to slave traders? What mental asylum you escape from?" He came over, dragging the sheet, and knelt by the pool. "Scorch is going to kill you."

"No she won't. I saved her life once." Of course, in her view that debt might now be repaid. "Besides, if I disappear, people will look for me. It will draw too much attention to her." I wondered who I was trying to convince, him or myself.

He pulled off the sheet and slid into the water. "Maybe."

I swam over to him. "Hey, it's fine."

But as we drifted together, our limbs entangled, I wondered if this would be the last time I held another human being.

⸺◦⸺

Jak took off after our bath, but not before extracting a promise that I would have third-meal with him, which most people ate before they slept at noon. Interesting timing, that. He wanted to come to the penthouse, too, which meant either he liked the place more than he would admit or else he didn't want me knowing where he had moved the Black Mark.

Out on the balcony of the penthouse, I released both of my beetle-bots, one to look for Oxil and the other Scorch. Then I went back inside and searched the meshes for information on Scorch. I found zilch: she hid better than a special operations agent. Finally, though, I located a news holo with her in the background. The image floated above a screen on my console. It showed a crowd of people in Cries watching a display about some government procession on the world Parthonia, in Selei City where the Assembly met. It was why I had moved there; the city that served as the seat of an interstellar government offered many opportunities for a discreet investigator.

The crowd had gathered in a plaza to watch the display on a holo-pedestal that probably doubled as artwork when it wasn't showing news. Scorch was studying the display intently. She had an odd look, a mixture of fascination and loathing. I didn't see why; the news was boring, just images of people filing into a building. The newscasters went on and on about the excitement of the event. Given that the Assembly met four times a year, every year, and that half the delegates attended as VR simulacrums from other places, they were pushing it with the excitement bit. It must have been a slow news day.

After the holo finished, I sat rubbing my chin. Why would Scorch care about who went to a routine Assembly session?

A light flickered on my gauntlet. Max's voice came out of the comm mesh. "Want to chat?"

I recognized the code phrase. "Go ahead. We're secure."

"Got a trace on Oxil," he said. "Your beetle picked her up by the lake behind the palace."

"Good work. Link me in."

As Max accessed my brain and linked me to the beetle, I closed my eyes. A vivid scene formed; I was standing on the shore of the Lake of Whispers, one of the few fresh water bodies on Raylicon, over a kilometer long. It spread out in a blue mirror, but one rippled with breezes. Imported trees grew around the edges and dropped streamers of leaves into the lake. Red and yellow flowers bloomed in untamed abundance. It was eerily beautiful, all the more so because such a profusion of plants was rare here. Raylicon hadn't dried out completely; it had fresh water underground if you went deep enough. But it wasn't easy to find.

Oxil stood a few paces away gazing at the lake. She wasn't doing much except enjoying the view. Breezes ruffled her spiky hair. Probably she was on a break from work.

After about five minutes, I said, "Max, this is boring."

"Sorry."

"Bring me out." I opened my eyes as the scene faded. "Let me know if she does anything."

"Will do. I have a report from the other beetle."

I sat up straighter. "It found Scorch?"

"Partially."

"How partially?"

"She is well shrouded. The bot can't record her voice or actions.

However, it did locate her out in the Vanished Sea. She is apparently meeting with someone."

"Who?" Few people braved that barren desert.

"I don't know."

I stood up. "Think I'll go for a visit."

I jogged across the sea basin, through shadows cast by the ridges that covered the ancient floor in gigantic corrugations. My feet pounded the ground, and the jammer in the pack strapped to my back shrouded my progress.

I ran at seventy kilometers per hour. Going on foot afforded better security than a flycar; it was easier to shroud a person than a vehicle. I would have to walk back, though, at least part of the way. At these speeds, the tissues of my body built up injury faster than the nanomeds could do repairs. Even with high-pressure hydraulics to support an augmented skeleton and a microfusion reactor to provide energy, the human body could handle the stress of such speeds only for so long before it began to break down.

It took me twelve minutes to cover fourteen kilometers. As I neared my destination, Max thought, Best to hide now.

I sighted on a bluff ahead. *Will that one work?*

Yes. They're on the other side.

I climbed into a crevice of the bluff. By wiggling through it on my stomach, I found a point where I could stay hidden but train my spyglass on the next bluff. Scorch was down there with a woman I didn't recognize, both of them half-hidden under an escarpment mottled with blue mineral deposits. A nondescript flycar waited in its shadow. Both Scorch and her companion had on clothes the same color as the blue and dark red desert, which made it hard to see them. My beetle was circling the bluff, but even this close it couldn't manage to send me more than a word here or there.

Easing down the bluff, I crept nearer, silent and shrouded. When I crouched in the shadow of a ripple of stone near the ground, I finally picked up their conversation.

". . . on the ship," Scorch was saying. Her spike of hair stood up behind her ear and glistened with oil. She held the carbine at her side.

"The ship is gone," the other woman said. She looked like a drifter from the port, with her ragged jumpsuit and scuffed boots. However, she had a top-notch shoulder holster—with a tangler.

"What about the passenger manifest?" Scorch asked.

"Took care of it." Her companion didn't look ruffled. "Passenger manifest has his fake name on it. Caul Wayer."

Scorch frowned. "Name on the ID I sold him was Caul Waver."

The other woman shrugged. "Waver, Wayer, port made a mistake. Happens a lot."

"It's done." Scorch motioned toward the tangler the other woman wore. "I'll take that back now."

Her companion pulled out the gun and tossed it to her. Scorch grabbed it out of the air, flipped it around—

And shot the drifter.

End V

VI
C A V E R N S

TWICE IN MY life I'd seen someone die by tangler fire. It wasn't any easier to take this time than before. The drifter fell to the ground in a violent seizure as chemicals from the shot scrambled her neural system. Then she convulsed. It took several minutes for her life to end, but it seemed like eternity. I didn't realize I'd lunged forward until my foot hit a rock and I sprawled on my stomach. The thudding of the drifter's limbs on the ground covered my fall; otherwise my aborted attempt to stop the murder might have ended in Scorch shooting me as well.

Scorch wasn't done yet, either. She used the laser carbine next and incinerated the drifter's body until nothing remained but a few ashes. Even as I watched, the breezes stirred them into the air. It wouldn't be long before they dispersed altogether.

Without a backward look, Scorch boarded the flycar. Within seconds it was soaring into the sky, headed back to Cries.

I didn't move at first. Even after my years in the army, I had never become inured to death. When my stomach settled, I walked over to the bluff where the drifter had died. Already most of the ashes were gone. I clicked a hollow disk off my gauntlet and scraped a few of the ashes into it.

Then I headed back to Cries.

—⸰—

"Message incoming," Max said.

I blinked, surfacing from the trance I had fallen into during my fourteen-kilometer trek across the Vanished Sea. I had just reached the outskirts of Cries.

"Message?" I asked.

"From Jak. Do you want to receive?"

"Go ahead."

His voice growled. "Got dinner, Bhaaj. Alone."

Damn. I had forgotten to meet him at the penthouse. "Sorry."

"Where are you?"

"Muttering Lane."

"Be there in—" He paused. "Three minutes."

"Thanks."

I kept walking. After a while, a gorgeous black hover car edged around the corner of a dilapidated warehouse and settled on the cobblestones. I activated the dart thrower in my left gauntlet. The darts only stunned, unlike the pulse gun in my shoulder holster. You could get a license to carry darts or a pulse gun—but not a tangler. Never a tangler. Police hated them. You couldn't trace the damn shot. They also killed slow and torturously. Darts only stunned, and with a pulse gun it was over in a fraction of a second. I didn't want to blast anyone, just protect myself if necessary.

When Jak jumped down from the car, I deactivated the dart thrower. I walked up to him and put my arms around his waist. He held me, my head against his shoulder.

"Want to tell me about it?" he asked.

"Not now." I let him go. "Take me home?"

"Yeah."

I took the passenger seat and he slid into the driver's side. Not that it mattered where we sat; he entered our destination into the car and let it take us back to my place. The rich leather upholstery, black and sleek, shifted under me, no doubt trying to ease my muscle tension.

"I don't think I'm hungry for dinner," I said.

"What happened, Bhaaj?"

I took a breath. Then I told him. When I finished, he said, "You could be next."

"I know."

"Caul Waver. An alias?"

"Apparently." I spoke into my gauntlet. "Max, any luck in finding that name on the passenger manifest of a ship?"

"Not much." Max sounded apologetic. "The port mesh system is too well-protected."

"I can have Royal check," Jak said.

I blinked at him. "Who is that?"

"Royal Flush."

"Oh. Yeah." I'd forgotten. He'd named his gauntlet EI after the legendary poker hand that in his youth had earned him the money to start the Black Mark. He'd been training that EI for decades. It was famous. Or maybe infamous was a better word. He never offered its services for free.

"What price?" I asked.

His gaze darkened. "That you don't get yourself killed."

I smiled wryly. "Deal."

While he told his system what we wanted, I watched, intrigued. He had one of the best under-city meshes on the planet. I didn't try too hard to see what he entered, though, knowing he considered it proprietary information.

He glanced at me. "Can you give me the ashes of the woman Scorch killed? If Royal can ID them, it might help his search."

I handed over the disk. "Max got a partial analysis. It's all in the disk memory."

"Good." Jak clicked the disk into his gauntlet. "You believe this Caul Waver is Prince Dayjarind?"

"Possibly." I thought back to Scorch's meeting with the drifter. "They said the name was on the manifest, but not that Waver was actually on the ship. It could be a ruse. Scorch killed that drifter so she wouldn't reveal what she knew. I'll bet the drifter killed Krestone." Thinking about the case helped me regain my equilibrium. "But what about that pin? What did it record?"

He shrugged. "Whatever Lavinda Majda talked about in the car."

"Maybe from before, too. Those pins last about an hour."

"You think Lavinda helped Dayj escape?"

"I suppose it's possible." I considered the other people in the flycar. "My guess is that Scorch was spying on Krestone, not Lavinda. I can't imagine one of the sisters betraying the family."

Jak scowled at me. "Freeing a demoralized young man is hardly a betrayal."

"I know. But they don't see it that way." I pushed back my dusty hair, which had tousled around my shoulders. "To them, it's a betrayal of Prince Dayjarind, too. They have a point, however much we don't like it. He's too inexperienced to deal under-city. Scorch would make byte fodder out of him."

"You think she sold him?"

"I'm praying I'm wrong."

Max suddenly spoke. "Incoming on Oxil."

"Oxil?" Jak squinted at me. "What the hell is that?"

"Just a second," I said. I closed my eyes as Max sent the VR feed to my brain.

A forest of drooping trees and wild flowers formed around me. Oxil was walking a few paces ahead as she spoke into a gauntlet comm. The beetle-bot hummed in closer so I could hear.

". . . nothing more," Oxil said. "Her dinner date gave her a damn alibi." A pause. "They may arrest her anyway. The source of her alibi isn't at all reliable."

I smiled, my eyes closed. "The Majda police don't like you, Jak."

"Feeling is mutual," he muttered.

Oxil leaned against the mossy trunk of a tree. I missed her next words, but then the beetle hummed in closer.

"—best I don't talk with you from here," Oxil was saying. "The risk of detection is too high." She paused. "All right. The cavern. One hour." She lowered her arm, and the view receded as my bot flew away before Oxil noticed it hovering about.

Then the beetle sighted two people through the trees. *Follow,* I thought.

We moved past the branches and came out at the Lake of Whispers. Corejida and Ahktar were standing together, their hands clasped as they gazed at the water.

Corejida was crying.

She made no sound, but tears ran down her cheeks. Ahktar slid his arm around her waist and she put hers around his. They held each other, their heads leaning together.

"They'll find him," Ahktar said.

"Yes." Corejida's voice shook. "Surely they will."

I felt very small. Their son's disappearance was killing them and so far I hadn't done a damn thing to help. Not knowing whether he was alive or dead had to make it even worse for them.

The scene faded and I opened my eyes to see Jak watching me. "Oxil works for Scorch," I said. "She must have been Dayj's inside contact."

"Scorch sold him an ID and ticket. Scared shitless Majda will find out." Talking about Scorch made him lapse into under-city dialect.

"Then should have killed me," I said.

"Knew people'd look for you. Maybe thought she owed you." His gaze darkened. "Might not stop her a second time. She paid her debt."

He had a point. "I don't find Dayj, Majda fires me. Then Scorch kills me."

"Yeah."

I wished he had a reason to argue to point.

Jak's gauntlet hummed. He tapped the comm. "What?"

Royal answered. "I've data on Caul Waver."

"That was fast," I said.

"You bet." The EI sounded smug. Given his programmer, that figured.

Jak smiled. "What do you have?"

"The drifter worked at the port," Royal said. "I checked meshes where she had access. Found the passenger manifest. It says Caul Waver left Raylicon seven days ago, bound for Metropoli."

Damn. I said, "Eleven billion people live on Metropoli."

"It won't be easy to find him," Jak said.

"If he even went there." It made sense, though. More people lived on Metropoli than any other Skolian world, and it had numerous seas teeming with life.

Jak met my gaze. "Time to tell Majda."

"If I tell Majda," I said, "they'll shift their focus to Metropoli." It would take immense resources to search such a heavily populated world. They would pull their attention away from Cries—which was probably exactly what Scorch wanted. It was the other reason she might have let me live, so I would follow Dayj's supposed trail to Metropoli. And lose him forever.

"If I tell Majda," I added, "I'll miss Oxil's meeting in the cavern." I had other reasons for playing it close right now, but I didn't want to tell Jak.

"You go to that cavern," Jak said, "you're going to die."

"No, I'm not."

"That's right. Because I'm coming with you."

"No." I didn't want Jak to risk his life because of my job. "I was hired to do this. You weren't."

"You remember how rizzed you got when I disappeared seven years ago to collect my money? You thought I had died."

"Yeah." I would never forget it. When he had showed up at the Black Mark after three tendays, grinning and smug, rich as sin, I'd been ready to throttle him.

His gaze darkened. "I won't go through that with you."

—⁘—

Jak and I walked with the evening crowds, mostly tourists and local residents out on the town. Actually, more accurately, under the town. This was one of the few under-city thoroughfares with legitimate businesses. City bots even came down here to clean up and do repairs. The city council had ideas to convert this area into a park, but so far they had done nothing more than talk. The under-city bosses had just enough influence above-city to push the idea far back in the urban planning queue.

My beetle had followed Scorch down here, but it lost her before she reached whatever entrance she used now for the cavern. Going in the same way I had before didn't strike me as a good idea, to put it mildly.

A man came up alongside Jak, a tourist out for a stroll judged by his clothes and friendly smile. I wasn't fooled. I knew him too well. Under that amiable exterior, he was deadly.

"Heya, Gourd," Jak said.

Gourd nodded to him. Then he looked across Jak at me. "Good to see you, Bhaaj."

"Yeah," I said. "Same here."

He spoke to Jak. "Got time?"

"Enough," Jak said.

I could tell Gourd wanted privacy. "I got to go," I said.

"No you don't." Jak glanced at his man. "What's up?"

"Commander Braze lost a hundred thousand on roulette."

Jak gave a satisfied smile. "Good."

"Not good. She's ready to drill someone. Says you got contraband holos in the casino that make people gamble too much."

"She can't do rizz," Jak answered. "Get herself court-martialed for gambling in Cries."

"She's got ties," Gourd said.

Jak frowned. "What ties?"

Gourd told him. It seemed Commander Braze had relatives with less than sterling backgrounds and enough connections under-city to add grief to Jak's life. Maybe a lot of grief.

"She wants her credit back," Gourd finished.

"Yeah, right," Jak said.

"Could make it hot for you."

"Tough."

"Real hot."

"I got connections, too, Gourd. People owe me favors. If I have to call them in, I will." Jak shook his head. "I give in to Braze, every rizz-punk will think they can take me."

Gourd didn't look surprised. He took off then, headed back to wherever they had moved the Black Mark.

I exhaled. This was the side of Jak I had let myself forget last night. It was also a major reason I had left Cries.

"You got trouble?" I asked.

"I'll manage. Always do."

I hoped so. It sounded like Braze's people had enough wealth to buy Jak a lot of misery. It probably wasn't the credits Braze wanted back as much as saving face over this business with Jak and his damn holos.

"Could be a mess," I said.

"No worry." Jak glanced around with that honed *awareness* of his that was could be so unnerving. "How you going to find Scorch?"

I didn't push about Braze. "I need another entrance. Know any?"

"No idea. Scorch changes doors like I move the Black Mark."

"So maybe we make our own door," I muttered.

Jak frowned at me. "What are you up to?"

"We need a better shroud." I tapped the pack slung over my shoulder. "You got anything?"

"Plenty." Then he said, "At the Black Mark."

I knew he wouldn't reveal its new location, especially not to me. We didn't know how this would play out, whether I would end up working with the police or in their custody. The less I knew about Jak's operations right now, the better.

"I can wait there." I motioned across the canal to a row of shops with holo-lights and canopies over outdoor café tables. "I'll have a kava."

He grinned. "Bhaaj acting like a tourist."

"Like hell," I grumbled. "Go on. Get out of here."

Laughing, he said, "Yeah. Be back."

As he set off at a brisk walk, I went to an ancient bridge that arched over the canal. It was built from red-streaked blue stone, with its edges carved in scallops and gargoyles. I had just reached its high point when Jak turned a corner. As soon as he was out of sight, I double-checked my jammer to ensure I was shrouded—including from Jak. I jogged back to the path where he and I had been walking and immediately turned down a side tunnel.

Then I set out for Scorch's cavern. Alone.

⊷

Seven years ago, I had mapped the cavities above Scorch's cavern while I was searching for Jak. To this day, I felt certain Scorch had been involved in that scheme to cheat him out of several million, but I had never found any evidence. Given that it involved Jak's illegal casino, I could hardly take my suspicions to the police. But I had never forgiven Scorch.

Now I crawled through cavities barely big enough for my body, with partial walls and ragged holes everywhere. Stalactites encrusted the openings. I wriggled on my stomach, pushing the pack ahead of me. Although it hadn't shrouded me from the security at the old entrance, it should be more difficult to monitor this maze. I was betting my life Scorch's defenses operated with less efficiency here.

The problem with shrouds was that they also interfered with any signals I might use to explore the cavern below. I couldn't risk many probes anyway—Scorch's security might pick them up—but I wished I had a better way to fix my location.

Finally I chose a place. If my map was accurate, I had reached the eastern edge of Scorch's operation. I took my pulse gun out of the pack and checked the ammunition. Three cartridges. I thumbed on the jammer's sonic damper—and fired at the tunnel.

Serrated projectiles tore into the ground and bored a small crater. Although the damper muffled the noise, it wasn't silent. I hoped it was enough. I fired again, drilling the hole deeper. Debris crumbled from its sides.

After a few moments, I quit drilling and waited until rocks quit trickling down the sides. Then, gripping my gun in one hand and my pack in the other, I eased into the chute. The sides felt hot. When my feet touched the uneven bottom, my head was a handspan below the top. Wedging myself lower, I knelt on the ground and held still, listening.

Nothing. No voices and or machinery. Either I hadn't drilled deep enough or I wasn't above an occupied area. If I had chosen well, it would be the latter; if I was wrong, I could drill for hours and never break through.

With my back against one wall and my boots braced against the other, I scooted up the chute and fired at the bottom again. Then I hit my heel into the ground with enhanced strength and speed, over and over. Still nothing. I fired again, deepening the chute, and hammered the ground with my boot. I might as well have been trying to drill through the blasted planet. Another shot, another kick—

My heel cracked the bottom.

I probed with my foot and knocked away pebbles. Freezing, I held my breath as rocks clattered to the ground. They dropped about as much as I expected for a cavern. No light came through the hole, which I hoped meant I had found a storage area. I needed extra care now. A scatter of debris wasn't likely to draw attention; it happened here all the time. But anything as heavy as me dropping from this height would set off alarms.

I took a light stylus out of my pack, slung its chain around my neck, and turned it on, giving myself a sphere of light. Then I set to work widening the hole. It took too long, but I managed with no more rocks falling. Finally I eased out, clenching my pack in my teeth. The frigging jammer was *heavy*.

And there I was, hanging from the ceiling.

The edges of the hole crumbled in my grip. I had hoped to come out near a stalagmite jutting up from the floor, but no rock formation was near enough to let me climb to the cavern below. The closest was over a meter away, a ridged pyramid of rock standing in a cluster of smaller stalagmites like a sentinel surrounded by flares.

It would only be seconds before my handholds gave away and I crashed to the floor. What the hell. I had nothing to lose. Inhaling sharply, I swung toward the stalagmite. That effort destroyed what little remained of my grip; I lost my hold in the same moment I hit the stalagmite. I threw my arms and legs around the pyramid and clenched hard.

Then I slipped. I managed to keep from sliding too fast, so when my boots hit the floor, they made almost no sound. I lowered into a crouch and put down the pack, my breath coming hard.

Then I waited.

After several moments, I switched off the damper. Although I wanted its silencing effect, I couldn't hear much through its field, either. If I had triggered alarms, I picked up no indication of it. That didn't mean it hadn't happened; last time, Scorch had known as soon as I entered her empire. At least the hole I had made didn't look much different from other cavities in the stalactite-encrusted ceiling. Still, even with my biomech, my shroud, and my knowledge of this area, I doubted I could evade Scorch's security for long.

I was in a storeroom, a small cavern that normally people entered by a narrow opening between two stalagmites. A length of canvas hung in the opening as a door. Crates with military markings stood in stacks all around the area. Scorch was selling illegal arms, mostly tanglers, but also laser carbines. Unfortunately, none of the crates were close enough to my hole in the ceiling to help me to climb out. I could move them, but it would make noise and even with my biomech augmentations it would take time, more than I would have if I had to escape fast.

The chances of my getting out of these caverns without Scorch knowing were just about zero. If she caught me here, I had no doubt that she would go for the kill this time.

I couldn't break open the crates. I tried shooting them, but it didn't work. Smashing them together would make too much noise even for the damper to hide, besides which, I doubted it would help if EM pulse projectiles hadn't done the trick. A fortune in weapons, and I couldn't steal a damn one. If Scorch was selling these to the Traders, I hoped she died a miserable death. Better yet, I hoped they double-crossed her and sold her into slavery. It was probably too late for Prince Dayjarind, but if Scorch had done what I thought, she deserved the worst. I didn't like her smuggling operation any better than I liked Jak's casino, but I could live with knowing they existed. If Scorch had committed treason, I couldn't look the other way.

I went to the canvas door and turned off my stylus. The darkness would have been absolute, but the IR in my eyes bathed the world in a lurid red glow with fuzzy rock formations. Although the stone generated too little heat for anything to stand out well, I could see where I was going. I reloaded my gun from the second cartridge, then pushed aside the canvas and stepped between the stalagmites, my weapon up and ready.

Outside, a pathway curved past. Columns made from joined stalactites and stalagmites delineated it, along with strange curtains of rock that looked filmy but felt like solid stone.

The path was empty. *Max,* I thought.

I'm here.

How are my vital signs?

Fine. Why do you ask?

Can you monitor other people?

Not like you. I get your medical information from the nanomeds in your body.

They might have nanomeds, too. Most people who could afford health meds carried them.

I know protocols for the chips in yours. I don't for theirs.

Can you hack them? Scorch's illegal biomech had to include meds. I had no doubt Oxil carried them as well; Majda spared no expense in outfitting their guards.

I can certainly try, Max said.

Good. Monitor the area for signals. At the least, he could warn me if anyone was nearby.

I set off on the path. In my IR vision, crystals glinted on the rocks like rubies. A drop of water fell from above and splashed on my nose. I had grown up here and my biomech was programmed to respond to different worlds, so I hadn't experienced any real difficulty with the lighter gravity on Raylicon. But now I was walking downhill, a grade steep enough to give me trouble in timing my steps. It slowed me down.

I have a signal, Max said.

Who?

I don't know. I can't crack their picoweb. They're up ahead, to the left.

I eased along a curtain of stone, my back to its rippled surface, my gun up. Ahead on the left, an oval glowed brighter red than the surrounding rock, indicating a higher temperature.

Is the person at that oval? I asked.

Behind it. Now Max sounded worried. So much for the supposed lack of afferent in his EI brain. I advise caution.

I edged up to the oval. A canvas door hung in it similar to the storeroom. *Max, listen. Access my hydraulics and guide my gun so it points directly at the person inside.*

I can't have a large effect on your limbs. But I can help. Max paused. I believe the person is several paces back from the entrance, to the left.

Got it. I swept aside the canvas, jerked up my gun—

And nearly blasted His Esteemed Highness, Prince Dayjarind Kazair Majda.

End VI

VII
D A Y J

HE SAT ON a rough pallet, staring into what was probably complete darkness for him; I doubted he had the IR enhancement of biomech in his body. Nanomeds to repair cells, delay aging, and keep him healthy, yes, but Majda wouldn't provide him with bioware used primarily in the military. Although I couldn't see him clearly, it didn't take a genius to tell he was frightened.

He spoke in a pure Iotic accent, his words deep and throaty. "Who is it? Who is there?"

Saints almighty. That voice alone could have women at his feet. Lowering my gun, I fumbled for the stylus around my neck. I came to my senses, though, before I turned it on. Scorch would monitor this cell even better than her storerooms. Gods knew, I had never expected she would keep Dayj for herself. It was truly insanity. She had to leave Raylicon; she could never pull it off here without news leaking. But she couldn't go now with every port under surveillance.

Manacles circled his left wrist and left ankle, with heavy chains that stretched to a massive hook in the wall. A blanket lay bunched up at one end of the pallet, and a jug stood nearby. His clothes were simple but clean, dark trousers and shirt, nothing like the expensive garments he had in the Majda holos.

I switched on the sonic damper. Then I said, "I'm here to help." My voice came out muffled. I went over and crouched next to him. "I'm Bhaaj."

He snapped up his free arm with his fist clenched while he protected his face with his other arm. That one action told me a great deal about his treatment here.

"I won't hurt you," I said. Up this close, I could see him better. I should have been ready, but no holo could prepare me for the full impact. Even with his face ragged from exhaustion and fear, he was so beautiful, it made me dizzy.

His voice rasped. "What do you want?"

"Your parents sent me." My mind spun with plans. His cell was a few paces across, little more than large hole created when mineral-laden water dissolved the softer rock and left a shell of harder stone. I located two holo-cams.

One was pointed straight at me.

Damn. It might be coincidence, but I couldn't take the chance. I spoke fast. "Your Highness, it won't be long before I'm discovered, if I haven't been already. We have to go now. I'm going to shoot your chains with an EM pulse gun."

He was looking at me now, though he probably couldn't see even an outline of my body. "How do I know you won't shoot me?"

"You have to trust me." I wondered if his voice rasped so badly because he had been shouting for help. No one would hear him down here except Scorch and the few people she let enter her empire. I aimed my gun at a point on the chain halfway between his wrist and the wall. Sweat gathered on my forehead. I didn't want to risk hitting him, but if he had to haul around too much of the chain, that would slow us down.

"I'm firing," I said. "Don't move."

His hand clenched on the pallet. "All right."

I held down the firing stud long enough for two projectiles to hit the chain, their explosive power muffled by the damper. The first damaged the link and the second cracked it in two. It took three shots to break the second chain. Having a stranger fire so near him in the dark had to be disturbing to Dayj, and he looked scared, but he maintained a remarkable composure, more than I had seen even with some ISC officers. I was beginning to wonder if his family knew him at all.

"You're free now," I said.

The chains scraped as he dragged them across the ground. "Thank you."

I grimaced. "Don't thank me yet. I don't know if I can get us out of here alive."

He felt around the wall until he found a handhold and then pulled himself up. As he stood, his leg buckled and he fell against the wall.

I jumped to my feet and reached for him. "What happened to your leg?"

Dayj jerked away when my palm brushed his arm. "Nothing."

"That wasn't nothing."

"I'm not sure. After one of the beatings, I couldn't walk for a few days." He took a shaky breath. "It's getting better. I don't think it's broken."

Gods al-flaming-mighty. "Who the blazes beat you?"

"She calls herself Scorch." His voice tightened. "She didn't like it when I refused her."

"She had no right to touch you." I didn't just mean the blows, either.

I wondered how Scorch's nose would feel, breaking under my fist. "Can you walk?"

"I think so." He took a step. His gait lurched, but he didn't fall. "Not fast, I am afraid."

"Here." I touched his arm, offering support. He tensed, but this time he didn't raise his fist or jerk away. So I slid my arm around his waist. He draped one arm over my shoulder and leaned on me while I helped him limp toward the doorway.

"Did Oxil bring you down here?" I asked as we pushed out past the canvas.

"Yes." He spoke bitterly. "I was so grateful to her for sneaking me out of the palace. Gods, I was a fool."

"You aren't a fool," I said. Lonely, yes, but if that made a person a fool, then half the human race was with him. I tried not to think of the past seven years since I had left Jak. "It isn't your fault other people commit crimes."

"I'm afraid I'm a rather poor judge of people." Dryly he said, "For all I know, Scorch could have sent you."

I started to swear colorfully at the suggestion, then remembered who I was with and shut up. "Sorry."

He actually laughed. It was soft and hoarse, but still a laugh. "I've heard much worse in the past few days."

Having listened to Scorch's vivid vocabulary myself, I could imagine. It amazed me that he could retain a sense of humor in all this.

We made our way uphill toward the storeroom. With his injured leg and my gravity problems, we had to go slow. Too slow. I thought of the dust in his gift box. His father had said he had kept it for years. "When did Oxil first bring you here?"

He glanced at me. "Four years ago."

"Did you meet Scorch then?"

"No. Not until I wanted to go offworld." He continued doggedly with his laborious steps. "Apparently she saw me, though, the first time I came down here."

Four years. That fit the date on the news broadcast I had seen with Scorch. She had worn one of her stranger expressions in that broadcast, an intensity that bordered on antipathy. I knew why, now. The delegates in that Assembly procession had included Roca Skolia, Dayj's intended. Scorch must have hated the woman who could claim Dayj. I thought of his words: *She didn't like it when I refused her.* I wouldn't intrude to ask what he meant. Assault took many forms, and if he fought, she would have ways to make him do what she wanted regardless of how he felt.

"I'm sorry," I said. "About everything."

He spoke in a low voice. "I just wanted to see the ocean."

"You will, someday."

"Perhaps." He didn't sound like he believed it any more than I did. I couldn't say the truth aloud, that we had little chance of escaping here. My pulse surged and I wanted to run.

The canvas door of a storeroom came into view, but it didn't look right. *Max,* I thought. *You have a map of this area now?*

Yes. The doorway you want is in about ten meters.

Thanks. I kept going, past a second canvas. I recognized the third one as the room with the gun crates.

A light appeared ahead.

Blast it! I drew Dayj behind one of the stalagmites at the storeroom and nudged him into the canvas. It wouldn't get him out of the caverns; even if he could have climbed to the hole in the ceiling, he didn't know how to navigate the maze of cavities above. But with all the bizarre rock formations and crates in there, he had plenty of places to hide.

Dayj slipped past the canvas. When he was gone, I switched off the damper.

A voice immediately became audible. "—see anyone here. They may have moved on."

I edged forward, crouched behind a row of stalagmites. At the last one, I looked outward to see one of Scorch's hired rizz-punks on the path. This one resembled the drifter Scorch had killed in the desert. I wondered if Scorch planned to murder everyone who knew she had kidnapped a Majda prince. Probably, if she intended to keep it secret. Her people were fools if they believed otherwise. It could explain why she had so few human guards here; the less people who knew, the better. For the same reason, she would erase the records her security systems kept of him.

I considered the guard as she ended her conversation. The darts in my gauntlets shot a powerful sedative. If I fired from this distance, I probably had about a forty-sixty chance of knocking her out. If I moved in closer, the odds improved, but a good chance existed she would see or hear me. Then I was dead.

Forty-sixty. The odds were too damn small. I gritted my teeth. Sometimes I hated this job.

I fired my pulse gun.

She never knew. The shots ripped through her, tearing apart her torso as they sent shock waves throughout her body. She collapsed, twisting as she fell, and smashed her light when she hit the ground. The tunnel went dark—

A laser flared from behind me, a brilliant light stabbing down the tunnel. It blasted a stalagmite only centimeters from where I crouched. I dropped and rolled fast as another laser shot exploded a stalactite. I barely scrambled out of the way before the spear of rock crashed to the ground. Shards flew everywhere and one stabbed my cheek.

The shooter was on the path to my left, where Dayj and I had been a few moments ago. She may have been following us. The storeroom where Dayj had hidden was also to my left, between me and this unknown shooter. The guard I had shot was farther up the path to my right. The rock formations where I was hiding bordered the trail and also extended into the darkness behind me, at right angles to the path. I crawled on my stomach behind the rocks, backing way from the trail, staying as low as possible. The darkness might help; it depended if the person firing at me had IR vision.

A familiar voice grated. "I know you're here, Bhaaj."

Scorch. Damn! I froze. She had every possible biomech enhancement: sight, hearing, muscles, skeleton, spinal node.

Max, can you locate her? I asked.

Estimate, he thought. Ten meters down the path.

Too close. I couldn't move, though. The noise would flag Scorch to my location, especially with her augmented hearing.

I peered through the rocks, but saw no one. Nor could I hear breathing. She was shrouded. If she stood in front of a stalagmite, her holosuit would project images of a stalagmite; if a wall rose to her left, the right side of her suit would show a wall. Conduits in the material would cool it and make it hard to pick her up on IR.

I closed my hand on the light stylus and slowly lifted the chain over my head. *Max, can you link to the chip that operates this light?*

Yes. I'm linked.

When I tell you, turn it on. I sighted on the fallen guard—and hurled the stylus at her. *Go!*

Light flared—and a laser beam hit the stylus dead on. In that instant, I fired toward the source of the beam, spraying the area with the

last of my second ammunition cartridge. The cavern echoed as projectiles shattered rock.

Darkness and silence descended.

Max, did I get her?

You hit a lot of rocks.

I know that.

I estimate the probability that you also hit Scorch is between
eleven and seventy-three percent.

Oh, well, that's definitive.

Sorry. It is the best I can do.

I was kneeling behind an outcropping, flanked by columns. That
Scorch hadn't returned fire could mean several things: I had hit her, she
couldn't find me, she had a strategy I hadn't guessed, or she was
recharging the carbine. The longer this went on, the more she had an advantage; I needed ammunition. I didn't think she had fired enough to use
a full charge, but that assumed she hadn't already used the carbine.

Footsteps came from my right, on the path where I had shot the
guard. Then Oxil edged around a curtain of rock, a pulse rifle gripped in
her hands. She looked down at the body of the guard I had shot, then
raised her gun. Scorch's shot had come from the opposite direction, so I
was penned now on both sides.

Max, I thought. *This is not good.*

I would call that an understatement.

Yeah, well, I would call it deadly.

Throw your gun. It will draw their fire. It is of no use to you without ammunition.

I have another cartridge. When I reload, though, they'll hear me. If
I moved fast enough, I might get Oxil before she killed me, but it would
leave me an easy target for Scorch. If she was still alive.

You need a diversion, Max thought. Throw your boot.

They'll hear me take it off. I touched my wrist. *I could get my
gauntlet off faster, with less noise.*

Without your gauntlets, you lose your connection to me.

I've two of them. I slid my right hand over my left gauntlet. *Retract
bio-threads from my left socket.*

Retracted. Max's thought had a tinny quality now.

I pressed the release and the gauntlet split open. No sound had betrayed me yet, but that wouldn't last. I steeled myself—then ripped off
the gauntlet and flung it at Oxil.

She fired immediately, hammering the rocks with projectiles. I scrambled to the left while I ripped the cartridge out of my pack. In that instant, a laser shot bored into the cranny I had just vacated. Hell and damnation. Scorch was alive and on to my tricks. I reloaded fast, all the time scuttling behind the stalagmites back toward the storeroom where Dayj had hidden.

When I finished reloading, I fired at Oxil, but she had already dodged out of sight. Laser fire melted stalagmites less than a meter away as I retreated. Scorch and I couldn't see each other. I edged back from the path, hoping it would throw off her estimate of my position. Then I stopped, my pulse racing, and listened.

Nothing.

I peered through the weird rocks. *Where'd Oxil go?*

She came this way, closer to Scorch's last location. She has hidden across the path.

I peered in that direction. A ragged fence of low rock pyramids bordered the other side of the trail. She could be anywhere behind it. I needed a better estimate. *Are you linked to the beetle I sent after Scorch earlier today?*

I lost contact when it reached the caverns.

We're here now, too. Maybe you can find it.

Searching.

Find it?

No.

Scorch's carbine could be recharging—

Got it!

Bring it here.

Working . . . Then he thought, I can link you into its cameras. It's too small to carry much power, so I can't do it until the beetle is within a few meters. Then you can see with its eyes. Temporarily.

I knew why he qualified his answer. *If it gets too close to Scorch or Oxil, they'll detect it.*

Yes. The bot is here. Linking.

My view of the cavern blurred. I closed my eyes and opened them. The scene refocused, still dim and red, but seen from higher up. Good. I was a beetle. We flew near the jagged ceiling on the other side of the path. Almost directly across from my hiding place, a brighter patch of red glowed behind two stalagmites.

Hey, I thought. *Max, bring me down lower.*

The lower you go, he thought. The greater your chance of detection.

I'll risk it. Circle over the last few meters.

The beetle drifted down in a spiral. The splotch of red resolved into Oxil crouched behind the pyramids of stone.

Hah! Got her.

You can't shoot her when she is behind those stalagmites.

Yeah, but knowing her location helps. I thought of Scorch. *Take the beetle up the path.*

Moving.

I floated through an inverted landscape of stone icicles that hung from the ceiling. Water dripped from them as if they were melting. Scorch shrouded herself well, though; nothing showed below except strange rocks.

A splintering crash came from the storeroom.

I snapped open my eyes and whipped up my gun.

Bhaaj, stop! Max thought. Dayj is in there.

In that same moment, Oxil lunged to her feet and fired at the storeroom. Simultaneously, a laser shot seared the canvas door, setting it aflame. As that all happened, I fired at Oxil, knowing exactly where to aim. With the canvas in flames now, light filled the cavern; Oxil stared straight at me as my shots tore through her, her face lit by the crackling fire.

Then she collapsed behind the stalagmites.

"Bhaaj!" a voice yelled. "Jump!"

I threw myself backward and slammed into a column. In the same moment, a laser shot from my left stabbed across my hiding place and missed me by only a handspan. Even as I returned Scorch's laser fire, I was looking to the right, up the path. The yell had come from there. I knew that voice.

Jak.

He was shrouded, but in the lurid firelight, the outline of his body showed. He had a weapon up and aimed, either a pulse rifle or a laser carbine. Looking down the path to the left, I finally located Scorch, a human-shaped ripple in the stalagmites.

Jak had his gun pointed straight at her.

She had her carbine pointed at me.

"You shoot me, Jak," Scorch called, "And I shoot her."

"You'll be dead before you fire," Jak said.

"I'm faster," she told him. "You got no biomech."

Well, hell. Both Scorch and I had augmented speed, but she had her gun up and mine was at my side. She only had to press the firing stud. I'd be dead before I got my weapon aimed.

"I got biomech," Jak told her.

"You're lying," Scorch said.

I knew Scorch well enough to recognize she wasn't sure. If she had thought she could move faster than Jak, I would be dead now. Unfortunately I knew another truth. Jak was bluffing. He had no biomech.

The burning canvas fell to the ground, flames dying, their light dimming. So at first I wasn't certain if what I saw in the entrance of the storeroom was real or a shadow. Then the "shadow" solidified—into a man.

Dayj.

He had a neural tangler clenched in his hand. The splintering we had heard must have been him cracking open one of the crates by smashing it into another. I must have been closer to breaking them than I realized.

"Dayj." Scorch was only a few steps away from him. Her outline faded as the fire died. "You can't shoot. You don't know how to use a tangler." She had an odd tone, as if she were talking to a child.

I hated her tone, but she was probably right. A tangler injected chemicals. It took experience to prepare and prime the gun, determine the dose, and decide where to shoot.

"You don't think I know?" Dayj's voice rasped, his Iotic accent a jarring contrast to the lurid scene, with the flames and glittering rock formations. "I watched, Scorch. I listened to you tell that drifter how to kill Captain Krestone, and I watched you get ready to kill your hired assassin."

Ah, no. Had Dayj just signed his death warrant? He might not realize it, but he had just told her he could testify against her as a witness. She had to kill him. Given all she had gone through to get him, though, she wouldn't want him dead. Letting him live would go against every tenet she lived by, but from what I had seen, she was obsessed with Dayj.

"Can't learn a tangler that way." Scorch's brusque voice gave me chills. "Even if you knew, you could never shoot. Drop the gun, Dayj."

I held my breath. If Scorch wavered even a moment, it would give Jak and me the opening we needed.

Dayj stared at her. The blaze of the canvas had died to embers and she was almost invisible now. If he waited any longer, Scorch would win. As soon as we could no longer see her, Jak's advantage disappeared. I glanced at Jak, moving only my eyes, not my head. His outline was also fading, which meant Scorch soon couldn't shoot him with accuracy, either, but it also acted as a flag, letting her know how little we could see her.

Dayj stood gripping a stalagmite, the chain hanging from the manacle on his wrist. He held the tangler in his other hand, aimed at Scorch. Watching him, I knew she was right. He couldn't commit murder. It wasn't in him. Chances were he hadn't primed the tangler properly, but if he believed he might kill her, it would stop him from shooting.

Or so I thought.

Then he fired.

Everything happened at once. Scorch only wavered for an instant, but it was enough. I threw myself forward and fired, crashing to the ground as her laser exploded a stalactite above my head. Melted debris showered me. Jak fired a fraction of a second later, but Scorch had already ducked to the side. And now she knew; he had bluffed about his speed.

Dayj lunged away from the storeroom. I could no longer see Scorch, but he had to be right next to her. I couldn't believe it. He was gambling that one of the most hardened under-city killers wouldn't immediately end his life. Incredibly, he was right. She hesitated only an instant, but it was long enough for him to yank the pack off her back so that it smashed a stalagmite. Although her shroud didn't fail completely, he must have damaged the jammer, because her visual disguise faded enough to let me see her blurred outline.

Even as Dayj had moved, I was jumping to my feet. Although I was going at many times normal speed, pushing hard, everything seemed to slow down. In the time it took Scorch to recover from Dayj's strike, I aimed—

And fired.

Projectiles ripped through Scorch. Her carbine discharged—and just missed Dayj. I hammered projectiles into her body, and they riveted her to the rock formation like a drill.

Suddenly the roar stopped. Scorch's body slid down the stalagmite and crumpled on the ground, leaving a smear of red.

"Ah, gods—" Dayj lurched back and dropped to his knees. Leaning forward with his arms around his stomach, he vomited on the ground.

I stood with my booted feet planted apart, both hands on my gun, my arms extended straight out from my body, my thumb still pressing the firing stud of my pulse gun.

"Bhaaj." Jak's voice came at my side. "You can stop."

I turned. When I aimed my gun at him, he put his hand on the barrel and carefully pushed it aside. "Stand down, Major," he said softly. "The engagement's over."

I stared at the gun I was still trying to fire. It took my adrenaline-inflamed mind that long to comprehend I had used up the ammunition. Then I took a deep breath. "Thanks."

"Yeah."

We went to Dayj then. He had his arms around his stomach and his head down. The remains of Scorch's body lay crumpled only paces away, but I couldn't look. Later, I'd have to face what I'd done here to-day and deal with it. Right now, Dayj needed us more.

I knelt next to him. "Are you all right?"

He lifted his head. "Who are you?"

Even in the waning light of the embers from the fire, I could see the haggard lines of his face. I spoke quietly. "My name is Bhaajan. I used to be an army officer. Now I do private investigations."

Dayj was gripping the tangler. I pried away his clenched fingers and took the gun. A quick check made the blood drain from my face. "These darts are loaded with water." They would disintegrate inside the body of whoever they hit, spreading their chemicals. Water, in this case.

"I've no idea how to use this weapon," he said hoarsely. "I don't even know what it is."

I stared at him, incredulous. "It's a tangler. One of the deadliest neural disruptors ever made."

He met my gaze. "I couldn't think of anything else to do that would give you a chance."

I set the gun on the ground. "You have guts." What an understate-ment. He had bluffed one of the most brutal under-city criminals on Raylicon with a water gun.

"Gods," Jak muttered to him. "Remind me never to let you in the Black Mark." He glanced around. "We should get moving. I'm sur-prised nothing has shot at us."

"It is probably because you are so close to me," Dayj said. "Her au-tomated systems won't harm me. She reprogrammed them after a laser nearly killed me when I tried to escape."

"We're also shrouded," I said. "From most sensors."

"I can see you," Dayj said. "Your skin shimmers."

"It's holographic powder. The effect breaks down up close." I rose to my feet and offered him a hand.

Dayj stood up and tried to take a step. As his leg gave out, both Jak and I grabbed for him. We each slid an arm around his waist, and he put his arms over our shoulders. Then we started up the path where Jak had come down.

"We can go out a back door I know," I said.

"Got a closer one," Jak said. "I've a jeeper waiting."

"A closer one?" I said. He might as well have just punched my gut. "You knew about another entrance?

Jak cleared his throat. "Uh—yeah."

"You, who supposedly didn't know a way in here?" Now that I thought about it, he hadn't had time to get a shroud, go back to the café, and then come here. He must have come straight to the cavern.

"Bhaaj—"

"You bastard." The muscles in my arm stiffened. "You ditched me. You never intended to go back to the café."

Jak stared at me across Dayj, his gaze dark and foreboding. "Of course *you* would never ditch *me*. And never mind that I just helped save your stubborn ass."

"My ass was fine," I growled.

"Excuse me," Dayj said. "But if the two of you continue this, you will break my spine."

My cheeks flamed. I hadn't realized I was gripping him so hard. At the same time I said, "My apologies, Your Highness," Jak turned red and said, "Oh. Sorry about that." I loosened my hold and Jak let go of him completely.

Within moments, we reached an exit that let us out into a decrepit canal. A jeeper waited, stocky and squat under an overhang created by a collapsed wall. Holo-paint sheened the armored surfaces of the vehicle; right now its mottled rust and blue exterior matched the surrounding canal rock.

As I helped Dayj into the jeeper, Jak surveyed the area. "No one has come after us yet."

Dayj paused on the doorway. "Scorch didn't want people to know she had me prisoner." In a dull voice, he added, "Anyone who knew, she killed."

I spoke in a low voice. "It's not your fault."

Jak swung into the driver's seat. "Her behavior makes no sense."

I sat with Dayj in the back. "Why not?"

Jak powered up the jeeper. After it rose into the air and headed down the canal, he swiveled around in his seat to look at Dayj. "She threw her reason to the wind over you."

It made sense to me. I'd thrown my reason to the wind over Jak more than once.

"Who are you?" Dayj asked him.

"Jak."

"I thank you for your help."

Jak nodded awkwardly. "I set a course for the palace."

"No," I said. "Wait." I turned to Dayj. "Is that what you want?"

He went very still. "I have a choice?"

I took a breath and plunged ahead. "I've told your family you went offworld. The port lists a ticket bought by someone with the ID Scorch sold you. It says you went to Metropoli. This jeeper and the caverns are protected from surveillance." I felt as if the world were spinning. If the Majdas found out what I was doing, my life would be worth nothing. "You probably can't leave Raylicon now, but if the search moves to Metropoli, it will ease up here. Eventually you could leave. Go wherever you want."

Jak stared at me. "I can't be hearing this."

"Why?" Dayj asked me. "Why would you do this for me? Do you realize what my family will do if they find out? Or the reward they will give you for bringing me back?"

"This isn't about a reward," I said. "Or their revenge. Some things are more important. Like freedom. You shouldn't have to live that way."

"What way?" He sounded tired. "As one of the richest people in an interstellar empire? There is a real hardship."

"You're a prisoner in your own home."

"The Houses have a rationale that goes back millennia." He rubbed his eyes, then dropped his arm. "It is a rich tradition, Major, not one to throw away lightly."

I wondered who he meant to convince, himself or me. "Then why did you run away?"

Softly he said, "Because I was starving."

I gentled my voice the best I knew how. "Skolians have settled hundreds of worlds. If you want a densely populated place with many seas, it doesn't have to be Metropoli. You can go somewhere they'd never know."

His look said it all, then. The longing, the loneliness, the frustrated dreams, the *hope*: it was all there in his dark eyes. He spoke with difficulty. "When I was lying in my cell down there, in the caverns, I remembered a gift my parents had given me when I was little, a globe of Raylicon with deserts in gold and ruby, the dead seas in crystal, and clouds in diamond. I thought it was the most beautiful thing I'd ever seen. But they wouldn't let me play with it. I would have broken it, you see." In a low voice he said, "That is my life, Major. I can only look at it, I cannot touch it."

I swallowed. "I'm sorry."

"But you see, that present—while I lay in the dark, I remembered *why* my parents gave it to me. I remembered their love." He spoke with difficulty. "I want to leave. But I cannot."

I thought of Corejida and Ahktar at the Lake of Whispers, both crying. It gave me a strange feeling, one I couldn't define. Envy? Grief? No one had ever stood on a shore or anywhere else and wept for me.

"You're sure?" I asked.

He nodded. "I'm sure."

Jak spoke quietly. "Perhaps after all this, you can convince them to give you more freedom."

Dayj tried to smile. "Perhaps I can."

We all knew that none of us believed that hope.

End VII

VIII
HOMECOMING

IT WAS STILL night when the jeeper reached Majda territory. The comm crackled with a woman's voice. "You have entered restricted airspace. Identify yourself and await instructions."

I leaned forward, between the pilot's and copilot's seats, and spoke into the comm. "This is Major Bhaajan. Notify General Majda that I'm coming in."

"Please hold, Major," the woman said.

"Understood." Apparently the jeeper's shroud didn't work all that well given how fast they had identified us. But it probably hid the people inside. I reached forward to deactivate it. Once they knew we carried Dayj, we shouldn't have trouble.

"Wait," Dayj said. "Not yet."

Jak glanced at him. "It's too late to turn back now."

"I know," Dayj said. "I just—I want a few more minutes of freedom. Even knowing it's about to end."

A new voice snapped out of the comm, hard and clipped. "Major, this is Captain Takkar. Where the hell have you been?"

I crossed my arms. "Around."

"Don't rizz with me, Bhaajan. You've hidden continuously since we told you to cut it with the shroud. You had better have a damn good explanation. And this one had better not involve some disreputable undercity kingpin."

Jak's eyes gleamed. "Don't you like me, Captain?"

Takkar swore in a manner she would never have done had she known a Majda prince could hear. I glanced at Dayj. He smiled slightly and shrugged.

I had other issues with the captain. I spoke into the comm. "Tell me something, Takkar. Where is Lieutenant Oxil?"

"She's off-duty," Takkar said. "Why?"

"You don't wonder where she is?"

"No. Why do you?"

"I've my reasons."

"What reasons?"

"I'll explain when we land."

"You're damn right you will," Takkar said. "The police are escorting you into the south park area."

"Understood," I said. Takkar sounded angry but not defensive. It was hard to tell from a voice over the comm, but my intuition said she didn't know about Oxil.

"Captain," I said. "Can you have the Majda sisters meet us when we land?"

"Why?" Takkar asked.

"I have news for them."

Tension snapped in her voice. "What did you find out?"

"I'll tell them."

Takkar just grunted.

I toggled off the reception and sat back with Dayj. "How well do you know Captain Takkar?"

"She's been with our police force for decades." Dayj smiled, his teeth a flash of white. "I've always liked her."

It was the first time I had seen his full smile, and I barely heard a word after that. No wonder Scorch had fallen so hard. She must have seen that dazzling smile of his when she spied on his visits with Oxil to the aqueducts. She had tried to attain the unattainable and paid for it with her life.

"Do you think Takkar knows about Oxil?" I asked Dayj.

"No. The captain is loyal to my family."

Although I disliked Takkar enough to wish he was wrong, it fit my impression. "They'll probably give her a lie detector test."

"Probably." He shook his head. "The first time Oxil snuck me out to the canals, I thought she would expect something in return. But she never asked for anything."

"She wanted you to trust her."

He looked out the window at the forest below. "I did. I was stupid."

"Dayj, no. They were scum. And Oxil was the fool. Scorch would never have let her live. She intended to kill anyone who knew you were down there."

He glanced at me with his dark gaze. "Except you did it for her."

That hit like ice water. I had no answer. He had seen me shoot Scorch, possibly Oxil and the guard as well. Records would also exist on Scorch's security system. Any lie detector test would verify I believed my actions were necessary to protect Dayj and myself, but no matter how they looked at it, I had killed three people. That first guard hadn't known I was there. Even if the police cleared me of murder, I would know the truth; I was capable of actions that made me no better than the criminals I tracked.

"Bhaaj, stop," Jak said.

I looked up at him. "Hey." I tried to smile. "It's not every day I get to ride with a disreputable under-city kingpin."

"Your lucky night." His smile didn't reach his eyes. He knew what I was thinking. He had held me in the past when darkness haunted my memories. This time I wouldn't even have him for long—for he would stay in Cries, which I could never do.

———

Escorted by Majda police, Jak landed the jeeper on a long, sloping lawn outside the palace. As soon as the engines powered down, I opened the door and jumped out. Eight police officers waited, along with Takkar and the new security chief. The Majda sisters were also there. From Takkar's thunderous expression, I thought she would have me slapped in the modern-day equivalent of irons. However, as impatient as she and the others looked, they stayed back while General Majda approached me.

I've always prided myself on being hard to intimidate, but even my confidence waned when I faced Vaj Majda. I tended to forget how tall she was, two meters. Her dark, upturned eyes seemed to miss nothing, and right now they were focused on me with unrelenting intensity.

We met a few paces from the jeeper. I bowed from the waist. "My greetings, General."

She spoke in her husky voice. "You've been difficult to find, Major."

"I know. I had good reason."

"And that is?"

I looked back at the jeeper, but Dayj hadn't come out. Jak stepped into the doorway and jumped down to the ground.

"Major Bhaajan." The General's voice tightened ominously. "How you spend your personal time is your affair. I assume you have reason to bring your—companion here."

"He helped." I started to say more, but then I stopped.

Dayj had appeared in the doorway of the jeeper.

A cry came from behind us, and then Corejida was striding past. Dayj jumped down and within moments he and his mother were embracing. Corejida kept saying, "I can't believe it." The chain attached to Dayj's wrist hung down her back, but I didn't think she noticed. The other chain, the one on his ankle, lay across the grass. Tears ran down her face and she made no attempt to hide them, contrary to the reputation of the noble Houses for restrained emotions.

"Gods," Vaj murmured. Her voice caught. It was the first time I had seen her control slip. "Thank you, Major."

I nodded, though I grieved for the freedom Dayj would never know. "He's going to need a doctor." I hesitated, uncertain how much to say about what Scorch had done to him. "A counselor, too, I think."

Majda inclined her head to me. "We will see to his health, both physical and emotional."

"And intellectual?" I knew I should keep my mouth shut, but the words came out anyway.

"Dayj has his books."

"It isn't enough." I plunged ahead. "General, I ask your forgiveness if I offend. But please listen." I motioned toward Dayj. "He's a lot smarter than you think. A lot more talented. He needs independence. He's suffocating here."

Anger flashed in her eyes. "I forgive your offense, Major, because you brought him home. But do not overstep yourself."

"He ran away." I had to speak even if it meant I lost the goodwill I had earned by finding him. "Doesn't that tell you anything? Gods know, I can see you all love him. He's a fortunate man in that." More quietly I added, "If you love him, let him have his dreams."

I thought she would have me thrown off the grounds then. If a gaze could truly have pierced, she would have sliced me to ribbons. "If he ran away of his own free will," she asked coldly, "why is he in chains now?"

"Because he trusted too easily. He never learned to survive on his own."

"All the more reason he should remain here."

"He came home because he loves you all." I was digging myself a deeper hole, but I owed Dayj. He had saved my life by bluffing Scorch. "But he wanted to weep and they weren't tears of joy."

Majda clasped her hands behind her back. "You take liberties I have not granted."

"You don't strike me as someone who prefers pretty words to the truth," I said. Behind her, people were running down the lawn from the palace, including Ahktar. He must have thrown on his robe without bothering to fasten the ties. It billowed out behind him, flying in the wind like a cape.

Vaj turned to watch them. "Everyone has their version of the truth, Major."

When Ahktar reached Dayj and Corejida, he threw his arms around them. While they hugged, other people gathered around, two of them doctors judging by the scanners they turned on Dayj. A police officer knelt by Dayj's ankle and began working on the manacle.

"I do know this," Majda told me. "I will be forever grateful that you brought him back to us."

I couldn't say any more. I should have realized a few words from an outsider couldn't change anything.

Majda went to Dayj then and greeted him. Although far more re-strained than her sister and brother-in-law, the General left no doubt of the truth in her last words.

Jak came over to me. "I don't know if he's incredibly lucky or one of the most unfortunate people I've ever met."

I exhaled softly. "Both, I think."

End VIII

IX
NEW LEAVES

JAK TOSSED MY jacket onto the bed. "You want to carry this or pack it?"

I stuffed the jacket into my duffle. "Both."

He wouldn't meet my gaze. We had already gone through the penthouse twice to make sure I wasn't leaving anything behind. Now we were stalling. I had nothing left in my work to keep me here; this morning a sum of credit far greater than I had expected had appeared in my bank account. Dayj told the police I acted to defend him from murder, and Majda accepted it. No charges would be brought against me. In fact, Takkar was ready to escort me off the planet herself, barred the opportunity to slap me in jail. I was free to go.

Except.

I stood by the bed while Jak paced around, checking for lost items. I tried to make a joke. "You'll wear a path in this expensive carpet." Ha, ha.

Jak turned without a smile. He made a stark contrast to the white wall, in his black trousers and muscle shirt. The holster strapped around his torso held an EM pulse gun against his ribs. Since the business with Scorch, we both went armed everywhere.

I shifted my weight. The obvious thing was for me to ask for a ride to the starport. I opened my mouth, but somehow, instead I said, "Come with me."

I immediately wanted to kick myself. What the blazes was wrong with me? Of course he wouldn't come. He had everything here, money, power, influence. Granted, his life skirted the borders of legality, to put it kindly, but Jak had never let that dissuade him. It *did* make a difference to me. He couldn't live my life any more than I could live his.

"You stay," he said.

"Took me a long time to get out."

He crossed his arms and his biceps bulged. "This is your home."

I wished he would stop looking so good. It made it hard to think clearly. "Can't ever come home."

"It's my home."

"Make a new one?"

"You make an old one."

To hell with the under-city terse inability to express anything. "I can't, Jak. This place is my nightmare. I tried to come home once before, after I retired from the army, and it didn't work. I've made a new life in Selei City. I want that life, not a past with so many ghosts and so much grief."

His jaw twitched. "I'm a ghost you want to forget?"

"No!" I spread my hands out from my body. "Come with me."

"You stay."

We stood looking at each other, nothing left to say.

"I've an incoming message," the penthouse EI announced.

"For flaming sakes," I muttered. "Your timing honks."

"Do you wish me to play it later?" the EI asked.

"Who is it from?"

"It isn't signed."

"Oh, well, great." I glared at no one in particular, because I didn't have the words to tell Jak how I felt. He stood waiting, and I knew he would never say how much this hurt, either. We made quite a pair, him and me, both equally inarticulate.

"Major Bhaajan?" the EI prodded.

"Project the message on the wall," I growled.

"It isn't visual."

Great. People used audio-only mail if they had something to hide. "One of Scorch's people sending us death threats?"

"I don't know," the EI said.

"Just play it." I was in no mood for breathy threats but we might as well get it over with.

The voice that rose into the air was anything but breathy. Rich and deep, it made the hairs on my neck stand up.

"My greetings, Major Bhaajan," Prince Dayjarind said.

Jar stared at me. "Gods *almighty.*"

I couldn't believe it, either. "He has *no* access to any mesh outside the palace. No way could he send me a letter."

"Major," the EI said. "Do you wish me to continue the message or would you prefer to continue conversing?"

"You know," Jak said, "that EI can be annoying."

I grimaced. "Yeah." To the EI I said, "Keep playing it."

"I would like to thank you, Major," Dayj continued. "I am unfamiliar with public meshes, so please excuse my clumsiness if I break protocols. This is my first message."

"He sounds a lot better now," Jak said.

"He does." It was an understatement. Dayj's voice had lost its hoarse, desperate quality.

"It is hard to know how to say this," Dayj went on. "I have had many talks with my family. As a result, next year I will attend school, probably Imperial University on Parthonia if I pass the entrance exams. My uncle is a psychology professor there, so I can live with him and his family."

I gaped at Jak. "He's going to *college*." I wished I could have been a beetle-bot in the room during his negotiations with his family. "That's incredible."

"Maybe they finally woke up," Jak said.

"Aunt Vaj isn't happy with the decision," Dayj said. "But she has given me the blessing of Majda. Her decision to accept it apparently has something to do with a conversation she had with you. Whatever you said, thank you."

Jak cocked an eyebrow at me. "You talking tough with Majda?"

"I said a few things."

"You got a suicide wish, Bhaaj."

I winced. "Just ornery."

"I must go," Dayj said. His voice lightened. "But I look forward to the future. Please give my thanks to your friend, the man with the jeeper. May you be well, Major Bhaajan. I wish you the best."

Then the room was silent.

"This is a good thing," Jak said.

"It is." I smiled. "Who would've thought?"

He scowled. "It shouldn't have taken almost losing him forever to make them wake up and realize he had to go."

"Sometimes you have to take risks." I went over and clasped his hands, a gesture of affection atypical of me, to say the least. He looked flustered. "Come with me, Jak. You don't have to stay here, running your damn casino. You could do so much more."

"I like running my damn casino." He didn't drop my hands, though.

"Haven't you ever wanted to see new places? Travel? Go to the stars?" I knew as soon as the gleam came into his eyes that he hadn't lost that desire. Wanderlust. He had always wanted to travel. "A whole universe is out there for you to conquer."

His wicked grin flashed. "I would, you know."

Gods he was sexy when he smiled that way. "Worth a try."

"Got no job in Selei City."

I didn't tell him that I had plenty of money now to support us both. He had his pride. "Find one."

He laughed. "What, no offer to make me a kept man, Bhaaj? Damn, woman, you can afford it. You're sinfully rich."

I flushed. "Figured you wouldn't want that."

"I know. That makes a difference."

"Enough to come?"

"You know the answer." After a moment, he added, "Might visit, though."

My breath caught. He had never made that offer before. "I'd like that."

He spoke dryly, "Got Braze's family and Scorch's people after me. Maybe this is a good time to fold up the Black Mark for a while." His eyes gleamed. "Maybe open it somewhere else."

"Jak." He had better not try that in Selei City.

He laughed, deep and full. "I swear, those glares of yours could incinerate a man." His smile became something gentler, more frightening than his grin, something that almost looked like love. "Just a visit, while things cool down here. Later—we'll see."

"Sounds good." If he came for a visit, it gave me time to work on him. He'd like it there, I knew. Maybe, given enough time, he'd consider something more permanent.

"Got a lot to take care of here first," he said.

"I'll help." I wasn't giving him time to change his mind.

Jak pulled me into his arms. "I dunno, Bhaaj. Think Selei City can handle us both?"

A laugh built up in me then, a really good one, the kind I hadn't felt in a long time. "We'll have to see."

He winked at me. "So we will."

I looked forward to finding that answer.

End IX

❖ CAMOUFLAGE ❖

by Robert Reed

I

THE HUMAN MALE had lived on the avenue for some thirty-two years. Neighbors generally regarded him as being a solitary creature, short-tempered on occasion, but never rude without cause. His dark wit was locally famous, and a withering intelligence was rumored to hide behind the brown-black eyes. Those with an appreciation of human beauty claimed that he was not particularly handsome, his face a touch asymmetrical, the skin rough and fleshy, while his thick mahogany-brown hair looked as if it was cut with a knife and his own strong hands. Yet that homeliness made him intriguing to some human females, judging by the idle chatter. He wasn't large for a human, but most considered him substantially built. Perhaps it was the way he walked, his back erect and shoulders squared while his face tilted slightly forwards, as if looking down from a great height. Some guessed he had been born on a high-gravity world, since the oldest habits never died. Or maybe this wasn't his true body, and his soul still hungered for the days when he was a giant. Endless speculations were woven about the man's past. He had a name, and everybody knew it. He had a biography, thorough and easily observed in the public records. But there were at least a dozen alternate versions of his past and left-behind troubles. He was a failed poet, or a dangerously successful poet, or a refugee who had escaped some political mess—unless he was some species of criminal, of course. One certainty was his financial security; but where his money came from was a subject of considerable debate. Inherited, some claimed. Others voted for gambling winnings or lucrative investments on now-distant colony worlds. Whatever the story, the man had the luxury of filling his days doing very little, and during his years on this obscure avenue, he had helped his neighbors with unsolicited gifts of money and sometimes more impressive flavors of aid.

Thirty-two years was not a long time. Not for creatures that routinely traveled between the stars. Most of the ship's passengers and all of its crew were ageless souls, durable and disease-free, with enhanced minds possessing a stability and depth of memory ready to endure a million years of comfortable existence. Which was why three decades was little different than an afternoon, and why for another century or twenty, locals would still refer to their neighbor as the newcomer.

Such was life onboard the Great Ship.

There were millions of avenues like this one. Some were short enough to walk in a day, while others stretched for thousands of uninterrupted kilometers. Many avenues remained empty, dark and cold as when humans first discovered the Great Ship. But some had been awakened, made habitable to human owners or the oddest alien passengers. Whoever built the ship—presumably an ancient, long-extinct species—it had been designed to serve as home for a wide array of organisms. That much was obvious. And there was no other starship like the Great Ship: larger than most worlds and durable enough to survive eons between the galaxies, and to almost every eye, lovely.

The wealthiest citizens from thousands of worlds had surrendered fortunes for the pleasure of riding inside this fabulous machine, embarking on a half-million-year voyage to circumnavigate the galaxy. Even the poorest passenger living in the tiniest of quarters looked on the majesty of his grand home and felt singularly blessed.

This particular avenue was almost a hundred kilometers long and barely two hundred meters across. And it was tilted. Wastewater made a shallow river that sang its way across a floor of sugar-and-pepper granite. For fifty thousand years, the river had flowed without interruption, etching out a shallow channel. Locals had built bridges at the likely places, and along the banks they erected tubs and pots filled with soils that mimicked countless worlds, giving roots and sessile feet happy places to stand. A large pot rested outside the man's front door—a vessel made of ceramic foam trimmed with polished brass and covering nearly a tenth of a hectare. When the man first arrived, he poisoned the old jungle and planted another. But he wasn't much of a gardener, apparently. The new foliage hadn't prospered, weed species and odd volunteers emerging from the ruins.

Along the pot's edge stood a ragged patch of Ilano vibra—an alien flower famous for its wild haunting songs. "I should cut that weed out of there," he would tell neighbors. "I pretty much hate the racket it's making." Yet he didn't kill them or tear out the little voice boxes. And after a

decade or two of hearing his complaints, his neighbors began to understand that he secretly enjoyed their complicated, utterly alien melodies.

Most of his neighbors were sentient, fully mobile machines. Early
in the voyage, a charitable foundation dedicated to finding homes and
livelihoods for freed mechanical slaves leased the avenue. But over the
millennia, organic species had cut their own apartments into the walls,
including a janusian couple downstream, and upstream, an extended
family of harum-scarums.

The human was a loner, but by no means was he a hermit.

True solitude was the easiest trick to manage. There were billions of
passengers onboard, but the great bulk of the ship was full of hollow
places and great caves, seas of water and ammonia and methane, as well
as moon-sized tanks filled with liquid hydrogen. Most locations were
empty. Wilderness was everywhere, cheap and inviting. Indeed, a brief
journey by cap-car could take the man to any of six wild places—alien
environments and hidden sewage conduits and a maze-like cavern that
was rumored to never have been mapped. That was one advantage: At
all times, he had more than one escape route. Another advantage was his
neighbors. Machines were always bright in easy ways, fountains of information if you knew how to employ them, but indifferent to the sub-
tleties of organic life, if not out and out blind.

Long ago, Pamir had lived as a hermit. That was only sensible at the
time. Ship captains rarely abandoned their posts, particularly a captain
of his rank and great promise.

He brought his fall upon himself, with the help of an alien.

An alien who happened to be his lover, too.

The creature was a Gaian and a refugee, and Pamir broke several
rules, helping find her sanctuary deep inside the ship. But another Gaian
came searching for her, and in the end, both of those very odd creatures
were nearly dead. The ship was never at risk, but a significant facility
was destroyed, and after making things as right as possible, Pamir vanished into the general population, waiting for the proverbial coast to
clear.

Thousands of years had brought tiny changes to his status. By most
accounts, the Master Captain had stopped searching for him. Two or
three or four possible escapes from the ship had been recorded, each
placing him on a different colony world. Or he had died in some ugly
fashion. The best story put him inside a frigid little cavern. Smugglers
had killed his body and sealed it into a tomb of glass, and after centuries

without food or air, the body had stopped trying to heal itself. Pamir was a blind brain trapped inside a frozen carcass, and the smugglers were eventually captured and interrogated by the best in that narrow field. According to coerced testimonies, they confessed to killing the infamous captain, though the precise location of their crime was not known and would never be found.

Pamir spent another few thousand years wandering, changing homes and remaking his face and name. He had worn nearly seventy identities, each elaborate enough to be believed, yet dull enough to escape notice. For good reasons, he found it helpful to wear an air of mystery, letting neighbors invent any odd story to explain the gaps in his biography. Whatever they dreamed up, it fell far from the truth. Machines and men couldn't imagine the turns and odd blessings of his life. Yet despite all of that, Pamir remained a good captain. A sense of obligation forced him to watch after the passengers and ship. He might live on the run for the next two hundred millennia, but he would always be committed to this great machine and its precious, nearly countless inhabitants.

Now and again, he did large favors.

Like with the harum-scarums living next door. They were a bipedal species—giants by every measure—adorned with armored plates and spine-encrusted elbows and an arrogance earned by millions of years of wandering among the stars. But this particular family was politically weak, and that was a bad way to be among harum-scarums. They had troubles with an old Mother-of-fathers, and when Pamir saw what was happening, he interceded. Over the course of six months, by means both subtle and decisive, he put an end to the feud. The Mother-of-fathers came to her enemies' home, walking backwards as a sign of total submission; and with a plaintive voice, she begged for death, or at the very least, a forgetting of her crimes.

No one saw Pamir's hand in this business. If they had, he would have laughed it off, and moments later, he would have vanished, throwing himself into another identity in a distant avenue.

Large deeds always demanded a complete change of life.

A fresh face.

A slightly rebuilt body.

And another forgettable name.

That was how Pamir lived. And he had come to believe that it wasn't a particularly bad way to live. Fate or some other woman-deity had given him this wondrous excuse to be alert at all times, to accept nothing as it first appeared, helping those who deserved to be helped, and when the time came, remaking himself all over again.

And that time always came . . .

I I

"Hello, my friend."

"Hello to you."

"And how are you this evening, my very good friend?"

Pamir was sitting beside the huge ceramic pot, listening to his Ilano vibra. Then with a dry smirk, he mentioned, "I need to void my bowels."

The machine laughed a little too enthusiastically. Its home was half a kilometer up the avenue, sharing an apartment with twenty other legally sentient AIs who had escaped together from the same long-ago world. The rubber face and bright glass eyes worked themselves into a beaming smile, while a happy voice declared, "I am learning. You cannot shock me so easily with this organic dirty talk." Then he said, "My friend," again, before using the fictitious name.

Pamir nodded, shrugged.

"It is a fine evening, is it not?"

"The best ever," he deadpanned.

Evening along this avenue was a question of the clock. The machines used the twenty-four-hour ship-cycle, but with six hours of total darkness sandwiched between eighteen hours of brilliant, undiluted light. That same minimal aesthetics had kept remodeling to a minimum. The avenue walls were raw granite, save for the little places where organic tenants had applied wood or tile facades. The ceiling was a slick arch made of medium-grade hyperfiber—a mirror-colored material wearing a thin coat of grime and lubricating oils and other residues. The lights were original, as old as the ship and laid out in the thin dazzling bands running lengthwise along the ceiling. Evening brought no softening of brilliance or reddening of color. Evening was a precise moment, and when night came . . . in another few minutes, Pamir realized . . . there would be three warning flashes, and then a perfect smothering blackness.

The machine continued to smile at him, meaning something by it. Cobalt-blue eyes were glowing, watching the human sit with the singing weeds.

"You want something," Pamir guessed.

"Much or little. How can one objectively measure one's wishes?"

"What do you want with me? Much, or little?"

"Very little."

"Define your terms," Pamir growled.

"There is a woman."

Pamir said nothing, waiting now.

"A human woman, as it happens." The face grinned, an honest delight leaking out of a mind no bigger than a fleck of sand. "She has hired me for a service. And the service is to arrange an introduction with you."

Pamir said, "An introduction," with a flat, unaffected voice. And through a string of secret nexuses, he brought his security systems up to full alert.

"She wishes to meet you."

"Why?"

"Because she finds you fascinating, of course."

"Am I?"

"Oh, yes. Everyone here believes you are most intriguing." The flexible face spread wide as the mouth grinned, never-used white teeth shining in the last light. "But then again, we are an easily fascinated lot. What is the meaning of existence? What is the purpose of death? Where does slavery end and helplessness begin? And what kind of man lives down the path from my front door? I know his name, and I know nothing."

"Who's this woman?" Pamir snapped.

The machine refused to answer him directly. "I explained to her what I knew about you. What I positively knew, and what I could surmise. And while I was speaking, it occurred to me that after all of these nanoseconds of close proximity, you and I remain strangers."

The surrounding landscape was unremarkable. Scans told Pamir that every face was known, and the nexus traffic was utterly ordinary, and when he extended his search, nothing was worth the smallest concern. Which made him uneasy. Every long look should find something suspicious.

"The woman admires you."

"Does she?"

"Without question." The false body was narrow and quite tall, dressed in a simple cream-colored robe. Four spidery arms emerged from under the folds of fabric, extending and then collapsing across the illusionary chest. "Human emotions are not my strength. But from what she says and what she does not say, I believe she has desired you for a very long time."

The Ilano vibra were falling silent now.

Night was moments away.

"All right," Pamir said. He stood, boots planting themselves on the hard pale granite. "No offense meant here. But why the hell would she hire you?"

"She is a shy lady," the machine offered. And then he laughed, deeply amused by his own joke. "No, no. She is not at all shy. In fact, she is a very important soul. Perhaps this is why she demands an intermediary."

"Important how?"

"In all ways," his neighbor professed. Then with a genuine envy, he added, "You should feel honored by her attentions."

A second array of security sensors was waiting. Pamir had never used them, and they were so deeply hidden no one could have noticed their presence. But they needed critical seconds to emerge from their slumber, and another half-second to calibrate and link together. And then, just as the first of three warning flashes rippled along the mirrored ceiling, what should have been obvious finally showed itself to him.

"You're not just my neighbor," he told the rubber face.

A second flash passed overhead. Then he saw the shielded cap-car hovering nearby, a platoon of soldiers nestled in its belly.

"Who else stands in that body?" Pamir barked.

"I shall show you," the machine replied. Then two of the arms fell away, and the other two reached up, a violent jerk peeling back the rubber mask and the grit-sized brain, plus the elaborate shielding. A face lay behind the face. It was narrow, and in a fashion lovely, and it was austere, and it was allowing itself a knife-like smile as a new voice said to this mysterious man:

"Invite me inside your home."

"Why should I?" he countered, expecting some kind of murderous threat.

But instead of threatening, Miocene said simply, "Because I would like your help. In a small matter that must remain—I will warn you—our little secret."

III

Leading an army of captains was the Master Captain, and next in command was her loyal and infamous First Chair. Miocene was the second most powerful creature in this spectacular realm. She was tough and brutal, conniving and cold. And of all the impossible crap to happen, this was the worst. Pamir watched his guest peel away the last of her elaborate disguise. The AI was propped outside, set into a diagnostic mode. The soldiers remained hidden by the new darkness and their old tricks. It was just the two of them inside the apartment, which made no sense. If Miocene knew who he was, she would have simply told her soldiers to catch him and abuse him and then drag him to the ship's brig.

So she didn't know who he was.

Maybe.

The First Chair had a sharp face and black hair allowed to go a little white, and her body was tall and lanky and ageless and absolutely poised. She wore a simple uniform, mirrored in the fashion of all captains and decorated with a minimum of epaulets. For a long moment, she stared into the depths of Pamir's home. Watching for something? No, just having a conversation through a nexus. Then she closed off every link with the outer world, and turning toward her host, she used his present name.

Pamir nodded.

She used his last name.

Again, he nodded.

And then with a question mark riding the end of it, she offered a third name.

He said, "Maybe."

"It was or wasn't you?"

"Maybe," he said again.

She seemed amused. And then, there was nothing funny about any of this. The smile tightened, the mouth nearly vanishing. "I could look farther back in time," she allowed. "Perhaps I could dig up the moment when you left your original identity behind."

"Be my guest."

"I am your guest, so you are safe." She was taller than Pamir by a long measure—an artifact of his disguise. She moved closer to the way-ward captain, remarking, "Your origins don't interest me."

"Well then," he began.

And with a wink, he added, "So is it true, madam? Are you really in love with me?"

She laughed abruptly, harshly. Stepping away from him, she again regarded the apartment, this time studying its furnishings and little dec-orations. He had a modest home—a single room barely a hundred me-ters deep and twenty wide, the walls paneled with living wood and the ceiling showing the ruddy evening sky of a random world. With a calm voice, she announced, "I adore your talents, whoever you are."

"My talents?"

"With the aliens."

He said nothing.

"That mess with the harum-scarums . . . you found an elegant solu-tion to a difficult problem. You couldn't know it at the time, but you helped the ship and my Master, and by consequence, you've earned my thanks."

"What do you wish from me tonight, madam?"

"Tonight? Nothing. But tomorrow—early in the morning, I would hope—you will please apply your talents to a small matter. A relatively simple business, we can hope. Are you familiar with the J'Jal?"

Pamir held tight to his expression, his stance. Yet he couldn't help but feel a hard kick to his heart, a well-trained paranoia screaming, "Run! Now!"

"I have some experience with that species," he allowed. "Yes, madam."

"I am glad to hear it," said Miocene.

As a fugitive, Pamir had lived among the J'Jal on two separate oc-casions. Obviously, the First Chair knew much more about his past. The pressing question was if she knew only about his life five faces ago, or if she had seen back sixty-three faces—perilously close to the day when he permanently removed his captain's uniform.

She knew his real identity, or she didn't.

Pamir strangled his paranoia and put on a wide grin, shoulders man-aging a shrug while a calm voice inquired, "And why should I do this er-rand for you?"

Miocene had a cold way of smirking. "My request isn't reason enough?"

He held his mouth closed.

"Your neighbors didn't ask for your aid. Yet you gave it willingly, if rather secretly." She seemed angry but not entirely surprised. Behind those black eyes, calculations were being made, and then with a pragmatic tone, she informed him, "I will not investigate your past."

"Because you already have," he countered.

"To a point," she allowed. "Maybe a little farther than I first implied. But I won't use my considerable resources any more. If you help me."

"No," he replied.

She seemed to flinch.

"I don't know you," he lied. "But madam, according to your reputation, you are a bitch's bitch."

In any given century, how many times did the First Chair hear an insult delivered to her face? Yet the tall woman absorbed the blow with poise, and then she mentioned a figure of money. "In an open account, and at your disposal," she continued. "Use the funds as you wish, and when you've finished, use some or all of the remaining wealth to vanish again. And do a better job of it this time, you should hope."

She was offering a tidy fortune.

But why would the second most powerful entity on the ship dangle such a prize before him? Pamir considered triggering hidden machines. He went as far as activating a tiny nexus, using it to bring a battery of weapons into play. With a thought, he could temporarily kill Miocene. Then he would slip out of the apartment through one of three hidden routes, and with luck, escape the pursuing soldiers. And within a day, or two at most, he would be living a new existence in some other little avenue . . . or better, living alone in one of the very solitary places where he had stockpiled supplies . . .

Once again, Miocene confessed, "This is a confidential matter."

In other words, this was not official business for the First Chair.

"More to the point," she continued, "you won't help me as much as you will come to the aid of another soul."

Pamir deactivated the weapons, for the moment.

"Who deserves my help?" he inquired.

"There is a young male you should meet," Miocene replied. "A J'Jal man, of course."

"I'm helping him?"

"I would think not," she replied with a snort.

Then through a private nexus, she fed an address to Pamir. It was in the Fall Away district—a popular home for many species, including the J'Jal.

"The alien is waiting for you at his home," she continued.

Then with her cold smirk, she added, "At this moment, he is lying on the floor of his backmost room, and he happens to be very much dead."

IV

Every portion of the Great Ship had at least one bloodless designation left behind by the initial surveys, while the inhabited places wore one or twenty more names, poetic or blunt, simple or fabulously contrived. In most cases, the typical passenger remembered none of those labels. Every avenue and cavern and little sea was remarkable in its own right, but under that crush of novelty, few were unique enough to be famous.

Fall Away was an exception.

For reasons known only to them, the ship's builders had fashioned a tube from mirrored hyperfiber and cold basalt—the great shaft beginning not far beneath the heavy armor of the ship's bow and dropping for thousands of perfectly vertical kilometers. Myriad avenues funneled down to Fall Away. Ages ago, the ship's engineers etched roads and paths in the cylinder's surface, affording views to the curious. The ship's crew built homes perched on the endless brink, and they were followed by a wide array of passengers. Millions now lived along its spectacular length. Millions more pretended to live there. There were more famous places onboard the Great Ship, and several were arguably more beautiful. But no other address afforded residents an easier snobbery. "My home is on Fall Away," they would boast. "Come enjoy my view, if you have a free month or an empty year."

Pamir ignored the view. And when he was sure nobody was watching, he slipped inside the J'Jal's apartment.

The Milky Way wasn't the largest galaxy, but it was most definitely fertile. Experts routinely guessed that three hundred million worlds had evolved their own intelligent, technologically adept life. Within that great burst of natural invention, certain patterns were obvious. Half a dozen metabolic systems were favored. The mass and composition of a home world often shoved evolution down the same inevitable pathways. Humanoids were common; human beings happened to be a young example of an ancient pattern. Harum-scarums were another, as were the Glory and the Aabacks, the Mnotis and the Striders.

But even the most inexpert inorganic eye could tell those species apart. Each humanoid arose on a different life-tree. Some were giants, others quite tiny. Some were built for enormous worlds, while others were frail little wisps. Thick pelts of fur were possible, or bright masses of downy feathers. Even among the naked mock-primates, there was an enormous range when it came to hands and faces. Elaborate bones shouted, "I am nothing like a human." While the flesh itself was full of golden blood and DNA that proved its alienness.

And then, there were the J'Jal.

They had a human walk and a very human face, particularly in the normally green eyes. They were diurnal creatures. Hunter-gatherers from a world much like the Earth, they had roamed an open savanna for millions of years, using stone implements carved with hands that at first glance, and sometimes with a second glance, looked entirely human.

But the similarities reached even deeper. The J'Jal heart beat inside a spongy double-lung, and every breath pressed against a cage of rubbery white ribs, while the ancestral blood was a salty ruddy mix of iron inside a protein similar to hemoglobin. In fact, most of their proteins had a telltale resemblance to human types, as did great portions of their original DNA.

A mutation-by-mutation convergence was a preposterous explanation.

Ten million times more likely was a common origin. The Earth and J'Jal must have once been neighbors. Ages ago, one world evolved a simple, durable microbial life. A cometary impact splashed a piece of living crust into space, and with a trillion sleeping passengers safely entombed, the wreckage drifted free of the solar system. After a few light-years of cold oblivion, the crude ark slammed into a new world's atmosphere, and at least one microbe survived, happily eating every native pre-life ensemble of hydrocarbons before conquering its new realm.

Such things often happened in the galaxy's early times. At least half a dozen other worlds shared biochemistries with the Earth. But only the J'Jal world took such a similar evolutionary pathway.

In effect, the J'Jal were distant cousins.

And for many reasons, they were poor cousins, too.

———⚡———

Pamir stood over the body, examining its position and condition. Spider-legged machines did the same. Reaching inside the corpse with sound and soft bursts of X-rays, the machinery arrived at a rigorous conclusion they kept to themselves. With his own eyes and instincts, their owner wished to do his best, thank you.

It could have been a human male lying dead on the floor.

The corpse was naked, on his back, legs together and his arms thrown up over his head with hands open and every finger extended. His flesh was a soft brown. His hair was short and bluish-black. The J'Jal didn't have natural beards. But the hair on the body could have been human—a thin carpet on the nippled chest that thickened around the groin.

In death, his genitals had shriveled back into the body.

No mark was visible, and Pamir guessed that if he rolled the body over, there wouldn't be a wound on the backside either. But the man was utterly dead. Sure of it, he knelt down low, gazing at the decidedly human face, flinching just a little when the narrow mouth opened and a shallow breath was drawn into the dead man's lungs.

Quietly, Pamir laughed at himself.

The machines stood still, waiting for encouragement.

"The brain's gone," he offered, using his left hand to touch the forehead, feeling the faint warmth of a hibernating metabolism. "A shaped plasma bolt, something like that. Ate through the skull and cooked his soul."

The machines rocked back and forth on long legs.

"It's slag, I bet. The brain is. And some of the body got torched too. Sure." He rose now, looking about the bedroom with a careful gaze.

A set of clothes stood nearby, waiting to dress their owner.

Pamir disabled the clothes and laid them on the ground beside the corpse. "He lost ten or twelve kilos of flesh and bone," he decided. "And he's about ten centimeters shorter than he used to be."

Death was a difficult trick to achieve with immortals. And even in this circumstance, with the brain reduced to ruined bioceramics and mindless glass, the body had persisted with life. The surviving flesh had healed itself, within limits. Emergency genetics had been unleashed, reweaving the original face and scalp and a full torso that couldn't have seemed more lifelike. But when the genes had finished, no mind was found to interface with the rejuvenated body. So the J'Jal corpse fell into a stasis, and if no one had entered this apartment, it would have remained where it was, sipping at the increasingly stale air, its lazy metabolism eating its own flesh until it was a skeleton and shriveled organs and a gaunt, deeply mummified face.

He had been a handsome man, Pamir could see.

Regardless of the species, it was an elegant, tidy face.

"What do you see?" he finally asked.

The machines spoke, in words and raw data. Pamir listened, and then he stopped listening. Again, he thought about Miocene, asking himself why the First Chair would give one little shit about this very obscure man.

"Who is he?" asked Pamir, not for the first time.

A nexus was triggered. The latest, most thorough biography was delivered. The J'Jal had been born onboard the ship, his parents wealthy enough to afford the luxury of propagation. His family's money was made on a harum-scarum world, which explained his name. Sele'ium—a play on the harum-scarum convention of naming yourself after the elements. And as these things went, Sele'ium was just a youngster, barely five hundred years old, with a life story that couldn't seem more ordinary.

Pamir stared at the corpse, unsure what good it did.

Then he forced himself to walk around the apartment. It wasn't much larger than his home, but with a pricey view making it twenty times more expensive. The furnishings could have belonged to either species. The color schemes were equally ordinary. There were a few hundred books on display—a distinctly J'Jal touch—and Pamir had a machine read each volume from cover to cover. Then he led his helpers to every corner and closet, to new rooms and back to the same old rooms again, and he inventoried every surface and each object, including a sampling of dust. But there was little dust, so the dead man was either exceptionally neat, or somebody had carefully swept away every trace of their own presence, including bits of dried skin and careless hairs.

"Now what?"

He was asking himself that question, but the machines replied, "We do not know what is next, sir."

Again, Pamir stood over the breathing corpse.

"I'm not seeing something," he complained.

A look came over him, and he laughed at himself. Quietly. Briefly. Then he requested a small medical probe, and the probe was inserted, and through it he delivered a teasing charge.

The dead penis pulled itself out of the body.

"Huh," Pamir exclaimed.

Then he turned away, saying, "All right," while shaking his head. "We're going to search again, this place and the poor shit's life. Mote by mote and day by day, if we have to."

V

Built in the upper reaches of Fall Away, overlooking the permanent clouds of the Little-Lot, the facility was an expansive collection of natural caverns and minimal tunnels. Strictly speaking, the Faith of the Many Joinings wasn't a church or holy place, though it was wrapped securely around an ancient faith. Nor was it a commercial house, though money and barter items were often given to its resident staff. And it wasn't a brothel, as far as the ship's codes were concerned. Nothing sexual happened within its walls, and no one involved in its mysteries gave his or her body for anything as crass as income. Most passengers didn't even realize that a place such as this existed. Among those who did, most regarded it as an elaborate and very strange meetinghouse—likeminded souls passed through its massive wooden door to make friends, and when possible, fall in love. But for the purposes of taxes and law, the captains had decided on a much less romantic designation: The facility was an exceptionally rare thing to which an ancient human word applied.

It was a library.

On the Great Ship, normal knowledge was preserved inside laser files and superconducting baths. Access might be restricted, but every word and captured image was within reach of buried nexuses. Libraries were an exception. What the books held was often unavailable anywhere else, making them precious, and that's why they offered a kind of privacy difficult to match, as well as an almost religious holiness to the followers of the Faith.

"May I help you, sir?"

Pamir was standing before a set of tall shelves, arms crossed and his face wearing a tight, furious expression. "Who are you?" he asked, not bothering to look at the speaker.

"My name is Leon'rd."

"I've talked to others already," Pamir allowed.

"I know, sir."

"They came at me, one by one. But they weren't important enough." He turned, staring at the newcomer. "Leon'rd," he grunted. "Are you important enough to help me?"

"I hope so, sir. I do."

The J'Jal man was perhaps a little taller than Pamir. He was wearing a purplish-black robe and long blue hair secured in back as a simple horsetail. His eyes were indistinguishable from a human's green eyes. His skin was a pinkish brown. As the J'Jal preferred, his feet were bare. They could be human feet, plantigrade and narrow, with five toes and a similar architecture of bones, the long arches growing taller when the nervous toes curled up. With a slight bow, the alien remarked, "I am the ranking librarian, sir. I have been at this post for ten millennia and eighty-eight years. Sir."

Pamir had adapted his face and clothing. What the J'Jal saw was a security officer dressed in casual garb. A badge clung to his sleeve, and every roster search identified him as a man with honors and a certain clout. But his disguise reached deeper. The crossed arms flexed for a moment, hinting at lingering tensions. His new face tightened until the eyes were squinting, affecting a cop's challenging stare; and through the pinched mouth, he said, "I'm looking for somebody."

To his credit, the librarian barely flinched.

"My wife," Pamir said. "I want to know where she is."

"No."

"Pardon me?"

"I know what you desire, but I cannot comply."

As they faced each other, a giant figure stepped into the room. The harum-scarum noticed the two males facing off, and with an embarrassment rare for the species, she carefully backed out of sight.

The librarian spoke to his colleagues, using a nexus.

Every door to this chamber was quietly closed and securely locked.

"Listen," Pamir said.

Then he said nothing else.

After a few moments, the J'Jal said, "Our charter is clear. The law is defined. We offer our patrons privacy and opportunity, in that order. Without official clearance, sir, you may not enter this facility to obtain facts or insights of any type."

"I'm looking for my wife," he repeated.

"And I can appreciate your—"

"Quiet," Pamir growled, his arms unfolding, the right hand holding a small, illegal plasma torch. With a flourish, he aimed at his helpless target, and he said one last time, "I am looking for my wife."

"Don't," the librarian begged.

The weapon was pointed at the bound volumes. The smallest burst would vaporize untold pages.

"No," Leon'rd moaned, desperately trying to alert the room's weapon suppression systems. But none was responding.

Again, he said, "No."

"I love her," Pamir claimed.

"I understand."

"Do you understand love?"

Leon'rd seemed offended. "Of course I understand—"

"Or does it have to be something ugly and sick before you can appreciate, even a little bit, what it means to be in love."

The J'Jal refused to speak.

"She's vanished," Pamir muttered.

"And you think she has been here?"

"At least once, yes."

The librarian was swiftly searching for a useful strategy. A general alarm was sounding, but the doors he had locked for good reasons suddenly refused to unlock. His staff and every other helping hand might as well have been on the far side of the ship. And if the gun discharged, it would take critical seconds to fill the room with enough nitrogen to stop the fire and enough narcotics to shove a furious human to the floor.

Leon'rd had no choice. "Perhaps I can help you, yes."

Pamir showed a thin, unpleasant grin. "That's the attitude."

"If you told me your wife's name—"

"She wouldn't use it," he warned.

"Or show me a holo of her, perhaps."

The angry husband shook his head. "She's changed her appearance. At least once, maybe more times."

"Of course."

"And her gender, maybe."

The librarian absorbed that complication. He had no intention of giving this stranger what he wanted, but if they could just draw this ugly business out for long enough . . . until a platoon of security troops could swoop in and take back their colleague . . .

"Here," said Pamir, feeding him a minimal file.

"What is this?"

"Her boyfriend, from what I understand."

Leon'rd stared at the image and the attached biography. The soft green eyes had barely read the name when they grew huge—a meaningful J'Jal expression—and with a sigh much like a human sigh, he admitted, "I know this man."

"Did you?"

Slowly, the implication of those words was absorbed.

"What do you mean? Is something wrong?"

"Yeah, my wife is missing. And this murdered piece of shit is the only one who can help me find her. Besides you, that is."

Leon'rd asked for proof of the man's death.

"Proof?" Pamir laughed. "Maybe I should call my boss and tell her that I found a deceased J'Jal, and you and I can let the law do its important and loud and very public work?"

A moment later, with a silent command, the librarian put an end to the general alert. There was no problem here, he lied; and with the slightest bow, he asked, "May I trust you to keep this matter confidential, sir?"

"Do I look trustworthy?"

The J'Jal bristled but said nothing. Then he stared at shelves at the far end of the room, walking a straight line that took him to a slender volume that he withdrew and opened, elegant fingers beginning to flip through the thin plastic pages.

With a bully's abruptness, Pamir grabbed the prize. The cover was a soft wood stained blue to identify its subject as being a relative novice. The pages were plastic, thin but dense, with a running account of the dead man's progress. Over the course of the last century, the librarians had met with Sele'ium on numerous occasions, and they had recorded his uneven progress with this very difficult faith. Audio transcripts drawn from a private journal let him speak again, explaining his mind to himself and every interested party. "My species is corrupt and tiny," Sele'ium had confessed with a remarkably human voice. "Every species is tiny and foul, and only together, joined in a perfect union, can we create a worthy society—a universe genuinely united."

A few pages held holos—stark, honest images of religious devotion that most of the galaxy would look upon as abominations. Pamir barely lingered on any picture. He had a clear guess about what he was looking for, and it helped that only one of the J'Jal's wives was human.

The final pages were key. Pamir stared at the last image. Then with a low snort and a disgusted shake of the head, he announced, "This must be her."

"But it isn't," said the librarian.

"No, it's got to be," he persisted. "A man should be able to recognize his own wife. Shouldn't he?"

Leon'rd showed the barest of grins. "No. I know this woman rather well, and she is not—"

"Where's her book?" Pamir snapped.

"No," the librarian said. "Believe me, this is not somebody you know."

"Prove it."

Silence.

"What's her name?"

Leon'rd straightened, working hard to seem brave.

Then Pamir placed the plasma torch against a random shelf, allowing the tip of the barrel to heat up to where smoke rose as the red wood binding of a true believer began to smolder.

The woman's journal was stored in a different room, far deeper inside the library. Leon'rd called for it to be brought to them, and then he stood close while Pamir went through the pages, committing much of it to a memory nexus. At one point, he said, "If you'd let me just borrow these things."

The J'Jal face flushed, and a tight hateful voice replied, "If you tried to take them, you would have to kill me."

Pamir showed him a wink.

"A word for the not-so-wise?" he said. "If I were you, I wouldn't give my enemies any easy ideas."

VI

How could one species prosper, growing in reach and wealth as well as in numbers, while a second species, blessed with the same strengths, exists for a hundred times longer and still doesn't matter to the galaxy?

Scholars and bigots had deliberated that question for ages.

The J'Jal evolved on a lush warm world, blue seas wrapped around green continents, the ground fat with metal ores and hydrocarbons, and a massive moon riding across the sky, helping keep the axis tilted just enough to invite mild seasons. Perhaps that wealth had been a bad thing. Born on a poorer world, humans had evolved to live in tiny, adaptable bands of twenty or so—everyone related to everyone, by blood or by marriage. But the early J'Jals moved in troops of a hundred or more, which meant a society wrapped around a more tolerant politics. Harmony was a given. Conflicts were resolved quietly, if possible; nothing was more precious to the troop than its own venerable peace. And with natural life spans reaching three centuries, change was a slow, fitful business brought on by consensus, or when absolutely necessary, by surrendering your will to the elders.

But quirks of nature are only one explanation for the future. Many great species had developed patiently. Some of the most famous, like the Ritkers and harum-scarums, were still tradition-bound creatures. Even humans had that sorry capacity: The wisdom of dead Greeks and lost Hebrews was followed long after their words had value. But the J'Jal were much more passionate about ancestors and their left-behind thoughts. For them, the past was a treasure, and their early civilizations were hide-bound and enduring machines that would remember every wrong turn and every quiet success.

After a couple hundred thousand years of flint and iron, humans stepped into space, while it took the J'Jal millions of years to contrive reasons for that kind of adventure.

That was a murderous bit of bad fortune.

The J'Jal solar system had metal-rich worlds and watery moons, and its neighbor suns were mature G-class stars where intelligence arose many times. While the J'Jal sat at home, happily memorizing the speeches of old queens, three different alien species colonized their outer worlds—ignoring galactic law and ancient conventions in the process.

Unknown to the J'Jal, great wars were being waged in their sky.

The eventual winner was a tiny creature accustomed to light gravity and the most exotic technologies. The K'Mal were cybernetic and quick-lived, subject to fads and whims and sudden convulsive changes of government. By the time the J'Jal launched their first rocket, the K'Mal outnumbered them in their own solar system. Millions of years later, that moment in history still brought shame. The J'Jal rocket rose into a low orbit, triggering a K'Mal fleet to lift from bases on the moon's hidden face. The rocket was destroyed, and suddenly the J'Jal went from being the masters of Paradise to an obscure creature locked on the surface of one little world.

Wars were fought, and won.

Peaces held, and collapsed, and the new wars ended badly.

True slavery didn't exist for the losers, even in the worst stretches of the long Blackness. And the K'Mal weren't wicked tyrants or unthinking administrators. But a gradual decay stole away the wealth of the J'Jal world. Birthrates plunged. Citizens emigrated, forced to work in bad circumstances for a variety of alien species. Those left home lived on an increasingly poisonous landscape, operating the deep mantle mines and the enormous railguns that spat the bones of their world into someone else's space.

While humans were happily hamstringing mammoths on the plains of Asia, the J'Jal were a beaten species scattered thinly across a hundred worlds. Other species would have lost their culture, and where they survived, they might have split into dozens of distinct and utterly obscure species. But the J'Jal proved capable in one extraordinary endeavor: Against every abuse, they managed to hold tight to their shared past, beautiful and otherwise; and in small ways, and then in slow large ways, they adapted to their far flung existence.

VII

"You'll be helping another soul."

Miocene had promised that much and said little else. She knew the dead J'Jal would point him to the library, and she had to know that he was bright enough to realize it was the human woman who mattered. Why the First Chair cared about the life of an apparently unremarkable passenger, Pamir couldn't guess. Or rather, he could guess too easily, drawing up long lists of motivations, each entry reasonable, and most if not all of them ridiculously wrong.

The human was named Sorrel, and it had been Sorrel since she was born two centuries ago. Unless she was older than that, and her biography was a masterful collection of inspired lies.

Like most of the library's patrons, she made her home on Fall Away. Yet even among that wealthy company, she was blessed. Not one but two trust funds kept her economy well fed. Her rich father had emigrated to a colony world before she was born, leaving his local assets in her name. While the mother—a decorated member of the diplomatic corps—had died on the ill-fated Hakkaleen mission. In essence, Sorrel was an orphan. But by most signs, she didn't suffer too badly. For the next several decades, she had appeared happy and unremarkable, wealthy and untroubled, and nothing Pamir found said otherwise.

What was the old harum-scarum saying?

"Nothing is as massive as the universe, but nothing is half as large as a sentient, imaginative mind."

Some time ago, the young woman began to change.

Like many young adults, Sorrel took an early vow of celibacy. With a million years of life stretching before her, why hurry into sex and love, disappointment and heartbreak? She had human friends, but because of her mother's diplomatic roots, she knew quite a few aliens too. For several years, her closest companions were a janusian couple—double organisms where the male was a parasite rooted in his spouse's back. Then her circle of alien friends widened . . . which seemed perfectly normal. Pamir searched the archives of forgotten security eyes and amateur documentaries, finding glimpses of luncheons and shopping adventures in the company of other species. Oxygen breathers; the traditional human allies. Then came the luxury cruise across a string of little oceans spread through the interior of the Great Ship—a brief voyage accomplished in the midst of the circumnavigation of the Milky Way—and near the end of that tame adventure, while drifting on a dim cold smooth-as-skin methane sea, she took her first lover.

He was a J'Jal, as it happened.

Pamir saw enough on the security eyes to fill in the blanks.

Cre'llan was a spectacularly wealthy individual, and ancient, and in a Faith that cherished its privacy, he flaunted his membership and his beliefs. Elaborate surgeries had reshaped his penis to its proper form. Everyone involved in the Many Joinings endured similar cosmetic work; a uniform code applied to both genders, and where no gender existed, one was invented for them. During his long life, Cre'llan had married hundreds if not thousands of aliens, and then on that chill night he managed to seduce a young virginal human.

After the cruise, Sorrel tried to return to her old life. But three days later she visited the library, and within the week, she underwent her own physical reconfigurations.

Pamir had seen glimpses of the surgery in her journal—autodocs and J'Jal overseers hovering around a lanky pale body. And when he closed his eyes now, concentrating on the buried data reserve, he could slowly and carefully flip his way through the other pages of that elaborate but still incomplete record.

After a year as a novice, Sorrel purchased a bare rectangle of stone and hyperfiber some fifty kilometers directly beneath the library. The apartment she built was deep and elaborate, full of luxurious rooms as well as expansive chambers that could be configured to meet the needs of almost any biology. But while every environmental system was the best available, sometimes those fancy machines didn't interact well with one another, and with the right touch, they were very easy to sabotage.

⸺⸺⸺

"Is it a serious problem, sir?"

"Not for me," Pamir allowed. "Not for you, I'd guess. But if you depend on peroxides, like the Ooloops do, then the air is going to taste sour. And after a few breaths, you'll probably lose consciousness."

"I understand," the apartment offered.

Pamir was standing in the service hallway, wearing his normal rough face as well as the durable jersey and stiff back of a life-long technician. "I'll need to wander, if I'm going to find your trouble. Which is probably an eager filter, or a failed link of code, or a leak, or who knows what."

"Do whatever is necessary," the soft male voice replied.

"And thanks for this opportunity," Pamir added. "I appreciate new business."

"Of course, sir. And thank you."

The apartment's usual repair firm was temporarily closed due to a bureaucratic war with the Office of Environments. A search of available candidates had steered the AI towards the best candidate. Pamir was releasing a swarm of busy drones that vanished inside the walls, and he continued walking down the hallway, pausing at a tiny locked door. "What's past here?"

"A living chamber."

"For a human?"

"Yes, sir."

Pamir stepped back. "I don't need to bother anyone."

"No one will be." The lock and seal broke. "My lady demands that her home be ready for any and all visitors. Your work is a priority."

Pamir nodded, stepping through the narrow slot.

His first thought was that captains didn't live half as well as this. The room was enormous yet somehow intimate, carpeted with living furs, art treasures standing about waiting to be admired, chairs available for any kind of body, and as an added feature, at least fifty elaborate games laid out on long boards, the pieces playing against each other until there was a winner, after which they would play again. Even the air tasted of wealth, scrubbed and filtered, perfumed and pheromoned. And in that perfect atmosphere, the only sound was the quiet precise and distant singing of a certain alien flower.

Llano vibra.

Pamir looked at monitors and spoke through nexuses, and he did absolutely nothing of substance. What he wanted to accomplish was already done. By a handful of means, the apartment was now invested with hidden ears and eyes. Everything else was for his senses and to lend him more credibility.

A tall diamond wall stood on the far side of the enormous bedroom, and beyond, five hectares of patio hung over the open air. A grove of highly bred Ilano vibra was rooted in a patio pot, its music passing through a single open door. The young woman was sitting nearby, doing nothing. Pamir looked at Sorrel for a moment, and then she lifted her head to glance in his general direction. He tried to decide what he was seeing. She was clothed but barefoot. She was strikingly lovely, but in an odd fashion that he couldn't quite name. Her pale skin had a genuine glow, a capacity to swallow up the ambient light and cast it back into the world in a softer form. Her hair was silver-white and thick, with the tips suddenly turning to black. She had a smooth girlish face and a tiny nose and blue-white eyes pulled close together, and her mouth was broad and elegant and exceptionally sad.

It was the sadness that made her striking, Pamir decided.

Then he found himself near the door, staring at her, realizing that nothing was simple about her sadness or his reactions.

Sorrel glanced at him a second time.

A moment later, the apartment inquired, "Is the lady a point of technical interest, sir?"

"Sure." Pamir laughed and stepped back from the diamond wall.

"Have you found the problem? She wishes to know."

"Two problems, and yes. They're being fixed now."

"Very well. Thank you."

Pamir meant to mention his fee. Tradesmen always talked money. But there came a sound—the soft musical whine of a rope deploying—that quickly fell away into silence.

The apartment stopped speaking to him.

"What—?" Pamir began. Then he turned and looked outside again. The woman wasn't alone anymore. A second figure had appeared, dressed like a rock climber and running across the patio towards Sorrel. He was a human or J'Jal, and apparently male. From where Pamir stood, he couldn't tell much more. But he could see the urgency in the intruder's step and a right hand that was holding what could be a weapon, and an instant later, Pamir was running too, leaping through the open door as the stranger closed on the woman.

Sorrel stared at the newcomer.

"I don't recognize his face," the apartment warned her, shouting now. "My lady—!"

The inertia vanished from her body. Sorrel leapt up and took two steps backwards before deciding to stand and fight. It was her best hope, Pamir agreed. She lifted her arms and lowered them again. She was poised if a little blank in the face, as if she was surrendering her survival to a set of deeply buried instincts.

The stranger reached for her neck with his left hand.

With a swift clean motion, she grabbed the open hand and twisted the wrist back. But the running body picked her off her feet, and both of them fell to the polished opal floor of the patio.

The man's right hand held a knife.

With a single plunge, the stranger pushed the blade into her chest, aiming for the heart. He was working with an odd precision, or perhaps by feel. He was trying to accomplish something very specific, and when she struggled, he would strike her face with the back of his free hand.

The blade dove deeper.

A small, satisfied moan leaked out of him, as if success was near, and then Pamir drove his boot into the smiling mouth.

The stranger was human, and furious.

He climbed to his feet, fending off the next three blows, and then he reached back and pulled out a small railgun that he halfway aimed, letting loose a dozen flecks of supersonic iron.

Pamir dropped, hit in the shoulder and arm.

The injured woman lay between them, bleeding and pained. The hilt of the knife stood up out of her chest, a portion of the hyperfiber blade reflecting the brilliant red of the blood.

With his good arm, Pamir grabbed the hilt and tugged.

There was a soft clatter as a Darmion crystal spilled out of her body along with the blade. This was what the thief wanted. He saw the glittering shape and couldn't resist the urge to grab at the prize. A small fortune was within reach, but then his own knife was driven clear through his forearm, and he screamed in pain and rage.

Pamir cut him twice again.

The little railgun rose up and fired once, twice, and then twice more.

Pamir's body was dying, but he still had the focus and strength to lift the man—a bullish fellow with short limbs and an infinite supply of blood, it seemed. Pamir kept slashing and pushing, and somewhere the railgun was dropped and left behind, and now the man struck him with a fist and his elbows and then tried to use his knee. Pamir grabbed the knee as it rose, borrowing its momentum as well as the last of his own strength to shove the thief against a railing of simple oak, and with a last grunt, flung him over the edge.

Only Pamir was standing there now.

Really, it was a beautiful view. With his chest ripped open and a thousand emergency genes telling his body to rest, he gazed out into the open expanse of Fall Away. Thirty kilometers across and lit by a multitude of solar-bright lights, it was a glory of engineering, and perhaps, a masterpiece of art. The countless avenues that fed into Fall Away often brought water and other liquids, and the captains' engineers had devised a system of airborne rivers—diamond tubes that carried the fluids down in a tangle of spirals and rings, little lakes gathering in pools held aloft by invisible means. And always, there were flyers moving in the air—organic and not, alive and not—and there was the deep musical buzz of a million joyous voices, and there were forests of epiphytes clinging to the wall, and there was a wet wind that hadn't ceased in sixty thousand years, and Pamir forgot why he was standing here. What was this place? Turning around, he discovered a beautiful woman with a gruesome wound in her chest telling him to sit, please. Sit. Sir, she said, please, please, you need to rest.

VIII

The Faith of the Many Joinings.

Where it arose first was a subject of some contention. Several widely scattered solar systems were viable candidates, but no single expert held the definitive evidence. Nor could one prophet or pervert take credit for this quasi-religious belief. But what some of the J'Jal believed was that every sentient soul had the same value. Bodies were facades, and metabolisms were mere details, and social systems varied in the same way that individual lives varied, according to choice and whim and a deniable sense of right. What mattered were the souls within all of these odd packages. What a wise soul wished to do was to befriend entities from different histories, and when possible, fall in love with them, linking their spirits together through the ancient pleasures of the flesh.

There was no single prophet, and the Faith had no birthplace. Which was a problem for the true believers. How could such an intricate, odd faith arise simultaneously in such widely scattered places? But what was a flaw might be a blessing, too. Plainly, divine gears were turning the universe, and this unity was just further evidence of how right and perfect their beliefs had to be. Unless the Faith was the natural outgrowth of the J'Jal's own nature: A social species is thrown across the sky, and every home belongs to more powerful species, and the entire game of becoming lovers to the greater ones is as inevitable and unremarkable as standing on their own two bare feet.

Pamir held to that ordinary opinion.

He glanced at his own bare feet for a moment, sighed and then examined his arm and shoulder and chest. The wounds had healed to where nothing was visible. Unscarred flesh had spread over the holes, while the organs inside him were quickly pulling themselves back into perfect condition. He was fit enough to sit up, but he didn't. Instead, he lay on the soft chaise set on the open-air patio, listening to the Ilano vibra. He was alone, the diamond wall to the bedroom turned black. For a moment, he thought about things that were obvious, and then he played with the subtle possibilities that sprang up from what was obvious.

The thief—a registered felon with a long history of this exact kind of work—had fallen for several kilometers before a routine security patrol noticed him, plucking him out of the sky before he could spoil any-body else's day.

The unlucky man was under arrest and would probably serve a cen-tury or two for his latest crime.

"This stinks," Pamir muttered.

"Sir?" said the apartment. "Is there a problem? Might I help?"

Pamir considered, and said, "No."

He sat up and said, "Clothes," and his technician's uniform pulled itself around him. Its fabric had healed, if not quite so thoroughly as his own body. He examined what could be a fleck of dried blood, and after a moment, he said, "Boots?"

"Under your seat, sir."

Pamir was giving his feet to his boots when she walked out through the bedroom door.

"I have to thank you," Sorrel remarked. She was tall and elegant in a shopworn way, wearing a long gray robe and no shoes. In the face, she looked pretty but sorrowful, and up close, that sadness was a deep thing reaching well past today. "For everything you did, thank you."

A marathon of tears had left her eyes red and puffy.

He stared, and she stared back. For a moment, it was as if she saw nothing. Then Sorrel seemed to grow aware of his interest, and with a shiver, she told him, "Stay as long as you wish. My home will feed you, and if you want, you can take anything that interests you. As a me-mento . . ."

"Where's the crystal?" he interrupted.

She touched herself between her breasts. The Darmion was back home, resting beside her enduring heart. According to half a dozen species, the crystal gave its possessor a keen love of life and endless joy—a bit of mystic noise refuted by the depressed woman who was wearing it.

"I don't want your little rock," he muttered.

She didn't seem relieved or amused. With a nod, she said, "Thank you," one last time, planning to end this here.

"You need a better security net," Pamir remarked.

"Perhaps so," she admitted, without much interest.

"What's your name?"

She said, "Sorrel," and then the rest of it. Human names were long and complex and unwieldy. But she said it all, and then she looked at him in a new fashion. "What do I call you?"

He used his most recent identity.

"Are you any good with security systems?" Sorrel inquired.

"Better than most."

She nodded.

"You want me to upgrade yours?"

That amused her somehow. A little smile broke across the milky face, and for a moment, the bright pink tip of her tongue pointed at him. Then she shook her head, saying, "No, not for me," as if he should have realized as much. "I have a good friend . . . a dear old friend . . . who has some rather heavy fears . . ."

"Can he pay?"

"I will pay. Tell him it's my gift."

"So who's this worried fellow?"

She said, "Gallium," in an alien language.

Genuinely surprised, Pamir asked, "What the hell is a harum-scarum doing, admitting he's scared?"

Sorrel nodded appreciatively.

"He admits nothing," she added. Then again, she smiled . . . a warmer expression, this time. Fetching and sweet, even wonderful, and for Pamir, that expression seemed to last long after he walked out of the apartment and on to his next job.

XI

The harum-scarum was nearly three meters tall, massive and thickly armored, loud and yet oddly serene at the same time, passionate about his endless bravery and completely transparent when he told his lies. His home was close to Fall Away, tucked high inside one of the minor avenues. He was standing behind his final door—a slab of hyperfiber-braced diamond—and with a distinctly human gesture, he waved off the uninvited visitor. "I do not need any favors," he claimed, speaking through his breathing mouth. "I am as secure as anyone and twelve times more competent than you when it comes to defending myself." Then with a blatant rudeness, he allowed his eating mouth to deliver a long wet belch.

"Funny," said Pamir. "A woman wishes to buy my services, and you are Gallium, her dear old friend. Is that correct?"

"What is the woman's name?"

"Why? Didn't you hear me the first time?"

"Sorrel, you claimed." He pretended to concentrate, and then with a little too much certainty said, "I do not know this ape-woman."

"Is that so?" Pamir shook his head. "She knows you."

"She is mistaken."

"So then how did you know she was human? Since I hadn't quite mentioned that yet."

The question won a blustery look from the big black eyes. "What are you implying to me, little ape-man?"

Pamir laughed at him. "Why? Can't you figure it out for yourself?"

"Are you insulting me?"

"Sure."

That won a deep silence.

With a fist only a little larger than one of the alien's knuckles, Pamir wrapped on the diamond door. "I'm insulting you and your ancestors. There. By the ship's codes and your own painful customs, you are now free to step out here, in the open, and beat me until I am dead for a full week."

The giant shook with fury, and nothing happened. One mouth expanded, gulping down deep long breaths, while the other mouth puckered into a tiny dimple—a harum-scarum on the brink of a pure vengeful rage. But Gallium forced himself to do nothing, and when the anger finally began to diminish, he gave an inaudible signal, causing the outer two doors to drop and seal tight.

Pamir looked left and then right. The narrow avenue was well-lit and empty, and by every appearance, it was safe.

Yet the creature had been terrified.

One more time, he paged his way through Sorrel's journal. Among those husbands were two harum-scarums. No useful name had been mentioned in the journal, but it was obvious which of them was Gallium. Lying about his fear was in character for the species. But how could a confirmed practitioner of this singular faith deny that he had even met the woman?

Pamir needed to find the other husbands.

A hundred different routes lay before him. But as harum-scarums liked to say, "The shortest line stretches between points that touch."

Gallium's security system was ordinary, and it was porous, and with thousands of years of experience in these matters, it took Pamir less than a day to subvert codes and walk through the front doors.

"Who is with me?" a voice cried out from the farthest room.

In J'Jal, curiously.

Then, "Who's there?" in human.

And finally, as an afterthought, the alien screamed, "You are in my realm, and unwelcome." In his own tongue, he promised, "I will forgive you, if you run away at this moment."

"Sorrel won't let me run," Pamir replied.

The last room was a minor fortress buttressed with slabs of high-grade hyperfiber and bristling with weapons, legal and otherwise. A pair of rail-guns followed Pamir's head, ready to batter his mind if not quite kill it. Tightness built in his throat, but he managed to keep the fear out of his voice. "Is this where you live now? In a little room at the bottom of an ugly home?"

"You like to insult," the harum-scarum observed.

"It passes my time," he replied.

From behind the hyperfiber, Gallium said, "I see an illegal weapon."

"Good. Since I'm carrying one."

"If you try to harm me, I will kill you. And I will destroy your mind, and you will be no more."

"Understood," Pamir said.

Then he sat—a gesture of submission on almost every world. He sat on the quasi-crystal tiling on the floor of the bright hallway, glancing at the portraits on the nearby walls. Harum-scarums from past ages stood in defiant poses. Ancestors, presumably. Honorable men and woman who could look at their cowering descendant with nothing but a fierce contempt.

After a few moments, Pamir said, "I'm pulling my weapon into plain view."

"Throw it beside my door."

The plasma gun earned a respectful silence. It slid across the floor and clattered to a stop, and then a mechanical arm unfolded, slapping a hyperfiber bowl over it, and then covering the bowl an explosive charge set to obliterate the first hand that tried to free the gun within.

The hyperfiber door lifted.

Gallium halfway filled the room beyond. He was standing in the middle of a closet jammed with supplies, staring at Pamir, the armored plates of his body flexing, exposing their sharp edges.

"You must very much need this work," he observed.

"Except I'm not doing my work," Pamir replied. "Frankly, I've sort of lost interest in the project."

Confused, the harum-scarum stood taller. "Then why have you gone to such enormous trouble?"

"What you need," Pamir mentioned, "is a small, well-charged plasma gun. That makes a superior weapon."

"They are illegal and hard to come by," argued Gallium.

"Your rail-guns are criminal, too." Just like with the front doors, there was a final door made of diamond reinforced with a meshwork of hyperfiber. "But I bet you appreciate what the shaped plasma can do to a living mind."

Silence.

"Funny," Pamir continued. "Not that long ago, I found a corpse that ran into that exact kind of tool."

The alien's back couldn't straighten anymore, and the armor plates were flexing as much as possible. With a quiet voice—an almost begging voice—Gallium asked the human, "Who was the corpse?"

"Sele'ium."

Again, silence.

"Who else has died that way?" Pamir asked. It was a guess, but not much of one. When no answer was offered, he added, "You've never been this frightened. In your long, ample life, you have never imagined that fear could eat at you this way. Am I right?"

Now the back began to collapse.

A miserable little voice said, "It just worsens."

"Why?"

The harum-scarum dipped his head for a moment.

"Why does the fear get worse and worse?"

"Seven of us now."

"Seven?"

"Lost." A human despair rode with that single word. "Eight, if you are telling the truth about the J'Jal."

"What eight?" Pamir asked.

Gallium refused to say.

"I know who you are," he continued. "Eight of Sorrel's husbands, and you. Is that right?"

"Her past husbands," the alien corrected.

"What about current lovers—?"

"There are none."

"No?"

"She is celibate," the giant said with a deep longing. Then he dropped his gaze, adding, "When we started to die, she gave us up. Physically, and legally as well."

Gallium missed his human wife. It showed in his stance and voice and how the great hand trembled, reaching up to touch the cool pane of diamond while he added, "She is trying to save us. But she doesn't know how—"

A sudden ball of coherent plasma struck the pane just then. No larger than a human heart, it dissolved the diamond and the hand, and the grieving face, and everything that lay beyond those dark lonely eyes.

✕

Pamir saw nothing but the flash, and then came a concussive blast that threw him off his feet. For an instant, he lay motionless. A cloud of atomized carbon and flesh filled the cramped hallway. He listened and heard nothing. At least for the next few moments, he was completely deaf. Keeping low, he rolled until a wall blocked his way. Then he started to breathe, scalding his lungs, and he held his breath, remaining absolutely still, waiting for a second blast to shove past.

Nothing happened.

With his mouth to the floor, Pamir managed a hot but breathable sip of air. The cloud was thinning. His hearing was returning, accompanied by a tireless high-pitched hum. A figure swam into view, tall and menacing—a harum-scarum, presumably one of the dead man's honored ancestors. He remembered that the hallway was littered with the portraits. Pamir saw a second figure, and then a third. He was trying to recall how many images there had been . . . because he could see a fourth figure now, and that seemed like one too many . . .

The plasma gun fired again. But it hadn't had time enough to build a killing charge, and the fantastic energies were wasted in a light show and a burst of blistering wind.

Again the air filled with dirt and gore.

Pamir leaped up and retreated.

Gallium was a nearly headless corpse, enormous even when mangled and stretched out on his back. The little room was made tinier with him on the floor. When their owner died, the rail-guns had dropped into their diagnostic mode, and waking them would take minutes, or days. The diamond door was shredded and useless. When the cloud fell away again, in another few moments, Pamir would be exposed and probably killed.

Like Gallium, he first used the J'Jal language.

"Hello," he called out.

The outer door was open and still intact, but its simple trigger was useless to him. It was sensitive only to pressure from a familiar hand. Staring out into the hallway, he shouted, "Hello," once again.

In the distance, a shape began to resolve itself.

"I am dead," he continued. "You have me trapped here, my friend." Nothing.

"Do what you wish, but before you cook me, I would love to know what this is about."

The shape seemed to drift one way, then back again.

Pamir jerked one of the dead arms off the floor. Then he started to position it, laying the broad palm against the wall, close to the door's trigger. But that was the easy part of this, he realized.

"You're a clever soul," he offered. "Allow a human to open the way for you. I outsmart the harum-scarum's defenses, and then you can claim both of us."

How much time before another recharge?

A few seconds, he guessed.

The corpse suddenly flinched and the arm dropped with a massive thunk.

"Shit," Pamir muttered.

On a high shelf was a plate, small but dense as metal. He took hold of it, made a few practice flings with his wrist, and then once again called out, "I wish you would tell me what this is about. Because I haven't got a clue."

Nothing.

In human, Pamir said, "Who the hell are you?"

The cloud was clearing again, revealing the outlines of a biped standing down the hallway, maybe ten meters from him.

Kneeling, Pamir again grabbed the dead arm. Emergency genes and muscle memory began to fight against him, the strength of a giant forcing him to grunt as he pushed the hand to where it was set beside the trigger. Then he threw all of his weight on the hand, forcing it to stay in place. For a moment, he panted. Then he grabbed the heavy plate with his left hand, and with a gasping voice, he said, "One last chance to explain."

The biped was beginning to aim.

"Bye-bye, then."

Pamir flipped the plate, aiming at a target barely three meters away. And in the same instant, he let the dead hand fall onto the trigger. A slab of hyperfiber slid from the ceiling, and the final door was shut. It could withstand two or three blasts from a plasma gun, but eventually it would be gnawed away. Which was why he flipped the plate onto the floor where it skipped and rolled, clipping the edge of the shaped charge of explosives that capped his own gun.

There was a sudden sharp thunder.

The door was left jammed shut by the blast. Pamir spent the next twenty minutes using a dead hand and every override to lift the door far enough to crawl underneath. But a perfectly symmetrical blast had left his own weapon where it lay, untouched beneath a bowl of mirror-bright hyperfiber.

His enemy would have been blown back up the hallway.

Killed briefly, or maybe just scared away.

Pamir lingered for a few minutes, searching the dead man's home for clues that refused to be found, and then he slipped back out into the public avenue—still vacant and safe to the eye, but possessing a palpable menace that he could now feel for himself.

XI

A ninety-second tube ride placed him beside Sorrel's front door. The apartment addressed him by the only name it knew, observing, "You are injured, sir." Performing its own rapid examination, a distinct alarm entered into an otherwise officious voice. "Do you know how badly you are injured, sir?"

"I've got a fair guess," Pamir allowed, an assortment of shrapnel still buried inside his leg and belly, giving him a rolling limp. "Where's the lady?"

"Where you left her, sir. On the patio."

Everyone was terrified, it seemed, except for her. But why should she worry? Sorrel had only been knifed by a quick-and-dirty thief, which on the scale of crimes was practically nothing.

"Have her come to her bedroom."

"Sir?"

"I'm not talking to her in the open. Tell her."

"What about her friend—?"

"Another husband is dead."

Silence.

"Will you tell her—?" Pamir began.

"She is already on her way, sir. As you have requested." Then after a pause, the apartment suggested, "About Gallium, please . . . I think you should deliver that sorry news . . ."

He told it.

She was dressed now in slacks and a silk blouse made by the communal spiders of the Kolochon district, and her bare feet wore black rings on every toe, and while she sat on one of the dozens of self-shaping chairs, listening to his recount of the last brutal hour, her expression managed to grow even more sad as well as increasingly detached. Sorrel made no sound, but always there was a sense that she was about to speak. The sorry and pained and very pretty face would betray a new thought, or the pale eyes would recognize something meaningful. But the mouth never quite made noise. When she finally uttered a few words, Pamir nearly forgot to listen.

"Who are you?"

Did he hear the question correctly?

Again, she asked, "Who are you?" Then she leaned forward, the blouse dipping in front. "You aren't like any environmental technician I've known, and I don't think you're a security specialist either."

"No?"

"You wouldn't have survived the fight, if you were just a fix-it man." She almost laughed, a little dimple showing high on the left cheek. "And even if you had lived, you would still be running now."

"I just want you to point me in the safest direction," he replied.

She didn't respond, watching him for what seemed like an age. Then sitting back in the deep wide chair, she asked, "Who pays you?"

"You do."

"That's not what I mean."

"But I'm not pushing too hard for my wages," he offered.

"You won't tell me who?"

"Confess a few things to me first," he replied.

She had long hands, graceful and quick. For a little while, the hands danced in her lap, and when they finally settled, she asked, "What can I tell you?"

"Everything you know about your dead husbands, and about those who just happen to be alive still." Pamir leaned forward, adding, "In particular, I want to hear about your first husband. And if you can, explain why the Faith of the Many Joinings seemed like such a reasonable idea."

XII

She had seen him earlier on the voyage and spoken with him on occasion—a tall and slender and distinguished J'Jal man with a fondness for human clothes, particularly red woolen suits and elaborately knotted white silk ties. Cre'llan seemed handsome, although not exceptionally so. He was obviously bright and engaging. Once, when their boat was exploring the luddite islands in the middle of the Gone-A-Long Sea, he asked if he might join her, sitting on the long chaise lounge beside hers. For the next little while—an hour, or perhaps the entire day—they chatted amiably about the most ordinary of things. There was gossip to share, mostly about their fellow passengers and the boat's tiny crew. There were several attempts to list the oceans that they had crossed to date, ranking them according to beauty and then history and finally by their inhabitants. Which was the most intriguing port? Which was the most ordinary? What aliens had each met for the first time? What were their first impressions? Second impressions? And if they had to live for the next thousand years in one of these little places, which would they choose?

Sorrel would have eventually forgotten the day. But a week later, she agreed to a side trip to explore Greenland.

"Do you know the island?"

"Not at all," Pamir lied.

"I never made sense of that name," Sorrel admitted, eyes narrowing as if to reexamine the entire question. "Except for some fringes of moss and the like, the climate is pure glacial. The island has to be cold, I was told. It has to do with the upwellings in the ocean and the sea's general health. Anyway, there is a warm current upwind from it, which brings the moisture, and the atmosphere is a hundred kilometers tall and braced with demon-doors. The snows are endless and fabulous, and you can't sail across the Gone-A-Long Sea without visiting Greenland once. At least that's what my friends told me."

"Was Cre'llan in your group?"

"No." Somehow that amused her. She gave a little laugh, adding, "Everybody was human, except for the guide, who was an AI with a human-facsimile body."

Pamir nodded.

"We power-skied up onto the ice during an incredibly hard snowfall. But then our guide turned to us, mentioning that it was a clear day, as they went. And we should be thankful we could see so much."

At most, they could see twenty meters in any direction. She was with a good friend—a child of the Great Ship like Sorrel, but a thousand years older. Sorrel had known the woman her entire life. They had shared endless conversations and gone to the same fine parties, and their shopping adventures had stretched on for weeks at a time. They always traveled together. And in their combined lives, nothing with real substance had occurred to either of them.

The glacier was thick and swiftly built up by the waves of falling snow. Sorrel and her companion skied away from the rest of the group, scaling a tall ridge that placed them nearly a kilometer above the invisible sea. Then the snow began to fall harder—fat wet flakes joining into snowballs that plunged from the white sky. They were skiing close together, linked by a smart-rope. Sorrel happened to be in the lead. What happened next, she couldn't say. Her first guess, and still her best guess, was that her friend thought of a little joke to play. She disabled the rope and untied herself, and where the ridge widened, she attempted to slip ahead of Sorrel, probably to scare her when she was most vulnerable.

Where the friend fell was a bit of a mystery.

Later, coming to the end of the ridge, Sorrel saw that she was alone. But she naturally assumed her companion had grown tired and gone back to rejoin the others. There wasn't cause for worry, and she didn't like worry, and so Sorrel didn't give it another thought.

But the other tourists hadn't seen her missing friend, either.

A search was launched. But the heavy snowfall turned into what can only be described as an endless avalanche from the sky. In the next hour, the glacier rose by twenty meters. By the time rescue crews could set to work, it was obvious that the missing passenger had stumbled into one of the vast crevices, and her body was dead, and without knowing her location, the only reasonable course would be to wait for the ice to push to the sea and watch for her battered remains.

In theory, a human brain could withstand that kind of abuse.

But the AI guide didn't believe in theory. "What nobody tells you is that this fucking island was once an industrial site. Why do you think the engineers covered it up? To hide their wreckage, of course. Experimental hyperfibers, mostly. Very sharp and sloppy, and the island was built with their trash, and if you put enough pressure on even the best bioceramic head, it will crack. Shatter. Pop, and die, and come out into the sea as a few handfuls of fancy sand."

Her friend was dead.

Sorrel never liked the woman more than anyone else or felt any bond unique just to the two of them. But the loss was heavy and persistent, and for the next several weeks, she thought about little else.

Meanwhile, their voyage through the Great Ship reached a new sea.

One night, while surrounded by a flat gray expanse of methane, Sorrel happened upon the J'Jal man wearing his red jacket and red slacks, and the fancy white tie beneath his nearly human face. He smiled at her, his expression genuine with either species. Then quietly, he asked, "Is something wrong?"

Nobody in her own group had noticed her pain. Unlike her, they were convinced that their friend would soon enough return from the oblivion.

Sorrel sat with the J'Jal. And for a very long while, they didn't speak. She found herself staring at his bare feet, thinking about the fragility of life. Then with a dry low voice, she admitted, "I'm scared."

"Is that so?" Cre'llan said.

"You know, at any moment, without warning, the Great Ship could collide with something enormous. At a third the speed of light, we might strike a sunless world or a small black hole, and billions would die inside this next instant."

"That may be true," her companion purred. "But I have invested my considerable faith in the talents of our captains."

"I haven't," she countered.

"No?"

"My point here . . ." She hesitated, shivering for reasons other than the cold. "My point is that I have lived for a few years, and I can't remember ever grabbing life by the throat. Do you know what I mean?"

"Very well," he claimed.

His long toes curled and then relaxed again.

"Why don't you wear shoes?" she finally asked.

And with the softest possible touch, Cre'llan laid his hand on hers. "I am an alien, Sorrel." He spoke while smiling, quietly telling her, "And it would mean so much to me if you could somehow, in your soul, forget what I am."

—◦—

"We were lovers before the night was finished," she admitted. A fond look passed into a self-deprecating chuckle. "I thought all J'Jal men were shaped like he was. But they aren't, he explained. And that's when I learned about the Faith of the Many Joinings."

Pamir nodded, waiting for more.

"They did eventually find my lost friend, you know." A wise sorry laugh came out of her. "A few years later, a patrol working along the edge of the glacier kicked up some dead bones and then the skull with her mind inside. Intact." Sorrel sat back in her chair, breasts moving under the blouse. "She was reconstituted and back inside her old life within the month, and do you know what? In the decades since, I haven't spoken to my old friend more than three times.

"Funny, isn't it?"

"The Faith," Pamir prompted.

She seemed to expect the subject. With a slow shrug of the shoulders, Sorrel observed, "Whoever you are, you weren't born into comfort and wealth. That shows, I think. You've had to fight in your life . . . probably through much of your life . . . for things that any fool knows are important. While someone like me—less than a fool by a long way—walks through paradise without ever asking herself, 'What matters?' "

"The Faith," he repeated.

"Think of the challenge," she said. Staring through him, she asked, "Can you imagine how very difficult it is to be involved—romantically and emotionally linked—with another species?"

"It disgusts me," he lied.

"It disgusts a lot of us," she replied. For an instant, she wore a doubting gaze, perhaps wondering if he was telling the truth about his feelings. Then she let the doubt fall aside. "I wasn't exceptionally horrified by the idea of sex outside my species," she admitted. "Which is why I wasn't all that interested either. Somewhere in the indifferent middle, I was. But when I learned about this obscure J'Jal belief . . . how an assortment of like-minded souls had gathered, taking the first critical steps in what might well be the logical evolution of life in our universe . . ."

Her voice drifted away.

"How many husbands did you take?"

She acted surprised. "Why? Don't you know?"

Pamir let her stare at him.

Finally, she said, "Eleven."

"You are Joined to all of them."

"Until a few years ago, yes." The eyes shrank, and with the tears, they brightened. "The first death looked like a random murder. Horrible, but imaginable. But the second killing was followed a few months later by a third. The same weapon was used in each tragedy, with the same general manner of execution . . ." Her voice trailed away, the mouth left open and empty. One long hand wiped at the tears, accomplishing little but pushing moisture across the sharp cheeks. "Since the dead belonged to different species, and since the members of the Faith . . . my husbands and myself . . . are sworn to secrecy—"

"Nobody noticed the pattern," Pamir interrupted.

"Oh, I think they saw what was happening," she muttered. "After the fifth or sixth death, security people made inquiries at the library. But no one there could admit anything. And then the killings slowed, and the investigation went away. No one was offered protection, and my name was never mentioned. At least that's what I assume, since nobody was sent to interview me." Then with a quiet, angry voice, Sorrel added, "After they linked the murders to the library, they didn't care what happened."

"How do you know that?"

She stared at Pamir, regarding him as if he were a perfect idiot.

"What? Did the authorities assume this was some ugly internal business among the Joined?"

"Maybe," she said. "Or maybe they received orders telling them to stop searching."

"Who gave the orders?"

She looked at a point above his head and carefully said, "No."

"Who wouldn't want these killings stopped?"

"I don't . . ." she began. Then she shook her head, adding, "I can't. Ask all you want, but I won't tell you anything else."

He asked, "Do you consider yourself in danger?"

She sighed. "Hardly."

"Why not?"

She said nothing.

"Two husbands are left alive," Pamir reminded her.

A suspicious expression played over him. Then she admitted, "I'm guessing you know which two."

"There's the Glory." Glories were birdlike creatures, roughly human-shaped but covered with a bright and lovely plumage. "One of your more recent husbands, isn't he?"

Sorrel nodded, and then admitted, "Except he died last year. On the opposite side of the Great Ship, alone. The body was discovered only yesterday."

Pamir flinched, saying, "My condolences."

"Yes. Thank you."

"And your first lover?"

"Yes."

"The J'Jal in the red suit."

"Cre'llan, yes. I know who you mean."

"The last man standing," he mentioned.

That earned a withering stare from a pained cold face. "I don't marry lightly. And I don't care what you're thinking."

Pamir stood and walked up beside her, and with his own stare, he assured, "You don't know what I'm thinking. Because I sure as hell don't know what I've got in my own soggy head."

She dipped her eyes.

"The J'Jal," he said. "I can track him down for myself, or you can make the introductions."

"It isn't Cre'llan," she whispered.

"Then come with me," Pamir replied. "Come and look him in the eye and ask for yourself."

XIII

As a species, the J'Jal were neither wealthy nor powerful, but among them were a few individuals of enormous age who had prospered in a gradual, relentless fashion. On distant worlds, they had served as cautious traders and inconspicuous landowners and sometimes as the bearers of alien technologies; and while they would always be aliens on those places, they had adapted well enough to feel as if they were home. And then the Great Ship had arrived. Their young and arrogant human cousins promised to carry them across the galaxy—for a fee. The boldest of these wealthy J'Jal left a hundred worlds behind, spending fortunes for the honor of gathering together again. They had no world of their own, yet some hoped to eventually discover some new planet reminiscent of their cradle world—an empty world they could claim for their own. Other J'Jals believed that the Earth and its humans were the logical, even poetic goal for their species—a place where they might blend into the ranks of their highly successful relatives.

"But neither solution gives me any particular pleasure," said the gentleman wearing red. With a nearly human voice, he admitted, "The boundaries between the species are a lie and impermanent, and I hope for a radically different future."

According to his official biography, Cre'llan was approximately the same age as *Homo sapiens*.

"What's your chosen future?" Pamir inquired.

The smile was bright and a little cold. "My new friend," the J'Jal said. "I think you already have made a fair assessment of what I wish for. And more to the point, I think you couldn't care less about whatever dream or utopia I just happen to entertain."

"I have some guesses," Pamir agreed. "And you're right, I don't give a shit about your idea of paradise."

Sorrel sat beside her ancient husband, holding his hand fondly. Divorced or not, she missed his company. They looked like lovers waiting for a holo portrait to be taken. Quietly, she warned Cre'llan, "He suspects you, darling."

"Of course he does."

"But I told him . . . I explained . . . you can't be responsible for any of this . . ."

"Which is the truth," the J'Jal replied, his smile turning into a grim little sneer. "Why would I murder anyone? How could it possibly serve my needs?"

The J'Jal's home was near the bottom of Fall Away, and it was enormous. This single room covered nearly a square kilometer, carpeted with green woods broken up with quick little streams, the ceiling so high that a dozen tame star-rocs could circle above and never brush wings. But all of that grandeur and wealth was dwarfed by the outside view: The braided rivers that ran down the middle of Fall Away had been set free some fifty kilometers above their heads, every diamond tube ending at the same point, their contents exploding out under extraordinary pressure. A flow equal to ten Amazons roared past Cre'llan's home, water and ammonia mixing with a spectacular array of chemical wastes and dying phytoplankton. Aggressive compounds battered their heads together and reacted, bleeding colors in the process. Shapes appeared inside the wild foam, and vanished again. A creative eye could see every face that he had ever met, and he could spend days watching for the faces that he had worn during his own long, strange life.

The window only seemed to be a window. In reality, Pamir was staring at a sheet of high-grade hyperfiber, thick and very nearly impervious to any force nature could throw at it. The view was a projection, a convincing trick. Nodding, he admitted, "You must feel remarkably safe, I would think."

"I sleep quite well," Cre'llan replied.

"Most of the time, I can help people with their security matters. But not you." Pamir was entirely honest, remarking, "I don't think the Master Captain has as much security in place. That hyperfiber. The AI watchdogs. Those blood-and-meat hounds that sniffed our butts on the way in." He showed a wide smile, and then mentioned, "If I'm not mistaken, you'd never have to leave this one room. For the next ten thousand years, you could sit where you're sitting today and eat what falls off these trees, and no one would have to touch you."

"If that was what I wished, yes."

"But he is not the killer," Sorrel muttered.

Then she stood and stepped away from the ancient creature, her hand grudgingly releasing his grip. She approached Pamir, kneeling before him. Suddenly she looked very young, serious and determined. "I know this man," she implored. "You have no idea what you're suggesting, if you think that he could hurt anyone . . . for any reason . . ."

"I once lived as a J'Jal," Pamir allowed.

Sorrel leaned away from him, taken by surprise.

"I dyed my hair blue and tinkered with these bones, and I even doctored my genetics, far enough to pass half-assed scans." Pamir gave no specifics, but he understood he was telling too much. Nonetheless, he didn't feel as if he had any choice. "I even kept a J'Jal lover. For a while, I did. But then she saw through my disguise, and I had to steal away in the middle of the night."

The other two watched him now, bewildered and deeply curious.

"Anyway," he continued. "During my stay with the J'Jal, a certain young woman came of age. She was very desirable. Extraordinarily beautiful, and her family was one of the wealthiest onboard the ship. Before that year was finished, the woman had acquired three devoted husbands. But someone else fell in love with her, and he didn't want to share. One of the new husbands was killed. After that, the other husbands went to the public hall and divorced her. They never spoke to the girl again. She was left unattached, and alone. What rational soul would risk her love under those circumstances?" Pamir shook his head while studying Cre'llan. "As I said, I slipped away in the night. And then several decades later, an elder J'Jal proposed to the widow. She was lonely, and he was not a bad man. Not wealthy, but powerful and ancient, and in some measure, wise. So she accepted his offer, and when nothing tragic happened to her new husband, not only did everyone understand who had ordered the killing. They accepted it, too. In pure J'Jal fashion."

With a flat, untroubled voice, Cre'llan said, "My soul has never been thought of as jealous."

"But I'm now accusing you of jealousy," Pamir countered.

Silence.

"Conflicts over females is ordinary business for some species," he continued. "Monopolizing a valuable mate can be a good evolutionary strategy, for the J'Jal as well as others, too. And tens of millions of years of civilization hasn't changed what you are, or what you can be."

Cre'llan snorted, declaring, "That old barbarism is something I would never embrace."

"Agreed."

The green gaze narrowed. "Excuse me, sir. I don't think I understand. What exactly are you accusing me of?"

"This is a beautiful, enormous fortress," Pamir continued. "And as you claim, you're not a jealous creature. But did you invite these other husbands to live with you? Did you offer even one of them your shelter and all of this expensive security?"

Sorrel glanced at the J'Jal, her breath catching for an instant.

"You didn't offer," Pamir continued, "because of a very reasonable fear: What if one of your houseguests wanted Sorrel for himself?"

An old tension rippled between the lovers.

"Every other husband was a suspect, in your mind. With those two harum-scarums being the most obvious candidates." He looked at Sorrel again. "Gallium would be his favorite—a relatively poor entity born into a biology of posturing and violence. His species is famous for stealing mates. Both sexes do it, every day. But now Gallium is dead, which leaves your husband with no one to worry about, it seems."

"But I am not the killer," Cre'llan repeated.

"Oh, I agree," Pamir said. "You are innocent, yes."

The statement seemed to anger both of them. Sorrel spoke first, asking, "When did you come to that conclusion?"

"Once I learned who your husbands were," Pamir replied. "Pretty much instantly." Then he sat forward in his chair, staring out at the churning waters. "No, Cre'llan isn't the murderer."

"You understand my nature?" the J'Jal asked.

"Maybe, but that doesn't particularly matter." Pamir laughed. "No," he said. "You're too smart and far too old to attempt this sort of bullshit with a human woman. Talk all you want about every species being one and the same. But the hard sharp damning fact is that human beings are not J'Jal. Very few of us, under even the most difficult circumstances, are going to look past the fact that their spouse is a brutal killer."

Cre'llan gave a little nod, the barest smile showing.

Sorrel stood, nervous hands clenching into fists. She looked vulnerable and sweet and very sorry. The beginnings of recognition showed in the blue-white eyes, and she started to stare at the J'Jal, catching herself now and forcing her eyes to drop.

"And something else was obvious," Pamir mentioned. "Pretty much from the beginning, I should think."

With a dry little voice, Cre'llan asked, "What was obvious?"

"From the beginning," Pamir repeated.

"What do you mean?" Sorrel asked.

"Okay," Pamir said, watching her face and the nervous fists. "Let's suppose that I'm killing your husbands. I want my rivals dead, and I want a reasonable chance of surviving to the end. Of course, I would start with Cre'llan. Since he enjoys the most security . . . better than everyone else combined, probably . . . I would hit him before he could smell any danger . . ."

That earned a cold silence.

Pamir shook his head. "The killer wants the husbands out of your life. From the start, I think he knew exactly what was required. The other ten husbands had to be murdered, since they loved you deeply and you seemed to love them. But this J'Jal . . . well, he's a different conundrum entirely, I'm guessing . . ."

Cre'llan appeared interested but distant. When he breathed, it was after a long breathless pause, and he sounded a little weak when he said, "I don't know what you are talking about."

"You told me," Pamir said to Sorrel.

"What did I—?"

"How you met him during the cruise. And what happened to you and your good friend just before you went to bed with this alien man—"

"I don't understand," she muttered.

Cre'llan snapped, "Be quiet."

Pamir felt a pleasant nervousness in his belly. "Cre'llan wanted you, I'm guessing. He wanted you badly. You were a wealthy, unattached human woman—the J'Jal adore our species—and you would bring him a fair amount of status. But to seduce you . . . well, he needed help. Which is why he paid your friend to vanish on the ice in Greenland, faking her own death . . .

"He wanted to expose you emotionally, with a dose of mortality—"

"Stop that," she told him.

Cre'llan said, "Idiot," and little more.

"The AI guide was right," Pamir told her. "The chances of a mind surviving the weight of that ice and the grinding against the hyperfiber shards . . . well, I found it remarkable to learn that your good friend was found alive.

"So I made a few inquiries.

"I can show you, if you wish. A trail of camouflaged funds leads from your friend back to a company formed just hours before her death.

The mysterious company made a single transfer of funds, declared bankruptcy and then dissolved. Your friend was the recipient. She was reborn as a very wealthy soul, and the principal stockholder in that short-lived company happened to have been someone with whom your first lover and husband does quite a lot of business."

Sorrel sat motionless. Her mouth closed and opened, in slow motion, and then it began to close again. Her legs tried to find the strength to carry her away, but she looked about for another moment or two, finding no door or hatchway to slip through in the next little while. She was caught, trapped by things awful and true. And then, just as Pamir thought that she would crack into pieces, the young woman surprised him.

Calmly, she told Cre'llan, "I divorce you."

"Darling—?" he began.

"Forever," she said. And then she pulled from a pocket what seemed like an ordinary knife. Which it was. A sapphire blade no longer than her hand was unfolded, and it took her ten seconds to cut the Darmion crystal out of her chest—ripped free for the second time in as many days—and then before she collapsed, she flung the gory gift at the stunned and sorry face.

XIV

Pamir explained what had happened as he carried her into her apartment. Then he set her on a great round bed, pillows offering themselves to her head while a small autodoc spider-walked its way across the pale blue sheets, studying her half-healed wound, then with more penetrating eyes, carefully examining the rest of her body.

Quietly, the apartment offered, "I have never known her to be this way."

In his long life, Pamir had rarely seen any person as depressed, as forlorn. Sorrel was pale and motionless, lying on her back, and even with her eyes open, something in her gaze was profoundly blind. She saw nothing, heard nothing. She was like a person flung off the topmost portion of Fall Away, tumbling out of control, gusts of wind occasionally slamming her against the hard walls, battering a soul that couldn't feel the abuse anymore.

"I am worried," the apartment confessed.

"Reasonable," Pamir replied.

"It must be a horrid thing, losing everyone who loves you."

"But someone still loves her," he countered. Then he paused, thinking hard about everything again.

"Tell me," he said. "What is your species-strain?"

"Is that important?"

"Probably not," said Pamir.

The AI described its pedigree, in brief.

"What's your lot number?"

"I do not see how that matters."

"Never mind," he said, walking away from their patient. "I already know enough as it is."

Pamir ate a small meal and drank some sweet alien nectar that left him feeling a little sloppy. When the head cleared, he slept for a minute or an hour, and then he returned to the bedroom and the giant bed. Sorrel was where he had left her. Her eyes were closed now, empty hands across her belly, rising and falling and rising with a slow steady rhythm that he couldn't stop watching.

"Thank you."

The voice didn't seem to belong to anyone. The young woman's mouth happened to be open, but it didn't sound like the voice he expected. It was sturdy and calm, the old sadness wiped away. It was a quiet polite and rather sweet voice that told him, "Thank you," and then added, "For everything, sir."

The eyes hadn't opened.

She had heard Pamir approach, or felt his presence.

He sat on the bed beside her, and after a long moment said, "You know. You'd be entitled to consider me—whoever I am—as being your main suspect. I could have killed the husbands. And I certainly put an end to you and Cre'llan."

"It isn't you."

"Because you have another suspect in mind. Isn't that it?"

She said nothing.

"Who do you believe is responsible?" he pressed.

Finally, the eyes pulled open, slowly, and they blinked twice, tears pooling but never quite reaching the point where they would flow.

"My father," she said.

"He killed your husbands?"

"Obviously."

"He's light-years behind us now."

Silence.

Pamir nodded, and after a moment, he asked, "What do you know about your father?"

"Quite a lot," she claimed.

"But you've never seen him," he reminded her.

"I have studied him." She shook her head and closed her eyes again. "I've examined his biography as well as I can, and I think I know him pretty well."

"He isn't here, Sorrel."

"No?"

"He emigrated before you were even born."

"That's what my mother told me, yes."

"What else?" Pamir leaned closer, adding, "What did she tell you about the man . . . ?"

"He is strong and self-assured. That he knows what is right and best. And he loves me very much, but he couldn't stay with me." Sorrel chewed on her lip for a moment. "He couldn't stay here, but my father has agents and ways, and I would never be without him. Mother promised me."

Pamir just nodded.

"My father doesn't approve of the Faith."

"I can believe that," he said.

"My mother admitted, once or twice . . . that she loved him very much, but he doesn't have a diplomat's ease with aliens. And his heart can be hard, and he has a capacity to do awful things, if he sees the need . . ."

"No," Pamir whispered.

The pale blue eyes opened. "What do you mean?"

"Your father didn't do any of this," he promised. Then he thought again, saying, "Well, maybe a piece of it."

"What do you mean—?"

Pamir set his hand on top of her mouth, lightly. Then as he began to pull his hand back, she took hold of his wrist and forearm, easing the palm back down against lips that pulled apart, teeth giving him a tiny swift bite.

A J'Jal gesture, that was.

He bent down and kissed the open eyes.

Sorrel told him, "You shouldn't."

"Probably not."

"If the murderer knows you are with me—"

He placed two fingers deep into her mouth, J'Jal fashion. And she sucked on them, not trying to speak now, eyes almost smiling as Pamir calmly and smoothly slid into bed beside her.

XV

One of the plunging rivers pulled close to the wall, revealing what it carried. Inside the diamond tube was a school of finned creatures, not pseudofish nor pseudowhales, but instead a collection of teardrop-shaped machines that probably fused hydrogen in their hearts, producing the necessary power to hold their bodies steady inside a current that looked relentless, rapid and chaotic, turbulent and exceptionally unappealing.

Pamir watched the swimming machines for a moment, deciding that this was rather how he had lived for ages now.

With a shrug and a soft laugh, he continued the long walk up the path, moving past a collection of modest apartments. The library was just a few meters farther along—a tiny portal carved into the smooth black basaltic wall. Its significance was so well hidden that a thousand sightseers passed this point every day, perhaps pausing at the edge of the precipice to look down, but more likely continuing on their walk, searching richer views. Pamir turned his eyes toward the closed doorway, pretending a mild curiosity. Then he stood beside the simple wall that bordered the outer edge of the trail, hands on the chill stone, eyes gazing down at the dreamy shape of the Little-Lot.

The massive cloud was the color of butter and nearly as dense. A trillion trillion microbes thrived inside its aerogel matrix, supporting an ecosystem that would never touch a solid surface.

The library door swung open—J'Jal wood riding on creaky iron hinges.

Pamir opened a nexus and triggered an old, nearly forgotten captain's channel. Then he turned towards the creaking sound and smiled. Sorrel was emerging from the library, dressed in a novice's blue robe and blinking against the sudden glare. The massive door fell shut again, and quietly, she said to him, "All right."

Pamir held a finger to his closed mouth.

She stepped closer and through a nexus told him, "I did what you told me."

"Show it."

She produced the slender blue book.

"Put it on the ground here."

This was her personal journal—the only volume she was allowed to remove from the library. She set it in front of her sandaled feet, and then asked, "Was I noticed, do you think?"

"I promise. You were seen."

"And do we just wait now?"

He shook his head. "No, no. I'm far too impatient for that kind of game."

The plasma gun was barely awake when he fired it, turning plastic pages and the wood binding into a thin cloud of superheated ash.

Sorrel put her arms around herself, squeezing hard.

"Now we wait," he advised.

Not for the first time, she admitted, "I don't understand. Still. Who do you think is responsible?"

Again, the heavy door swung open.

Without looking, Pamir called out, "Hello, Leon'rd."

The J'Jal librarian wore the same purplish-black robe and blue ponytail, and his expression hadn't changed in the last few days—a bilious outrage focused on those who would injure his helpless dependents. He stared at the ruins of the book, and then he glared at the two humans, focusing on the male face until a vague recognition tickled.

"Do I know you?" he began.

Pamir was wearing the same face he had worn for the last thirty-two years. A trace of a smile was showing, except around the dark eyes. Quietly, fiercely, he said, "I found my wife, and thanks for the help."

Leon'rd stared at Sorrel, his face working its way through a tangle of wild emotions. "Your wife?" he sputtered.

Then he tipped his head, saying, "No, she is not."

"You know that?" Pamir asked.

The J'Jal didn't respond.

"What do you know, Leon'rd?"

For an instant, Leon'rd glanced back across a shoulder—not at the library door but at the nearby apartments. The man was at his limits. He seemed frail and tentative, hands pressing at the front of his robe while the long toes curled under his bare feet. Everything was apparent. Transparent. Obvious. And into this near-panic, Pamir said, "I know what you did."

"No," the J'Jal replied, without confidence.

"You learned something," Pamir continued. "You are a determined scholar and a talented student of other species, and some years ago, by design or by dumb luck, you unraveled something. Something that was supposed to be a deep, impenetrable secret."

"No."

"A secret about my wife," he said.

Sorrel blinked, asking, "What is it?"

Pamir laughed harshly. "Tell her," he advised.

The blood had drained out of Leon'rd's face.

"No, I agree," Pamir continued. "Let's keep this between you and me, shall we? Because she doesn't have any idea, either—"

"About what?" the woman cried out.

"She is not your wife," the librarian snapped.

"The hell she isn't." He laughed. "Check the public records. Two hours ago, in a civil ceremony overseen by two Hyree monks, we were made woman and male-implement in a legally binding manner—"

"What do you know about me?" Sorrel pressed.

Pamir ignored her. Staring at the J'Jal, he said, "But somebody else knows what we do. Doesn't he? Because you told him. In passing, you said a few words. Perhaps. Unless of course you were the one who devised this simple, brutal plan, and he is simply your accomplice."

"No!" Leon'rd screamed. "I did not dream anything."

"I might believe you." Pamir glanced at Sorrel, showing a tiny wink. "When I showed him an image of one of your dead husbands, his reaction wasn't quite right. I saw surprise, but the J'Jal eyes betrayed a little bit of pleasure, too. Or relief, was it? Leon'rd? Were you genuinely thrilled to believe that Sele'ium was dead and out of your proverbial hair?"

The librarian looked pale and cold, arms clasped tight against his shivering body. Again, he glanced at the nearby apartments. His mouth opened and then pulled itself closed, and then Pamir said, "Death."

"What did you say?" Leon'rd asked.

"There are countless wonderful and inventive ways to fake your own death," Pamir allowed. "But one of my favorites is to clone your body and cook an empty, soulless brain, and then stuff that brain inside that living body, mimicking a very specific kind of demise."

"Sele'ium?" said Sorrel.

"What I think." Pamir was guessing, but none of the leaps were long or unlikely. "I think your previous husband was a shrewd young man. He grew up in a family that had lived among the harum-scarums. That's where his lineage came from, wasn't it, Leon'rd? So it was perfectly natural, even inevitable, that he could entertain thoughts about killing the competition, including his own identity . . ."

"Tell me what you know," Sorrel begged.

"Almost nothing," Pamir assured. "Leon'rd is the one who is carrying all the dark secrets on his back. Ask him."

The J'Jal covered his face with his hands. "Go away," he whimpered.

"Was Sele'ium a good friend of yours and you were trying to help? Or did he bribe you for this useful information?" Pamir nodded, adding, "Whatever happened, you pointed him toward Sorrel, and you must have explained, 'She is perhaps the most desirable mate on the Great Ship—' "

A sizzling blue bolt of plasma struck his face, melting it and obliterating everything beyond.

The headless body wobbled for a moment and then slumped and dropped slowly, settling against the black wall, and Leon'rd leaped backwards, while Sorrel stood over the remains of her newest husband, her expression tight but calm—like the face of a sailor who has already ridden through countless storms.

XVI

Sele'ium looked like a pedestrian wandering past, his gaze distracted and his manner a little nervous. He seemed embarrassed by the drama that he had happened upon. He looked human. The cold blond hair and purplish-black skin were common on high-UV worlds, while the brown eyes were as ordinary as could be. He wore sandals and trousers and a loose-fitting shirt, and he stared at the destroyed body, seeing precisely what he expected to see. Then he glanced at Sorrel, and with a mixture of warmth and pure menace, he said, "You do not know . . . you cannot . . . how much I love you . . ."

She recoiled in horror.

He started to speak again, to explain himself.

"Get away!" she snapped. "Leave me alone!"

His reaction was to shake his head with his mouth open—a J'Jal refusal—and then he calmly informed her, "I am an exceptionally patient individual."

Which wrung a laugh out of her, bitter and thin.

"Not today, no," he conceded. "And not for a thousand years, perhaps. But I will approach you with a new face and name—every so often, I will come to you—and there will be an hour and a certain heartbeat when you come to understand that we belong to one another—"

The corpse kicked at the empty air.

Sele'ium glanced at what he had done, mildly perturbed by the distraction. Then slowly, he realized that the corpse was shrinking, as if it were a balloon slowly losing its breath. How odd. He stared at the mysterious phenomenon, not quite able to piece together what should have been obvious. The headless ruin twitched hard and then harder, one shrinking leg flinging high. And then from blackened wound rose a puff of blue smoke, and with it, the stink of burnt rubber and cooked hydraulics.

With his left hand, Sele'ium yanked the plasma gun from inside his shirt—a commercial model meant to be used as a tool, but with its safeties cut away—and he turned in a quick circle, searching for a valid target.

"What is it?" Leon'rd called out.

"Do you see him—?"

"Who?"

The young J'Jal was more puzzled than worried. He refused to let himself panic, his mind quickly ticking off the possible answers, settling on what would be easiest and best.

In the open air, of course.

"Just leave us," Leon'rd begged. "I will not stand by any longer!"

Sele'ium threw five little bolts into the basalt wall, punching out holes and making a rain of white-hot magma.

Somewhere below, a voice howled.

Sorrel ran to the wall and looked down, and Sele'ium crept beside her, the gun in both hands, its reactor pumping energies into a tiny chamber, readying a blast that would obliterate everything in its path.

He started to peer over, and then thought better of it.

One hand released the weapon and the arm wrapped around Sorrel's waist, and when she flung her elbow into his midsection, he bent low. He grunted and cursed softly and then told her, "No."

With his full weight, he drove the woman against the smooth black wall, and together, his face on her left shoulder, they bent and peered over the edge.

Pamir grabbed the plasma gun, yanking hard.

And Sorrel made herself jump.

Those two motions combined to lift her and Sele'ium off the path, over the edge and plummeting down. Pamir's gecko-grip was ripped loose from the basalt, and he was falling with them, one hand on the gun, clinging desperately, while the other arm began to swing, throwing its fist into the killer's belly and ribs. Within moments, they were falling as fast as possible. A damp singing wind blew past them, and the wall was a black smear to one side, and the rest of Fall Away was enormous and distant and almost changeless. The airborne rivers and a thousand flying machines were out of reach and useless. The three of them fell and fell, and sometimes a voice would pass through the roaring wind— a spectator standing on the path, remarking in alarm, "Who were they?" Three bodies, clinging and kicking. Sele'ium punished Pamir with his own free hand, and then he let himself be pulled closer, and with a mouth that wasn't more than a few days old, he bit down on a wrist, hard, trying to force the stranger to release his hold on the plasma gun.

Pamir cried out and let go.

But as Sele'ium aimed at his face, for his soul, Pamir slammed at the man's forearm and pushed it backwards again, and he put a hard knee into the elbow, and a weapon that didn't have safeties released its stored energies, a thin blinding beam that coalesced inside the dying man's head, his brain turning to light and ash, a supersonic *crack* leaving the others temporarily deafened.

Pamir kicked the corpse away and clung to Sorrel, and she held tight to him, and after another few minutes, as they plunged toward the yellow depths of a living, thriving cloud, he shouted into her better ear, explaining a thing or two.

XVII

Again, it was nearly nightfall.

Once again, Pamir sat outside his apartment, listening to the wild songs of the Ilano vibra. Nothing looked out of the ordinary. Neighbors strolled past or ran past or flew by on gossamer wings. The janusian couple paused long enough to ask where he had been these last days, and Pamir said a few murky words about taking care of family troubles. The harum-scarum family was outside their apartment, gathered around a cooking pit, eating a living passion ox in celebration of another day successfully crossed. A collection of machines stopped to ask about the facsimile that they had built for Pamir, as a favor. Did it serve its intended role? "Oh, sure," he said with a nod. "Everybody was pretty much fooled, at least until the joke was finished."

"Was there laughter?" asked one machine.

"Constant, breathless laughter," Pamir swore. And then he said nothing else about it.

A single figure was approaching. He had been watching her for the last kilometer, and as the machines wandered away, he used three different means to study her gait and face and manner. Then he considered his options, and he decided to remain sitting where he was, his back against the huge ceramic pot and his legs stretched out before him, one bare foot crossed over the other.

She stopped a few steps short, watching him but saying nothing.

"You're thinking," Pamir told her. "Throw me into the brig, or throw me off the ship entirely. That's what you're thinking now."

"But we had an agreement," Miocene countered. "You were supposed to help somebody, and you have, and you most definitely have earned your payment as well as my thanks."

"Yeah," he said, "but I know you. And you're asking yourself, 'Why not get rid of him and be done with it?' "

The First Chair was wearing a passenger's clothes and a face slightly disguised, eyes blue and the matching hair curled into countless tight knots, the cheeks and mouth widened but nothing about the present smile any warmer than any other smile that had ever come from this hard, hard creature.

"You know me," she muttered.

A moment later, she asked, "Will you tell me who you are?"

"Don't you know yet?"

She shook her head, and with a hint of genuine honesty, she admitted, "Nor do I particularly care, one way or the other."

Pamir grinned and leaned back a little more.

"I suppose I could place you in custody," Miocene continued. "But a man with your skills and obvious luck . . . well, you probably have twelve different ways to escape from our detention centers. And if I sent you falling onto a colony world or an alien world . . . I suppose in another thousand years or so, you would find your way back again, like a dog or an ugly habit."

"Fair points," he admitted.

Then with a serious, warm voice, he asked, "How is Sorrel?"

"That young woman? As I understand it, she has put her apartment up for sale, and she has already moved away. I'm not sure where—"

"Bullshit," he interrupted.

Miocene grinned, just for a moment. "Perhaps I do have an idea or two. About who you might be . . ."

"She knows now."

The woman's face seemed to narrow, and the eyes grew larger and less secure. "Knows what?" she managed.

"Who her father is," said Pamir. "Her true father, I mean."

"One man's conjecture," the First Chair reminded him. Then with a dismissive shake of the head, she added, "A young woman in a gullible moment might believe you. But she won't find any corroboration, not for the next thousand years . . . and eventually, she will have to believe what she has always believed . . ."

"Maybe."

Miocene shrugged. "It's hardly your concern now. Is it?"

"Perhaps it isn't," he allowed. Then as the overhead lights flickered for the first time, he sat up straighter. "The thief was your idea, wasn't he? The one who came to steal away the Darmion crystal?"

"And why would I arrange such a thing?"

"What happened afterwards was exactly what you were hoping for," he said. "An apparently random crime leaves Sorrel trusting me, and the two of us emotionally linked to each other."

With a narrow grin, Miocene admitted, "But I was wrong in one way."

"Were you?"

"I assumed that the killer, whoever he was, would likely put an end to you. Exposing himself in the process, of course."

A second ripple of darkness passed along the avenue. Pamir showed her a stern face, and quietly, he said, "Madam First Chair. You have always been a remarkable and wondrously awful bitch."

"I didn't know it was Sele'ium," she admitted.

"And you didn't know why he was killing the husbands, either." Pamir stood up now, slowly. "Because the old librarian, Leon'rd, pieced together who Sorrel was. He told Sele'ium what he had learned, and he mentioned that Sorrel's father was a woman, and as it happens, that woman is the second most important person onboard the Great Ship."

"There are some flaws in the public records, yes." She nodded, adding, "These are problems that I'm taking care of now."

"Good," he said.

Miocene narrowed her gaze. "And yes, I am a difficult soul. The bitch queen, and so on. But what I do in my life is enormous and very complicated, and for a multitude of good reasons, it is best if my daughter remains apart from my life and from me."

"Maybe so," he allowed.

"Look at these last few days. Do you need more reasons than this?" she asked. Then she took a step closer, adding, "But you are wrong, in one critical matter. Whoever you are."

"Wrong where?"

"You assume I wanted you to be killed, and that's wrong. It was a possibility and a risk. But as a good captain, I had to consider the possibility and make contingency plans, just in case." She took another little step, saying, "No, what all of this has been . . . in addition to everything else that it seems to have been . . . is what I have to call an audition."

"An audition?" Pamir muttered, genuinely puzzled.

"You seem to be a master at disappearing," Miocene admitted. Then she took one last step, and in a whisper, she said, "There may come a day when I cannot protect my daughter anymore, and she'll need to vanish in some profound and eternal fashion . . ."

A third ripple of darkness came, followed by the full seamless black of night.

"That's your task, if you wish to take it," she said, speaking into the darkness. "Whoever you happen to be . . . are you there, can you hear me . . . ?"

XVIII

Sorrel had been walking for weeks, crossing the Indigo Desert one step at a time. She traveled alone with her supplies in a floating pack tied to her waist. It was ten years later, or ten thousand. She had some trouble remembering how much time had passed, which was a good thing. She felt better in most ways, and the old pains had become familiar enough to be ignored. She was even happy, after a fashion. And while she strolled upon the fierce landscape of fire-blasted stone and purple succulents, she would sing, sometimes human songs and occasionally tunes that were much harder to manage and infinitely more beautiful.

One afternoon, she heard notes answering her notes.

Coming over the crest of a sharp ridge, she saw something utterly unexpected—a thick luxurious stand of irrigated Ilano vibra.

Louder now, the vegetation sang to her.

She started to approach.

In the midst of the foliage, a shape was sitting. A human shape, perhaps. Male, by the looks of it. Sitting with his back to her, his face totally obscured by the shaggy black hair. Yet he seemed rather familiar, for some reason. Familiar in the best ways, and Sorrel stepped faster now, and smiled, and with a parched voice, she tried to sing in time with the alien weed.

❖ THE BIG DOWNTOWN ❖
by Jack McDevitt

I

I WOKE UP on the couch in my office, listening to the wind. Sunlight was coming through the drawn blinds. "*Kristi.*" Pete's voice. The office AI. "*You have a call. I wouldn't have bothered you but the guy sounds desperate.*"

It was almost nine. Time to open up. "What's he want, Pete?"

"*Something about a missing person.*"

Lord, I didn't want to get up. "Who is it? Who's calling?"

"*Says his name is Jules Steinmetz. Kristi, I think you need to talk to him.*"

I was using my sweater for a pillow. Somewhere in the building a door slammed. The Madson is probably the only place in D.C. where you still have to close the doors yourself. I got up, put the coffee on, straightened my hair and blouse, sat down behind the desk, and told Pete to put him through.

Steinmetz blinked on in the middle of the office. The guy looked scared. His jaws were clamped tight and there were rings around his eyes. His hair was uncombed and he stared at me with a bleakness that you just don't want to see first thing in the morning. He was wearing a wrinkled white pullover and black slacks. "*Ms. Walker?*" he said. "*I don't know what to do.*"

"Okay, Mr. Steinmetz." I tried to sound as if everything were under control. "Try to relax. What's going on?"

"*The police are saying it was an accident.*"

"What was an accident?"

"*The boat.*" His eyes closed and his face twisted as he fought back tears.

"I'm coming in on this a bit late. Who's missing? Why don't you start from the beginning and tell me what happened?"

"*Sylvia. The police think she was out in Eliot's boat when Walter hit last week—.*"

Walter was the hurricane that had ripped up the area that past Wednesday. "Wait a minute." I switched on the desk lamp. "What's Sylvia's last name, please?"

"Ames. Sylvia Ames."

A few people had died in the storm, including several who'd been out in boats. They still can't convince everybody that hurricanes are dangerous, even this far north. "Who's Sylvia? What's her connection to you?"

"She's my fiancée," he said.

"And Eliot?"

"*K. C. Eliot.*" He made a face, showing me that Eliot was a guy, and Steinmetz didn't much care for him. "He's an artist."

"Okay," I said. "Sylvia and Eliot were out on a boat and they got caught by the storm. That's what the police say?"

"*Yes. It can't be right.*"

"Why not?"

"*She's my fiancée.*" He delivered the three words syllable by syllable, as if I'd missed the significance first time around. "*She's not going to go out on a boat ride with somebody else.*"

Well, I thought, stranger things have happened. "What's her connection with Eliot?"

"*She's an artist's model.*"

"And she was posing for him?"

"*Yes.*"

"On the boat?"

"*No. Of course not. In his studio.*"

"Where's the studio?"

He gave me an address in Alexandria. "How'd they get on the boat?"

"*I don't know. The police have a witness, a guy down at the docks, who says he saw Eliot take his boat out when the storm was approaching. Says he got on the radio and tried to warn him.*"

"What kind of boat?"

"*A sailboat.*"

"Where was the storm?"

"*A few hours away. Maybe eight. I mean, Sylvia's no fool. She was going to finish up at the studio and then we were going to head inland. Get away from it.*"

"She was supposed to meet you somewhere?"

"*I was going to pick her up at her apartment. She never showed up.*"

"Okay. The witness saw them take the boat out?"

"*He says there were three of them. Eliot, another guy, and a tall blond. They're assuming the blond is Sylvia.*"

"Why are you so sure it couldn't have been her? Other than that she's your fiancée?"

"*She wouldn't have done that. She posed part time. Her real job was being a medical technician.*" He was having trouble breathing. "*Ms. Walker, the police say they've done all they can. I need somebody to find her.*"

"Jules," I said, softening my voice, "it's been six days. You're telling me no one's heard from her since the day of the storm?"

"*Yes.*"

"Have they recovered any bodies from the bay?"

"*No. They found the boat. Up near Annapolis.*"

"Okay. When did they take the boat out? It was Wednesday, right? Same day as the storm."

"*Yes. The witness says they left about eleven. In the morning.*"

The storm had arrived around seven that night. Not a big one, especially, but there is no such thing as a moderate hurricane. Winds at one-ten. They'd evacuated most of the area. There was still a major cleanup going on. "How long have you been engaged, Jules?"

"*I know what you're thinking. She wouldn't have done that.*"

"Wouldn't have cheated."

"*No.*"

Love is wonderful. But it looked to me as if she'd gone out there with the intention of taking on two guys. They'd gotten carried away, lost track of the storm, and there you are.

"How long had she been modeling for Eliot?"

"*Off and on for a year.*"

I spelled out what it would cost him for me to look into it. He agreed. Anything. Just find her.

"Jules," I said, "I have to tell you at the outset that I don't have much hope. She's been missing since the storm, and an eyewitness described someone who looked like her getting on the boat." I held out my hands. "We have to face the facts."

He stood looking at me, big, pleading, scared. "*Something else you should know,*" he said.

"What's that?"

"She didn't particularly like Eliot. If she were going to cheat, he wouldn't have been the guy."

"I'll get back to you," I said, "as soon as I have something."

⎯⁂⎯

I started by checking my client's background. Jules was a biologist at the University of Maryland. He'd done a couple of flights with Academy missions, charting life forms elsewhere. Originally from Hamburg. Thirty-one years old. Author of two books on biosystem patterns. Whatever they are.

Sylvia, as a model, had maintained an online sales pitch. Her hologram appeared beside the bookcase, seated fetchingly on a gray fabric sofa. Off-the-shoulder black velvet gown. Soft long hair and incandescent brown eyes. A live one. A burgundy voice indicated she was available for modeling assignments. Make appointment.

"Hello, Sylvia," I said.

She smiled. *"Good morning, Kristi."*

"Where have you gone, babe?"

"I don't know. I wish I could help."

I could see why Jules was upset. She was twenty-four. A graduate of Michener Medical in Alexandria. With honors. Virginia native.

And then there was Kevin Charles Eliot. A little guy, as nearly as I could tell. Middle-aged. A bit unkempt. I'd have liked to see a picture of him standing beside Sylvia. It looked as if he'd be almost eye-level with her bumpers.

He'd been having a mildly successful career, by which I mean he sold enough of his work to make a living. But not much more. And my first thought was: How did he afford a sailboat?

Eliot had lived in the D.C. area all his life. According to the bio he'd posted, he seemed not to have done anything, ever, other than paint. He specialized in portraits. You wanted a picture done of Uncle Ralph, something that made Ralph look like a person of significance, Eliot was your guy. Some of his work found its way into galleries, and he even had some art critics gushing. Although I noticed none of the gushes were recent.

When I called Judy Bergdorf, who did the art sections for *The Washington Post*, she told me that Eliot had been ambitious to achieve the top rung, as every artist is. *"But he just didn't have the talent."*

Actually, he looked pretty good to me.

"*No imagination,*" she said. "*Technically, he's about as good as they come, but he doesn't have the spark that you need to make the museums.*"

"That sounds pretty abstract," I told her. "What's 'spark'?"

"*Look at any of his work. The subjects don't come alive. Not the way they do, say, for Bronson. Or Meriwether. You look in their eyes and there's nobody looking back at you.*"

"Okay," I said. "Thanks."

"*In all fairness to him,*" she continued, "*hardly anybody else can do it either.*"

"Did you know him personally, Judy?"

"*More or less.*" Judy was about fifty, but she looked twenty years younger. "*Does this have anything to do with the accident, Kristi?*"

"Yeah," I said. "I'm interested in the woman who was with him." I walked over and looked out the window. A bus was landing at the rooftop station across the street. "Did he have any enemies you know of? Anybody who might want to see him dead?"

"*No,*" she said. "*These guys, the artists, tend not to like each other very much, but the competition doesn't get that hot.*"

"Anybody other than an artist?"

"*Not that I know of.*"

"Okay. Would you think he'd be the kind of guy who'd take a sailboat out into a storm?"

"*K.C.?*" She laughed. "*I wondered about that when I first heard what had happened. He always seemed to me like a safety-first kind of guy.*"

———※———

I poured myself a cup of coffee, got comfortable, tied into Weather Central and reran the hurricane.

Walter had first touched land in Georgia. It had then, as hurricanes usually do, thrown a sharp northerly turn and roared into the Carolinas. It cut a path of destruction inland to Columbia, and turned northeast again toward the Atlantic. It churned back out to sea, hammered Myrtle Beach and the coastal communities, rolled over the Outer Banks and Norfolk, and, on Wednesday, September 17, just after sunset, it blew into Chesapeake Bay.

The track it had followed had been Hurricane Alley a long time.

Nothing much had changed about that. But global warming had given us bigger storms and more of them. As these things went, Walter was only average. But that was enough.

I watched it move north as evening fell. Most of the towns on both sides of the bay had been evacuated. The sky remained bright and sunny until late afternoon and then, as if someone had thrown a switch, the world got dark.

The Weather Central re-creation filled the office. Virginia's eastern shore lay on my right, near the bookcase and below my graduation picture from the police academy. Gloucester Point, Lancaster, and the mouth of the Potomac were on the left. No lights moved along the big highways. At the beginning, there were a few taxis in the air, and maybe a couple commercial carriers, but they got out of the way quickly. The hurricane took over the bay, and the only light visible in all that churning panorama came from a table lamp on my desk. It was rough water. You wouldn't have wanted to be out there. Not in a warship, let alone a sailboat.

I looked at the map. Eliot's boat had been docked at Chesapeake Beach. It was a long way from his studio. If they were there at eleven, they could have gone out for a brief run, and Sylvia could still have made it back home by three to meet Jules. But it seemed like a lot of running around for damned little time on the water.

I wondered how experienced a sailor Eliot had been. Actually, the fact he'd gone out in the face of the storm pretty much answered that question.

So I went back to watching Walter come north, watched the rising water push into the Potomac, watched the storm spread out across both shores. It arrived in full force off Chesapeake Beach and Eliot's dock at seven o'clock, give or take. It knocked some buildings flat. Wrecked a few boats that had not been put away. And finally moved into Maryland.

2

I called Jack Calloway at the station to see what, if anything, he had. Jack's a small, quiet guy with the kind of carefully trimmed mustache that you'd find on a real estate agent. Black skin, black eyes, and a receding hairline. If you didn't look closely you might not take him too seriously. But that would be a mistake. He was in fact a good man to have at your back. We'd worked together when I was on the force.

"*I don't think there's any big mystery, Kristi,*" he said. "*It's pretty obvious your young lady was making out on the side. I mean, she was a nude model. Did you know that?*"

"I didn't have the details."

"*Okay. So it's not a big leap from there to the bedroom.*"

"We can debate that later, Jack. It still doesn't explain why they'd go out into the bay with a hurricane coming in."

"*People do things like that all the time. The storm is why they do it.*" He was in his office, leaning back against his desk. Several plaques were visible behind him.

"You found the boat," I said.

"*The Coast Guard did. They found what was left of it.*"

"Where?"

"*Up near Annapolis. It was wedged against one of the Tolley Bridge supports.*" He showed me a picture. The hull was caved in along the port side. The mast was busted. "*The Coast Guard got an S.O.S. from them. But it was too late. The station was already locked down and they couldn't send anybody out.*"

"Where was the boat when the S.O.S. came in?"

"*I don't know. Middle of the bay somewhere.*"

"And by then the storm had already hit?"

"*Apparently. Look, they were having a pretty good time in the cabin, probably drinking, and nobody paying attention. And suddenly the storm's on top of them. It wouldn't be the first time it happened.*"

"Did anybody see them out on the bay? Were they adrift at any time?"

"*Nobody we know of. With the storm coming, most folks were headed inland.*" He looked as if he'd been through this conversation several times already.

"So the investigation's closed?" I said.

"*There never was a criminal investigation. No reason to think there was anything here to concern ourselves with. You have anything new to offer?*" He folded his hands and propped his chin on them.

"No," I said. "You have any idea who the third person was?"

"*No. We've got a few missing persons, but nobody who seems likely.*" He shrugged. "*Easiest is just to wait until the body comes ashore.*"

I rode a taxi over to Chesapeake Beach, not so much because it was a long drive and a lot quicker to go by air, but because it gave me a chance to look at the countryside. I hadn't been out of the metropolitan area since the storm hit, and I wanted to see for myself how much damage there was.

There were some smashed houses scattered across the landscape. Everything's supposed to be resistant to hurricanes, but there's just so much you can do before the cost becomes exorbitant. I'd spent that Wednesday night huddled in my apartment wondering whether the place would blow away.

The real problem was that, since the storms had become so severe and so frequent, insurance premiums had gone through the roof, and nobody was covered anymore. So you get an event like this, and your house blows away, you're wiped out. To make matters worse, the experts are saying global warming is past the point where it can be easily controlled, and conditions, at least for the foreseeable future, will continue to deteriorate.

—§—

It was threatening rain when my taxi descended into Chesapeake Beach. The sky had turned gray, and a cold wind blew off the bay. If there had at one time actually been a beach, it was long gone, submerged beneath the rising waters of the past century and a half. You could see where the town had retreated from the bay, where a few stone buildings, not worth saving, had been overtaken and now lay offshore.

The taxi set down on a pad outside a seafood restaurant. One wall had been blown in. A couple of guys were working on it. Immediately north of the pad were a half dozen short piers and a ramshackle wooden building marked Roney's Boathouse. It appeared untouched. I told the cab to wait.

I walked over to the boathouse and found a thin, bored-looking guy with a lot of gray hair and a thick gray beard scraping the hull of a jetboat. "Name's Marty," he said. "What can I do for you?"

"Hi, Marty. Kristi Walker." I gave him a big smile. The book says you get a better response from people if you show them your ID. But I've discovered from long experience that guys like this one are more inclined to speak freely to a woman than they are to a P.I. "I wanted to talk with you about K. C. Eliot. One of your customers."

"You a cop?" he asked, uncertain.

"Private," I said. "You don't mind talking to me?" I threw in another smile.

"No. No, I don't mind. What do you want to know?" He put his scraper down and did an appraisal. He answers my questions; I let him look.

Marty was the guy the police had interviewed. "Was anybody else here when Eliot took the boat out? Anybody other than you?"

"No." He grinned. "Wasn't anybody left in *town*. Goddamn storm was coming and they'd all cleared out. I was getting ready to put the last boats away."

"The last boats?"

"There were three of them docked outside. We were supposed to bring them in until the storm passed."

"Okay."

"Then I was going to get out of town myself."

"Did you get the other boats in?"

He looked at me as though the question made no sense. "Two of them," he said.

"Why only two?"

"The third one was Eliot's."

"You're saying that Eliot had arranged to have his boat moved inside, but then he took it out on the bay instead?"

"That's right."

"Did he tell you why?"

"Not really."

"Did you talk with him?"

"On the radio."

"You didn't go out when you saw him on the pier?"

"I was working. Didn't know they were there until they were climbing aboard. I went out and tried to call them back but he just waved and kept going. I couldn't figure that at all. So I used the radio."

"You warned him about the storm."

"Yeah. Asked him where he was going."

"What did he say?"

"Told me he'd only be out a little while. Told me not to worry. He'd take care of the boat himself." He pointed me toward a couple of chairs set around a wooden board on a pair of sawhorses.

"You told the police there were two people with him."

"Yep. A man and a woman."

I showed Sylvia to him. "Is this the woman?" I'd switched her into more casual clothing.

"*Hello, Marty,*" she said. "*Nice to meet you.*"

He looked at her admiringly, and then frowned. "Could be. Hard to tell. I didn't get a good look. She was blond, like this one."

"When you talked to him, was it strictly audio?"

"Yes."

"No visual?"

"No."

"The other male. Had you ever seen him before?"

"No. He wasn't from around here."

"Can you describe him?"

"Big guy. Middle-aged."

"That's it?"

"Black hair. Clean-shaven." He got up, wandered over to a coffee machine and took down two cups. "Want one?"

"Yes. Sure."

"He was wearing a khaki jacket."

There were several boats, on carriers, inside the building. "You came through the storm pretty well," I said.

"Roney's has been here a long time. What'd you say your name was again?"

"Kristi."

"Kristi. Sorry. My memory's not what it used to be. Anyhow, it's going to take more than a hurricane to knock us down."

"When you talked to Eliot on the radio, how did he sound?"

"How do you mean?"

"Did he sound normal? Worried? Anything out of the ordinary?"

He thought about it. "No. I don't recall anything unusual. Except he didn't particularly want to talk to me."

"Really."

"Eliot's usually pretty talkative. Not this time. Hi Marty, we're fine, good-bye. And that was pretty much it."

We sat for a couple of minutes, talking idly, while I finished my coffee. It had started to rain, and the rain quickly became a downpour. It pounded on the roof.

I got up, thanked him, gave him my card, and told him if anything else occurred to him, or if he saw any of these people again, to give me a call. "Oh," I said. "One more question."

He was studying the card. "Yeah?"

"You ever see the blond here before?"

He shook his head. "Nope."

"You're sure?"

"Yep. She'd of been hard to forget."

I went up to Annapolis and looked at the wreckage. They'd pulled it away from the bridge and beached it. I knew a couple of the cops up there and one of them, Angelo Reynoso, escorted me to the site. It had been a sixteen-footer, the kind of boat you see all over Chesapeake Bay.

"I understand they got off an S.O.S.," I said.

He looked at the wreckage with the world-weariness in his eyes that all cops acquire if they hang around long enough. "That's what I hear, Kris. It was too late, though. The storm had already shut down the station. Wasn't anything anybody could do."

"What did Eliot say? Send help?"

"I understand it was the AI. It just kept repeating that they needed assistance."

"The AI?"

"Yes."

"That seems strange, doesn't it? What would you do if you woke up out there with a storm coming on?"

"I'd get on the radio and make some noise."

I climbed into the boat. It was full of water and sand. There were two radios, one aft at the helm, the other in the cabin. They were identical models, the Spindrift 280.

"Bed's been slept in," said Angelo. Yeah. It looked as if they'd been having a good time. I checked the head. Two toothbrushes. "They found her purse over in the corner."

"It *was* Sylvia Ames's purse?"

"Yeah. Did you know her?"

"No," I said. "Her boy friend's my client."

His voice dropped an octave. "That has to be tough."

I called Spindrift and got an A.I. "I'd like some information on the 280 marine radio, please."

"*Of course,*" it said, in a silky female voice. "*What did you want to know?*"

I asked about range. And then: "Does it have a relay function?"

"*Yes, it does.*"

"Thank you very much."

Angelo looked interested. "You think the S.O.S. might have come from a remote location?"

"It's possible. A directed signal aimed at the boat and then broadcast from there. Who knows?"

"You think it was a murder."

"I'm looking at the possibilities, Anj."

"You always did have a lot of imagination, love."

3

I started wandering around town, getting to know the art community. Aside from the artists, there were agents, suppliers, gallery operators, sales people, even a guy who configured AI's who were making paintings. I had no idea that we had AI's doing art. I'd heard about it, but hadn't believed it. I do now. I saw some of their work and they're better than human. In some ways.

Word got out that I was on the street, and by the third day I was hearing things like, We were expecting you, and Heard you were coming.

Everybody knew Eliot, but nobody really admitted to being a friend. He was not, according to the consensus, in any kind of trouble. And no one knew of a reason anybody would want him dead.

I saved the most likely location for last: The Renaissance Gallery, in Arlington, was owned by Mary and James Colter. It had, on occasion, handled Eliot's work. James was there when I showed up.

The place looked good. Subdued lighting, satin curtains, thick carpets, just-audible classical music. Oil paintings were on display on two levels. I'm no art critic, but James smoothly assured me the artists were among the best currently working in the N.A.U. and Europe. "May I ask how your interests lie?" he asked.

James Colter didn't so much walk through the gallery as he swept through. A monarch moving among his monuments. It was easy to visualize him seated on a chair hauled about by peasants. He was fifty, with dark brown hair, and a tendency to keep his voice low as if we were in a church.

How did my interests lie?

This guy got to see my ID. "Do you have anything by K. C. Eliot?" I asked.

"Why, yes, Ms. Walker." His attitude changed slightly. The monarch was still there, but he became more distant. Consumed by pressing duties, you know. "As it happens we have." He led me into the rear. We climbed a circular staircase to the mezzanine, and he pointed to a portrait of a young man clad in hunting gear. The young man stood beside a tree, gazing serenely back at us. "This is one of his very best. He called it 'After the Hunt.' " He smiled, casting away the title. "As you can see, his balance is superb."

"Yes," I said. "Remarkable."

"This is about ten years old. Eliot hadn't planned to sell it. He used it as a demonstration piece. But, as a result of his unfortunate death, it came into our hands."

"It's quite good," I said.

"Yes." James stood back so as not to block my view.

"Do you have anything else of his?"

"No. Nothing, I'm sorry to say."

"Prints, maybe?"

He coughed politely. "We don't carry prints."

I asked how much the painting might bring. He cited a number which was considerably higher than my conversation with Judy Bergdorf suggested. "How well did you know him?" I asked.

"Eliot? Not well at all, actually." He glanced at the time. "I only knew him as a professional."

"Did he have any friends?"

"Not really. He wasn't a sociable sort."

"What about a girlfriend?"

We were starting back downstairs, but he paused with his fingers lightly holding the handrail. "Yes," he said. "There was a young lady."

"Can you tell me her name?"

"Janice Something."

The name turned out to be JoBeth Androska. JoBeth had been with Eliot a couple of times when he'd visited the gallery. "Average-looking woman," according to James. She worked at the Moonlight Hotel on Wilson Boulevard.

I drove over, got lucky, and found her on duty. She looked good, certainly better than James had implied. She teared up when I told her why I was there. It took a few minutes to pry her loose from the counter. We eventually found chairs in the lobby. "It's terrible," she said. "I just don't know what to think."

"I'm sorry," I said.

"It's not knowing that drives me crazy. And the other thing is that I can't believe he'd have taken the boat out with that storm coming in. It just wasn't like him."

She started to dissolve in front of me. Then she looked around, saw that everyone in the lobby was watching, and swallowed hard. "Let's go back to the employees' lunchroom."

The lunchroom was a bare-bones place, where maybe ten people could eat. There was a long table in the center. We sat down at it, and she asked whether I thought there was any chance K. C. might be alive.

I didn't want to lie to her. I thought Eliot and Sylvia were dead. And the third person too, whoever he might turn out to be.

Her voice gave way. "I should be used to it by now," she said. "But it just doesn't seem possible." She shook her head. "Until there's a body—"

"How was he doing as an artist?" I asked, trying to sound as if I just wanted to change the subject.

"Okay." She picked up a napkin, folded it in half, and folded it again. "He thought his work was improving. Getting better all the time."

"I mean financially."

"All right." She cleared her throat. "He was never going to make big money. He knew that."

"His studio was in Alexandria."

"Yes."

"What's happening over there now?"

"At the studio? Not much. The rent was paid through the end of the month. The executor is running an estate sale tomorrow. This weekend we're going to clear what's left."

"Who's the executor?"

"I am."

"JoBeth, I wonder if you'd mind telling me what the estate is worth?"

Big smile. "It was a surprise to me."

"How much of a surprise?"

"The accountant's going to give me the numbers within the next few days. But it looks like about six hundred thousand."

Not bad for a struggling artist. That was about nine years' pay for me. "And it's going to whom?"

She looked uncomfortable. "He left everything to me."

"Nothing to the family?"

"He didn't have a family. Folks are dead. He was an only child."

"Okay."

"I didn't do it." She was sniffling.

"I know."

"Thank you."

She excused herself, went through a back door, and returned with a glass of water. Belatedly she asked if I wanted any. "Is this going to take much longer? They need me back at the desk."

"No. Just a minute or two. There was a second man with him when he took the boat out. Do you have any idea who that might have been? Big guy, black hair. About fifty, fifty-five."

"I don't know."

"Have you ever known him to do anything like this before?"

"You mean take a model out on the boat?"

"Yeah."

"Never. He was strictly professional about that."

"How about riding into a storm? Was he inclined to take chances?"

"K. C.? He's the most cautious man I know. No, he'd never do anything like that."

"But he did."

She nodded. "I don't understand it."

That didn't surprise me. In my experience women almost never know their men very well. "JoBeth, I'd like to ask a favor."

"Go ahead."

"Are you off this evening?"

"Yes. I'm done at six."

"I wonder if you'd mind letting me look around K. C.'s studio?"

She thought about it. "Why? What could it possibly have to do with the boat coming apart in a storm?"

I reached over and laid a hand on her forearm. She was trembling. "I won't know until I've looked."

⁓

The studio was located on the second floor of a stone building at the south end of Fletcher Street, over a men's clothing store. It was mostly empty when I got there, the furniture gone, personal stuff gone, just a few packing cases left in the middle of the room.

JoBeth stood inside the doorway. This is where he had his easel. Over there is where the model usually posed. Bedroom in there. Kitchen back that way.

He'd lived there. And I gathered that they'd both lived there, off and on. Never a formal arrangement. Weekends. Otherwise hit or miss. I thought about the nude models and wondered whether a girlfriend can get used to that. But I couldn't see any point asking.

The place looked as if it had cost money. It was big, and if it wasn't exactly luxurious, it wasn't nickels and dimes either. "Did he do anything else besides art?" I asked. "I mean, did he have any other employment?"

"No," she said. "This was his life, right here."

"Any other means of income?"

"Not that I know of."

I took another look around the studio. Two long windows looking down on Fletcher Street. Nice curtains. Paneled walls. Brass bathroom fixtures. A tub you could swim in. "If you don't mind my asking, Jo-Beth, the rent here must have been fairly high."

"It is. I didn't realize how high until I got talking to the landlord a few days ago."

"How'd he manage it?"

She touched the curtains gently. Swayed, and held on. "I don't know. I guess he was doing better than I thought."

"What's in the cases?"

"Odds and ends. Brushes, canvas, paint."

"He was working on a portrait of Sylvia Ames when things went wrong."

"Yes."

"Did you know Sylvia?"

She nodded. "I knew her." She touched one of the boxes gently, with a fingertip. "I was okay with it. It's what he did. He was very professional."

"Okay."

"Nobody who came here, who modeled for him, ever had a complaint."

"You don't think anything was going on? On the boat?"

"No. I don't believe it."

"Did he complete the portrait?"

"No. Did you want to see it? I have it right here."

"Please."

It was in back, leaning against a wall, front facing in as if it were an embarrassment. She held it for me. "It's just a preliminary sketch. He was just starting."

Sylvia would have been portrayed almost in profile, clasping roses to her breast, long hair combed down over one shoulder.

She put it back, face in again. "Does he customarily do that?" I asked. "Make a preliminary sketch before starting the final work?"

"Oh, yes. He always does it. Uses charcoal."

"JoBeth," I said, "how long had he been in this studio?"

"He moved over here about three years ago. Right around the time I met him."

"Where was he before then?"

She gave an address on Warlock Avenue. One of the seedier sections of town.

"Thanks," I said. "Are there more sketches around? Or finished work?"

She shook her head no. "Maybe one or two. The last year or so, he's worked mostly on commission. Somebody wants a portrait, he does it, and the portrait goes out."

"But that wasn't the case with Sylvia."

"No. He still had hopes of making a name for himself. But it's hard. It's not simply a matter of talent. I mean, he had the talent. But a lot of it's politics."

"How do you mean?"

"Schmoozing with the gallery owners. And the distributors. And the critics. Especially the critics. K. C. never did any of that. He let his work stand for itself." She sighed, stricken by the unfairness of it all. "He has an archive. It contains everything he's ever done."

꧁꧂

The archive was recorded in the AI's files, but the files had been transferred to her place, so that's where we went. She lived about a mile away, in a small apartment looking down on a large Italian restaurant. *Louie's.* She broke out a bottle and we drank a round to the missing artist. Then she directed the AI to produce the archive.

There were a few landscapes, but mostly he did portraits. I guess I'd expected to see more nudes, but there were all kinds of people, kids on a wooden bridge, an elderly woman gazing across an open field, a young mother nursing her infant. There were several of the sort you find in boardrooms, an intimidating founder looking out past the rabble. His most common subjects were elderly men and women who looked boring. Stuffy. "He hated doing those," she said. "Paintings of stuck-up people who had never done anything. But it's where the money was."

One in particular caught my eye: a bearded man wearing a safari hat and a hunting jacket. He seemed a bit pompous, but there was simultaneously something heroic about the figure.

"That's Harold Clayborn," she said. When I showed no sign of recognition, she added, "Midnight."

Ah, yes. Midnight Clayborn, an adventurer who'd written books about his travels around the globe, and to a handful of other worlds.

"Does Clayborn have the painting?" I asked.

"Yes. He commissioned K. C. to do it."

"I'm impressed." Clayborn claimed to have found Sennacherib's throne. I wasn't sure what else he'd done, but his books were enormously popular. "Did you get to meet him?"

"No." She looked disappointed. "He was before my time."

"Are there any other famous people here?" I asked.

She considered it. "I don't think so."

Among the landscapes, there was a painting of a young man gazing across the Hudson. A couple of country scenes. And a moonlit beach.

"The critics said he had no imagination," she said. "But look at those."

The beach looked romantic. The moon was full, and its golden track ran to the horizon. But the fact was I'd seen a thousand like it. "Yes," I said. "Critics are not to be taken seriously."

"Absolutely right. Kristi, he had a passion for his art. *Loved* what he did. When he wasn't painting, we were out at the museums and the galleries. When the Retreat opened a few months ago, we were there. The first day."

I wasn't clear on what she was saying. The Retreat was a structure found in a star system that supported no life. It had been a single building on an airless moon orbiting a gas giant. It was empty when an Academy team found it, ten or eleven years ago, and it didn't look as if anybody had been there for a long time. But two *things* had lived and died there. They'd had a library and a shower and oversized furniture and apparently whatever else they needed to make themselves comfortable.

The Academy arranged to have the place disassembled and brought to Arlington and then put back together. It had taken a long time, but they'd done it and the place had opened to an excited public and outraged preservationists that past spring.

But what did it have to do with art?

"Let me show you," she said.

She signaled the AI and a portrait materialized. "This was found hanging in the main room when they first got to the Retreat." I'd seen it before. It was faded, had spent too much time in vacuum and, I guess, in pretty cold temperatures. Don't know what that does to a painting. But maybe it was just as well. The subject wasn't somebody you'd want to meet on a D.C. street at night.

They called it *The Stranger*. It had smoldering eyes and a reptilian smile and shadows in the wrong places. It wore a dark robe and a hood was pulled down over the forehead. I recalled that the experts thought it was an accurate rendering, possibly a self-portrait, of one of the two creatures that had lived in the Retreat.

"K. C. wanted to see how art would look through nonhuman eyes," she said. "Did you see the mile-long lines that first day? When they first opened? We were there." She shook her head angrily. "And people accuse him of having no soul." She poured another round, and we drank to his soul.

"How'd he meet Clayborn?" I asked.

"One of the gallery owners knew him. Annie Detmer. When he mentioned getting a portrait done, she recommended K. C."

I turned back to the Clayborn painting. "He did a nice job."

"Yes, he did, didn't he? Later, Clayborn bought some of his other paintings."

"Really?"

"Yes. He was K. C.'s best customer."

"How many paintings did he buy?"

She had to think. "I believe it was five."

"Do you know how much he paid?"

"I can't imagine why it would matter. But I don't know. I have no idea."

"Did K. C. ever hint about the amount?"

"I suppose he did. He told me that Clayborn appreciated his work. And what he meant by that, I'm sure, is that he paid pretty generously." Her eyes became defensive.

"What else?" I asked.

"How do you mean?"

"There's something you're not telling me."

She took a deep breath. "I'm not sure it's anything."

"Try me."

"He was getting money from Clayborn."

"You mean other than the payments for the paintings?"

She wavered, looked like maybe yes, maybe no. "I just know payments came in."

"Regularly?"

"I don't know."

"How'd the money come?"

"What do you mean?"

"How did Clayborn make the payment? Transferral? Check? What?"

"Transferral."

"Okay," I said. "Anybody else?"

"Anybody else what?"

This kid wasn't the quickest babe on the block. "Was anybody else giving him money?"

"Not that I know of."

"Do you have access to his bank records?"

"No," she said.

"But you're his executor."

She managed a smile. "Right," she said.

It took a while, but eventually the numbers came through. Eliot had incorporated himself as Rising Wind Enterprises. And there were the purchases from Clayborn, six in all, beginning almost four years earlier. But only six. Where were the other payments?

"I don't know," she said. "K. C. told me he was sending money."

Well, there were some large deposits. Thirty thousand here, forty thousand there. Over the years they added up to almost three-quarters of a million. But this money came from a numbered account. I checked the designator. The account was listed to the International Bank, which rode serenely on the space station. "You think this is Clayborn's money?" I asked.

JoBeth didn't know. Maybe.

I looked up everything I could find about Midnight Clayborn. He became famous twenty-five years ago when Adam Hutton wrote his biography *Midnight*. The nickname had come from an incident early in his career. Arab bandits had seized some kids at an excavation site. The kids had belonged to Clayborn's workers. The incident occurred while he was digging at Ugarit. The kidnappers had demanded money, but they were a particularly bloodthirsty crew with a history of occasionally murdering hostages. Six kids were involved. And Clayborn had no inclination to rely on the honor of cutthroats.

Consequently he organized a rescue operation. A friend created a distraction by crash-landing a flyer nearby, and Clayborn with a few picked men charged into the bandit camp precisely at midnight, as the guards were being changed. There was a brief exchange of gunfire, during which he was wounded, but several of the bandits were killed, and the others fled. The hostages were rescued unharmed, and Harold Clayborn had earned the sobriquet by which the world has known him since.

He was a popular area speaker, forever talking to service organizations, graduating classes, academic groups. His next scheduled event was at the Adventurers' Club Friday evening. That was only two days away.

I was sitting in my office looking at his hologram when Jack called. (Clayborn was wearing the same safari hat as in Eliot's painting. He was a little younger, and looked quite capable of riding down a bunch of bandits.)

"Yeah, Jack," I said. "What can I do for you?"

"*You busy?*"

"What's happening?"

"*Why don't you come down to the station? I'll wait for you.*"

4

Eliot's body had been found lying face down in the marsh grass on the western shore, a few miles north of Lexington Park.

The lab unit was there when we arrived. It was a desolate stretch of swamp, and it had been difficult to find dry ground for the emergency vehicles. We came down on a hilltop surrounded by ooze. Jack passed me a pair of boots from the locker. I took off my shoes and pulled them on. "Be careful getting out," he said. "Don't sink."

Eliot's body had come to rest against an embankment. It had been spotted by a couple of bird-watchers in a boat. It now lay in the EV, where the technicians were going over it. The team leader was Catherine Sabatina. Cathie was abrasive, but she was good at her job. She turned as we approached.

"Good to see you, Jack," she said. She nodded my way. "The victim has a severe head contusion. Might have come from a collision with a spar when he went overboard," she said. "Or somebody might have used an oar handle on him."

"Okay," he said. "What else have we got?"

"He's been in the water about two weeks."

"Cause of death?"

"Let you know when we get him back to the lab."

It was getting dark. A cold wind blew off the bay. I could see a couple of boats out about a mile, sailboats, drifting past. Their lights were just coming on.

Cathie and her team climbed into the EV. It lifted off and turned west.

"Blow to the head," I said.

He nodded. "That's what it sounds like." We sloshed back through the muck, got onto dry land, and pulled off the boots. "What have you got on this, Kristi? Anything?"

I told him what I'd been doing.

"So what's next?"

"Not sure yet. I'll let you know."

A few hours later I got a call from him. Eliot had drowned.

⎯⎯§⎯⎯

I was thinking it was time I met Midnight Clayborn. The Friday evening address at the Adventurers' Club sounded like the right venue. I got on the circuit and checked it out. Was the public welcome?

"Sorry, but no," they told me. *"Members only. And guests."*

I called around. Found somebody who knew somebody, and got an introduction to Pavel Gurov, a volcanologist. Pavel—Pasha to his friends—was a member, but hadn't been planning on attending. He would reconsider, and would be delighted to invite me as his guest if I would consent to have a drink afterward with him. He was a bit stiff, a guy who'd spent too much time in the field, but he seemed okay. I said sure. Then I called JoBeth and asked whether her AI was capable of imitating K. C.'s voice.

"Sure," she said. She sounded suspicious. But I tried to allay her concerns. Then I told her what I wanted her to do.

⎯⎯§⎯⎯

The Adventurers' Club meets monthly at the Brandeis Hotel, just off Massachusetts Avenue. Pasha and I rolled in with about fifteen minutes to spare.

The Brandeis is one of these ancient places, built in the latter part of the twenty-first century. It has lots of heavy paneling and oddball lighting and what the travel agents like to call character, which means the elevators creak.

The members, as you would expect, were predominantly but not exclusively male. There were about eighty people present, milling around and nursing drinks, when a bell dinged and we filed into one of the banquet rooms. A dinner consisting mostly of inedible pork and vegetables showed up. We were seated in groups of eight, and I could see Clayborn at the head table. A few drums and spears had been placed strategically around the room, and a dark blue banner with THE ADVENTURERS' CLUB marked in silver Arabic-style letters was mounted along the front wall. A lectern stood in front of the banner.

I was, by the way, wearing an auburn wig that changed my hair from short to shoulder-length. It was the best disguise I could think of. I knew by then I'd be sitting down with Midnight at some point and asking him questions, and I didn't want him remembering me from this event.

We got the food down as best we could, and eventually a small portly man, who did not look at all like an adventurer, got up from the head table, walked over to the lectern, and welcomed us. It was good to see us again. He announced that one of the members had passed away since they'd last gathered, read the minutes of the last meeting, gave way to the treasurer for a financial report, and to the membership secretary for remarks about the membership drive. I wondered, but did not ask, what the qualifications for membership were.

Finally it was time to introduce the guest of honor. "Dr. Harold C. Clayborn." Clayborn rose to considerable applause. "*Midnight* Clayborn," the moderator added.

The applause went through the roof.

He was tall, leading-man handsome, though his best days were behind him. His hair was peppered with gray, but he moved with the smooth lankiness of a practiced athlete. He wore a bright red jacket, a white shirt, and gray slacks with a crease that could have cut the pork. He looked perfectly at home.

The moderator remarked how he needed no introduction, but then spent five minutes detailing his accomplishments, both on- and off-world. Finally he gave way to Clayborn, and another round of applause. Clayborn said hello in a rich baritone voice. "It's good to be with you," he said, "with people who've gone past the humdrum existence of civilized life, and reached out for something more." He was good, and I could see they loved him. "It's a pleasure to be here."

More applause.

"The past is prologue, somebody said. And if that's true, it's equally true that the experience of other civilizations, of offworld cultures, qualifies as an alternate past, as a catalog of events that might have happened here. And that is precious knowledge for the same reason our own experience is precious, because we can learn from it."

I listened for several minutes, then excused myself from the table and retreated outside into the lobby, where I sat down in a leather chair and called JoBeth.

"*Hello,*" she said.

"Ready to go," I told her.

"*You're sure I won't get into trouble?*" she asked. "*I really don't like doing this.*"

"It's okay, JoBeth," I said. "Just think of it as an experiment."

"*All right. I assume you know what you're doing.*"

Next I called Pete at the office and told him what I needed. Then I went back to listen to the rest of Midnight Clayborn's presentation.

He had a commanding presence. I don't intimidate easily, but there was something about him that seemed almost more than human. Even when he was blowing smoke, as he did that evening. "We have no idea what's out there," he was saying in his conclusion. "The interstellar deeps still defy us. We can travel in them, but we cannot cross them. How is it that we have bluejays and philosophers and, yes, organizations like The Adventurers' Club? The answers are out there. Somewhere. We've seen just enough to be sure. But I'm sorry to say it's going to fall to another generation to find them. To leave the Big Downtown, this little island of light, and figure out what the cosmos is really up to."

He thanked them and headed for his table. They stood and applauded until he returned to the lectern. Every time he tried to sit, it started again. Finally the emcee intervened.

"Isn't he marvelous?" said Pasha.

Everyone gathered around to shake his hand. In the midst of it, he had to answer a call. I watched sudden surprise appear on his weather-beaten face as he listened to the voice in his link. His brow creased. He held up a hand to keep his admirers at bay.

What had just happened was that he'd received a message from his AI. There'd been a call at home. Audio only. The caller had identified himself as K. C. Eliot. Eliot had left a message: "*Need to talk to you. Call you later. Don't try to reach me.*"

When he was able, he broke away from the crowd, went out into the hall, made a call, and spoke for two or three minutes. It was an animated conversation, at least on his end. I was too far away to overhear, but he was shaking his head, and he wasn't happy. Several of his admirers spilled out of the meeting room and found him, so he had to cut the conversation short.

He was engulfed again. At that point I signaled Pete. He called me and I answered in front of Pasha. I listened for a moment and then tried to look concerned. "When?" I asked. I nodded, and bit my lip. "Okay. I'll be there as quickly as I can manage it."

"What's wrong?" Pasha asked.

"My mother. She's been taken ill. I'm terribly sorry, but I have to get right over there."

Pasha was about thirty. Reasonably attractive. Blond hair, mustache, blue eyes, good smile. Not the world's best sense of humor, but it might show up, given a chance. I hated to lie to him. "I have to hustle," I said. That meant an aircab. I thanked him for the evening, delivered a chaste kiss, promised to get in touch, and hurried out of the dining room. I tossed my wig in my handbag and, when Clayborn arrived in the lobby, I assumed a safe distance and fell in behind him. He walked into the parking garage and I called for a cab. In case you're not familiar with the megalopolis rules, private flight vehicles are not permitted. You want to take to the air, you grab a bus or a taxi. Otherwise you stay on the ground. I watched him get into a black Cavallo and start down out of the garage.

The cab was waiting outside when I hit the front door. I climbed in, showed it my account, then disabled the AI, and took over manual control. You're not supposed to do that unless there's an emergency, but I figured this qualified. When the Cavallo bounced out onto Massachusetts Avenue, I was directly overhead.

He went six blocks, pulled up in front of the Memorial Hotel, turned his car over to the attendants, and strode inside.

⁓

The landing pad was half a block away. I reactivated the AI, jumped out, hustled down the street and charged into the hotel. Clayborn was standing in the restaurant queue.

I added dark glasses, and wished I'd thought to bring along a spare jacket. But I did the next best thing, checking the one I was wearing. Then I sat down in the lobby and tried to look as if I were expecting someone.

Prices at the Memorial are steep, so the help is all human. Even the entertainers. No avatars running around. Several executive-types were clustered near the front desk, wearing badges that carried their names and the label *BreezeWay*.

The restaurant was standard. Too many tables and chairs in too little space. Broad windows looked out on the traffic. It was late. The place was about a quarter full. After a minute or so the host took Clayborn to a corner table. They brought coffee, and he checked the time. He still looked unhappy.

I think I spotted the guy he was waiting for as soon as he came in the door. Tall. Taller even than Midnight. Hard features. Hair black, going gray at the temples. Well-dressed. Maybe fifty years old. He breezed through the people waiting at the host's station, located his man, and started in his direction.

The argument began before he'd even reached the table. It was low-key, no shouting or anything like that, but you couldn't miss it.

I took a picture and sent it to Jack. Minutes later he was on the link. *"George Antonelli,"* he said. *"He's an executive with H&B. One of their top people."*

"What's he do?"

"He's an engineer."

"Any connection with artists?"

"Not that I know of. Haven't really had time to look. What are they talking about?"

"I can't get close enough to tell. But Midnight's not happy."

"Okay. Be careful."

Anybody who goes into my line of work needs to be able to read lips. I couldn't see anything of what Antonelli was saying; the angle was wrong. But I was able to pick up some of Midnight's comments. *Damned right!* And *Why are they something something?* He kept looking around, conscious that he was in a public place. I considered walking over and saying hello, see how they'd react, but I thought better of it. Best to be conservative until you get a good idea what's going on.

The waiter showed up, poured coffee for Antonelli, refilled Clayborn's cup, and they ordered. When he'd gone, Clayborn didn't pick up where he'd left off, as I expected, but simply sat staring out the window.

Antonelli said something. Clayborn shook his head. No. Not possible. Somebody—He stopped and sighed. Both men checked the time, and checked it again. Coffee came. Antonelli tried it and pushed it away. He started talking again. Clayborn shook his head. No. It doesn't matter what you say.

After about ten minutes, Antonelli got up and left. He came out of the dining room like a thrown spear and went out through the front doors. A few minutes later their meals arrived.

I watched Clayborn finish eating. When he came out of the dining room, he headed directly for me and I wondered whether I'd made a mistake and he'd recognized me from the Adventurers' Club. No way he could miss me, and when he smiled in my direction, I had already begun preparing an explanation. But he went right by and into a convenience store.

I got up and headed for the exit.

5

From a distance, the Retreat looked like a two-story turtle shell, split down the middle. The split incorporated a courtyard, which had a bench, a curving walkway, an assortment of geraniums, and a few newly planted oak trees. There were two front doors, one in each wing. And lots of windows. The architecture was plain, without any serious effort at ornamentation, other than a few abutments and setbacks. There was a circular cupola on the roof at the rear. I saw no shielding of any kind, and it was hard to stand in front of this place and imagine it out on a moon, just sitting there. The guidebook said it had used an energy shield to seal itself off from the void, but it nevertheless looked fragile. I tried to imagine myself living there, looking out those windows at empty space, and nowhere to go. It wasn't my kind of situation.

It lies alongside the newly built Academy museum. I paid up, one price for the whole show, and went inside.

What strikes you about the Retreat is how big the occupants were. They have avatars of the two of them outside, in the courtyard, and you stand there and look up at them. I got to slightly above the male's belt line. They were wearing robes and hoods, with eyes that scared the kids. Their foreheads were arched, and their smiles sent a chill down my back.

You walk inside and the scale of the furniture reinforces initial impressions, makes it all real, the enormous sofa and chairs, and even the massive books, all too large for human comfort. It brought back memories of being five years old.

There were books everywhere. In the western wing, there'd been a library. (I don't know whether it had been the western wing on the moon, or even whether you could have a western wing on a satellite rolling through a polar orbit. But it was on the western side in Arlington.) The original books had all been replaced by dummy volumes. You couldn't remove any of them from the bookshelves. They had been frozen when the Survey team found the site, and this of course was supposed to be an effort to reproduce the original experience. In air-conditioned comfort. But the bindings, which resembled tooled leather, were soft. I doubted that had been their condition when the Academy team first found them.

One volume lay open on a table, and another on a chair. Two printed pages in each were exposed. The lines of symbols were exactly reproduced from the originals. No one had yet succeeded in deciphering any of the alien script. But the experts were confident they could do it. Eventually.

What struck you was the portrait of the male that JoBeth had shown me. It was considerably more disquieting in person than the picture had been in JoBeth's apartment. It looked exactly like the avatar out front, but you knew that was electronic fakery. This, God help us, was real. It was mounted behind the sofa, one of those eerie pictures that made you feel you were being watched. The guidebook said that the thing was thought to be a self-portrait. And that was more disconcerting still.

It was somewhat faded. The experts put its age at several centuries, maybe as much as a thousand years. The frame was chocolate brown, decorated with intertwining curved lines.

They keep a guard near the living-room portrait because it's a bottleneck. People pile up and nobody wants to leave.

There was a similar portrait of the female in one of the bedrooms. Her mood seemed lighter, and her eyes less threatening. But not so much that I'd have felt comfortable sharing a donut with her.

If you looked out the front windows, you didn't see the avatars, or the traffic on the Potomac Expressway, or the Old Pentagon Building, which should have been visible to the southeast. Instead you saw what the Survey team had seen: an enormous gas giant in the middle of the sky, its rings and moons rising high and dipping below the horizon. And, in the distance, a second ringed world. The Twins.

I'm not usually big on spectacle. I've been to the Canyon and to Yosemite and to the Alps, and I've even been to the Moon, but it just doesn't do much for me. Never did. Give me twenty seconds with a great view and I'm ready to eat. But that window! It literally made me dizzy.

The security chief was a heavyweight. Big man, lots of stomach pushing at his uniform. I showed him my ID and asked whether I could see the vid record for Friday, June 14.

"Opening day," he said.

"Yes. Please."

He led me into a viewing room and left me to it. "The AI's Hutch," he said.

"Hutch?"

"Private joke. She's a big wheel in the Academy."

So I sat down and showed K. C. Eliot to Hutch. "If he shows up somewhere I'd like to see it."

"*Eleven oh-four a.m., Kristi,*" she said. And showed me Eliot and JoBeth strolling through the Retreat living room. They stopped to look at the furniture, and through the front windows at the Twins. They glanced at a few of the books, and then wandered over and stood in front of the portrait. *The Stranger.* JoBeth said something. He nodded.

After a few minutes they moved off. Into the kitchen. Then upstairs. And finally they left.

"Thanks, Hutch," I said.

"*You're welcome. Did you want to see the rest?*"

"There's more?"

"*June 18.*"

"Run it."

Eliot was alone this time. He came in past the front security station and made directly for the living room. There, he bypassed everything else and took up a position in front of *The Stranger*. He stood studying it about fifteen minutes. It was a quiet time, and the guard didn't bother him. Then he left.

George Antonelli had no police record, and seemed never to have been in trouble. He was fifty-one, a graduate of Comstock and of West Haven Technical. He was married with two young kids.

He specialized in unique design projects, those one-of-a-kind engineering challenges where no previous experience existed, and which were not likely to be repeated. He had built the Mohan Bridge in California, and the Coronet Building in New York. But he was best known for his association with the Retreat.

He had supervised the operation to disassemble the place and bring it back to Arlington. There'd been a big fight about it because a lot of people thought it should have been left where it was. But in the end, the bureaucrats had their way, and they contracted with H&B to do the job. According to the accounts, H&B had sent their best man.

Many thought the task could not be accomplished. But Antonelli had taken the Retreat apart like a puzzle, lifted it into orbit, repackaged it, and turned it over to the cargo masters. They'd brought it to Earth orbit and delivered it to Arlington. Once there, Antonelli had taken charge again and reassembled the puzzle.

It had been, the guidebook said, a unique achievement. The actual move had required six years, although the process had taken considerably longer because of the various legal challenges and protests.

The effort had cost him his first marriage. His wife had apparently gotten tired of living without a husband and found somebody else. There had been no children.

His company, H&B, had in the meantime enjoyed a remarkable run of success. Several off-world projects had come their way, and they'd responded with energy and imagination. They'd built the black hole station at Carmalla, they'd set up a deep space transport system off Argon II, and they were in the process of designing the first serious space habitats. I couldn't help noticing that much of their business had been funneled through the Academy. Clayborn had sat on the Academy board of directors during this period. It wasn't hard to see how he and Antonelli had become acquainted.

They'd also brought back an alien starship from the same site. I wandered outside and strolled past it. It had been parked, God knew how long, on the same mountain shelf that the Retreat had occupied. I looked up at it, gray and innocuous. Kids chased each other up its ladder and peeked out through the airlock.

Inside the museum, there were artifacts from the mission, pictures of the participants, the jumpsuits they'd worn, schematics of their ship. You could visit the VR section and relive any of several experiences. You could watch the Academy team approach the Retreat for the first time, or Antonelli and his engineers begin the process of disassembling the building. You could visit the gift shop and buy alien dolls, or a model of the alien vessel. Also for sale were T-shirts, books, dinnerware and glasses engraved with the Academy crest. And prints of the two paintings.

The gift shop was busy on the day I was there, and the prints seemed by far the most popular items.

It struck me as odd that we didn't yet have a name for the two creatures who had inhabited that faraway rock. We still didn't know who they were, what they were doing there, or where they'd come from. They were simply strangers. In the deepest sense of the word.

I wondered what they'd have made of all the fuss, of the crowds and kids and balloons and flags and popcorn.

—⊸⊱—

I wished I had a contact at the Academy. I went back in the morning, introduced myself as a representative of the William L. Albright Corporation, told them we were planning to do some off-world construction, and that I wanted to speak with someone about how they'd managed the relocation of the Retreat.

I got bounced around a bit and finally landed in the office of a deputy assistant who had actually been on the vertical moon during the operation. That's the moon where the retreat was located. It has a polar orbit, putting it almost at ninety degrees to the rest of the system. It provides a remarkable view of the whole show, rings, moons, you name it.

His name was Al Perry, and he was more than willing to talk. Mostly, I suspect, because he thought being that far from home was pretty impressive stuff when you were dealing with a young woman. Well, reasonably young. Or maybe he thought I was a potential employer, and it looked good on his resumé.

Perry was about forty-five, a bit formal, prematurely receding hair, large head, short, not quite heavy, but headed in that direction.

I asked questions about the Retreat, how they'd handled the zero-gee problems, how they'd managed to take apart a structure that, as far as I could see, hadn't been designed to be taken apart. What kind of equipment they'd needed. How the pieces had been stored for the Earth-bound flight. How the alien ship had been moved. Had someone figured out how to make it work and piloted it home? (It had come back in the hold of the *Sebastian Toomy*.)

Gradually I shifted the conversation around to the people involved in the move. To the Academy onsite rep. To the crew of the *Toomy*. To the H&B team. And eventually we arrived at George Antonelli.

"Good man," Perry said. "Sharp as they come."

"That must have been a tricky assignment," I said, "working out there in a hostile environment, trying to juggle equipment on a narrow shelf. Obviously he got the job done."

"Yes," he said. "He had to break a few heads to do it, but he got it done."

"Tough boss, huh?"

"Well, I don't know if I'd put it quite that way. But he doesn't have much tolerance for stupidity."

"Yeah. I worked for a guy like that once. It can be a little bit draining."

He thought about it. "He got results."

"His people resent him? The reason I ask, we'll be out in the middle of nowhere too, for a long time. I think we'll need a guy who can get along with everybody."

"Yeah. Well, I didn't mean to suggest he couldn't get along with the help. He got along fine."

"Did they work around the clock, Al?"

"No. He didn't have enough people to run that kind of operation. It costs a lot of money to maintain a crew in a place like that. He only had maybe a dozen people. And they worked regular hours. When it was their time off, he didn't want to see them anywhere around the work-site."

"I see."

"He expected them to relax, watch VR, play cards, whatever." He sat back and put his hands behind his head.

"Was that your first time off-world, Al?"

"No. I've been out to a couple of the stations. But it's the first time I've been that far."

"A lot of light-years."

"Oh, yes." He looked behind him. There was a photograph of him standing on the shelf in front of the Retreat. He was wearing an old flannel shirt and a pair of shorts. Looked absolutely summery inside the force field pressure suit that they switch on and off.

"How long were you there?"

"About six months," he said.

"A long time in a place like that. Did you ever get to be alone in the Retreat? When nobody else was there?"

"Oh, yes," he said. "Sure."

"How'd it feel?"

"You want the truth?"

"Please."

"I was spooked. The place was really creepy when you were alone. And out there, it's always night."

"Well," I said, "at least you knew that if something did happen, the others would know about it right away."

"How do you mean?"

I shrugged. "Well, if you were down working in the Retreat and there was maybe an accident, the watch officer would see it right away. Right?"

His brow wrinkled. "We didn't have a watch officer."

"What would happen if, say, your suit started to fail?"

"If I were working alone, you mean?"

"Yeah."

"I'd call for help."

"Suppose you were unconscious?"

He thought about it. "Bye-bye," he said.

6

I spent the next couple of days watching Antonelli. I followed him to work, and followed him home. I watched him take his family to dinner at the Hong Kong Restaurant in Georgetown. He didn't do anything, or go anywhere, unusual.

While I waited for him to show me what was going on, I took to reading one of Clayborn's books, *The Life and Times of Midnight Clayborn*. It had been cowritten with somebody I'd never heard of.

The jacket featured a picture of a young Clayborn on horseback, riding down the hostage-takers under a full moon, while two children cringed against a low stone wall. There was a pyramid in the background.

I tried to remember whether the rescue had happened in Egypt. Not that it mattered. A little editorial license was understandable.

There'd been other exploits. At Umrich, where he'd recovered a set of stolen Assyrian steles, he was pursued and nearly killed by renegade Arabs. At Cislu, while he was exploring the palace of Maraki, a wall had caved in, trapping him in the foundation for seventy-two hours. He'd dug his way out. At Safe Harbor, a world populated by voracious predators, he'd beaten off a kobala, which is apparently a kind of shark with wings. He'd been caught in the middle of two wars and countless incidents of civil unrest. He'd been arrested several times, jailed, accused of stealing treasures from Egypt, Iraq, Jordan, Israel, Mexico, Brazil, and three extraterrestrial sites. It was all true, of course, but Clayborn explains that if he hadn't taken the artifacts, they would have been left to rot in the ground, or grabbed off by a dictator who would never have appreciated their value. "These things do not belong to individual governments," he writes in his epilogue. "They belong to the human race. And I made it my business to stake that claim."

He maintains that most of what he took ended in museums. A lot of it went back to the source countries, over his protests. But he'd made the artifacts so visible, had made the public so aware of their existence, that the chances of their being stolen or abused had, he says, dwindled considerably. In 2228, he had been awarded the Legion of Merit, and the following year had won the Americus.

He'd been married twice. His first wife had been lost in a wild boat ride down the Amazon. He doesn't have much to say about it in his book, but Archibald Tetis, in *Logic of Empire*, describes the incident, and states that Clayborn blamed himself and was inconsolable for months.

His second marriage lasted four years. This was to Janet Koleeva. They'd parted amicably. In his autobiography, Clayborn has nothing but good things to say about Janet, who'd been an historian attached to the University of Pennsylvania. Their careers, he said, were just on different vectors.

In his survey of modern archeological excavations, Michael McKenna says that no one contributed more to the field than Midnight Clayborn.

⸺⸱⸺

I was getting nowhere with my passive approach to things. So I decided to see Antonelli.

My sense of the guy was that if I showed up at his town house, I wouldn't get past the AI. If I tried his office, they'd demand to know what I wanted to talk to him about, and again I'd be refused entry. I knew what time he generally left for home. So I took station in the lobby, but I picked a day on which he was late. More than an hour late. I went outside and sat in my car to avoid calling attention to myself. But I hung on, and eventually he showed up.

George Antonelli looked like the kind of boss that people hate. His features had a sting in them. And he was a man with better things to do than talk with strangers. I didn't get a sidewise glance until I stepped in front of him and showed my badge. "My name's Walker, Mr. Antonelli," I said. "I'm a private detective, investigating the deaths of K. C. Eliot and Sylvia Ames. May I have a moment of your time, please?"

There was a brief glimmer of surprise. But he smothered it. "Who?" he asked, in a carefully controlled voice.

"K. C. Eliot," I said. "And Sylvia Ames."

"I don't know these people. I have no idea who they are."

"I only need a moment," I said.

"You're a *private* detective?"

"Yes. That's correct."

"I don't have to talk to you. Get out of my way."

He tried to push past me but I didn't move. "No," I said. "You don't. I can just turn over what I have to the police, and you can talk to them instead, if you want." Now I backed away and gave him room. "Your call."

He tried to smile. He wasn't good at it. "What do you want?"

"Tell me about Eliot."

He scrunched his face up as if trying to recall. "That's the guy who was in the news, right? The one they fished out of the bay?"

"You telling me a friend of yours shows up murdered and you took no notice?"

"What do you mean, a friend of mine? I told you I didn't know him."

"That's odd," I said. "Are you sure?"

"Yes. Of course I'm sure."

"Your name's in his files." Strictly speaking, that wasn't a lie. Everybody's name is listed in the registry, and the registry is, more or less, part of everyone's files. Nevertheless his eyes opened a bit more.

"I can't imagine why," he said. "I never heard of this guy."

"What about Sylvia?" I said.

His car arrived. A guy in a uniform got out and held the door for him. "Thanks, Al." Antonelli handed him a bill. "Listen, lady." He turned back to me. "I don't know Eliot, and I have no idea who Sylvia is."

"Mr. Antonelli," I said, "I know you're involved in this. Why don't you tell me what you know and make it easy on yourself? It's all going to come out eventually anyway."

He looked around to see if anyone was within earshot. Somebody, a woman, was coming out the front door. She nodded to him and started across the street. He stood with a phony smile pasted on his face until she was out of earshot. "Ms. Walker," he said, "if you have nothing but baseless accusations I think this interview's over."

"You want to tell me where you were on the afternoon of the seventeenth? The day the storm hit?"

"At home. With my wife and kids."

I made a pretense of recording it in my notebook. "You were there all day?"

He had to think about it. "Yes."

A good family guy. "You're sure."

"Of course I am."

"The police will want to verify that with your wife."

He shrugged. "They can verify to their heart's content."

"Mr. Antonelli, do you own a boat?"

"Yes. Maggie and I like to take the kids out on the Chesapeake. Is there a crime in that?"

"No," I said. "Where do you keep it docked?"

"Basil Point." He looked at the time. "Now, if you don't mind I really have to be going."

"Okay." I handed him a card. "In case you think of anything you want to tell me."

"Sure," he said.

⸻

I went back to Chesapeake Beach and showed a hologram of Antonelli to Marty. The hologram stood there, looking bored.

"George," I said, "say hello to Marty."

Antonelli rolled his eyes. Looked around the pier. "*Where are we?*"

"Walk down toward the end of the pier," I said.

He showed no sign of complying, so I directed the AI to take him over. Antonelli sighed and took a few steps. "*Satisfied?*" he asked.

I froze him in place. "Marty," I said, "is this by any chance the guy who was with Eliot and the woman when they took the sailboat out?"

He made a face. "I keep trying to tell you, I was too far away to get a good look."

"*Might* he have been?"

"Maybe. Can't be sure. It's possible."

From there I went to Basil Point. It's become a major tourist spot in the last few years. But in October it's bleak and deserted, nothing but empty streets and dead leaves.

I found Antonelli's boat at Ed's Marina. It was a twin-jet Yolanda yacht, luxurious, with wide decks and a blue and white hull. Its name, *Maggie*, was painted up front.

An elderly woman was in charge of the marina. "Ed's not here," she told me.

I showed her my ID. "Maybe you can help me."

She was gray and beefy and looked as if her feet hurt. Her name was Tina. "What do you need?"

"Tina," I said, "were you by any chance here on the seventeenth? The day of the hurricane?"

"Yeah," she said. "I was here."

I looked toward *Maggie*. "Do you happen to know whether anybody took it out that day?"

"Yeah. Nobody took it out."

"You're sure."

"Absolutely." She started to turn away.

"Do you keep track of everything that comes and goes?"

"No."

"Then how can you be so certain?"

"Because it was in maintenance that day. We were servicing the engine. Now, is there anything else?" She had other things to do.

"When did the owner make it available for service?"

"I think it was the day before. Tuesday."

"And he picked it up—?"

"A couple days after the hurricane, I think. Friday or Saturday. It was in the boathouse during the storm."

"How often," I asked, "does he get the engine serviced?"

"Every six months. Like clockwork. Antonelli's pretty serious about it. Takes good care of that boat."

"I would, too." She softened a little. "Tina, I wonder if I could have a look at the service records?"

She was reluctant. It was a nuisance. "I'm really busy," she said.

I showed her a fifty, and she took me into the boathouse and opened up. I looked back over the previous two years. Tina wandered off and I had to track her down again. She was out on the pier, talking to a customer. "Tina," I said, getting her off to one side, "you were right. He does get the service done regularly at six-month intervals."

"That's what I said."

"Except this last service. It wasn't really due until November. It was performed seven weeks early."

She shrugged. "I think he said it was running rough."

"You find anything wrong? Any problems?"

She shook her head. "Clean as a whistle."

7

Harold (Midnight) Clayborn lived in a mansion in Marquette, Virginia, on the bay shore. It was an imposing place, constructed of white stone and curving glass panels, with a courtyard and a tower in the eastern wing that served as an observatory. The house was surrounded by broad lawns, and the lawns by a high wall. There was a swimming pool in back, and a tennis court on the west side. Reluctantly, Jack took me out in a police flyer. We found the great man at home, and told him we wanted to talk to him.

"*Of course,*" he said. "*Anytime I can help the police. What's it about?*"

"It would be best," said Jack, "if we talk about it off-circuit."

"*Oh, yes. Of course. You're locked into the pad now. I'll see you in a few minutes.*" That voice was pure brandy.

The wind had shifted around to the south, brought in warm weather, and died. The result was that the area was enclosed in unseasonable fog. We dropped onto the pad and found Clayborn waiting. He came around to my side of the aircraft, and opened the door. "Hello," he said, with his customary charm. "We've got a few puddles. Watch your step."

Midnight Clayborn had come of age when we were discovering ruins on Quraqua. It was the first indication that we'd ever had company anywhere, and Midnight, as a graduate student, had wasted no time joining an expedition. Everyone who went to Quraqua during those early years eventually became famous. But in the end it was Clayborn's work at Ur and Troy, Thebes and Jerusalem, Pergamon and the Valley of the Kings, that turned him into a legend.

Jack did the introductions and explained that we wanted to talk to him about K. C. Eliot. Clayborn nodded and we started up the walkway toward the front door. "I was sorry to hear about K. C.," he said. "I don't really understand what happened. What could he have been thinking?"

"We were hoping you might be able to give us an idea, Dr. Clayborn. How well did you know him?"

"Not all that well, really." He shook his head. "Not socially at all. I bought some paintings from him. Admired his work. I thought he had great potential. But it never really developed. I think these last few years he'd plateaued."

We mounted the front steps onto a porch filled with deck chairs and potted plants. Doors opened, and we stepped into a world devoted to antiquity. The walls were covered with voodoo masks and daggers and sun disks and shields and native drums.

Steles with inscriptions in Sanskrit or Egyptian or God-knows-what stood in every corner. Shelves supported vases and pieces of ironware. Display cases held books and plates and statuary. And an assortment of metal boxes. It was a museum. I stopped to look at one of the boxes.

"It's a calibrator," he said. "It's from the C-site on Quraqua."

"A calibrator," said Jack.

"Yes. It came out of an electrical generating plant."

"How old is it?" I asked.

He opened the case and invited me to touch it. The metal was pitted. "About three thousand years," he said. "If we'd gotten to Quraqua a bit sooner, we might have been able to talk with them."

"Nobody at all left?" asked Jack. He was being polite. Other worlds were too far away to care about.

"No," he said. "Nobody. You go to a place like that and you know that the inhabitants have gone extinct, it changes you. Everything they had becomes almost sacred."

"But that's true of Ur and Troy, too," I said. "Everybody's gone."

He shook his head as we passed through a set of velvet curtains into a living room. "No. The children of Troy are still with us. They wear business suits now, and hang out at the pool. But they're still around. *Those* unfortunates—" he looked back in the direction of the box, "—they, and everything they ever were, are gone. Except a few odd pieces." His eyes closed momentarily. "I was glad to get back to the Big Downtown."

"What's the Big Downtown?" asked Jack.

"It's the way the far travelers refer to Earth. It's us. Once you've been off-world, I mean *really* off-world, not just to Moonbase, but out there—" he jabbed an index finger at the ceiling, "—and you find out how dark and empty everything is, you acquire a distinct taste for human company. For city lights and highways and theaters and bars. For the place where life is. The common wisdom is that everybody comes home a party animal."

"Is it true?" I asked.

He smiled. "I wouldn't know. Most of what's out there, pretty much all of it, is empty. Even places where it's warm and wet—" He shook his head. "It's lonely out there, Lieutenant. Lonelier than you could ever imagine."

Chestnut-colored drapes filtered the sunlight, and a fire crackled cheerfully behind a grate. Several original oil paintings decorated the walls, and I wondered if any of them had been done by Eliot. A book, a mystery novel, lay open on a side table. He motioned us into leather chairs, opened a liquor cabinet, and asked what we would like. "I know about policemen on duty," he said with a smile. "Some of these are non-alcoholic, if you wish, and I think you'll find them quite satisfying." I went for scotch and water. Jack was a straight arrow, and got something that looked green. Clayborn, the perfect host, went with the green stuff. Then he made himself comfortable in an armchair. "Now," he said, "what can I do for you?"

Jack and I have an understanding. I get to go along on these interviews when it affects the case I'm working on, but I stay in the background. As the representative of the official authorities, he controls the interview. "I wonder if you could tell us, Dr. Clayborn," he said, "if you know whether Eliot had any enemies? Anyone who'd want to see him dead?"

He held his glass up and stared at it. "You think Eliot was murdered?"

Jack was wearing his official face, thoughtful, businesslike, non-threatening. "At this point, we're just asking questions. We really don't know what happened."

"But you must have reason to suspect something wasn't right."

"It's only a routine inquiry." He produced a paper notebook. It was his signal to Clayborn that he was not using a voice recorder. People tend to be more forthcoming when they know that. "We don't yet understand what happened."

Clayborn shook his head. "I see. But I doubt I know anything that will help."

"Why don't you tell us about your relationship with him."

He sipped his drink and set the glass down. "As I said, there's not much to tell. I bought a few paintings from him. He seemed promising." He shook his head sadly. "Terrible waste."

It was my cue to break in. "Dr. Clayborn, you bought six of his paintings, is that correct?"

He used an index finger to count invisible acquisitions. "Yes," he said. "Six."

"It appears," said Jack, "you paid considerably more than market value for them. Can you tell us why?"

"Sure. I thought Eliot was going somewhere. The paintings were an investment. I expected the day would come when they'd be worth quite a lot."

"Nevertheless," continued Jack, "we've been given to understand the market value during the period you made the purchases was much less than you paid for them."

He finished off his drink, and asked whether anybody wanted more. We both passed, and he refilled his own glass. "I'm sure I could have bargained him down," he said. "But the truth is I liked the guy. I've been pretty fortunate in my life. It was a chance to give something back."

"How did you come to know him?" Jack asked.

"K. C.? I met him through Annie Detmer. She owns the Gaslight Gallery."

"Which is where?"

"In Wheaton. I've known her a long time. She holds periodic events. Runs a sale on a given artist, and has the artist over to talk to her customers. I was there one evening, just dropped in, didn't realize anything special was going on, and there was K. C."

"When was that?" asked Jack.

"Six or seven years ago, I guess. Give or take."

Jack made a note. Then: "Dr. Clayborn, do you maintain any numbered bank accounts?"

He looked at us and considered his answer. "Yes," he said. "You'd find out anyway, I suppose, if you really wanted to. I have a special account for business purposes."

"How do you mean?"

He made a noise deep in his throat. "You may be aware that I have something of an unsavory reputation in the academic world. If my name gets attached to a project, sometimes other sources of support dry up."

"Unsavory?" said Jack. "In what way?"

"Some of my colleagues would tell you I'm a grave robber."

Jack needed a long moment to think that one over. "Is it true?"

"Probably." He smiled. "Not that I've been unethical. The truth is
that some of the most precious sites on the planet are located in areas
whose governments are, um, less than reasonable. The Arab Triangle,
for example." He put the glass down and leaned forward, suddenly intent. "That's where we all began. And the details are still buried in those
deserts. But if you go out there and locate anything of value, you're pro-
hibited from taking it out of the country. The local government pays
what they call a compensatory amount, strictly nominal. Not that it matters."

"What *does* matter?"

"They sell the pieces to the highest bidder. It's strictly money. The
result is that major finds disappear into the holdings of private collectors."

"I see."

"They have no more claim to the artifacts than we do."

"So," I said, "whoever finds them—"

"Should keep them. That's exactly right, Kristi." He turned a penetrating gaze on me. "I don't want you to get the wrong idea. I've
profited from my finds. I won't deny that. I mean, I have to make a living too. But most of the stuff I've brought back, almost all of it, has
gone to museums or to research facilities. Some of it was donated outright."

I looked around at the furniture, the artifacts, the artwork. "You
seem to have done okay."

"Most of it's inherited money. My family owns Omnicomm."

"Okay." Jack sucked on his lower lip. "Do you know George Antonelli?"

"Yes," he said. "I know George."

"May I ask your connection with him?"

"He did a lot of work for the Academy when I was on the board of
directors. There's not much connection now. We have lunch once in a
while. That's about all."

"You're not friends."

"Well, more or less."

"Do you have any sort of ongoing project with him?"

"Why, no. As I told you, we get together once in a while to eat. When I'm down near the Capitol."

"Okay. You had a conversation with him in the Memorial Hotel Friday evening."

A surprised smile appeared at the corners of his mouth. "That's correct," he said. "Have you been watching me?"

"You want to tell us what that was about?"

He looked back at me. "You're the young lady from the Adventurers' Club."

"Yes," I said.

"Your hair was different then."

I smiled.

"Very good."

"Tell us," said Jack, "about your conversation with Antonelli."

The details seemed to escape him. "Whatever it was," he said, "there wasn't much to it. I think we were talking football."

"Football?"

"Yes. That's correct. And we talked a little bit about the presentation I'd done earlier in the evening at the Adventurers' Club. But I assume you already know all about that." Another smile for me.

"And that's all?"

"Yes. Sorry. But there was nothing very earthshaking."

"You were upset," I said.

"I'm a fan."

Jack was staring at his notebook. "Let's talk about the numbered account. Did you at any time transfer funds to Eliot?"

"No," he said. "Never."

"Just so I understand this, when you bought the paintings, Eliot was paid from a regular account?"

"Yes. That's right."

"Have you given any other money to Eliot?"

He looked as if he were having trouble remembering. So long ago. So trivial. "Why, no," he said. "I'm sure I haven't." His eyes met Jack's. "Lieutenant, am I suspected of something?"

Jack closed his notebook and put it away. "No. This is all routine, Dr. Clayborn. No need to be concerned." Unless of course you *are* complicit, Midnight. He glanced over at me. Did I have anything else to ask?

There were three original oil paintings in the room. One depicted a medieval crowd scene, a lot of people gathered around a fountain, wielding pitchers. Another was of a bearded man dressed in clothing from the late-twenty-first century. Loaded with dignity. And the third was a rendering of a beautiful dark-eyed dancer, caught in mid-flight across a stage, coming directly out of the portrait.

"Beautiful," I said.

He looked pleased. The bearded man, he explained, was a Kahollah. The fountain was a DeRenne, and the dancer was an Olandra. Two of the names rang bells. "I wonder," I said, "if we could see the Eliot paintings?"

"Ah." He looked apologetic. "I wish I could. They're not up at the moment."

"Oh?"

"They're being reframed. If you'd like to come back in a couple of days, I'd be happy to show them to you."

"That's quite all right," I said. "I think we've taken enough of your time, Dr. Clayborn."

He walked back with us to the flyer, told us he was sure we'd discover that it was just an accident out on the bay, that sometimes rational people do irrational things, and assured us we were welcome any time we wanted to return to his home.

We lifted away, up over the tennis court. The bay sparkled in the late afternoon sunlight. Jack sighed and sat back while we swung west and headed toward Alexandria. "I'm surprised," he said, "you didn't want to come back and look at the Eliot paintings."

"Not necessary. I got what I wanted."

"Which was—?"

"He has them in the attic. Once again, we see the wisdom of not calling ahead on these things. If we had, they'd have been up all over the house."

8

Later that afternoon I walked into the Gaslight Gallery in Wheaton. Annie Detmer was busy with customers, but she noticed me and her eyes widened enough to show me I was expected. I looked through the place while I waited. There was a nice mix of sculpture with the paintings, but I was mostly interested in whether any K. C. Eliot work would show up. I didn't see any.

Eventually, with a lot of chuckling and self-congratulation about spending what it takes, Annie's customers chose an abstract, a flurry of red and gold light cones that looked as if they were coming through an unwashed window. Annie collected her money and assured them they'd have the painting next day.

As they strolled out the front door, she approached me, and tried a smile that didn't quite fit. "Yes, miss," she said. "How may I help you?"

There wasn't much to Annie Detmer. She was old and faded and maybe after a big meal she would have made it to a hundred pounds. Her hair was washed-out and stiff. Her face sagged, and she looked tired. And there was a little of the deer-in-the-headlights in her expression.

I showed her my ID.

"I was sorry to hear about K. C.," she said. "I always thought he was going to be one of the great ones." She shrugged. "But I guess not." Another customer was coming in.

"Were you close to him?" I asked.

"No. Not really." She paused. "I liked him. I mean, he was a decent enough guy. And I think we were all rooting for him."

"Who's *we*?"

"Oh." She blinked. Several times. "It's just a figure of speech. But I think anyone who knew him would have wished him well."

I went through the questions. She'd known K. C. about ten years. The Gaslight had been the first gallery to sell one of his paintings. He'd been to Annie's place for dinner a couple of times. She didn't know anybody who didn't like him. Although that wasn't the same as saying he had a lot of friends. He was shy. Some people thought him standoffish. But she couldn't imagine anyone who'd want him dead. "You're wasting your time," she said. "I don't know what he was doing out on that boat, but I'm sure it was an accident. He just wasn't paying attention. It happens to all of us."

Sure. I know lots of people who'd take a sailboat into a hurricane.

I commented that the Gallery looked prosperous, which it did. She said that she managed to make a living, excused herself, and hurried off to take care of the new arrival.

I took my time, apparently browsing among the paintings, but trying to put things together.

Still more people came in. Annie stayed busy, but periodically

THE BIG DOWNTOWN

threw a surreptitious glance in my direction. Eventually the place emptied out again and she had no choice but to circle back to me. "Anything else I can help with?" she asked.

I'd noticed that she advertised a custom frame service. "To be honest," she said, "it's almost half the business."

"Really?"

She nodded. "Oh, yes. This is the only place in the city where you can match the frame with the artwork. You can't just put anything around a DeGrasse, you know."

"Of course not."

"When I write my memoirs, that'll be the title." She smiled tentatively. "Well." She was waiting for me to say how I had to be going.

I was looking at a sculpture of Hermes, bronze in motion. It would have looked good in my living room, but it was a trifle pricey. "Have you done any framing for Harold Clayborn?"

"Yes," she said. "Occasionally."

"Do you have anything of his now?"

"No." She looked at me suspiciously. "Why do you ask?"

"Just curious."

"Is there anything else I can show you?"

"No, thanks. I appreciate your time, Ms. Detmer."

"It's no trouble at all."

I started for the door, and paused. She stood rooted to the spot.

"There *is* one other thing. How well do you know George Antonelli?"

Bingo. She recognized the name, and I watched her shut down. "I don't know him," she said. "Never heard of him."

"You're sure?"

"Yes."

"Usually, a question like that, people need a minute to think."

"No," she said. "I don't know him."

⸺✴⸺

I'd taken my time confirming Antonelli's story with his wife. The fact is that a wife or a mother is usually something less than a convincing witness. In these kinds of situations, you know as soon as you leave the husband's office he's going to be calling home. So I like to delay a few days. Maybe give them a chance to forget the details of any story they've cooked up.

Her name was Margaret. She was the personnel officer at Menendez Laboratories in Georgetown. She went into work usually one or two days a week. I picked a day on which she was at home, and I was able to confirm that her husband had shown up at his office.

The town house was located in a clubby section of Westwood. I didn't see any properties out there that wouldn't have come in at three-quarters of a million. There was a park across the street, and beyond that you could see the Potomac. The sky had clouded over and, when I walked up onto the porch, a light drizzle was beginning.

I identified myself, waited, and the AI asked what I wanted.

"I'd like to speak with Margaret Antonelli, please."

"About what?" The thing spoke with Antonelli's voice, except that all the intonations had gone out of it. The tone was impersonal, if the language wasn't.

"I'm a private investigator. I'd like a couple of minutes of Ms. Antonelli's time to verify some information."

It began to rain harder. A gust blew some of it onto the porch.

The door opened. *"Please come in,"* said the AI.

Margaret Antonelli was waiting for me just inside. She was an attractive woman. Reminded me a little of my aunt Janna. A brunette about forty. Bright, amicable eyes. A good smile. I had not been impressed by her husband and my first reaction was to wonder that she hadn't been smart enough to sidestep him.

"Hello," she said. "I hope you didn't have any trouble getting past Wally."

She meant the AI, and I said no, everything was fine.

"Sometimes he's overprotective." She led the way into a sitting room.

The interior was not what I'd expected. Once you met Antonelli, you'd have looked for gaudy. Expensive gaudy, the kind of stuff intended to display wealth and taste. But the furnishings were subdued, conservative, quiet. We sat down in a couple of armchairs. "Now, Kristi—It *is* all right if I call you Kristi, isn't it?"

"Yes," I said. "Of course."

"Kristi, my friends call me Maggie." She turned on a lamp to dispell the general gloom outside. "How may I help you?"

"Maggie, I'm investigating the death of K. C. Eliot."

Her brow furrowed. "Who?"

"The artist. It seems he took his sailboat out the day Walter hit."

"That was dumb," she said. Then recognition took hold. "Eliot's the one you spoke about with my husband."

"Yes. That was Wednesday, September 17."

There was an explosion of giggles and a little blond girl charged into the room, trailing a balloon. At the same moment, I heard a child's laughter elsewhere in the house. "There are two of them," she said. "This is Jill. Say hello to Ms. Walker, Jill."

We went through a couple minutes of fun and games with Jill and her brother, Ed. He came in carrying a rubber bat. The kids were probably two and three.

"Anyway," I said when I was able to get back to the subject, "your husband says he was at home with you on the seventeenth. The day the storm hit."

"Yes?" she said. The smile had faded slightly.

"Is that so?"

"Oh, yes. He was here with me that day. We thought about leaving town, you know, with the children and all. But the house is solid. It's reinforced against hurricanes."

"So you stayed."

"Yes."

"Maggie," I asked, "were you here all day?"

"Yes, we were."

"Didn't go out at all?"

"Oh, we might have run down to the market. Nothing more than that." The kids were chasing each other around the room. Maggie shushed them and shooed them out.

"They must keep you pretty much pinned down," I said.

She brightened. "Not really. Wally takes good care of them."

The AI. Well, it made sense. Wally could tend to their needs, and you knew he wouldn't fall asleep. The perfect babysitter. "Thanks, Maggie," I said.

She looked at me oddly. "Kristi, may I ask a question?"

"Yes. Of course."

"What is it actually you're looking for? Didn't Eliot die in an accident? I don't understand the point of your questions."

"We're not sure," I said, "there wasn't more to it than that."

"But surely you don't think George would be involved. George wouldn't hurt a fly."

He could have fooled me. George struck me as being willing to employ whatever means necessary to get what he wanted.

I was on my way back to the office when I got a call from Jack. A second body had washed up.

9

It was the western shore again, only a few miles from the place where they'd found Eliot.

I looked at the body and remembered the hologram, the eyes, the easy smile. A beautiful young woman with her life in front of her. She didn't look so good after three weeks in the water. "No sign of violence," said Jack. He shrugged. It's a tough world.

"Are we sure it's Sylvia?"

He nodded. "It's her." We watched them lift her into the EV, close the doors, and get ready to depart.

"Where's the third body?" I asked.

He shrugged. "It'll turn up."

"You really think so?"

"I don't know. I know you think Clayborn's involved in this, but I'm an old believer in Occam's razor."

"Occam's razor?"

"The simplest, most straightforward explanation is the right one. They went out partying and they lost track of the time."

It was getting late and I was tired. "Gotta go, Jack," I said.

He put a hand on my shoulder. "There's something else, Kristi." He looked uncomfortable. "I had a call from the commissioner. He wants you to stop bothering the Antonellis."

I looked out across the bay. A pair of gulls wheeled past, chirping. "Maybe," I said, "you should have invited him down here to see Sylvia."

⸺⸱⸺

I went by Jules's office before heading home. As soon as he saw me, he knew. We went across the street to Mike's Bar & Grill and had a drink together and he thanked me and asked if I knew what had happened.

"I think she was murdered," I said. "I think she got unlucky. The killer was after Eliot, and she was there when he showed up."

"Why?"

"I'm not sure yet."

"Okay," he said. "I want you to finish the job. Get whoever did it."

"I intend to."

"Good."

It was dark when I got to the office. I parked around back in my private spot and climbed out of the car. I was thinking about Jules, and Sylvia, and I wasn't paying attention to anything else. That can be a mistake. I didn't realize I wasn't alone until something nailed me from behind. Lights exploded and I staggered forward and crashed against the door. There were voices. Laughter. Somebody said my name.

I tried to get up. Got to my knees. Then they hit me again. In the back. And down I went. I took a couple of kicks in the ribs.

"Hi, Kristi." I tried to twist around. See who was there.

Two of them. One short and heavy with a growth of black whiskers. One tall and lean with lots of nose. The Nose grabbed hold of my hair, dragged me to my feet, and held me. Whiskers did a quick groping search, found my weapon, jerked it and the holster free, and hit me in the stomach. But they didn't let me fall.

The fat little guy drew back as if he was going to hit me again, made me flinch, but only stroked my jaw. Then he caught my chin in the palm of his hand and squeezed. "You want to start minding your own business, Kristi." He had big ears and bad breath and a crooked smile and he needed dental work. He pushed his face into mine and crushed his lips against my mouth.

I was having trouble breathing as it was. I tried to slug him but I couldn't get a clear shot. His buddy let go of my hair and grabbed my arms.

"You taste good, Babe," said Whiskers. "Maybe I'll come back some time. Do you right."

I delivered a knee where it did some damage. He huffed and folded up while his partner got an arm around my throat and dragged my head back. "What you want to do, Kristi," he said, "is mind your own business. Forget Eliot. Let it go. Or we'll be back to talk to you again." Another punch. I couldn't really tell any more what was happening, other than that I was getting stomped. Then the lights went out.

⸺⸙⸺

I was still in the parking lot when I came out of it. Charlie Hazzard, who runs a bail bonding operation across the hall from my office, was bent over me, telling me not to move, asking what happened, assuring me help was on the way.

You don't pay attention, that's what you can expect.

I think I managed to say thanks. I went in and out a couple times. Lights descended and somebody was holding my wrist and the pain went away and so did everything else.

10

"You were lucky," Jack said.

"Easy for you to say." They'd taken me to the St. Teresa Medical Center where I was sharing a room with a woman who'd just gotten enhancement therapy so she could be smarter. She was lying there watching *Uncle Tim's Family* and I didn't think it was going to work.

"Look," Jack said. "They could have killed you."

"I got careless."

"Can't do that. Not in your business." It was hard to talk over Uncle Tim. "What are you going to do?"

"What I'm being paid to. Find out who killed Sylvia."

"There was water in her lungs. She drowned. Just like Eliot."

"Yeah. I figured. But now at least I assume even *you* understand it was no accident."

"That's cruel, Kristi."

"But earned." Sunlight came through the curtains and formed a checkered pattern across two walls.

"When are they going to let you go?"

"Tomorrow morning," I said. Nothing was broken. A few parts were bent and twisted, but I'd be okay. I was still pretty high on whatever it was they'd given me. I felt no inhibitions, and nothing hurt.

"You want me to assign someone to you? Just in case they try something again?"

"I'll be fine."

"Kristi—"

"I'll be fine, Jack."

"Okay. Have it your way. Can you identify them?"

"Yes."

"You want to take a look now? Are you up to it?"

"Yeah. I think I can manage."

He produced a disk and we had to ask the high I.Q. candidate if we could shut down Uncle Tim for a bit. She objected and we compromised and waited for the show to end. Then we took over the VR system.

Jack angled the projection so she couldn't see, and began showing me holograms of various solid citizens who specialized in assault. Fat ones and tall lean ones. "*You taste good. Babe,*" said the fat ones. The lean ones all said, "*You want to start minding your own business, Kristi.*" Whiskers turned out to be Andy McCarter. Better known as "Grapes." His pal was Rudy Bessinger. Both had long careers as strong-arm men. "Who do they work for?" I asked.

"AlphaBeta, Inc. They're enforcers for Roman Jankiewicz."

Well, that was a surprise. Jankiewicz made popovers and other synthetic drugs. Everything was strictly legal, although various citizens' groups had been trying for years to get legislation passed to put him and his pals out of business. The problem was the usual one, though. Jankiewicz put money in the right pockets. But what was his connection with K. C. Eliot?

"Grapes and Rudy hang out at AlphaBeta," Jack said. "Officially, they're lab assistants." He glanced down at his link. "I'll send a unit right over."

"No," I said.

"What do you mean *no*? You're not going to let them get away with this?"

"Wouldn't think of it. But I don't want them arrested. Not just yet, anyhow."

I was still limping when I got back to the office. The first thing I did was thank Charlie Hazzard for helping out. He turned pale at the thought of what had happened. Charlie's a good guy but he doesn't like violence. He told me I needed to find a different line of work. He looked at my black eye and the bruises on my throat and wondered why on earth I'd gotten into the business.

I admitted I wasn't sure. It was what I did. Most people spend their working lives in a service establishment or an office. Same stuff happens all the time. I didn't think I could live like that. I liked to think I was a little like Midnight Clayborn. But just a little.

Charlie said he hoped I'd find something different to do before I got seriously hurt. Then he went over to his safe and fished out my weapon and holster. I put it back on my belt, thanked him, told him I owed him a drink, and went home.

I gave myself a couple more days to heal and then I went back out along the Chesapeake, visiting every boating facility I could find on the west shore. I showed Mr. and Mrs. Antonelli to the proprietors, and Clayborn, and Jankiewicz, and Grapes and Rudy. I had them walk around and say hello and ask if they could rent a power boat for the day. "*Be back well before the hurricane hits,*" I had each of them say. "*And there's a bonus in it for you.*" I was looking for anybody who had sold or rented a boat to any of those people, or made pier space available to them, or done marine maintenance for them. Anybody who had so much as *seen* any of them. I spent three days and came away empty. So I switched over and started on the eastern shore.

On the second day, exactly one month after the hurricane, I pulled into Van Clay, a small fishing town, and heard there'd been a death and a fire that morning. "Hap Carlucci," the attendant told me while I was getting my fuel cells checked. "The boathouse burned to the ground and Hap was inside."

I drove over and took a look. The place was still smoldering. The pier and the boathouse had both been made of wooden planks. It was a smoking ruin. Several boats had been lost. And of course Hap, who'd been a retired police officer trying to make ends meet. The cops were not happy.

I talked to Myra Corvella, the police chief. "It was murder," she said. "Somebody walked in, took out Hap, spilled fuel all over the place, and set the fire."

"I'm sorry."

"*Somebody's* going to be sorry." Myra was a big woman, gray eyes, attractive in a masculine sort of way, husky voice. "Now then, Ms. Walker," she said, "what are you doing in town? Do you have any idea who did this?"

"I don't know. If I can pin it down, you'll be first to find out. Did they rent boats? Hap's place?"

"Yes."

"Did the records survive?"

She looked past my shoulder at the smoke, drifting slowly inland. "I doubt it."

This felt like Grapes and Rudy. I was trying to think how they'd known.

—⁂—

There was no point continuing my hunt along the east shore. I left the car on automatic and rode back to the office half asleep. When it pulled into my parking place, I looked around to make sure I had no company, and got out.

I wondered if somebody had been eavesdropping on me. And it occurred to me that maybe the reason for my getting jumped had been more than simply an attempt to scare me off.

They'd planted a bug.

I swept the office. And found it in my holster. At the bottom, out of sight.

Okay. I left it in place, called Jack, and told him about the fire on the east shore.

"*We've heard,*" he said. "*I didn't know it was connected with you. Okay, I'll touch base with Myra. See what she has. See whether we can help.*"

"Good."

"*What are you going to do?*"

"I think I know what's behind this. Jankiewicz lives out on Reagan Drive. I'm going to pay him a visit this evening. Late. After he goes to bed."

"*Don't do it, Kristi. Not alone. I'll go with you.*"

"We won't get anything out of him if we're both there. Let me try it my way."

"*No. It's too dangerous.*"

"Don't worry about it. The bottom-feeders will be off for the evening."

"*I'm telling you, Kristi—*"

"Don't worry, Jack. Those two nitwits are no threat."

I turned on the VR, tuned to the news, took the bug out of my holster and set it on a table where it could listen to the broadcast. Then I went into the washroom where I was well away from it, and gave Pete his instructions.

An hour after I went out the door, he was to shut off the VR, produce some background sounds that suggested I was moving around the office. Then he was to make it sound as if the office door had opened and closed. We would get footsteps down the corridor, down the staircase, and out of the building. Car doors would open and close. The engine would start, and we'd get the sounds of a vehicle pulling off the parking lot and heading out onto the expressway.

In addition, he was to monitor my commlink, and relay any transmissions through the bug. "I want whoever's listening in to get everything."

"Won't they figure out it's a plant?"

"Things'll be happening too fast, Pete. I hope."

I changed into a dark shirt and slacks and soft shoes, and had the AI take pictures of me slinking around in the outfit with a gun in my hand. I filtered out the office background so all I had was a Kristi Walker hologram. Pete put it on a chip, I inserted the chip into my projector, and put the projector in its accustomed place over my left breast pocket. It looked like an imitation silver clover.

When it got dark, I left as quietly as I could. The VR stayed on. Amos Wolbry was commenting somberly on the situation in the Middle East. As far as an eavesdropper would be concerned, I was still sitting there watching the news.

—⁑—

Roman Jankiewicz lived in Exeter, Virginia. It was one of those quiet suburban neighborhoods, well off the main thoroughfare. Lots of kids, ball fields, hedges, and churches. His house was located across the street from an American Rangers hall.

I stayed well away from it. I left the car around a corner, cut through a patch of woods, and came out a block away. From that distance I couldn't be sure which house was his. But for the moment I didn't care about that. What I did care about was the big Warrior parked in the street. There was somebody in it.

I should mention that I've worked hard on my martial arts skills, but when it comes down to it, I've always found a good stick works best. There were a few broken branches lying around. I tried several, and selected one that felt right.

The houses were separated by hedges and driveways. I'd gone as far as I could under cover of the trees. I stepped out into plain sight and begin strolling casually along as if I were just going for a walk. I hid the stick as best I could.

It was mid-October cold and I had my jacket pulled up. I tried to stay away from the streetlights. If the guy in the car took a good look, I might have a problem. But, as I got closer, I saw no sign that he was paying attention.

It was Grapes.

And it was early. They wouldn't be expecting me for another hour or so. There were no other cars on the street. A couple were parked in driveways, but they looked empty. There was no sign of Rudy. He wouldn't be standing behind a tree. It was too early, and too cold. He was probably in the living room. Watching out a front window.

I got close enough to pick up the house. It was a split-level, curtains drawn on an illuminated front room. Other windows along the front, in the east and west wings, were dark. Rudy would be at one of those.

Grapes was on the same side of the street as the house, so any observer inside did not have a good angle. Moreover, there were a couple of trees in the way.

My commlink vibrated. It was Pete. But it was too quiet out there and I knew my voice would carry. I'd talk to him later. When I could.

Grapes was parked in the darkest spot he could find, about two hundred feet from the house. He didn't want to be too obvious.

I came up behind the Warrior. Grapes must have seen me, finally, because he tried to squirm around in the seat and look over his shoulder, but he was too fat. So he settled for squinting in the side mirror. Not the world's swiftest bodyguard. I figured I just looked like one of the locals. His windows were open. That made it easier.

I walked up to him and the first thing he saw was a gun aimed at his head. "It's not set on sleep, Grapes," I told him.

"Hey." He looked scared, angry, indignant. "What do you think you're doing?"

I pointed it at his eye. "How's it going?" I asked.

"Walker!" He glanced down at his wrist. At his commlink, hidden in the darkness.

"Don't do it," I said. "Don't do anything at all unless I tell you to. Raise your voice and you're dead."

"Okay," he said. "Take it easy."

"Open the door. Slowly."

"Okay. Okay. Look, about the other night—"

"Save it, Grapes. I don't hold grudges."

"Yeah. Well, I wouldn't blame you if you were mad. I mean, I guess we were a little rougher than we had to be." He stole a glance toward the house. Probably hoping Rudy and Jankiewicz were watching what was happening. That they'd be here in a minute to rescue his sorry ass.

He opened the door.

"All right. Get out of the car."

"Okay, Kristi," he said. "I'm gettin' out. You don't have to worry about me."

"Good."

He put his left foot out onto the road.

"Take it slow," I said. "Keep your hands where I can see them."

"Yeah. No, everything's okay. Listen, if you need anything, I'll do what I can—"

"I'm sure." He got out and I motioned him onto the sidewalk. We were in front of a dark house—the reason he'd picked the spot—surrounded by a neatly manicured hedge. "That way," I said, steering him toward the front gate. It squeaked as we went through onto the lawn.

"What are you going to do?" he asked. He seemed to have just noticed the branch in my right hand. "Kristi, I'll make it up to you. Don't get excited."

"I'm not excited, Grapes."

Generally if you stand in front of someone with a stick in your hand, he expects you to bring it down on his head. But that's a dangerous maneuver. The crack on the head is de rigueur in these situations, but first you have to disable the target.

The gun was in my left hand. I could see him measuring his chances, but before he could do anything I rammed the branch into his midsection, pool-cue style. He whuffed and went down on his knees. Then I banged him on the head with it and he let out a soft squeal and fell full-length on the grass.

I checked him to make sure he was still breathing. Then I gagged and cuffed him.

Meantime, the hour had expired, and I knew Pete was starting the sound effects back at the office. Anybody listening in on the bug would have thought I was just going out the door.

—⊶—

I moved through the hedges to the side of Jankiewicz's house, where there was a clear view of the front lawn. Then I activated the projector.

A black-clad version of myself, looking like a commando, appeared beside a tree. The hologram moved behind it, and then crossed to another tree closer to the front porch. I looked pretty good. More to the point, anybody watching out the front window couldn't miss the show.

I heard movement in the house. A window opened. Then a red beam licked out and hit the tree. And found the commando. She collapsed, went through a series of spasms, and finally lay still. I couldn't help admiring my acting ability.

The front door opened. "Got the bitch," said a voice I didn't recognize.

Rudy came out, followed by a little pipsqueak of a guy in a jogging suit. I knew him from his pictures. Jankiewicz. Gray hair, pinched features. He shuffled out onto the lawn. They were both carrying guns.

"How'd she get here so fast?" Jankiewicz wanted to know. "She just left her place."

"Where's Grapes?" asked Rudy. They kept their weapons trained on the downed hologram. "If she's hurt Grapes I'm going to kill the bitch."

Jankiewicz snarled. "Worry about that later. Get her behind the hedge until we figure out what to do with her."

The angle between them was too wide. I wouldn't be able to cover both from where I stood. So I set the gun for SLEEP and took out Rudy without warning. He went down like a sack of rocks. Simultaneously the hologram vanished, Jankiewicz jumped a foot, and I stepped out from my cover and told him to drop his weapon.

He started to turn but thought better of it and laid the gun on the grass. "Don't shoot," he said.

"Not unless you move."

"What do you want?"

I let him see I wasn't happy. "Why'd you sic your goons on me?"

"It was a mistake," he said. "We got the wrong person."

"Yeah. There's some truth to that."

"Hey, listen. I got no quarrel with you, Kristi."

"I've got one with you, *Roman*. That *is* your name, right?"

"Yes. Yes, it is. And I'm telling you the truth. It was a computer glitch."

"All right. Now, *Roman*, let me try to make something clear. I'm not going to have a lot of patience with your screwing around." I looked meaningfully at the gun and reset it. He couldn't tell how high, but I knew he'd be thinking worst case.

KILL.

He was small. Weak. Used to having other people provide muscle for him.

"Don't get excited," he said.

"Why does everybody here think I'm excited?"

"Listen." He was looking around desperately. Hoping somebody would show up. "We can cut a deal."

"Who wanted me out of the way? Was it Clayborn?"

"I don't know. This is assault. At least put the gun away."

I smiled at him, holstered the weapon, and knocked him down. Straight right to the jaw. "Sure. You'd want to take this case to court, wouldn't you?"

He sat on the grass, looking pitiful.

"Was it Antonelli?" I saw it in his eyes. "Thanks," I said.

"You didn't hear that from me."

"It doesn't matter, *Roman*. You and your boys killed the marina attendant in Van Clay. What's worse, you made me an accomplice. You listened in and you tried to get ahead of me."

"No," he said. "That wasn't me."

"Sure it was."

"It was them." He indicated Rudy and the Warrior. "I didn't have anything to do with it. I didn't know they were going to do anything like that. They weren't even working for me."

"They were working for Antonelli?"

He nodded. Yes.

"Because Antonelli rented a boat the day the storm was coming. And I'd have found out."

"You'll have to ask him."

"I'm asking *you*, Roman."

He looked at me and shook his head no. "I don't know."

"Your boys bugged me," I said.

No. "There's a mistake here somewhere."

"You were able to listen in. What about Antonelli?"

"What about him?"

"Was he able to listen, too? Was he on the circuit?"

"Yeah," he said. "It was his idea."

11

Jack drifted down in a cruiser, followed seconds later by a medical unit. "I see you've been rousting honest citizens again."

"Those two—" Rudy and Grapes. "Search their digs and their working stations at AlphaBeta. They used hyzine to get the fire going. If you don't find traces of it somewhere, I'll be surprised."

"And when we lean on them, what are they going to tell us?"

"You're going to be issuing a warrant for Antonelli."

"Are you serious?"

"You ever know me to fool around?" They were lifting Grapes into a stretcher. He was moaning softly.

"What about *him*?" Jankiewicz.

He was cuffed. The police were walking him toward a car. I strolled over. "Roman?"

"Yeah?" He sounded angry. Tougher now, with the cops there to protect him. "What do you want, Bitch?"

"What's your connection with Clayborn?"

He responded with a string of profanity.

"Okay," I said. "Jack, you've got accessory to murder with this one. For a start."

I got more unkind words.

"Hey," Jack said. "You want to tell me what this is all about?"

"Sure." I was watching them load Jankiewicz into the car when I remembered Pete's call. "Hang on a second, Jack." I made the connection and asked him what he wanted.

"*JoBeth tried to reach you.*"

"She leave a message?"

"*She says she found a box of Eliot's journals.*"

"Okay."

"*She says there's stuff about Antonelli and Clayborn.*"

"Good. That sounds like just what we need."

"*I'm supposed to tell you it was in one of the boxes that came over from the studio.*"

"All right. Put me through to her."

JoBeth's AI answered. Then JoBeth was on the circuit. "*Hello, Kristi,*" she said. "*You ought to see what I found.*"

"What did you find?"

"*I was going through the stuff I'd stashed,*" she said, "*when I first cleared out K. C.'s place. There's a diary. And an account book. Those payments you were looking for. They're all here. In detail. Where the money came from. How much. The whole operation.*"

"Good."

"*You were right about Antonelli. He's involved in it up to his eyeballs.*"

"All right. Put it somewhere safe."

"*Clayborn, too. Kristi, those sons of bitches murdered K. C.*"

"I know."

"*You think this'll be enough to prove it?*"

"I think so. Okay, listen, JoBeth, I want you to stay there. At your apartment. I've got something to clean up here. When I'm finished I'll be over."

"*Okay. I'll wait for you.*"

"You alone?"

"*Yes. Nobody here but me. And you don't have to tell me. I'll keep the door locked.*"

The cops were doing a search while I stood off to one side. They don't like me helping. A half hour or so after I'd spoken to JoBeth, my link vibrated again.

"Walker," I said.

"*Kristi.*" It was JoBeth again. "*I think I'm getting a visitor.*"

"How do you mean?"

"*The entry blinker's on. Somebody's trying to get in downstairs.*"

"Damn." The entry blinker was a warning lamp. Somebody without a key was trying to get through the front door. "Okay, you better get out of there, JoBeth. It's probably nothing, but play it safe."

"*You're damned right I'll play it safe.*"

"Clear out. Go across the street and wait in the restaurant. In Louie's. I'll meet you there."

"*I can't do that, Kristi. I have no way to get past whoever's in the front hallway.*"

"Isn't there a back door?"

"*Not one I can reach without saying hello.*"

"Okay. I'm on my way."

I heard sounds that suggested she was running around the apartment looking for a coat or something. "*I'm scared, Kristi,*" she said.

I was pushing Jack out the door. "We need to take the flyer," I told him.

"*Kristi, I've got no place to go.*"

"How about neighbors? Can you get into somebody else's apartment?"

"*I don't know. Maybe.*"

"Try it."

"*Okay.*"

"Take the diary."

"*I've got the diary.*"

"Leave the circuit open. We'll be there in a half hour."

⸺⸱⸺

I jumped into the flyer with Jack. "Where we going?" he asked.

I gave him the address.

"Is this an emergency? I can have a unit sent around."

"No," I said. "We should have time."

We lifted over the trees, swung in a wide arc and headed back toward Alexandria. Jack was up front with Pedro, the driver. I was in back. The eastern stars were lost in the glare coming off D.C.

"What's going on?" said Jack.

"When we get there," I told him, "I'm going to hand you at least one of the killers."

"*Kristi,*" JoBeth again. "*He's coming upstairs. How close are you?*"

"About twenty-five minutes."

"*I don't think I have that long.*" She sounded terrified.

Jack swung around in his seat, frowning. "What are you telling her? We'll be there in ten. But that's going to be too late." He punched a button on the console. "We need to send somebody."

"No," I said. "Jack, trust me. It's okay."

"Okay? Kristi, have you gone crazy?"

"JoBeth," I asked, "is there more than one person?"

"*No. I think only one.*"

The apartment house had six floors. "If you go up," I said, "can you get out onto the roof?"

"*Yes. I think so.*"

"Do it. Try to be quiet."

Jack was staring at me, his hand still on the comm unit. "Okay," I said. "Here's what's happening."

—◦—

Jack talked to Alexandria alerting them to the situation. "But don't send anybody till I tell you."

JoBeth got back on the circuit. "*I'm on the sixth floor. But the goddamn roof door won't open.*"

"Where's the intruder?"

"*I think he knows I'm here, Kristi. Where the hell are you?*"

"We're coming as fast as we can."

"*How fast is that?*"

"Twenty minutes. Maybe a little bit longer."

"There's Alexandria," said Pedro.

Jack was leaning forward in his seat, as if he could speed the flyer along.

I heard a bang on the circuit. "How are you coming with the door, JoBeth?"

"*It's open now. I'm on the roof.*"

"Good. Close it behind you."

"*Trying. It's warped.*"

"Can you lock it?"

"*I don't see a lock anywhere.*"

"Three minutes away," said Jack. "Time to bring in the troops."

"Go ahead." And, into the link: "JoBeth. Get away from the door. Is there any place you can hide?"

"*No. There's nowhere. I'm wide open up here.*" She was struggling for breath.

Jack called Alexandria. "Okay," he told them. "Send in backup."

Something in the flyer began to beep. We adjusted course slightly and started to decelerate.

"*He's here,*" she said. Her voice went up a few notches.

The carrier wave clicked off.

"JoBeth? You okay?"

She didn't answer.

"Is that the rooftop there?" asked Pedro.

"That's it," I said.

"The roof door's wide open," said Jack. "Can you see anybody?"

There was a parking lot on the west side of the building. But not enough clearance for the flyer.

"Land in the street, Pedro," I said. "By the front door."

He brought us down between the apartment house and Louie's Italian restaurant. Jack opened the door and scrambled out while Pedro shut off the engines. A ground unit pulled up.

"Perfect timing," Jack said. He directed one of the officers to cover the back.

In Louie's Restaurant, most of the diners had abandoned their food to crowd against the window. Among them was JoBeth.

She had, of course, not been in her apartment since the beginning of the operation.

The intruder tried to get out the rear door, but was apprehended by the officer and Pedro, who'd gone around to back him up. We could see them bringing their prisoner back through the parking lot.

"Is it Antonelli?" asked Jack.

"That'll be my guess."

"What about Eliot's diary?"

"It doesn't exist."

"So what have we proved?"

"We'll know for certain who's trying to cover things up. And if nothing else you can get the son of a bitch for breaking and entering."

More backup arrived.

JoBeth joined them. "How'd I do?" she asked.

I shook her hand. "Brilliant."

"Did they catch him?"

"Here they come now."

"Doesn't look like Antonelli to me," said Jack.

But it *was*. *Maggie* Antonelli. She strode forward looking angry and frustrated, and not at all like the amiable housewife I'd spoken with a few days earlier. She pulled momentarily away from the officers and confronted me. "This is *your* doing, Walker," she said. "I hope you're proud of yourself. What do you think's going to happen to my kids now?"

"How can they go wrong," I said, "with a mother like you?"

She tried to get free, to come at me, but the cops hustled her past.

We found a Lokker 380 in the alley behind the building. It was set at KILL.

"Did you know all along she was involved?" Jack asked.

"I'm not surprised. It took two people to kill Eliot and Sylvia."

"Antonelli was the second male."

"Sure. He had Eliot and Sylvia at gunpoint. Took them out, decked Eliot at his leisure and threw him into the bay."

"Poor Sylvia," he said.

"Yeah. He must have drowned her personally. Couldn't be sure she might not be a champion swimmer, so he would have taken her over the side and held her under. It wouldn't have been hard. He's pretty big."

"And Maggie rented a boat in Van Clay and went out to get him."

"Yes."

"You were that sure?"

"I was sure when Tina told me he'd insisted on having maintenance done that day on his yacht."

"He was establishing the fact that he hadn't used his boat."

"That's right. He was taking no chances. If he just left it at the dock unused, nobody might notice it was there."

"What about the S.O.S.? The storm had hit by the time that came in. Antonelli couldn't have still been in the boat."

"Directed transmission from shore. Relayed through the boat's radio and broadcast to the Coast Guard."

He looked happy. "Pretty good," he said.

"I get by."

"Well." He watched Maggie get into the ground unit and leave for the station.

"Inspiring woman," I said.

He nodded. "Let's go pick up Antonelli. The other one."

"Yeah." We walked back to the flyer.

"You still haven't told me what the motive was. What's it about?"

"Jack, let's go make our collection. I'll tell you on the way."

⸻

To no one's surprise, George Antonelli was gone when we arrived at his town house. He'd known what had happened to Maggie so he cleared out.

I went over to see Jules and brought him up to date on everything we knew.

The hunt continued almost three weeks. He was found hiding in a mountain cabin in Bolivia. As the police closed in, he took his own life. We all felt kind of badly about that.

12

And finally, Clayborn. I guess we wanted to go after him only after we'd wrapped Antonelli. I don't think it ever occurred to either of us that Clayborn would run. He just wasn't the type.

When we walked into his living room, he gave us the kind of big, welcoming smile you reserve for people you've been in combat with. "Good to see you, Lieutenant Calloway," he said. "And Kristi Walker." He looked at me, and I saw genuine warmth in his eyes. "I'm happy to say I knew from the beginning you would be a formidable pursuer. I never underestimated you the way George did." He waved us into seats. "I wish we might have met under different circumstances."

The guy was a charmer. Give him that. "Yeah," I said. "You have anything to do with sending the gorillas after me?"

He shook his head. "You should know better than to ask. I would never have countenanced anything like that. I didn't find out until after you'd arrested Jankiewicz. Had I known, I'd have taken care of him myself."

We'd remained standing.

"For the record," he continued, "I didn't know the Antonellis were going to do what they did either. I wouldn't have allowed it."

"You want to call your lawyer?" asked Jack.

"Eventually, I suppose I'll have to."

"Eliot was blackmailing you," I said.

"That's right."

"The price kept going up. And you made the mistake of telling Antonelli."

"Yes. But I should tell you that it wasn't George's fault. Left to himself he'd just have let it go. He'd 've let me worry about it. It was Maggie."

"Maggie told you that?" asked Jack.

"No. George would have taken the blame on himself. But it *was* Maggie. They stood to lose everything if it came out about the painting. George would have been disgraced. Jailed. There would have been lawsuits." He shook his head sadly at the perfidy of the world. "They had two kids. Maggie came from nothing. She wasn't going back."

Jack nodded. "Where is it?"

Clayborn led the way upstairs, into the back of the house. "How long have you known?" he asked, directing the question toward me.

"Since Jankiewicz showed up. I already had an artist, a gallery operator who had a sideline making frames, and the guy who was responsible for taking the Retreat apart so it could be moved to Arlington. Then I got a chemist." It had been the last piece.

We stopped in front of a door at the end of the passageway. He unlocked it and turned on the lights. On the far wall hung *The Stranger*.

"Antonelli got the painting for you," I said. "He made the switch out at the Twins. While they were taking the Retreat apart."

"That's so. He took the painting as soon as we had the replacement ready. Years before the Retreat was shipped."

"Eliot painted the replacement."

"Sure. He was perfect for it. He was a superb technician."

"Annie Detmer supplied the frame."

He walked over and stood beside the painting. Admiring it. "Yes."

"And Jankiewicz aged it. Made it look like the original."

He nodded. Glanced at Jack. "It's the first time in my life I've wantonly broken the law, Lieutenant." He held out his wrists.

Jack produced a pair of cuffs.

I caught his eyes. "What happened to keeping treasures out of the hands of private collectors?"

"I don't know," he said. "I guess talking's easy."

After they'd left the room, I stood looking up at it. *The Stranger*. I don't know much about art, but this one had something the copy in the museum lacked. I almost thought the thing was smiling at me.

I wondered whether it would have been any more difficult to fathom than Clayborn.

❖ IDENTITY THEFT ❖
by Robert J. Sawyer

THE DOOR TO my office slid open. "Hello," I said, rising from my chair. "You must be my nine o'clock." I said it as if I had a ten o'clock and an eleven o'clock, but I didn't. The whole Martian economy was in a slump, and, even though I was the only private detective on Mars, this was the first new case I'd had in weeks.

"Yes," said a high, feminine voice. "I'm Cassandra Wilkins."

I let my eyes rove up and down her body. It was very good work; I wondered if she'd had quite so perfect a figure before transferring. People usually ordered replacement bodies that, at least in broad strokes, resembled their originals, but few could resist improving them. Men got buffer, women got curvier, and everyone modified their faces, removing asymmetries, wrinkles, and imperfections. If and when I transferred myself, I'd eliminate the gray in my blond hair and get a new nose that would look like my current one had before it'd been broken a couple of times.

"A pleasure to meet you, Ms. Wilkins," I said. "I'm Alexander Lomax. Please have a seat."

She was a little thing, no more than a hundred and fifty centimeters, and she was wearing a stylish silver-gray blouse and skirt, but no makeup or jewelry. I'd expected her to sit down with a catlike, fluid movement, given her delicate features, but she just sort of plunked herself into the chair. "Thanks," she said. "I do hope you can help me, Mr. Lomax. I really do."

Rather than immediately sitting down myself, I went to the coffeemaker. I filled my own mug, then opened my mouth to offer Cassandra a cup, but closed it before doing so; transfers, of course, didn't drink. "What seems to be the problem?" I said, returning to my chair.

It's hard reading a transfer's expression: the facial sculpting was usually very good, but the movements were somewhat restrained. "My husband—oh, my goodness, Mr. Lomax, I hate to even say this!" She looked down at her hands. "My husband . . . he's disappeared."

I raised my eyebrows; it was pretty damned difficult for someone to disappear here. New Klondike was only three kilometers in diameter, all of it locked under the dome. "When did you last see him?"

"Three days ago."

My office was small, but it did have a window. Through it, I could see one of the supporting arches that helped to hold up the transparent dome over New Klondike. Outside the dome, a sandstorm was raging, orange clouds obscuring the sun. Auxiliary lights on the arch compensated for that, but Martian daylight was never very bright. That's a reason why even those who had a choice were reluctant to return to Earth: after years of only dim illumination, apparently the sun as seen from there was excruciating. "Is your husband, um, like you?" I asked.

She nodded. "Oh, yes. We both came here looking to make our fortune, just like everyone else."

I shook my head. "I mean is he also a transfer?"

"Oh, sorry. Yes, he is. In fact, we both just transferred."

"It's an expensive procedure," I said. "Could he have been skipping out on paying for it?"

Cassandra shook her head. "No, no. Joshua found one or two nice specimens early on. He used the money from selling those pieces to buy the New You franchise here. That's where we met—after I threw in the towel on sifting dirt, I got a job in sales there. Anyway, of course, we both got to transfer at cost." She was actually wringing her synthetic hands. "Oh, Mr. Lomax, please help me! I don't know what I'm going to do without my Joshua!"

"You must love him a lot," I said, watching her pretty face for more than just the pleasure of looking at it; I wanted to gauge her sincerity as she replied. After all, people often disappeared because things were bad at home, but spouses are rarely forthcoming about that.

"Oh, I do!" said Cassandra. "I love him more than I can say. Joshua is a wonderful, wonderful man." She looked at me with pleading eyes. "You have to help me get him back. You just have to!"

I looked down at my coffee mug; steam was rising from it. "Have you tried the police?"

Cassandra made a sound that I guessed was supposed to be a snort: it had the right roughness, but was dry as Martian sand. "Yes. They—oh, I hate to speak ill of anyone, Mr. Lomax! Believe me, it's not my way, but—well, there's no ducking it, is there? They were useless. Just totally useless."

I nodded slightly; it's a story I heard often enough—I owed most of what little livelihood I had to the local cops' incompetence and indifference. "Who did you speak to?"

"A—a detective, I guess he was; he didn't wear a uniform. I've forgotten his name."

"What did he look like?"

"Red hair, and—"

"That's Mac," I said. She looked puzzled, so I said his full name. "Dougal McCrae."

"McCrae, yes," said Cassandra. She shuddered a bit, and she must have noticed my surprised reaction to that. "Sorry," she said. "I just didn't like the way he looked at me."

I resisted running my eyes over her body just then; I'd already done so, and I could remember what I'd seen. I guess her original figure hadn't been like this one; if it had, she'd certainly be used to admiring looks from men by now.

"I'll have a word with McCrae," I said. "See what's already been done. Then I'll pick up where the cops left off."

"Would you?" Her green eyes seemed to dance. "Oh, thank you, Mr. Lomax! You're a good man—I can tell!"

I shrugged a little. "I can show you two ex-wives and a half-dozen bankers who'd disagree."

"Oh, no," she said. "Don't say things like that! You *are* a good man, I'm sure of it. Believe me, I have a sense about these things. You're a good man, and I know you won't let me down."

Naïve woman; she'd probably thought the same thing about her husband—until he'd run off. "Now, what can you tell me about your husband? Joshua, is it?"

"Yes, that's right. His full name is Joshua Connor Wilkins—and it's Joshua, never just Josh, thank you very much." I nodded. Guys who were anal about being called by their full first names never bought a round, in my experience. Maybe it was a good thing that this clown was gone.

"Yes," I said. "Go on." I didn't have to take notes, of course. My office computer was recording everything, and would extract whatever was useful into a summary file for me.

Cassandra ran her synthetic lower lip back and forth beneath her artificial upper teeth, thinking for a moment. Then: "Well, he was born in Calgary, Alberta, and he's thirty-eight years old. He moved to Mars seven mears ago." Mears were Mars-years; about double the length of those on Earth.

"Do you have a picture?"

"I can access one," she said. She pointed at my desk terminal. "May I?"

I nodded, and Cassandra reached over to grab the keyboard. In doing so, she managed to knock over my coffee mug, spilling hot joe all over her dainty hand. She let out a small yelp of pain. I got up, grabbed a towel, and began wiping up the mess. "I'm surprised that hurt," I said. "I mean, I *do* like my coffee hot, but . . ."

"Transfers feel pain, Mr. Lomax," she said, "for the same reason that biologicals do. When you're flesh-and-blood, you need a signaling system to warn you when your parts are being damaged; same is true for those of us who have transferred. Admittedly, artificial bodies are much more durable, of course."

"Ah," I said.

"Sorry," she replied. "I've explained this so many times now—you know, at work. Anyway, please forgive me about your desk."

I made a dismissive gesture. "Thank God for the paperless office, eh? Don't worry about it." I gestured at the keyboard; fortunately, none of the coffee had gone down between the keys. "You were going to show me a picture?"

"Oh, right." She spoke some commands, and the terminal responded—making me wonder what she'd wanted the keyboard for. But then she used it to type in a long passphrase; presumably she didn't want to say hers aloud in front of me. She frowned as she was typing it in, and backspaced to make a correction; multiword passphrases were easy to say, but hard to type if you weren't adept with a keyboard—and the more security conscious you were, the longer the passphrase you used.

Anyway, she accessed some repository of her personal files, and brought up a photo of Joshua-never-Josh Wilkins. Given how attractive Mrs. Wilkins was, he wasn't what I expected. He had cold, gray eyes, hair buzzed so short as to be nonexistent, and a thin, almost lipless mouth; the overall effect was reptilian. "That's before," I said. "What about after? What's he look like now that he's transferred?"

"Umm, pretty much the same," she said.

"Really?" If I'd had that kisser, I'd have modified it for sure. "Do you have pictures taken since he moved his mind?"

"No actual pictures," said Cassandra. "After all, he and I only just transferred. But I can go into the NewYou database, and show you the plans from which his new face was manufactured." She spoke to the terminal some more, and then typed in another lengthy passphrase. Soon enough, she had a computer-graphics rendition of Joshua's head on my screen.

"You're right," I said, surprised. "He didn't change a thing. Can I get copies of all this?"

She nodded, and spoke some more commands, transferring various documents into local storage.

"All right," I said. "My fee is two hundred solars an hour."

"That's fine, that's fine, of course! I don't care about the money, Mr. Lomax—not at all. I just want Joshua back. Please tell me you'll find him."

"I will," I said, smiling my most reassuring smile. "Don't you worry about that. He can't have gone far."

—⊶—

Actually, of course, Joshua Wilkins *could* perhaps have gone quite far—so my first order of business was to eliminate that possibility.

No spaceships had left Mars in the last ten days, so he couldn't be off-planet. There was a giant airlock in the south through which large spaceships could be brought inside for dry-dock work, but it hadn't been cracked open in weeks. And, although a transfer could exist freely on the Martian surface, there were only four personnel air locks leading out of the dome, and they all had security guards. I visited each of those air locks and checked, just to be sure, but the only people who had gone out in the last three days were the usual crowds of hapless fossil hunters, and every one of them had returned when the dust storm began.

I remember when this town had started up: "The Great Fossil Rush," they called it. Weingarten and O'Reilly, two early private explorers who had come here at their own expense, had found the first fossils on Mars, and had made a fortune selling them back on Earth. More valuable than any precious metal; rarer than anything else in the solar system—actual evidence of extraterrestrial life! Good fist-sized specimens went for millions in online auctions; excellent football-sized ones for billions. There was no greater status symbol than to own the petrified remains of a Martian pentaped or rhizomorph.

Of course, Weingarten and O'Reilly wouldn't say precisely where they'd found their specimens, but it had been easy enough to prove that their spaceship had landed here, in the Isidis Planitia basin. Other treasure hunters started coming, and New Klondike—the one and only town on Mars—was born.

Native life was never widely dispersed on Mars; the single ecosystem that had ever existed here seemed to have been confined to an area not much bigger than Rhode Island. Some of the prospectors—excuse me, fossil hunters—who came shortly after W&O's first expedition found a few nice specimens, although most had been badly blasted by blowing sand.

Somewhere, though, was the mother lode: a bed that produced fossils more finely preserved than even those from Earth's famed Burgess Shale. Weingarten and O'Reilly had known where it was—they'd stumbled on it by pure dumb luck, apparently. But they'd both been killed when their heat shield separated from their lander when reentering Earth's atmosphere after their third expedition here—and, in the twenty mears since, no one had yet rediscovered it.

People were still looking, of course. There'd always been a market for transferring consciousness; the potentially infinite lifespan was hugely appealing. But here on Mars, the demand was particularly brisk, since artificial bodies could spend days or even weeks on the surface, searching for paleontological gold, without worrying about running out of air. Of course, a serious sandstorm could blast the synthetic flesh from metal bones, and scour those bones until they were whittled to nothing; that's why no one was outside right now.

Anyway, Joshua-never-Josh Wilkins was clearly not outside the dome, and he hadn't taken off in a spaceship. Wherever he was hiding, it was somewhere in New Klondike. I can't say he was breathing the same air I was, because he wasn't breathing at all. But he was *here*, somewhere. All I had to do was find him.

I didn't want to duplicate the efforts of the police, although "efforts" was usually too generous a term to apply to the work of the local constabulary; "cursory attempts" probably was closer to the truth, if I knew Mac.

New Klondike had twelve radial roadways, cutting across the nine concentric rings of buildings under the dome. My office was at dome's edge; I could have taken a hovertram into the center, but I preferred to walk. A good detective knew what was happening on the streets, and the hovertrams, dilapidated though they were, sped by too fast for that.

I didn't make any bones about staring at the transfers I saw along the way. They ranged in style from really sophisticated models, like Cassandra Wilkins, to things only a step up from the tin woodman of Oz. Of course, those who'd contented themselves with second-rate synthetic forms doubtless believed they'd trade up when they eventually happened upon some decent specimens. Poor saps; no one had found truly spectacular remains for mears, and lots of people were giving up and going back to Earth, if they could afford the passage, or were settling in to lives of, as Thoreau would have it, quiet desperation, their dreams as dead as the fossils they'd never found.

I continued walking easily along; Mars gravity is about a third of Earth's. Some people were stuck here because they'd let their muscles atrophy; they'd never be able to hack a full gee again. Me, I was stuck here for other reasons, but I worked out more than most—Gully's Gym, over by the shipyards—and so still had reasonably strong legs; I could walk comfortably all day if I had to.

The cop shop was a five-story building—it could be that tall, this near the center of the dome—with walls that had once been white, but were now a grimy grayish pink. The front doors were clear alloquartz, same as the overhead dome, and they slid aside as I walked up to them. At the side of the lobby was a long red desk—as if we don't see enough red on Mars—with a map showing the Isidis Planitia basin; New Klondike was a big circle off to one side.

The desk sergeant was a flabby lowbrow named Huxley, whose uniform always seemed a size too small for him. "Hey, Hux," I said, walking over. "Is Mac in?"

Huxley consulted a monitor, then nodded. "Yeah, he's in, but he don't see just anyone."

"I'm not just anyone, Hux. I'm the guy who picks up the pieces after you clowns bungle things."

Huxley frowned, trying to think of a rejoinder. "Yeah, well . . ." he said, at last.

"Oooh," I said. "Good one, Hux! Way to put me in my place."

He narrowed his eyes. "You ain't as funny as you think you are, Lomax," he said.

"Of course I'm not," I said. "Nobody could be *that* funny. I nodded at the secured inner door. "Going to buzz me through?"

"Only to be rid of you," said Huxley. So pleased was he with the wit of this remark that he repeated it: "Only to be rid of you."

Huxley reached below the counter, and the inner door—an unmarked black panel—slid aside. I pantomimed tipping a nonexistent hat at Hux, and headed into the station proper. I then walked down the corridor to McCrae's office; the door was open, so I rapped my knuckles against the plastic jamb.

"Lomax!" he said, looking up. "Decided to turn yourself in?"

"Very funny, Mac," I said. "You and Hux should go on the road together."

He snorted. "What can I do for you, Alex?"

Mac was a skinny biological, with shaggy orange eyebrows shielding his blue eyes. "I'm looking for a guy named Joshua Wilkins."

Mac had a strong Scottish brogue—so strong, I figured it must be an affectation. "Ah, yes," he said. "Who's your client? The wife?"

I nodded.

"A bonnie lass," he said.

"That she is," I said. "Anyway, you tried to find her husband, this Wilkins . . ."

"We looked around, yeah," said Mac. "He's a transfer, you knew that?"

I nodded.

"Well," Mac said, "she gave us the plans for his new face—precise measurements, and all that. We've been feeding all the video made by public security cameras through facial-recognition software. So far, no luck."

I smiled. That's about as far as Mac's detective work normally went: things he could do without hauling his bony ass out from behind his desk. "How much of New Klondike do they cover now?" I asked.

"It's down to sixty percent of the public areas," said Mac. People kept smashing the cameras, and the city didn't have the time or money to replace them.

"You'll let me know if you find anything?"

Mac drew his shaggy eyebrows together. "You know the privacy laws, Alex. I can't divulge what the security cameras see."

I reached into my pocket, pulled out a fifty-solar coin, and flipped it. It went up rapidly, but came down in what still seemed like slow motion to me, even after all these years on Mars; Mac didn't require any special reflexes to catch it in midair. "Of course," he said, "I suppose we could make an exception . . ."

"Thanks. You're a credit to law-enforcement officials everywhere."

He snorted again, then: "Say, what kind of heat you packing these days? You still carrying that old Smith & Wesson?"

"I've got a license," I said, narrowing my eyes.

"Oh, I know, I know. But be careful, eh? The times, they are a-changin'. Bullets aren't much use against a transfer, and getting to be more of those each day."

I nodded. "So I've heard. How do you guys handle them?"

"Until recently, as little as possible," said Mac. "Turning a blind eye, and all that."

"Saves getting up," I said.

Mac didn't take offense. "Exactly. But let me show you something." We left his office, went further down the corridor and entered another room. He pointed to a device on the table. "Just arrived from Earth," he said. "The latest thing."

It was a wide, flat disk, maybe half a meter in diameter, and five centimeters thick. There were a pair of U-shaped handgrips attached to the edge, opposite each other. "What is it?" I asked.

"A broadband disrupter," he said. He picked it up and held it in front of himself, like a gladiator's shield. "It discharges an oscillating multi-frequency electromagnetic pulse. From a distance of four meters or less, it will completely fry the artificial brain of a transfer—killing it as effectively as a bullet kills a human."

"I don't plan on killing anyone," I said.

"That's what you said the last time."

Ouch. Still, maybe he had a point. "I don't suppose you have a spare one I can borrow?"

Mac laughed. "Are you kidding? This is the only one we've got so far."

"Well, then," I said, heading for the door, "I guess I'd better be careful."

My next stop was the NewYou building. I took Third Avenue, one of the radial streets of the city, out the five blocks to it. The building was two stories tall and was made, like most structures here, of red laser-fused Martian sand bricks. Flanking the main doors were a pair of wide alloquartz display windows, showing dusty artificial bodies dressed in fashions from about two mears ago; it was high time somebody updated things.

Inside, the store was part showroom and part workshop, with spare parts scattered about: here, a white-skinned artificial hand; there, a black lower leg; on shelves, synthetic eyes and spools of colored monofilament than I guessed were used to simulate hair. There were also all sorts of internal parts on worktables: motors and hydraulic pumps and joint hinges. A half-dozen technicians were milling around, assembling new bodies or repairing old ones.

Across the room, I spotted Cassandra Wilkins, wearing a beige suit today. She was talking with a man and a woman, who were biological; potential customers, presumably. "Hello, Cassandra," I said, after I'd closed the distance between us.

"Mr. Lomax!" she said, excusing herself from the couple. "I'm so glad you're here—so very glad! What news do you have?"

"Not much," I said. "I've been to visit the cops, and I thought I should start my investigation here. After all, your husband owned this franchise, right?"

Cassandra nodded enthusiastically. "I knew I was doing the right thing hiring you," she said. "I just knew it! Why, do you know that lazy detective McCrae never stopped by here—not even once!"

I smiled. "Mac's not the outdoorsy type," I said. "And, well, you get what you pay for."

"Isn't that the truth?" said Cassandra. "Isn't that just the God's honest truth!"

"You said your husband moved his mind recently?"

She nodded her head. "Yes. All of that goes on upstairs, though. This is just sales and service down here."

"Can you show me?" I asked.

She nodded again. "Of course—anything you want to see, Mr. Lomax!" What I wanted to see was under that beige suit—nothing beat the perfection of a transfer's body—but I kept that thought to myself. Cassandra looked around the room, then motioned for another staff member—also female, also a transfer, also gorgeous, and this one did wear tasteful makeup and jewelry—to come over. "I'm sorry," Cassandra said to the two customers she'd abandoned a few moments ago. "Miss Takahashi here will look after you." She then turned to me. "This way."

We went through a curtained doorway and up a set of stairs. "Here's our scanning room," said Cassandra, indicating the left-hand one of a pair of doors; both doors had little windows in them. She stood on tiptoe to look in the scanning-room window, and nodded, apparently satisfied by what she saw, then opened the door. Two people were inside: a balding man of about forty, who was seated, and a standing woman who looked twenty-five; the woman was a transfer herself, though so there was no way of knowing her real age. "So sorry to interrupt," Cassandra said. She looked at the man in the chair, while gesturing at me. "This is Alexander Lomax. He's providing some, ah, consulting services for us."

The man looked at me, surprised, then said, "Klaus Hansen," by way of introduction.

"Would you mind ever so much if Mr. Lomax watched while the scan was being done?" asked Cassandra.

Hansen considered this for a moment, frowning his long, thin face. But then he nodded. "Sure. Why not?"

"Thanks," I said. "I'll just stand over here." I moved to the far wall and leaned back against it.

The chair Hansen was sitting in looked a lot like a barber's chair. The female transfer who wasn't Cassandra reached up above the chair and pulled down a translucent hemisphere that was attached by an articulated arm to the ceiling. She kept lowering it until all of Hansen's head was covered, and then she turned to a control console.

The hemisphere shimmered slightly, as though a film of oil was washing over its surface; the scanning field, I supposed.

Cassandra was standing next to me, arms crossed in front of her chest. It was an unnatural-looking pose, given her large bosom. "How long does the scanning take?" I asked.

"It's a quantum-mechanical process," she replied. "So the scanning is rapid. But it'll take about ten minutes to move the data into the artificial brain. And then . . ."

"And then?" I said.

She lifted her shoulders, as if the rest didn't need to be spelled out. "Why, and then Mr. Hansen will be able to live forever."

"Ah," I said.

"Come along," said Cassandra. "Let's go see the other side." We left that room, closing its door behind us, and entered the one next door. This room was a mirror image of the previous one, which I guess was appropriate. Standing erect in the middle of the room, supported by a metal armature, was Hansen's new body, dressed in a fashionable blue suit; its eyes were closed. Also in the room was a male NewYou technician, who was biological.

I walked around, looking at the artificial body from all angles. The replacement Hansen still had a bald spot, although its diameter had been reduced by half. And, interestingly, Hansen had opted for a sort of permanent designer-stubble look; the biological him was clean-shaven at the moment.

Suddenly the simulacrum's eyes opened. "Wow," said a voice that was the same as the one I'd heard from the man next door. "That's incredible."

"How do you feel, Mr. Hansen?" asked the male technician.

"Fine," he said. "Just fine."

"Good," the technician said. "There'll be some settling-in adjustments, of course. Let's just check to make sure all your parts are working . . ."

"And there it is," said Cassandra, to me. "Simple as that." She led me out of the room, back into the corridor.

"Fascinating," I said. I pointed at the left-hand door. "When do you take care of the original?"

"That's already been done. We do it in the chair."

I stared at the closed door, and I like to think I suppressed my shudder enough so that Cassandra was unaware of it. "All right," I said. "I guess I've seen enough."

Cassandra looked disappointed. "Are you sure don't want to look around some more?"

"Why?" I said. "Is there anything else worth seeing?"

"Oh, I don't know," said Cassandra. "It's a big place. Everything on this floor, everything downstairs . . . everything in the basement."

I blinked. "You've got a basement?" Almost no Martian buildings had basements; the permafrost layer was very hard to dig through.

"Yes," she said. "Oh, yes." She paused, then looked away. "Of course, no one ever goes down there; it's just storage."

"I'll have a look," I said.

And that's where I found him.

He was lying behind some large storage crates, face down, a sticky pool of machine oil surrounding his head. Next to him was a fusion-powered jackhammer, the kind many of the fossil hunters had for removing surface rocks. And next to the jackhammer was a piece of good old-fashioned paper. On it, in block letters, was written, "I'm so sorry, Cassie. It's just not the same."

It's hard to commit suicide, I guess, when you're a transfer. Slitting your wrists does nothing significant. Poison doesn't work, and neither does drowning.

But Joshua-never-anything-else-at-all-anymore Wilkins had apparently found a way. From the looks of it, he'd leaned back against the rough cement wall, and, with his strong artificial arms, had held up the jackhammer, placing its bit against the center of his forehead. And then he'd held down on the jackhammer's twin triggers, letting the unit run until it had managed to pierce through his titanium skull and scramble the soft material of his artificial brain. When his brain died, his thumbs let up on the triggers, and he dropped the jackhammer, then tumbled over himself. His head had twisted sideways when it hit the concrete floor. Everything below his eyebrows was intact; it was clearly the same face Cassandra Wilkins had shown me.

I headed up the stairs and found Cassandra, who was chatting in her animated style with another customer.

"Cassandra," I said, pulling her aside. "Cassandra, I'm very sorry, but . . ."

She looked at me, her green eyes wide. "What?"

"I've found your husband. And he's dead."

She opened her pretty mouth, closed it, then opened it again. She looked like she might fall over, even with gyroscopes stabilizing her. I put an arm around her shoulders, but she didn't seem comfortable with it, so I let her go. "My . . . God," she said at last. "Are you . . . are you positive?"

"Sure looks like him," I said.

"My God," she said again. "What . . . what happened?"

No nice way to say it. "Looks like he killed himself."

A couple of Cassandra's coworkers had come over, wondering what all the commotion was about. "What's wrong?" asked one of them—the same Miss Takahashi I'd seen earlier.

"Oh, Reiko," said Cassandra. "Joshua is dead!"

Customers were noticing what was going on, too. A burly flesh-and-blood man, with arms as thick around as most men's leg's, came across the room; he seemed to be the boss here. Reiko Takahashi had already drawn Cassandra into her arms—or vice-versa; I'd been looking away when it had happened—and was stroking Cassandra's artificial hair. I let the boss do what he could to calm the crowd, while I used my commlink to call Mac and inform him of Joshua Wilkins's suicide.

—o—

Detective Dougal McCrae of New Klondike's finest arrived about twenty minutes later, accompanied by two uniforms. "How's it look, Alex?" Mac asked.

"Not as messy as some of the biological suicides I've seen," I said. "But it's still not a pretty sight."

"Show me."

I led Mac downstairs. He read the note without picking it up.

The burly man soon came down, too, followed by Cassandra Wilkins, who was holding her artificial hand to her artificial mouth.

"Hello, again, Mrs. Wilkins," said Mac, moving to interpose his body between her and the prone form on the floor. "I'm terribly sorry, but I'll need you to make an official identification."

I lifted my eyebrows at the irony of requiring the next of kin to actually look at the body to be sure of who it was, but that's what we'd gone back to with transfers. Privacy laws prevented any sort of ID chip or tracking device being put into artificial bodies. In fact, that was one of the many incentives to transfer; you'd no longer left fingerprints or a trail of identifying DNA everywhere you went.

Cassandra nodded bravely; she was willing to accede to Mac's request. He stepped aside, a living curtain, revealing the artificial body with the gaping head wound. She looked down at it. I'd expected her to quickly avert her eyes, but she didn't; she just kept staring.

Finally, Mac said, very gently, "Is that your husband, Mrs. Wilkins?"

She nodded slowly. Her voice was soft. "Yes. Oh, my poor, poor Joshua . . ."

Mac stepped over to talk to the two uniforms, and I joined them. "What do you do with a dead transfer?" I asked. "Seems pointless to call in the medical examiner."

By way of answer, Mac motioned to the burly man. The man touched his own chest and raised his eyebrows in the classic, "Who, me?" expression. Mac nodded again. The man looked left and right, like he was crossing some imaginary road, and then came over. "Yeah?"

"You seem to be the senior employee here," said Mac. "Am I right?"

The man nodded. "Horatio Fernandez. Joshua was the boss, but, yeah, I guess I'm in charge until head office sends somebody new out from Earth."

"Well," said Mac, "you're probably better equipped than we are to figure out the exact cause of death."

Fernandez gestured theatrically at the synthetic corpse, as if it were—well not *bleedingly* obvious, but certainly apparent.

Mac nodded. "It's just a bit too pat," he said, his voice lowered conspiratorially. "Implement at hand, suicide note." He lifted his shaggy orange eyebrows. "I just want to be sure."

Cassandra had drifted over without Mac noticing, although of course I had. She was listening in.

"Yeah," said Fernandez. "Sure. We can disassemble him, check for anything else that might be amiss."

"No," said Cassandra. "You can't."

"I'm afraid it's necessary," said Mac, looking at her. His Scottish brogue always put an edge on his words, but I knew he was trying to sound gentle.

"No," said Cassandra, her voice quavering. "I forbid it."

Mac's voice got a little firmer. "You can't. I'm legally required to order an autopsy in every suspicious case."

Cassandra wheeled on Fernandez. "Horatio, I order you not to do this."

Fernandez blinked a few times. "Order?"

Cassandra opened her mouth to say something more, then apparently thought better of it. Horatio moved closer to her, and put a hulking arm around her small shoulders. "Don't worry," he said. "We'll be gentle." And then his face brightened a bit. "In fact, we'll see what parts we can salvage—give them to somebody else; somebody who couldn't afford such good stuff if it was new." He smiled beatifically. "It's what Joshua would have wanted."

The next day, I was siting in my office, looking out the small window. The dust storm had ended. Out on the surface, rocks were strewn everywhere, like toys on a kid's bedroom floor. My wrist commlink buzzed, and I looked at it in anticipation, hoping for a new case; I could use the solars. But the ID line said NKPD. I told the device to accept the call, and a little picture of Mac's red-headed face appeared on my wrist. "Hey, Lomax," he said. "Come on by the station, would you?"

"What's up?"

The micro-Mac frowned. "Nothing I want to say over open airwaves."

I nodded. Now that the Wilkins case was over, I didn't have anything better to do anyway. I'd only managed about seven billable hours, damnitall, and even that had taken some padding.

I walked into the center along Ninth Avenue, entered the lobby of the police station, traded quips with the ineluctable Huxley, and was admitted to the back.

"Hey, Mac," I said. "What's up?"

"'Morning, Alex," Mac said, rolling the R in "Morning." "Come in; sit down." He spoke to his desk terminal, and turned its monitor around so I could see it. "Have a look at this."

I glanced at the screen. "The report on Joshua Wilkins?" I said.

Mac nodded. "Look at the section on the artificial brain."

I skimmed the text, until I found that part. "Yeah?" I said, still not getting it.

"Do you know what 'baseline synaptic web' means?" Mac asked.

"No, I don't. And you didn't either, smart-ass, until someone told you."

Mac smiled a bit, conceding that. "Well, there were lots of bits of the artificial brain left behind. And that big guy at NewYou—Fernandez, remember?—he really got into this forensic stuff, and decided to run it through some kind of instrument they've got there. And you know what he found?"

"What?"

"The brain stuff—the raw material inside the artificial skull—was pristine. It had never been imprinted."

"You mean no scanned mind had ever been transferred into that brain?"

Mac folded his arms across his chest and leaned back in his chair. "Bingo."

I frowned. "But that's not possible. I mean, if there was no mind in that head, who wrote the suicide note?"

Mac lifted those shaggy eyebrows of his. "Who indeed?" he said. "And what happened to Joshua Wilkins's scanned consciousness?"

"Does anyone at NewYou but Fernandez know about this?" I asked.

Mac shook his head. "No, and he's agreed to keep his mouth shut while we continue to investigate. But I thought I'd clue you in, since apparently the case you were on isn't really closed—and, after all, if you don't make money now and again, you can't afford to bribe me for favors."

I nodded. "That's what I like about you, Mac. Always looking out for my best interests."

Perhaps I should have gone straight to see Cassandra Wilkins, and made sure that we both agreed that I was back on the clock, but I had some questions I wanted answered first. And I knew just who to turn to. Raoul Santos was the city's top computer expert. I'd met him during a previous case, and we'd recently struck up a small-f friendship—we both shared the same taste in bootleg Earth booze, and he wasn't above joining me at some of New Klondike's sleazier saloons to get it. I used my commlink to call him, and we arranged to meet at the Bent Chisel.

The Bent Chisel was a little hellhole off of Fourth Avenue, in the sixth concentric ring of buildings. I made sure I had my revolver, and that it was loaded, before I entered. The bartender was a surly man named Buttrick, a biological who had more than his fair share of flesh, and blood as cold as ice. He wore a sleeveless black shirt, and had a three-day growth of salt-and-pepper beard. "Lomax," he said, acknowledging my entrance. "No broken furniture this time, right?"

I held up three fingers. "Scout's honor."

Buttrick held up one finger.

"Hey," I said. "Is that any way to treat one of your best customers?"

"My best customers," said Buttrick, polishing a glass with a ratty towel, "pay their tabs."

"Yeah," I said, stealing a page from Sgt. Huxley's *Guide to Witty Repartee*. "Well." I headed on in, making my way to the back of the bar, where my favorite booth was located. The waitresses here were topless, and soon enough one came over to see me. I couldn't remember her name offhand, although we'd slept together a couple of times. I ordered a scotch on the rocks; they normally did that with carbon-dioxide ice here, which was much cheaper than water ice on Mars. A few minutes later, Raoul Santos arrived. "Hey," he said, taking a seat opposite me. "How's tricks?"

"Fine," I said. "She sends her love."

Raoul made a puzzled face, then smiled. "Ah, right. Cute. Listen, don't quit your day job."

"Hey," I said, placing a hand over my heart, "you wound me. Down deep, I'm a stand-up comic."

"Well," said Raoul, "I always say people should be true to their innermost selves, but . . ."

"Yeah?" I said. "What's your innermost self?"

"Me?" Raoul raised his eyebrows. "I'm pure genius, right to the very core."

I snorted, and the waitress reappeared. She gave me my glass. It was just a little less full than it should have been: either Buttrick was trying to curb his losses on me, or the waitress was miffed that I hadn't acknowledged our former intimacy. Raoul placed his order, talking directly into the woman's breasts. Boobs did well in Mars gravity; hers were still perky even though she had to be almost forty.

"So," said Raoul, looking over steepled fingers at me. "What's up?" His face consisted of a wide forehead, long nose, and receding chin; it made him look like he was leaning forward even when he wasn't.

I took a swig of my drink. "Tell me about this transferring game."

"Ah, yes," said Raoul. "Fascinating stuff. Thinking of doing it?"

"Maybe someday," I said.

"You know, it's supposed to pay for itself within three mears," he said, " 'cause you no longer have to pay life-support tax after you've transferred."

I was in arrears on that, and didn't like to think about what would happen if I fell much further behind. "That'd be a plus," I said. "What about you? You going to do it?"

"Sure. I want to live forever; who doesn't? 'Course, my dad won't like it."

"Your dad? What's he got against it?"

Raoul snorted. "He's a minister."

"In whose government?" I asked.

"No, no. A *minister*. Clergy."

"I didn't know there were any of those left, even on Earth," I said.

"He *is* on Earth, but, yeah, you're right. Poor old guy still believes in souls."

I raised my eyebrows. "Really?"

"Yup. And because he believes in souls, he has a hard time with this idea of transferring consciousness. He would say the new version isn't the same person."

I thought about what the supposed suicide note said. "Well, is it?"

Raoul rolled his eyes. "You, too? Of course it is! The mind is just software—and since the dawn of computing, software has been moved from one computing platform to another by copying it over, then erasing the original."

I frowned, but decided to let that go for the moment. "So, if you do transfer, what would you have fixed in your new body?"

Raoul spread his arms. "Hey, man, you don't tamper with perfection."

"Yeah," I said. "Sure. Still, how much could you change things? I mean, say you're a midget; could you choose to have a normal-sized body?"

"Sure, of course."

I frowned. "But wouldn't the copied mind have trouble with your new size?"

"Nah," said Raoul. The waitress returned. She bent over far enough while placing Raoul's drink on the table that her breast touched his bare forearm; she gave me a look that said, "See what you're missing, tiger?" When she was gone, Raoul continued. "See, when we first started copying consciousness, we let the old software from the old mind actually try to directly control the new body. It took months to learn how to walk again, and so on."

"Yeah, I read something about that, years ago," I said.

Raoul nodded. "Right. But now we don't let the copied mind do anything but give orders. The thoughts are intercepted by the new body's main computer. *That* unit runs the body. All the transferred mind has to do is *think* that it wants to pick up this glass, say." He acted out his example, and took a sip, then winced in response to the booze's kick. "The computer takes care of working out which pulleys to contract, how far to reach, and so on."

"So you could indeed order up a body radically different from your original?" I said.

"Absolutely," said Raoul. He looked at me through hooded eyes. "Which, in your case, is probably the route to go."

"Damn," I said.

"Hey, don't take it seriously," he said, taking another sip, and allowing himself another pleased wince. "Just a joke."

"I know," I said. "It's just that I was hoping it wasn't that way. See, this case I'm on: the guy I'm supposed to find owns the NewYou franchise here."

"Yeah?" said Raoul.

"Yeah, and I think he deliberately transferred his scanned mind into some body other than the one that he'd ordered up for himself."

"Why would he do that?"

"He faked the death of the body that looked like him—and, I think he'd planned to do that all along, because he never bothered to order up any improvements to his face. I think he wanted to get away, but make it look like he was dead, so no one would be looking for him anymore."

"And why would he do that?"

I frowned, then drank some more. "I'm not sure."

"Maybe he wanted to escape his spouse."

"Maybe—but she's a hot little number."

"Hmm," said Raoul. "Whose body do you think he took?"

"I don't know that, either. I was hoping the new body would have to be at least roughly similar to his old one; that would cut down on the possible suspects. But I guess that's not the case."

"It isn't, no."

I nodded, and looked down at my drink. The dry-ice cubes were sublimating into white vapor that filled the top part of the glass.

"Something else is bothering you," said Raoul. I lifted my head, and saw him taking a swig of his drink. A little bit of amber liquid spilled out of his mouth and formed a shiny bead on his recessed chin. "What is it?"

I shifted a bit. "I visited NewYou yesterday. You know what happens to your original body after they move your mind?"

"Sure," said Raoul. "Like I said, there's no such thing as moving software. You copy it, then delete the original. They euthanize the biological version, once the transfer is made, by frying the original brain."

I nodded. "And if the guy I'm looking for put his mind into the body intended for somebody else's mind, and that person's mind wasn't copied anywhere, then . . ." I took another swig of my drink. "Then it's murder, isn't it? Souls or no souls—it doesn't matter. If you shut down the one and only copy of someone's mind, you've murdered that person, right?"

"Oh, yes," said Raoul. "Deader than Mars itself is now."

I glanced down at the swirling fog in my glass. "So I'm not just looking for a husband who's skipped out on his wife," I said. "I'm looking for a cold-blooded killer."

⟞⟓⟝

I went by NewYou again. Cassandra wasn't in—but that didn't surprise me; she was a grieving widow now. But Horatio Fernandez—he of the massive arms—was on duty.

"I'd like a list of all the people who were transferred the same day as Joshua Wilkins," I said.

He frowned. "That's confidential information."

There were several potential customers milling about. I raised my voice so they could hear. "Interesting suicide note, wasn't it?"

Fernandez grabbed my arm and led me quickly to the side of the room. "What the hell are you doing?" he whispered angrily.

"Just sharing the news," I said, still speaking loudly, although not quite loud enough now, I thought, for the customers to hear. "People thinking of uploading should know that it's not the same—at least, that's what Joshua Wilkins said in that note."

Fernandez knew when he was beaten. The claim in the putative suicide note was exactly the opposite of NewYou's corporate position: transferring was supposed to be flawless, conferring nothing but benefits. "All right, all right," he hissed. "I'll pull the list for you."

"Now that's service," I said. "They should name you employee of the month."

He led me into the back room and spoke to a computer terminal. I happened to overhear the passphrase for accessing the customer database; it was just six words—hardly any security at all.

Eleven people had moved their consciousnesses into artificial bodies that day. I had him transfer the files on each of the eleven into my wrist commlink. "Thanks," I said, doing that tip-of-the-nonexistent-hat thing I do. Even when you've forced a man to do something, there's no harm in being polite.

⟞⟓⟝

If I was right that Joshua Wilkins had appropriated the body of somebody else who had been scheduled to transfer the same day, it shouldn't be too hard to figure out whose body he'd taken; all I had to do, I figured, was interview each of the eleven.

My first stop, purely because it happened to be the nearest, was the home of a guy named Stuart Berling, a full-time fossil hunter. He must have had some recent success, if he could afford to transfer.

Berling's home was part of a row of townhouses off Fifth Avenue, in the fifth ring. I pushed his door buzzer, and waited impatiently for a response. At last he appeared. If I wasn't so famous for my poker face, I'd have done a double take. The man who greeted me was a dead ringer for Krikor Ajemian, the holovid star—the same gaunt features and intense eyes, the same mane of dark hair, the same tightly trimmed beard and mustache. I guess not everyone wanted to keep even a semblance of their original appearance.

"Hello," I said. "My name is Alexander Lomax. Are you Stuart Berling?"

The artificial face in front of me surely was capable of smiling, but choose not to. "Yes. What do you want?"

"I understand you only recently transferred your consciousness into this body."

A nod. "So?"

"So, I work for the NewYou—the head office on Earth. I'm here to check up on the quality of the work done by our franchise here on Mars." Normally, this was a good technique. If Berling was who he said he was, the question wouldn't faze him. But if we was really Joshua Wilkins, he'd know I was lying, and his expression might betray this. But transfers didn't have faces that were as malleable; if this person was startled or suspicious, nothing in his plastic features indicated it.

"So?" Berling said again.

"So I'm wondering if you were satisfied by the work done for you?"

"It cost a lot," said Berling.

I smiled. "Yes, it does. May I come in?"

He considered this for a few moments, then shrugged. "Sure, why not?" He stepped aside.

His living room was full of work tables, covered with reddish rocks from outside the dome. A giant lens on an articulated arm was attached to one of the work tables, and various geologist's tools were scattered about.

"Finding anything interesting?" I asked, gesturing at the rocks.

"If I was, I certainly wouldn't tell you," said Berling, looking at me sideways in the typical paranoid-prospector's way.

"Right," I said. "Of course. So, *are* you satisfied with the NewYou process?"

"Sure, yeah. It's everything they said it would be. All the parts work."

"Thanks for your help," I said, pulling out my PDA to make a few notes, and then frowning at its blank screen. "Oh, damn," I said. "The silly thing has a loose fusion pack. I've got to open it up and reseat it." I showed him the back of the unit's case. "Do you have a little screwdriver that will fit that?"

Everybody owned some screwdrivers, even though most people rarely needed them, and they were the sort of thing that had no standard storage location. Some people kept them in kitchen drawers, others kept them in tool chests, still others kept them under the bathroom sink. Only a person who had lived in this home for a while would know where they were.

Berling peered at the little slot-headed screw, then nodded. "Sure," he said. "Hang on."

He made an unerring beeline for the far side of the living room, going to a cabinet that had glass doors on its top half, but solid metal ones on its bottom. He bent over, opened one of the metal doors, reached in, rummaged for a bit, and emerged with the appropriate screwdriver.

"Thanks," I said, opening the case in such a way that he couldn't see inside. I then surreptitiously removed the little bit of plastic I'd used to insulate the fusion battery from the contact it was supposed to touch. Meanwhile, without looking up, I said, "Are you married, Mr. Berling?" Of course, I already knew the answer was yes; that fact was in his NewYou file.

He nodded.

"Is your wife home?"

His artificial eyelids closed a bit. "Why?"

I told him the honest truth, since it fit well with my cover story: "I'd like to ask her whether she can perceive any differences between the new you and the old."

Again, I watched his expression, but it didn't change. "Sure, I guess that'd be okay." He turned and called over his shoulder, "Lacie!"

A few moments later, a homely flesh-and-blood woman of about fifty appeared. "This person is from the head office of NewYou," said Berling, indicating me with a pointed finger. "He'd like to speak to you."

"About what?" asked Lacie. She had a deep, not-unpleasant voice.

"Might we speak in private?" I said.

Berling's gaze shifted from Lacie to me, then back to Lacie. "Hrmpph," he said, but then, a moment later, added, "I guess that'd be all right." He turned around and walked away.

I looked at Lacie. "I'm just doing a routine follow-up," I said. "Making sure people are happy with the work we do. Have you noticed any changes in your husband since he transferred?"

"Not really."

"Oh?" I said. "If there's anything at all . . ." I smiled reassuringly. "We want to make the process as perfect as possible. Has he said anything that's surprised you, say?"

Lacie crinkled her face. "How do you mean?"

"I mean, has he used any expressions or turns of phrase you're not used to hearing from him?"

A shake of the head. "No."

"Sometimes the process plays tricks with memory. Has he failed to know something he should know?"

"Not that I noticed," said Lacie.

"What about the reverse? Has he known anything that you wouldn't expect him to know?"

She lifted her eyebrows. "No. He's just Stuart."

I frowned. "No changes at all?"

"No, none . . . well, almost none."

I waited for her to go on, but she didn't, so I prodded her. "What is it? We really would like to know about any difference, any flaw in our transference process."

"Oh, it's not a flaw," said Lacie, not meeting my eyes.

"No? Then what?"

"It's just that . . ."

"Yes?"

"Well, just that he's a demon in the sack now. He stays hard forever."

I frowned, disappointed not to have found what I was looking for on the first try. But I decided to end the masquerade on a positive note. "We aim to please, ma'am. We aim to please."

—⁌—

I spent the next several hours interviewing four other people; none of them seemed to be anyone other than who they claimed to be.

Next on my list was Dr. Rory Pickover, whose home was an apartment in the innermost circle of buildings, beneath the highest point of the dome. He lived alone, so there was no spouse or child to question about any changes in him. That made me suspicious right off the bat: if one were going to choose an identity to appropriate, it ideally would be someone without close companions. He also refused to meet me at his home, meaning I couldn't try the screwdriver trick on him.

I thought we might meet at a coffee shop or a restaurant—there were lots in New Klondike, although none were doing good business these days. But he insisted we go outside the dome—out onto the Martian surface. That was easy for him; he was a transfer now. But it was a pain in the ass for me; I had to rent a surface suit.

We met at the south air lock just as the sun was going down. I suited up—surface suits came in three stretchy sizes; I took the largest. The fish-bowl helmet I rented was somewhat frosted on one side; sandstorm-scouring, no doubt. The air tanks, slung on my back, were good for about four hours. I felt heavy in the suit, even though in it I still weighed only about half of what I had back on Earth.

Rory Pickover was a paleontologist—an actual scientist, not a treasure-seeking fossil hunter. His pre-transfer appearance had been almost stereotypically academic: a round, soft face, with a fringe of graying hair. His new body was lean and muscular, and he had a full head of dark brown hair, but the face was still recognizably his. He was carrying a geologist's hammer, with a wide, flat blade; I rather suspected it would nicely smash my helmet. I had surreptitiously transferred the Smith & Wesson from the holster I wore under my jacket to an exterior pocket on the rented surface suit, just in case I needed it while we were outside.

We signed the security logs, and then let the technician cycle us through the air lock.

Off in the distance, I could see the highland plateau, dark streaks marking its side. Nearby, there were two large craters and a cluster of smaller ones. There were few footprints in the rusty sand; the recent storm had obliterated the thousands that had doubtless been there earlier. We walked out about five hundred meters. I turned around briefly to look back at the transparent dome and the buildings within.

"Sorry for dragging you out here," said Pickover. He had a cultured British accent. "I don't want any witnesses." Even the cheapest artificial body had built-in radio equipment, and I had a transceiver inside my helmet.

"Ah," I said, by way of reply. I slipped my gloved hand into the pocket containing the Smith & Wesson, and wrapped my fingers around its reassuring solidity.

"I know you aren't just in from Earth," said Pickover, continuing to walk. "And I know you don't work for NewYou."

We were casting long shadows; the sun, so much tinier than it appeared from Earth, was sitting on the horizon; the sky was already purpling, and Earth itself was visible, a bright blue-white evening star.

"Who do you think I am?" I asked.

His answer surprised me, although I didn't let it show. "You're Alexander Lomax, the private detective."

Well, it didn't seem to make any sense to deny it. "Yeah. How'd you know?"

"I've been checking you out over the last few days," said Pickover. "I'd been thinking of, ah, engaging your services."

We continued to walk along, little clouds of dust rising each time our feet touched the ground. "What for?" I said.

"You first, if you don't mind," said Pickover. "Why did you come to see me?"

He already knew who I was, and I had a very good idea who he was, so I decided to put my cards on the table. "I'm working for your wife."

Pickover's artificial face looked perplexed. "My . . . wife?"

"That's right."

"I don't have a wife."

"Sure you do. You're Joshua Wilkins, and your wife's name is Cassandra."

"What? No, I'm Rory Pickover. You know that. You called me."

"Come off it, Wilkins. The jig is up. You transferred your consciousness into the body intended for the real Rory Pickover, and then you took off."

"I—oh. Oh, Christ."

"So, you see, I know. Too bad, Wilkins. You'll hang—or whatever the hell they do with transfers—for murdering Pickover."

"No." He said it softly.

"Yes," I replied, and now I pulled out my revolver. It really wouldn't be much use against an artificial body, but until quite recently Wilkins had been biological; hopefully, he was still intimidated by guns. "Let's go."

"Where?"

"Back under the dome, to the police station. I'll have Cassandra meet us there, just to confirm your identity."

The sun had slipped below the horizon now. He spread his arms, a supplicant against the backdrop of the gathering night. "Okay, sure, if you like. Call up this Cassandra, by all means. Let her talk to me. She'll tell you after questioning me for two seconds that I'm not her husband. But—Christ, damn, Christ."

"What?"

"I want to find him, too."

"Who? Joshua Wilkins?"

He nodded, then, perhaps thinking I couldn't see his nod in the growing darkness, said, "Yes."

"Why?"

He tipped his head up, as if thinking. I followed his gaze. Phobos was visible, a dark form overhead. At last, he spoke again. "Because *I'm* the reason he's disappeared."

"What?" I said. "Why?"

"That's why I was thinking of hiring you myself. I didn't know where else to turn."

"Turn for what?"

Pickover looked at me. "I did go to NewYou, Mr. Lomax. I knew I was going to have an enormous amount of work to do out here on the surface now, and I wanted to be able to spend days—weeks!—in the field, without worrying about running out of air, or water, or food."

I frowned. "But you've been here on Mars for six mears; I read that in your file. What's changed?"

"*Everything,* Mr. Lomax." He looked off in the distance. "Everything!" But he didn't elaborate on that. Instead, he said. "I certainly know this Wilkins chap you're looking for; I went to his store, and had him transfer my consciousness from my old biological body into this one. But he also kept a copy of my mind—I'm sure of that."

I raised my eyebrows. "How do you know?"

"Because my computer accounts have been compromised. There's no way anyone but me can get in; I'm the only one who knows the passphrase. But someone *has* been inside, looking around; I use quantum encryption, so you can tell whenever someone has even *looked* at a file." He shook his head. "I don't know how he did it—there must be some technique I'm unaware of—but somehow Wilkins has been extracting information from the copy of my mind. That's the only way I can think of that anyone might have learned my passphrase."

"You think Wilkins did all this to access your bank accounts? Is there really enough money in them to make it worth starting a new life in somebody else's body? It's too dark to see your clothes right now, but, if I recall correctly, they looked a bit . . . shabby."

"You're right. I'm just a poor scientist. But there's something I know that could make the wrong people rich beyond their wildest dreams."

"And what's that?" I said.

He continued to walk along, trying to decide, I suppose, whether to trust me. I let him think about that, and at last, Dr. Rory Pickover, who was now just a starless silhouette against a starry sky, said, in a soft, quiet voice, "I know where it is."

"Where what is?"

"The alpha deposit."

"The what?"

"Sorry," he said. "Paleontologist's jargon. What I mean is, I've found it: I've found the mother lode. I've found the place where Weingarten and O'Reilly had been excavating. I've found the source of the best preserved, most-complete Martian fossils."

"My God," I said. "You'll be *rolling* in it."

Perhaps he shook his head; it was now too dark to tell. "No, sir," he said, in that cultured English voice. "No, I won't. I don't want to *sell* these fossils. I want to preserve them; I want to protect them from these plunderers, these . . . these *thieves*. I want to make sure they're collected properly, scientifically. I want to make sure they end up in the best museums, where they can be studied. There's so much to be learned, so much to discover!"

"Does Wilkins know now where this . . . what did you call it? This alpha deposit is?"

"No—at least, not from accessing my computer files. I didn't record the location anywhere but up here." Presumably he was tapping the side of his head.

"But you think Wilkins extracted the passphrase from a copy of your mind?"

"He must have."

"And now he's presumably trying to extract the location of the alpha deposit from that copy of your mind."

"Yes, yes! And if he succeeds, all will be lost! The best specimens will be sold off into private collections—trophies for some trillionaire's estate, hidden forever from science."

I shook my head. "But this doesn't make any sense. I mean, how would Wilkins even know that you had discovered the alpha deposit?"

Suddenly Pickover's voice was very small. "I'd gone in to NewYou—you have to go in weeks in advance of transferring, of course, so you can tell them what you want in a new body; it takes time to custom-build one to your specifications."

"Yes. So?"

"So, I wanted a body ideally suited to paleontological work on the surface of Mars; I wanted some special modifications—the kinds of the things only the most successful prospectors could afford. Reinforced knees; extra arm strength for moving rocks; extended spectral response in the eyes, so that fossils will stand out better; night vision so that I could continue digging after dark; but . . ."

I nodded. "But you didn't have enough money."

"That's right. I could barely afford to transfer at all, even into the cheapest off-the-shelf body, and so . . ."

He trailed off, too angry at himself, I guess, to give voice to what was in his mind. "And so you hinted that you were about to come into some wealth," I said, "and suggested that maybe he could give you what you needed now, and you'd make it up to him later."

Pickover sounded sad. "That's the trouble with being a scientist; sharing information is our natural mode."

"Did you tell him precisely what you'd found?" I asked.

"No. No, but he must have guessed. I'm a paleontologist, I've been studying Weingarten and O'Reilly for years—all of that is a matter of public record. He must have figured out that I knew where their fossil beds are. After all, where else would a guy like me get money?" He sighed. "I'm an idiot, aren't I?"

"Well, Mensa isn't going to be calling you any time soon."

"Please don't rub it in, Mr. Lomax. I feel bad enough as it is, and—" His voice cracked; I'd never heard a transfer's do that before. "And now I've put all those lovely, lovely fossils in jeopardy! Will you help me, Mr. Lomax? Please say you'll help me!"

I nodded. "All right. I'm on the case."

⚊⚋⚊

We went back into the dome, and I called Raoul Santos on my commlink, getting him to meet me at Rory Pickover's little apartment at the center of town. It was four floors up, and consisted of three small rooms—an interior unit, with no windows.

When Raoul arrived, I made introductions. "Raoul Santos, this is Rory Pickover. Raoul here is the best computer expert we've got in New Klondike. And Dr. Pickover is a paleontologist."

Raoul tipped his broad forehead at Pickover. "Good to meet you."

"Thank you," said Pickover. "Forgive the mess, Mr. Santos. I live alone. A lifelong bachelor gets into bad habits, I'm afraid." He'd already cleared debris off of one chair for me; he now busied himself doing the same with another chair, this one right in front of his home computer.

"What's up, Alex?" asked Raoul, indicating Pickover with a movement of his head. "New client?"

"Yeah," I said. "Dr. Pickover's computer files have been looked at by some unauthorized individual. We're wondering if you could tell us from where the access attempt was made."

"You'll owe me a nice round of drinks at the Bent Chisel," said Raoul.

"No problem," I said. "I'll put it on my tab."

Raoul smiled, and stretched his arms out, fingers interlocked, until his knuckles cracked. Then he took the now-clean seat in front of Pickover's computer and began to type. "How do you lock your files?" he asked, without taking his eyes off the monitor.

"A verbal passphrase," said Pickover.

"Anybody besides you know it?"

Pickover shook his artificial head. "No."

"And it's not written down anywhere?"

"No, well . . . not as such."

Raoul turned his head, looking up at Pickover. "What do you mean?"

"It's a line from a book. If I ever forgot the exact wording, I could always look it up."

Raoul shook his head in disgust. "You should always use random passphrases." He typed keys.

"Oh, I'm sure it's totally secure," said Pickover. "No one would guess—"

Raoul interrupted. "Your passphrase being, 'Those privileged to be present . . . ' "

I saw Pickover's jaw drop. "My God. How did you know that?"

Raoul pointed to some data on the screen. "It's the first thing that was inputted by the only outside access your system has had in weeks."

"I thought passphrases were hidden from view when entered," said Pickover.

"Sure they are," said Raoul. "But the comm program has a buffer; it's in there. Look."

Raoul shifted in the chair so that Pickover could see the screen clearly over his shoulder. "That's . . . well, that's very strange," said Pickover.

"What?"

"Well, sure that's my passphrase, but it's not quite right."

I loomed in to have a peek at the screen, too. "How do you mean?" I said.

"Well," said Pickover, "see, my passphrase is 'Those privileged to be present at a family festival of the Forsytes'—it's from the opening of *The Man of Property*, the first book of *The Forsyte Saga* by John Galsworthy. I love that phrase because of the alliteration—'privilege to be present,' 'family festival of the Forsytes.' Makes it easy to remember."

Raoul shook his head in you-can't-teach-people-anything disgust. Pickover went on. "But, see, whoever it was typed in even more."

I looked at the glowing string of letters. In full it said: *Those privileged to be present at a family festival of the Forsytes have seen them dine at half past eight, enjoying seven courses.*

"It's too much?" I said.

"That's right," said Pickover, nodding. "My passphrase ends with the word 'Forsytes.' "

Raoul was stroking his receding chin. "Doesn't matter," he said. "The files would unlock the moment the phrase was complete; the rest would just be discarded—systems that principally work with spoken commands don't require you to press the enter key."

"Yes, yes, yes," said Pickover. "But the rest of it isn't what Galsworthy wrote. It's not even close. *The Man of Property* is my favorite book; I know it well. The full opening line is 'Those privileged to be present at a family festival of the Forsytes have seen that charming and instructive sight—an upper middle-class family in full plumage.' " Nothing about the time they ate, or how many courses they had."

Raoul pointed at the text on screen, as if it had to be the correct version. "Are you sure?" he said.

"Of course!" said Pickover. "Galsworthy's public domain; you can do a search online and see for yourself."

I frowned. "No one but you knows your passphrase, right?"

Pickover nodded vigorously. "I live alone, and I don't have many friends; I'm a quiet sort. There's no one I've ever told, and no one who could have ever overheard me saying it, or seen me typing it in."

"Somebody found it out," said Raoul.

Pickover looked at me, then down at Raoul. "I think . . ." he said, beginning slowly, giving me a chance to stop him, I guess, before he said too much. But I let him go on. "I think that the information was extracted from a scan of my mind made by NewYou."

Raoul crossed his arms in front of his chest. "Impossible."

"What?" said Pickover, and "Why?" said I.

"Can't be done," said Raoul. "We know how to copy the vast array of interconnections that make up a human mind, and we know how to reinstantiate those connections in an artificial substrate. But we don't know how to decode them; nobody does. There's simply no way to sift through a digital copy of a mind and extract specific data."

Damn! If Raoul was right—and he always was in computing matters—then all this business with Pickover was a red herring. There probably was no bootleg scan of his mind; despite his protestations of being careful, someone likely had just overheard his passphrase, and decided to go spelunking through his files. While I was wasting time on this, Joshua Wilkins was doubtless slipping further out of my grasp.

Still, it was worth continuing this line of investigation for a few minutes more. "Any sign of where the access attempt was made?" I asked Raoul.

He shook his head. "No. Whoever did it knew what they were doing; they covered their tracks well. The attempt came over an outside line—that's all I can tell for sure."

I nodded. "Okay. Thanks, Raoul. Appreciate your help."

Raoul got up. "My pleasure. Now, how 'bout that drink."

I opened my mouth to say yes, but then it hit me—what Wilkins must be doing. "Umm, later, okay? I've—I've got some more things to take care of here."

Raoul frowned; he'd clearly hoped to collect his booze immediately. But I started maneuvering him toward the door. "Thanks for your help, Raoul. I really appreciate it."

"Um, sure, Alex," he said. He was obviously aware he was being given the bum's rush, but he wasn't fighting it too much. "Anytime."

"Yes, thank you awfully, Mr. Santos," said Pickover.

"No problem. If—"

"See you later, Raoul," I said, opening the door for him. "Thanks so much." I tipped my nonexistent hat at him.

Raoul shrugged, clearly aware that something was up, but not motivated sufficiently to find out what. He went through the door, and I hit the button that caused it to slide shut behind him. As soon as it was closed, I put an arm around Pickover's shoulders, and propelled him back to the computer. I pointed at the line Raoul had highlighted on the screen, and read the ending of it aloud: " ' . . . dine at half past eight, enjoying seven courses.' "

Pickover nodded. "Yes. So?"

"Numbers are often coded info," I said. " 'Half past eight; seven courses.' What's that mean to you?"

"To me?" said Pickover. "Nothing. I like to eat much earlier than that, and I never have more than one course."

"But it could be a message," I said.

"From who?"

There was no easy way to tell him this. "From you to you."

He drew his artificial eyebrows together in puzzlement. "What?"

"Look," I said, motioning for him to sit down in front of the computer, "Raoul is doubtless right. You can't sift a digital scan of a human mind for information."

"But that must be what Wilkins is doing."

I shook my head. "No," I said. "The only way to find out what's in a mind is to ask it interactively."

"But . . . but no one's asked me my passphrase."

"No one has asked *this* you. But Joshua Wilkins must have transferred the extra copy of your mind into a body, so that he could deal with it directly. And that extra copy must be the one that's revealed your codes to him."

"You mean . . . you mean there's another me? Another *conscious* me?"

"Looks that way."

"But . . . no, no. That's . . . why, that's *illegal*. Bootleg copies of human beings—my God, Lomax, it's obscene!"

"I'm going to go see if I can find him," I said.

"It," said Pickover, forcefully.

"What?"

"It. Not him. I'm the only 'him'—the only real Rory Pickover."

"So what do you want me to do when I find it?"

"Erase it, of course. Shut it down." He shuddered. "My God, Lomax, I feel so . . . so violated! A stolen copy of my mind! It's the ultimate invasion of privacy . . ."

"That may be," I said. "But the bootleg is trying to tell you something. He—it—gave Wilkins the passphrase, and then tacked some extra words onto it, in order to get a message to you."

"But I don't recognize those extra words," said Pickover, sounding exasperated.

"Do they *mean* anything to you? Do they suggest anything?"

Pickover reread what was on the screen. "I can't imagine what," he said, "unless . . . no, no, I'd never think up a code like that."

"You obviously just *did* think of it. What's the code?"

Pickover was quiet for a moment, as if deciding if the thought was worth giving voice. Then: "Well, New Klondike is circular in layout, right? And it consists of concentric rings of buildings. Half past eight—that would be between Eighth and Ninth Avenue, no? And seven courses—in the seventh circle out from the center? Maybe the damned bootleg is trying to draw our attention to a location, a specific place here in town."

"Between Eighth and Ninth, eh? That's a rough area. I go to a gym near there."

"The old shipyards," said Pickover. "Aren't they there?"

"Yeah." I started walking toward the door. "I'm going to investigate."

"I'll go with you," said Pickover.

I looked at him and shook my head. He would doubtless be more of a hindrance than a help. "It's too dangerous," I said. "I should go alone."

Pickover looked for a few moments like he was going to protest, but then he nodded. "All right. I hope you find Wilkins. But if you find another me . . ."

"Yes?" I said. "What would you like me to do?"

Pickover gazed at me with pleading eyes. "Erase it. Destroy it." He shuddered again. "I never want to see the damned thing."

I had to get some sleep—damn, but sometimes I do wish I were a transfer. I took the hovertram out to my apartment, and let myself have five hours—Mars hours, admittedly, which were slightly longer than Earth ones—and then headed out to the old shipyards. The sun was just coming up as I arrived there. The sky through the dome was pink in the east and purple in the west.

Some active maintenance and repair work was done on spaceships here, but most of these ships were no longer spaceworthy and had been abandoned. Any one of them would make a good hideout, I thought; spaceships were shielded against radiation, making it hard to scan through their hulls to see what was going on inside.

The shipyards were large fields holding vessels of various sizes and shapes. Most were streamlined—even Mars's tenuous atmosphere required that. Some were squatting on tail fins; some were lying on their bellies; some were supported by articulated legs. I tried every hatch I could see on these craft, but, so far, they all had their air locks sealed tightly shut.

Finally, I came to a monstrous abandoned spaceliner—a great hull, some three hundred meters long, fifty meters wide, and a dozen meters high. The name *Mayflower II* was still visible in chipped paint near the bow—which is the part I came across first—and the slogan "Mars or Bust!" was also visible.

I walked a little farther alongside the hull, looking for a hatch, until—

Yes! I finally understood what a fossil hunter felt like when he at last turned up a perfectly preserved rhizomorph. There was an outer air-lock door here, and it was open. The other door, inside, was open, too. I stepped through the chamber, entering the ship proper. There were stands for holding space suits, but the suits themselves were long gone.

I walked over to the far end of the room, and found another door— one of those submarine-style ones with a locking wheel in the center. This one was closed, and I figured it would probably have been sealed shut at some point, but I tried to turn the wheel anyway, just to be sure, and damned if it didn't spin freely, disengaging the locking bolts. I pulled the door open, and stepped through it, into a corridor. The door was on spring-loaded hinges; as soon as I let go of it, it closed behind me, plunging me into darkness.

Of course, I'd brought a flashlight. I pulled it off my belt and thumbed it on.

The air was dry and had a faint odor of decay to it. I headed down the corridor, the pool of illumination from my flashlight going in front of me, and—

A squealing noise. I swung around, and the beam from my flashlight caught the source before it scurried away: a large brown rat, its eyes two tiny red coals in the light. People had been trying to get rid of the rats—and cockroaches and silverfish and other vermin that had somehow made it here from Earth—for mears.

I turned back around and headed deeper into the ship. The floor wasn't quite level: it dipped a bit to—to, starboard, they'd call it—and I also felt that I was gaining elevation as I walked along. The ship's floor had no carpeting; it was just bare, smooth metal. Oily water pooled along the starboard side; a pipe must have ruptured at some point. Another rat scurried by up ahead; I wondered what they ate here, aboard the dead hulk of the ship.

I thought I should check in with Pickover—let him know where I was. I activated my commlink, but the display said it was unable to connect. Of course: the radiation shielding in the spaceship's hull kept signals from getting out.

It was getting awfully cold. I held my flashlight straight up in front of my face, and saw that my breath was now coming out in visible clouds. I paused and listened. There was a steady dripping sound: condensation, or another leak. I continued along, sweeping the flashlight beam left and right in good detective fashion as I did so.

There were doors at intervals along the corridor—the automatic sliding kind you usually find aboard spaceships. Most of these panels had been pried open, and I shone my flashlight into each of the revealed rooms. Some were tiny passenger quarters, some were storage, one was a medical facility—all the equipment had been removed, but the examining beds betrayed the room's function.

I checked yet another set of quarters, then came to a closed door, the first one I'd seen along this hallway.

I pushed the open button, but nothing happened; the ship's electrical system was dead. Of course, there was an emergency handle, recessed into the door's thickness. I could have used three hands just then: one to hold my flashlight, one to hold my revolver, and one to pull on the handle. I tucked the flashlight into my right armpit, held my gun with my right hand, and yanked on the recessed handle with my left.

The door hardly budged. I tried again, pulling harder—and almost popped my arm out of its socket. Could the door's tension control have been adjusted to require a transfer's strength to open it? Perhaps.

I tried another pull, and to my astonishment, light began to spill out from the room. I'd hoped to just yank the door open, taking advantage of the element of surprise, but the damned thing was only moving a small increment with each pull of the handle. If there was someone on the other side, and he or she had a gun, it was no doubt now leveled directly at the door.

I stopped for a second, shoved the flashlight into my pocket, and— damn, I hated having to do this—holstered my revolver so that I could free up my other hand to help me pull the door open. With both hands now gripping the recessed handle, I pulled with all my strength, letting out an audible grunt as I did so.

The light from within stung my eyes; they'd grown accustomed to the soft beam from the flashlight. Another pull, and the door panel had now slid far enough into the wall for me to slip into the room by turning sideways. I took out my gun, and let myself in.

A voice, harsh and mechanical, but no less pitiful for that: "*Please . . .*"

My eyes swung to the source of the sound. There was a worktable, with a black top, attached to the far wall. And strapped to that table—

Strapped to that table was a transfer's synthetic body. But this wasn't like the fancy, almost-perfect simulacrum that my client Cassandra inhabited. This was a crude, simple humanoid form, with a boxy torso and limbs made up of cylindrical metal segments. And the face—

The face was devoid of any sort of artificial skin. The eyes, blue in color and looking startlingly human, were wide, and the teeth looked like dentures loose in the head. The rest of the face was a mess of pulleys and fiber optics, of metal and plastic.

"*Please . . .*" said the voice again. I looked around the rest of the room. There was a fusion battery, about the size of a softball, with several cables snaking out of it, including some that led to portable lights. There was also a closet, with a simple door. I pulled it open—this one slid easily—to make sure no one else had hidden in there while I was coming in. An emaciated rat that had been trapped there at some point scooted out of the closet, and through the still partially open corridor door.

I turned my attention to the transfer. The body was clothed in simple denim pants and a T-shirt.

"Are you okay?" I said, looking at the skinless face.

The metal skull moved slightly left and right. The plastic lids for the glass eyeballs retracted, making the non-face into a caricature of imploring. "*Please . . . ,*" he said for a third time.

I looked at the metal restraints holding the artificial body in place: thin nylon bands, pulled taut, that were attached to the tabletop. I couldn't see any release mechanism. "Who are you?" I said.

I was half-prepared for the answer, of course. "Rory Pickover." But it didn't sound anything like the Rory Pickover I'd met: the cultured British accent was absent, and this synthesized voice was much higher pitched.

Still, I shouldn't take this sad thing's statement at face value—especially since it had hardly any face. "Prove it," I said. "Prove you're Rory Pickover."

The glass eyes looked away. Perhaps the transfer was thinking of how to satisfy my demand—or perhaps he was just avoiding my eyes. "My citizenship number is 48394432."

I shook my head. "No good," I said. "It's got to be something *only* Rory Pickover would know."

The eyes looked back at me, the plastic lids lowered, perhaps in suspicion. "It doesn't matter who I am," he said. "Just get me out of here."

That sounded reasonable on the surface of it, but if this *was* another Rory Pickover . . .

"Not until you prove your identity to me," I said. "Tell me where the alpha deposit is."

"Damn you," said the transfer. "The other way didn't work, so now you're trying this." The mechanical head looked away. "But this won't work, either."

"Tell me where the alpha deposit is," I said, "and I'll free you."

"I'd rather die," he said. And then, a moment later, he added wistfully, "Except . . ."

I finished the thought for him. "Except you can't."

He looked away again. It was hard to feel for something that looked so robotic; that's my excuse, and I'm sticking to it. "Tell me where

O'Reilly and Weingarten were digging. Your secret is safe with me."

He said nothing. The gun in my hand was now aimed at the robotic head. "Tell me!" I said. "Tell me before—"

Off in the distance, out in the corridor: the squeal of a rat, and—

Footfalls.

The transfer heard them, too. Its eyes darted left and right in what looked like panic.

"Please," he said, lowering his volume. As soon as he started speaking, I put a vertical index finger to my lips, indicating that he should be quiet, but he continued: "Please, for the love of God, get me out of here. I can't take any more."

I made a beeline for the closet, stepping quickly in and pulling that door most of the way shut behind me. I positioned myself so that I could see—and, if necessary, shoot—through the gap. The footfalls were growing louder. The closet smelled of rat. I waited.

I heard a voice, richer, more human, than the supposed Pickover's. "What the—?"

And I saw a person—a transfer—slipping sideways into the room, just as I had earlier. I couldn't yet see the face from this angle, but it wasn't Joshua. The body was female, and I could see that she was a brunette. I took in air, held it, and—

And she turned, showing her face now. My heart pounded. The delicate features. The wide-spaced green eyes.

Cassandra Wilkins.

My client.

She'd been carrying a flashlight, which she set now on another, smaller table. "Who's been here, Rory?" Her voice was cold.

"No one," he said.

"The door was open."

"You left it that way. I was surprised, but . . ." He stopped, perhaps realizing to say any more would be a giveaway that he was lying.

She tilted her head slightly. Even with a transfer's strength, that door must be hard to close. Hopefully she'd find it plausible that she'd given the handle a final tug, and had only assumed that the door had closed completely when she'd last left. Of course, I immediately saw the flaw with that story: you might miss the door not clicking into place, but you wouldn't fail to notice that light was still spilling out into the corridor. But most people don't consider things in such detail; I'd hoped she'd buy Pickover's suggestion.

And, after a moment more's reflection, she seemed to do just that, nodding her head, apparently to herself, then moving closer to the table onto which the synthetic body was strapped. "We don't have to do this again," said Cassandra. "If you just tell me . . ."

She let the words hang in the air for a moment, but Pickover made no response. Her shoulders moved up and down a bit in a philosophical shrug. "It's your choice," she said. And then, to my astonishment, she hauled back her right arm and slapped Pickover hard across the robotic face, and—

And Pickover screamed.

It was a long, low, warbling sound, like sheet-metal being warped, a haunted sound, an inhuman sound.

"*Please* . . ." he hissed again, the same plaintive word he'd said to me, the word I, too, had ignored.

Cassandra slapped him again, and again he screamed. Now, I've been slapped by lots of women over the years: it stings, but I've never screamed. And surely an artificial body was made of sterner stuff than me.

Cassandra went for a third slap. Pickover's screams echoed in the dead hulk of the ship.

"Tell me," she said.

I couldn't see his face; her body was obscuring it. Maybe he shook his head. Maybe he just glared defiantly. But he said nothing.

She shrugged again; they'd obviously been down this road before. She moved to one side of the bed and stood by his right arm, which was pinned to his body by the nylon strap. "You really don't want me to do this," she said. "And I don't have to, if . . ." She let the uncompleted of-fer hang there for a few seconds, then: "Ah, well." She reached down with her beige, realistic-looking hand, and wrapped three of her fingers around his right index finger. And then she started bending it backward.

I could see Pickover's face now. Pulleys along his jawline were working; he was struggling to keep his mouth shut. His glass eyes were rolling up, back into his head, and his left leg was shaking in spasms. It was a bizarre display, and I alternated moment by moment between feeling sympathy for the being lying there, and feeling cool detachment be-cause of the clearly artificial nature of the body.

Cassandra let go of Pickover's index finger, and, for a second, I thought she was showing some mercy. But then she grabbed it as well as the adjacent finger, and began bending them both back. This time, de-spite his best efforts, guttural, robotic sounds did escape from Pickover.

"Talk!" Cassandra said. "*Talk!*"

I'd recently learned—from Cassandra herself—that artificial bodies had to have pain sensors; otherwise, a robotic hand might end up resting on a heating element, or too much pressure might be put on a joint. But I hadn't expected such sensors to be so sensitive, and—

And then it hit me, just as another of Pickover's warbling screams was torn from him. Cassandra knew all about artificial bodies; she sold them, after all. If she wanted to adjust the mind-body interface of one so that pain would register particularly acutely, doubtless she could. I'd seen a lot of evil things in my time, but this was perhaps the worst. Scan a mind, put it in a body wired for hypersensitivity to pain, and torture it until it gave up its secrets. Then, of course, you just wipe the mind, and—

"You *will* crack eventually, you know," she said, almost conversationally, as she looked at Pickover's fleshless face. "Given that it's inevitable, you might as well just tell me what I want to know."

The elastic bands that served as some of Pickover's facial muscles contracted, his teeth parted, and his head moved forward slightly but rapidly. I thought for half a second that he was incongruously blowing her a kiss, but then I realized what he was really trying to do: spit at her. Of course, his dry mouth and plastic throat were incapable of generating moisture, but his mind—a human mind, a mind accustomed to a biological body—had summoned and focused all its hate into that most primal of gestures.

"Very well," said Cassandra. She gave his fingers one more nasty yank backwards, holding them at an excruciating angle. Pickover alternated screams and whimpers. Finally, she let his fingers go. "Let's try something different," she said. She leaned over him. With her left hand, she pried his right eyelid open, and then she jabbed her right thumb into that eye. The glass sphere depressed into the metal skull, and Pickover screamed again. The artificial eye was presumably much tougher than a natural one, but, then again, the thumb pressing into it was also tougher. I felt my own eyes watering in a sympathetic response.

Pickover's artificial spine arched up slightly, as he convulsed against the two restraining bands. From time to time, I got clear glimpses of Cassandra's face, and the perfectly symmetrical artificial smile of glee on it was almost sickening.

At last, she stopped grinding her thumb into his eye. "Had enough?" she said. Because if you haven't . . ."

Pickover was indeed still wearing clothing; it was equally gauche to walk the streets nude whether you were biological or artificial. But now, Cassandra's hands moved to his waist. I watched as she undid his belt, unsnapped and unzipped his jeans, and then pulled the pants as far down his metallic thighs as they would go before she reached the restraining strap that held his legs to the table. Transfers had no need for underwear, and Pickover wasn't wearing any. His artificial penis and testicles now lay exposed. I felt my own scrotum tightening in dread.

And then Cassandra did the most astonishing thing. She'd had no compunctions about bending back his fingers with her bare hands. And she hadn't hesitated when it came to plunging her naked thumb into his eye. But now that she was going to hurt him down there, she seemed to want no direct contact. She started looking around the room; for a second, she was looking directly at the closet door. I scrunched back against the far wall, hoping she wouldn't see me. My heart was pounding.

Finally, she found what she was looking for: a wrench, sitting on the floor. She picked it up, raised the wrench above her head and, and looked directly into Pickover's one good eye—the other had closed as soon as she'd removed her thumb, and had never reopened as far as I could tell. "I'm going to smash your ball bearings into iron filings, unless . . ."

He closed his other eye now, the plastic lid scrunching.

"Count of three," she said. "One."

"I can't," he said in that low volume that served as his whisper. "You'd ruin them, sell them off—"

"Two."

"Please! They belong to science! To all humanity!"

"*Three!*"

Her arm slammed down, a great arc slicing through the air, the silver wrench smashing into the plastic pouch that was Pickover's scrotum. He let out a scream greater than any I'd yet heard, so loud, indeed, that it hurt my ears despite the muffling of the partially closed closet door.

She hauled her arm up again, but waited for the scream to devolve into a series of whimpers. "One more chance," she said. "Count of three." His whole body was shaking. I felt nauseous.

"One."

He turned his head to the side, as if by looking away he could make the torture stop.

"Two."

A whimper escaped his artificial throat.

"Three!"

I found myself looking away, too, unable to watch as—

"*All right!*"

It was Pickover's voice, shrill and mechanical, shouting.

"All right!" he shouted again. I turned back to face the tableau: the human-looking woman with a wrench held up above her head, and the terrified mechanical-looking man strapped to the table. "All right," he repeated once more, softly now. "I'll tell you what you want to know."

"You'll tell me where the alpha deposit is?" asked Cassandra lowering her arm.

"Yes," he said. "Yes."

"Where?

Pickover was quiet.

"Where?"

"God forgive me . . ." he said softly.

She began to raise her arm again. "*Where?*"

"Sixteen-point-four kilometers south-southwest of Nili Patera," he said. "The precise coordinates are . . ." and he spoke a string of numbers.

"You better be telling the truth," Cassandra said.

"I am." His voice was tiny. "To my infinite shame, I am."

Cassandra nodded. "Maybe. But I'll leave you tied up here until I'm sure."

"But I told you the truth! I told you everything you need to know."

"Sure you did," said Cassandra. "But I'll just confirm that."

I stepped out of the closet, my gun aimed directly at Cassandra's back. "Freeze," I said.

Cassandra spun around. "Lomax!"

"Mrs. Wilkins," I said, nodding. "I guess you don't need me to find your husband for you anymore, eh? Now that you've got the information he stole."

"What? No, no. I still want you to find Joshua. Of course I do!"

"So you can share the wealth with him?"

"Wealth?" She looked over at the hapless Pickover. "Oh. Well, yes, there's a lot of money at stake." She smiled. "So much so that I'd be happy to cut you in, Mr. Lomax—oh, you're a good man. I know you wouldn't hurt me!"

I shook my head. "You'd betray me the first chance you got."

"No, I wouldn't. I'll need protection; I understand that—what with all the money the fossils will bring. Having someone like you on my side only makes sense."

I looked over at Pickover and shook my head. "You tortured that man."

"That 'man,' as you call him, wouldn't have existed at all without me. And the real Pickover isn't inconvenienced in the slightest."

"But . . . *torture*," I said. "It's inhuman."

She jerked a contemptuous thumb at Pickover. "He's not human. Just some software running on some hardware."

"That's what you are, too."

"That's *part* of what I am," Cassandra said. "But I'm also *authorized*. He's bootleg—and bootlegs have no rights."

"I'm not going to argue philosophy with you."

"Fine. But remember who works for whom, Mr. Lomax. I'm the client—and I'm going to be on my way now."

I held my gun rock-steady. "No, you're not."

She looked at me. "An interesting situation," she said, her tone even. "I'm unarmed, and you've got a gun. Normally, that would put you in charge, wouldn't it? But your gun probably won't stop me. Shoot me in the head, and the bullet will just bounce off my metal skull. Shoot me in the chest, and at worst you might damage some components that I'll eventually have to get replaced—which I can, and at a discount, to boot.

"Meanwhile," she continued, "I have the strength of ten men; I could literally pull your limbs from their sockets, or crush your head between my hands, squeezing it until it pops like a melon and your brains, such as they are, squirt out. So, what's it going to be, Mr. Lomax? Are you going to let me walk out that door and be about my business? Or are you going to pull that trigger, and start something that's going to end with you dead?"

I was used to a gun in my hand giving me a sense of power, of security. But just then, the Smith & Wesson felt like a lead weight. She was right: shooting her with it was likely to be no more useful than just throwing it at her. Of course, there were crucial components in an artificial body's makeup; I just didn't happen to know what they were, and, anyway, they probably varied from model to model. If I could be sure to drop her with one shot, I'd do it. I'd killed before in self-defense, but . . .

But this wasn't self-defense. Not really. If I didn't start something, she was just going to walk out. Could I kill in cold . . . well, not cold *blood*. But she *was* right: she was a person, even if Pickover wasn't. She was the one and only legal instantiation of Cassandra Wilkins. The cops might be corrupt here, and they might be lazy. But even they wouldn't turn a blind eye on attempted murder. If I shot her, and somehow got away, they'd hunt me down. And if I didn't get away, she *would* be attacking me in self-defense.

"So," she said, at last. "What's it going to be?"

"You make a persuasive argument, Mrs. Wilkins," I said in the most reasonable tone I could muster under the circumstances.

And then, without changing my facial expression in the slightest, I pulled the trigger.

I wondered if a transfer's time sense ever slows down, or if it is always perfectly quartz-crystal timed. Certainly, time seemed to attenuate for me then. I swear I could actually see the bullet as it followed its trajectory from my gun, covering the three meters between the barrel and—

And not, of course, Cassandra's torso.

Nor her head.

She was right; I probably couldn't harm her that way.

No, instead, I'd aimed past her, at the table on which the *faux* Pickover was lying on his back. Specifically, I'd aimed at the place where the thick nylon band that crossed over his torso, pinning his arms, was anchored on the right-hand side—the point where it made a taut diagonal line between where it was attached to the side of the table and the top of Pickover's arm.

The bullet sliced through the band, cutting it in two. The long portion, freed of tension, flew up and over his torso like a snake that had just had forty thousand volts pumped through it.

Cassandra's eyes went wide in astonishment that I'd missed her, and her head swung around. The report of the bullet was still ringing in my ears, of course, but I swear I could also hear the *zzzzinnnng*! of the restraining band snapping free. To be hypersensitive to pain, I figured you'd have to have decent reaction times, and I hoped that Pickover had been smart enough to note in advance my slight deviation of aim before I fired it.

And, indeed, no sooner were his arms free than he sat bolt upright—his legs were still restrained—and grabbed one of Cassandra's arms, pulling her toward him. I leapt in the meager Martian gravity. Most of Cassandra's body was made of lightweight composites and synthetic materials, but I was still good old flesh and blood: I outmassed her by at least fifty kilos. My impact propelled her backwards, and she slammed against the table's side. Pickover shot out his other arm, grabbing Cassandra's second arm, pinning her backside against the edge of the table. I struggled to regain a sure footing, then brought my gun up to her right temple.

"All right, sweetheart," I said. "Do you really want to test how strong your artificial skull is?"

Cassandra's mouth was open; had she still been biological, she'd probably have been gasping for breath. But her heartless chest was perfectly still. "You can't just shoot me," she said.

"Why not? Pickover here will doubtless back me up when I say it was self-defense, won't you, Pickover?"

He nodded. "Absolutely."

"In fact," I said, "you, me, this Pickover, and the other Pickover are the only ones who know where the alpha deposit is. I think the three of us would be better off without you on the scene anymore."

"You won't get away with it," said Cassandra. "You can't."

"I've gotten away with plenty over the years," I said. "I don't see an end to that in sight." I cocked the hammer, just for fun.

"Look," she said, "there's no need for this. We can all share in the wealth. There's plenty to go around."

"Except you don't have any rightful claim to it," said Pickover. "You stole a copy of my mind, and tortured me. And you want to be rewarded for that?"

"Pickover's right," I said. "It's his treasure, not yours."

"It's *humanity's* treasure," corrected Pickover. "It belongs to all mankind."

"But I'm your client," Cassandra said to me.

"So's he. At least, the legal version of him is."

Cassandra sounded desperate. "But—but that's a conflict of interest!"

"So sue me," I said.

She shook her head in disgust. "You're just in this for yourself!"

I shrugged amiably, and then pressed the barrel even tighter against her artificial head. "Aren't we all?"

"Shoot her," said Pickover. I looked at him. He was still holding her upper arms, pressing them in close to her torso. If he'd been biological, the twisting of his torso to accommodate doing that probably would have been quite uncomfortable. Actually, now that I thought of it, given his heightened sensitivity to pain, even this artificial version was probably hurting from twisting that way. But apparently this was a pain he was happy to endure.

"Do you really want me to do that?" I said. "I mean, I can understand, after what she did to you, but . . ." I didn't finish the thought; I just left it in the air for him to take or leave.

"She *tortured* me," he said. "She deserves to die."

I frowned, unable to dispute his logic—but, at the same time, wondering if Pickover knew that he was as much on trial here as she was.

"Can't say I blame you," I said again, and then added another "but," and once more left the thought incomplete.

At last, Pickover nodded. "But maybe you're right. I can't offer her any compassion, but I don't need to see her dead."

A look of plastic relief rippled over Cassandra's face. I nodded. "Good man," I said. I'd killed before, but I never enjoyed it.

"But, still," said Pickover, "I would like *some* revenge."

Cassandra's upper arms were still pinned by Pickover, but her lower arms were free. To my astonishment, they both moved. The movement startled me, and I looked down, just in time to see them jerking toward her groin, almost as if to protect . . .

I found myself staggering backward; it took a second for me to regain my balance. "*Oh, my God . . .*"

Cassandra had quickly moved her arms back to a neutral, hanging-down position—but it was too late. The damage had been done.

"You . . ." I said. I normally was never at a loss for words, but I was just then. "You're . . ."

Pickover had seen it, too; his torso had been twisted just enough to allow him to do so.

"No woman . . ." he began slowly.

Cassandra hadn't wanted to touch Pickover's groin—even though it was artificial—with her bare hands. And when Pickover had suggested exacting revenge for what had been done to him, Cassandra's hands had moved instinctively to protect—

Jesus, why hadn't I see it before? The way she plunked herself down in a chair, the fact that she couldn't bring herself to wear makeup or jewelry in her new body; her discomfort at intimately touching or being intimately touched by men: it was obvious in retrospect.

Cassandra's hands had moved instinctively to protect *her own testicles*.

"You're not Cassandra Wilkins," I said.

"Of course I am," said the female voice.

"Not on the inside, you're not," I said. "You're a man. Whatever mind has been transferred into that body is male."

Cassandra twisted violently. Goddamned Pickover, perhaps stunned by the revelation, had obviously loosened his grip, because she got free. I fired my gun again and the bullet went straight into her chest; a streamer of machine oil, like from a punctured can, shot out, but there was no sign that the bullet had slowed her down.

"Don't let her get away!" shouted Pickover, in his rough mechanical voice. I swung my gun on him, and for a second I could see terror in his eyes, as if he thought I meant to off him for letting her twist away. But I aimed at the nylon strap restraining his legs and fired. This time, the bullet only partially severed the strap. I reach down and yanked at the remaining filaments, and so did Pickover. They finally broke and this strap, like the first, snapped free. Pickover swung his legs off the table, and immediately stood up. An artificial body had many advantages, among them not being woozy or dizzy after lying down for God-only-knew how many days.

In the handful of seconds it had taken to free Pickover, Cassandra had made it out the door that I'd pried partway open, and was now running down the corridor in the darkness. I could hear splashing sounds, meaning she'd veered far enough off the corridor's centerline to end up in the water pooling along the starboard side, and I heard her actually bump into the wall at one point, although she immediately continued on. She didn't have her flashlight, and the only illumination in the corridor would have been what was spilling out of the room I was now in—a fading glow to her rear as she ran along, whatever shadow she herself was casting adding to the difficulty of seeing ahead.

I squeezed out into the corridor. I still had my flashlight in my pocket; I fished it out and aimed it just in front of me; Cassandra wouldn't benefit much from the light it was giving off. Pickover, who, I noted, had now done his pants back up, had made his way through the half-open door and was now standing beside me. I started running, and he fell in next to me.

Our footfalls now drowned out the sound of Cassandra's; I guessed she must be some thirty or forty meters ahead. Although it was almost pitch black, she presumably had the advantage of having come down this corridor several times before; neither Pickover nor I had ever gone in this direction.

A rat scampered out of our way, squealing as it did so. My breathing was already ragged, but I managed to say, "How well can you guys see in the dark?"

Pickover's voice, of course, showed no signs of exertion. "Only slightly better than biologicals can."

I nodded, although he'd have to have had better vision than he'd just laid claim to in order to see it. My legs were a lot longer than Cassandra's, but I suspected she could pump them more rapidly. I swung the flashlight beam up, letting it lance out ahead of us for a moment. There she was, off in the distance. I dropped the beam back to the floor in front of me.

More splashing from up ahead; she'd veered off once more. I thought about firing a shot—more for the drama of it, than any serious hope of bringing her down—when I suddenly became aware that Pickover was passing me. His robotic legs were as long as my natural ones, and he could piston them up and down at least as quickly as Cassandra could.

I tried to match his speed, but wasn't able to. Even in Martian gravity, running fast is hard work. I swung my flashlight up again, but Pickover's body, now in front of me, was obscuring everything further down the corridor; I had no idea how far ahead Cassandra was now—and the intervening form of Pickover prevented me from acting out my idle fantasy of squeezing off a shot.

Pickover continued to pull ahead. I was passing open door after open door, black mouths gaping at me in the darkness. I heard more rats, and Pickover's footfalls, and—

Suddenly, something jumped on my back from behind me. A hard arm was around my neck, pressing sharply down on my Adam's apple. I tried to call out to Pickover, but couldn't get enough breath out . . . or in. I craned my neck as much as I could, and shone the flashlight beam up on the ceiling, so that some light reflected down onto my back from above.

It was Cassandra! She'd ducked into one of the other rooms, and lain in wait for me. Pickover was no detective; he had completely missed the signs of his quarry no longer being in front of him—and I'd had Pickover's body blocking my vision, plus the echoing bangs of his footfalls to obscure my hearing. I could see my own chilled breath, but, of course, not hers.

I tried again to call out to Pickover, but all I managed was a hoarse croak, doubtless lost on him amongst the noise of his own running. I was already oxygen-deprived from exertion, and the constricting of my throat was making things worse; despite the darkness I was now seeing white flashes in front of my eyes, a sure sign of asphyxiation. I only had a few seconds to act—

And act I did. I crouched down as low as I could, Cassandra still on my back, her head sticking up above mine, and I leapt with all the strength I could muster. Even weakened, I managed a powerful kick, and in this low Martian gravity, I shot up like a bullet. Cassandra's metal skull smashed into the roof of the corridor. There happened to be a lighting fixture directly above me, and I heard the sounds of shattering glass and plastic.

I was descending now in maddeningly slow motion, but as soon as I was down, Cassandra still clinging hard to me, I surged forward a couple of paces then leapt up again. This time, there was nothing but unrelenting bulkhead overhead, and Cassandra's metal skull slammed hard into it.

Again the slow-motion fall. I felt something thick and wet oozing through my shirt. For a second, I'd thought Cassandra had stabbed me—but no, it was probably the machine oil leaking from the bullet hole I'd put in her earlier. By the time we had touched down again, Cassandra had loosened her grip on my neck as she tried to scramble off me. I spun around and fell forward, pushing her backward onto the corridor floor, me tumbling on top of her. Despite my best efforts, the flashlight was knocked from my grip by the impact, and it spun around, doing a few complete circles before it ended up with its beam facing away from us.

I still had my revolver in my other hand, though. I brought it up, and, by touch, found Cassandra's face, probing the barrel roughly over it. Once, in my early days, I'd rammed a gun barrel into a thug's mouth; this time, I had other ideas. I got the barrel positioned directly over her left eye, and pressed down hard with it—a little poetic justice.

I said, "I bet if I shoot through your glass eye, aiming up a bit, I'll tear your artificial brain apart. You want to find out?"

She said nothing. I called back over my shoulder, "*Pickover!*" The name echoed down the corridor, but I had no idea whether he heard me. I turned my attention back to Cassandra—or whoever the hell this really was. I cocked the trigger. "As far as I'm concerned, Cassandra Wilkins is my client—but you're not her. Who are you?"

"I *am* Cassandra Wilkins," said the voice.

"No, you're not," I said. "You're a man—or, at least, you've got a man's mind."

"I can *prove* I'm Cassandra Wilkins," said the supine form. "My name is Cassandra Pauline Wilkins; my birth name is Collier. I was born in Sioux City, Iowa, on 30 October 2079. I immigrated to New Klondike in July 2102. My citizenship number is—"

"Facts. Figures." I shook my head. "Anyone could find those things out."

"But I know stuff no one else could possibly know. I know the name of my childhood pets; I know what I did to get thrown out of school when I was fifteen; I know precisely where the original me had a tattoo; I . . ."

She went on, but I stopped listening.

Jesus Christ, it was almost the perfect crime. No one could really get away with stealing somebody else's identity—not for long. The lack of intimate knowledge of how the original spoke, of private things the original knew, would soon enough give you away, unless—

Unless you were the *spouse* of the person whose identity you'd appropriated.

"You're not Cassandra Wilkins," I said. "You're Joshua Wilkins. You took her body; you transferred into it, and she transferred—" I felt my stomach tighten; it really was a nearly perfect crime. "And she transferred *nowhere*; when the original was euthanized, she died. And that makes you guilty of murder."

"You can't prove that," said the female voice. "No biometrics, no DNA, no fingerprints. I'm whoever I say I am."

"You and Cassandra hatched this scheme together," I said. "You both figured Pickover had to know where the alpha deposit was. But then you decided that you didn't want to share the wealth with anyone—not even your wife. And so you got rid of her, and made good your escape at the same time."

"That's crazy," the female voice said. "I *hired* you. Why on—on *Mars*—would I do that, then?"

"You expected the police to come out to investigate your missing-person report; they were supposed to find the body in the basement of NewYou. But they didn't, and you knew suspicion would fall on you—the supposed spouse!—if you were the one who found it. So you hired me—the dutiful wife, worried about her poor, missing hubby! All you wanted was for me to find the body."

"Words," said Joshua. "Just words."

"Maybe so," I said. "I don't have to satisfy anyone else. Just me. I will give you one chance, though. See, I want to get out of here alive—and I don't see any way to do that if I leave you alive, too. Do you? If you've got an answer, tell me—otherwise, I've got no choice but to pull this trigger."

"I promise I'll let you go," said Joshua.

I laughed, and the sound echoed in the corridor. "You promise? Well, I'm sure I can take that to the bank."

"No, seriously," said Joshua. "I won't tell anyone. I—"

"Are you Joshua Wilkins?" I asked.

Silence.

"*Are you?*"

I felt the face moving up and down a bit, the barrel of my gun shifting slightly in the eye socket as it did so. "Yes."

"Well, rest in peace," I said, and then, with relish, added, "*Josh.*"

I pulled the trigger.

The flash from the gun barrel briefly lit up the female, freckled face, which was showing almost human horror. The revolver snapped back in my hand, then everything was dark again. I had no idea how much damage the bullet would do to the brain. Of course, the artificial chest wasn't rising and falling, but it never had been. And there was nowhere to check for a pulse. I decided I'd better try another shot, just to be sure. I shifted slightly, thinking I'd put this one through the other eye, and—

And Joshua's arms burst up, pushing me off him. I felt myself go airborne, and was aware of Joshua scrambling to his feet. He scooped up the flashlight, and as he swung it and himself around, it briefly illuminated his face. There was a deep pit where one eye used to be.

I started to bring the gun up and—

And Joshua thumbed off the flashlight. The only illumination was a tiny bit of light, far, far down the corridor, spilling out from the torture room; it wasn't enough to let me see Joshua clearly. But I squeezed the trigger, and heard a bullet ricochet—either off some part of Joshua's metal internal skeleton, or off the corridor wall.

I was the kind of guy who always knew *exactly* how many bullets he had left: two. I wasn't sure I wanted to fire them both off blindly, but—

I could hear Joshua moving closer. I fired again. This time, the feminine voice box made a sound between an *oomph* and the word "ouch," so I knew I'd hit him.

One bullet to go.

I started walking backward—which was no worse than walking forward; I was just as likely to trip either way in this near-total darkness. The body in the shape of Cassandra Wilkins was much smaller than mine—but also, although it shamed the macho me to admit it, much stronger. It could probably grab me by the shoulders and pound my head up into the ceiling, just as I'd pounded hers—and I rather suspect mine wouldn't survive. And if I let it get hold of my arm, it could probably wrench the gun from me; five bullets hadn't been enough to stop the artificial body, but one was all it would take to ice me for good.

And so I decided it was better to have an empty gun than a gun that could potentially be turned on me. I held the weapon out in front, took my best guess, and squeezed the trigger one last time.

The revolver barked, and the flare from the muzzle lit the scene, stinging my eyes. The artificial form cried out—I'd hit a spot its sensors felt was worth protecting with a major pain response, I guess. But the being kept moving forward. Part of me thought about turning tail and running—I still had the longer legs, even if I couldn't move them as fast—but another part of me couldn't bring myself to do that. The gun was of no more use, so I threw it aside. It hit the corridor wall, making a banging sound, then fell to the deck plates, producing more clanging as it bounced against them.

Of course, as soon as I'd thrown the gun away, I realized I'd made a mistake. *I* knew how many bullets I'd shot, and how many the gun held, but Joshua probably didn't; even an empty gun could be a deterrent if the other person thought it was loaded.

We were facing each other—but that was all that was certain. Precisely how much distance there was between us I couldn't say. Although running produced loud, echoing footfalls, either of us could have moved a step or two forward or back—or left or right—without the other being aware of it. I was trying not to make any noise, and a transfer could stand perfectly still, and be absolutely quiet, for hours on end.

I had no idea how badly I'd hurt him. In fact, given that he'd played possum once before, it was possible the sounds of pain were faked, just to make me think he was damaged. My great grandfather said clocks used to make a ticking sound with the passing of each second; I'd never heard such a thing, but I was certainly conscious of time passing in increments as we stood there, each waiting for the other to make a move.

Suddenly, light exploded in my face. He'd thumbed the flashlight back on, aiming it at what turned out to be a very good guess as to where my eyes were. I was temporarily blinded, but his one remaining mechanical eye responded more efficiently, I guess, because now that he knew exactly where I was, he leapt, propelling himself through the air and knocking me down.

This time, both hands closed around my neck. I still outmassed Joshua and managed to roll us over, so he was on his back and I was on top. I arched my back and slammed my knee into his balls, hoping he'd release me . . .

. . . except, of course, he didn't have any balls; he only thought he did. *Damn!*

The hands were still closing around my gullet; despite the chill air, I felt myself sweating. But with his hands occupied, mine were free: I pushed my right hand onto his chest—startled by the feeling of artificial breasts there—and probed around until I found the slick, wet hole my first bullet had made. I hooked my right thumb into that hole, pulled sideways, and brought in my left thumb, as well, squeezing it down into the opening, ripping it wider and wider. I thought if I could get at the internal components, I might be able to rip out something crucial. The artificial flesh was soft, and there was a layer of what felt like foam rubber beneath it—and beneath that, I could feel hard metal parts. I tried to get my whole hand in, tried to yank out whatever I could, but I was fading fast. My pulse was thundering so loudly in my ears I couldn't hear anything else, just a *thump-thump-thumping*, over and over again, the *thump-thump-thumping* of . . .

Of footfalls! Someone was running this way, and—

And the scene lit up as flashlights came to bear on us.

"There they are!" said a harsh, mechanical voice that I recognized as belonging to Pickover. "There they are!"

"NKPD!" shouted another voice I also recognized—a deep, Scottish brogue. "Let Lomax go!"

Joshua looked up. "Back off!" he shouted—in that female voice. "If you don't, I'll finish him."

Through blurring vision, I thought I could see Mac hesitating. But then he spoke again. "If you kill him, you'll go down for murder. You don't want that."

Joshua relaxed his grip a bit—not enough to let me escape, but enough to keep me alive as a hostage, at least a little while longer. I sucked in cold air, but my lungs still felt like they were on fire. In the illumination from the flashlights I could see the improved copy of Cassandra Wilkins's face craning now to look at McCrae. Transfers didn't show as much emotion as biologicals did, but it was clear that Joshua was panicking.

I was still on top. I thought if I waited until Joshua was distracted, I could yank free of his grip without him snapping my neck. "Let go of him," Mac said firmly. It was hard to see him; he was the one holding the light source, after all, but I suddenly became aware that he was also holding a large disk. "Release his neck, or I'll deactivate you for sure."

Joshua practically had to roll his green eyes up into his head to see Mac, standing behind him. "You ever use one of those before?" he said, presumably referring to the disrupter disk. "No, I know you haven't—no transfer has been killed on Mars in weeks, and that technology only just came out. Well, I work in the transference business. I know the disruption isn't instantaneous. Yes, you can kill me—but not before I kill Lomax."

"You're lying," said McCrae. He handed his flashlight to Pickover, and brought the disk up in front of him, holding it vertically by its two U-shaped handles. "I've read the specs."

"Are you willing to take that chance?" asked Joshua.

I could only arch my neck a bit; it was very hard for me to look up and see Mac, but he seemed to be frowning, and, after a second, he turned partially away. Pickover was standing behind him, and—

And suddenly an electric whine split the air, and Joshua was convulsing beneath me, and his hands were squeezing my throat even more tightly than before. The whine—a high keening sound—must have been coming from the disrupter. I still had my hands inside Joshua's chest and could feel his whole interior vibrating as his body racked. I yanked my hands out and grabbed onto his arms, pulling with all my might. His hands popped free from my throat, and his whole luscious female form was shaking rapidly. I rolled off him; the artificial body kept convulsing as the keening continued. I gasped for breath and all I could think about for several moments was getting air into me.

After my head cleared a bit, I looked again at Joshua, who was still convulsing, and then I looked up at Mac, who was banging on the side of the disrupter disk. I realized that, now that he'd activated it, he had no idea how to deactivate it. As I watched, he started to turn it over, presumably hoping there was some control he'd missed on the side he couldn't see—and I realized that if he completed his move, the disk would be aimed backward, in the direction of Pickover. Pickover clearly saw this, too: he was throwing his robot-like arms up, as if to shield his face—not that that could possibly do any good.

I tried to shout "No!," but my voice was too raw, and all that came out was a hoarse exhalation of breath, the sound of which was lost beneath the keening. In my peripheral vision, I could see Joshua lying face down. His vicious spasms stopped as the beam from the disrupter was no longer aimed at him.

But even though I didn't have any voice left, Pickover did, and his shout of *"Don't!"* was loud enough to be heard over the electric whine of the disrupter. Mac continued to rotate the disk a few more degrees before he realized what Pickover was referring to. He flipped the disk back around, then continued turning it until the emitter surface was facing straight down. And then he dropped it, and it fell in Martian slo-mo, at last clanking against the deck plates, a counterpoint to the now-muffled electric whine. I hauled myself to my feet and moved over to check on Joshua, while Pickover and Mac hovered over the disk, presumably looking for the off switch.

There were probably more scientific ways to see if the transferred Joshua was dead, but this one felt right just then: I balanced on one foot, hauled back the other leg, and kicked the son of a bitch in the side of that gorgeous head. The impact was strong enough to spin the whole body through a quarter-turn, but there was no reaction at all from Joshua.

Suddenly, the keening died, and I heard a self-satisfied *"There!"* from Mac. I looked over at him, and he looked back at me, caught in the beam from the flashlight Pickover was holding. Mac's bushy orange eyebrows were raised and there was a sheepish grin on his face. "Who'd have thought the off switch had to be pulled out instead of pushed in?"

I tried to speak, and found that I did have a little voice now. "Thanks for coming by, Mac. I know how you hate to leave the station."

Mac nodded in Pickover's direction. "Yeah, well, you can thank this guy for putting in the call," he said. He turned, and faced Pickover full-on. "Just who the hell are you, anyway?"

I saw Pickover's mouth begin to open in his mechanical head, and a thought rushed through my mind. This Pickover was bootleg. Both the other Pickover and Joshua Wilkins had been correct: such a being shouldn't exist, and had no rights. Indeed, the legal Pickover would doubtless continue to demand that this version be destroyed; no one wanted an unauthorized copy of himself wandering around.

Mac was looking away from me, and toward the duplicate of Pickover. And so I made a wide sweeping of my head, left to right, then back again. Pickover apparently saw it, because he closed his mouth before sounds came out, and I spoke, as loudly and clearly as I could in my current condition. "Let me do the introductions," I said, and I waited for Mac to turn back toward me.

When he had, I pointed at Mac. "Detective Dougal McCrae," I said, then I took a deep breath, let it out slowly, and pointed at Pickover, "I'd like you to meet Joshua Wilkins."

Mac nodded, accepting this. "So you found your man? Congratulations, Alex." He then looked down at the motionless female body. "Too bad about your wife, Mr. Wilkins."

Pickover turned to face me, clearly seeking guidance. "It's so sad," I said quickly. "She was insane, Mac—had been threatening to kill her poor husband Joshua here for weeks. He decided to fake his own death to escape her, but she got wise to it somehow, and hunted him down. I had no choice but to try to stop her."

As if on cue, Pickover walked over to the dead artificial body, and crouched beside it. "My poor dear wife," he said, somehow managing to make his mechanical voice sound tender. He lifted his skinless face toward Mac. "This planet does that to people, you know. Makes them go crazy." He shook his head. "So many dreams dashed."

Mac looked at me, then at Pickover, then at the artificial body lying on the deck plating, then back at me. "All right, Alex," he said, nodding slowly. "Good work."

I tipped my nonexistent hat at him. "Glad to be of help."

I walked into the dark interior of the Bent Chisel, whistling.

Buttrick was behind the bar, as usual. "You again, Lomax?"

"The one and only," I replied cheerfully. That topless waitress I'd slept with a couple of times was standing next to the bar, loading up her tray. I looked at her, and suddenly her name came to me. "Hey, Diana!" I said. "When you get off tonight, how 'bout you and me go out and paint the town . . ." I trailed off: the town was *already* red; the whole damned planet was.

Diana's face lit up, but Buttrick raised a beefy hand. "Not so fast, lover boy. If you've got the money to take her out, you've got the money to settle your tab."

I slapped two golden hundred-solar coins on the countertop. "That should cover it." Buttrick's eyes went as round as the coins, and he scooped them up immediately, as if he was afraid they'd disappear—which, in this joint, they probably would.

"I'll be in the booth in the back," I said to Diana. "I'm expecting Mr. Santos; when he arrives, could you bring him over?"

Diana smiled. "Sure thing, Alex. Meanwhile, what can I get you? Your usual poison?"

I shook my head. "Nah, none of that rotgut. Bring me the best scotch you've got—and pour it over *water* ice."

Buttrick narrowed his eyes. "That'll cost extra."

"No problem," I said. "Start up a new tab for me."

A few minutes later, Diana came by the booth with my drink, accompanied by Raoul Santos. He took the seat opposite me. "This better be on you, Alex," said Raoul. "You still owe me for the help I gave you at Dr. Pickover's place."

"Indeed it is, old boy. Have whatever you please."

Raoul rested his receding chin on his open palm. "You seem in a good mood."

"Oh, I am," I said. "I got paid this week."

The man the world now accepted as Joshua Wilkins had returned to NewYou, where he'd gotten his face finished and his artificial body upgraded. After that, he told people it was too painful to continue to work there, given what had happened with his wife. So he sold the NewYou franchise to his associate, Horatio Fernandez. The money from the sale gave him plenty to live on, especially now that he didn't need food and didn't have to pay the life-support tax anymore. He gave me all the fees his dear departed wife should have—plus a very healthy bonus.

I'd asked him what he was going to do now. "Well," he said, "even if you're the only one who knows it, I'm still a paleontologist—and now I can spend days on end out on the surface. I'm going to look for new fossil beds."

And what about the other Pickover—the official one? It took some doing, but I managed to convince him that it had actually been the late Cassandra, not Joshua, who had stolen a copy of his mind, and that she was the one who had installed it in an artificial body. I told Dr. Pickover that when Joshua discovered what his wife had done, he destroyed the bootleg and dumped the ruined body that had housed it in the basement of the NewYou building.

Not too shabby, eh? Still, I wanted more. I rented a surface suit and a Mars buggy and headed out to 16.4 kilometers south-southwest of Nili Patera. I figured I'd pick myself up a lovely rhizomorph or a nifty pentaped, and never have to work again.

Well, I looked and looked and looked, but I guess the duplicate Pickover had lied about where the alpha deposit was; even under torture, he hadn't betrayed his beloved fossils. I'm sure Weingarten and O'Reilly's source is out there somewhere, though, and the legal Pickover is doubtless hard at work thinking of ways to protect it from looters.

I hope he succeeds. I really do.

But for now, I'm content just to enjoy this lovely scotch.

"How about a toast?" suggested Raoul, once Diana had brought him his booze.

"I'm game," I said. "To what?"

Raoul frowned, considering. Then his eyebrows climbed his broad forehead, and he said, "To being true to your innermost self."

We clinked glasses. "I'll drink to that."